CW00537326

PILGRENNON'S GAMBIT

MANDA BENSON

-Book two of Pilgrennon's Children-

TANGENTRINE

www.tangentrine.com

www.tangentrine.com

Copyright © Manda Benson 2024

Based on a concept first published in Pilgrennon's
Beacon, 2010
First edition published by Tangentrine 2024

British Library Cataloguing in Publication Data. A
catalogue record for this book is available from the
British Library.

This novel is a work of fiction. Any resemblance to
locations, incidents, or persons living or dead is purely
coincidental.

Pilgrennon's Gambit, *Pilgrennon's Children*, and their
respective characters are the intellectual property of
Manda Benson. All rights reserved. No part of this
publication may be reproduced, stored in a retrieval
system, or transmitted in any form or by any means,
electronic, mechanical, photocopying, recording,
or otherwise, without the prior permission of the
publishers.

Manda Benson asserts the moral right to be identified
as the author of this work.

ISBN: 978-1-917231-03-9

For My Dad

and with thanks to
J.D. Williams
Richard Zwicker

PART ONE
LONDON

PART ONE
LONDON

THE rain had stopped and the wind had fallen. A dense fog had come upon the sea air and formed a wall encircling the boat. Although the sun must be up by now, whichever direction Dana looked, the ocean surface blurred and disappeared at the same distance. The sound of the waves under the keel and the heavy throb of the motor seemed very thick and close in the cold, wet atmosphere.

Ivor paid little attention to the mist, and concentrated instead on the boat's on-board GPS navigation system. "Do let me know if I'm going wrong," he said. "This thing isn't exactly new or particularly reliable, and it wouldn't do to end up smashed on the rocks for you having misplaced faith in it and me."

They'd set out before first light, Ivor saying something about it being a shame Dana hadn't been able to see the Northern Lights before she went, the weather having conspired against them.

"You're not going back to that beach we were at yesterday, are you?" It seemed to Dana that she'd spent the whole of last night sliding into sleep and coming back to consciousness with a flashback of Jananin up on the moor above the beach, squinting over the barrel of her weapon, or a sensation of overbalancing and a start as the sand came up to meet her. When morning had finally come, she'd woken stiff with the bruises from yesterday's fall.

"No. Let's try to get to one of the other beaches to the north. There's one near Shawbost that's easy to get to the road from."

Dana could make out the coast of Lewis in her interpretation of GPS, although it was still some distance away. "Do you think..." Dana stared into the mist to the fore, but her eyes could discern nothing, and she had only her imagined map of the coastline to give any idea of what might be there. "Do you think she'll still be on Lewis?"

Ivor glanced up from the screen. "Our old friend Dr Blake? I'd expect so. I don't think she managed to find us by pure chance yesterday. Either she's managed to hack into the police's system, or she's got her own method of tracking you. Try not to worry about her, though. Like I said, I can't imagine she'd do anything to hurt you. Not unless she were to catch you with me again."

Dana put her hand in her skirt pocket and held one of the fuses she kept there tightly. What if Blake was waiting for them, standing on a cliff ready to blow up Ivor's boat? After a moment, she said, "I think she is called *Professor* Blake, now."

"Wouldn't surprise me. To be honest, it would surprise me more if a Nobel laureate *didn't* have a chair."

"Ivor, what is a Nobel laureate? And what's the difference between a doctor and a professor?"

"A doctor can be either a medical doctor, like a GP or a specialist, or someone who has done a PhD in a subject and written a thesis."

"What's a thesis?"

"It's a book of your experiments or knowledge that you develop while you do your PhD. Mine was about how autistic people think differently to neurotypical people. Blake's was something in material chemistry; not her synapse because she came up with that afterwards when she was working as a postdoctoral fellow."

"And what's a professor?"

"A professor is someone who is given a chair at a university."

"Are the chairs in university plastic ones, like in schools?"

"No, it's a metaphorical chair. Like a seat at the table where the decisions are made."

"Like King Arthur's round table?"

"Something like that."

Dana imagined Jananin Blake sitting on a plastic school chair at a table with knights. She supposed she had a sword and a knife she could take, so she would sort of fit in with them.

"And the Nobel prize is an award that gets given every year to the person whose scientific research is the most important and interesting that year, and the Nobel laureate is the person, or group, who receives that prize. Only one each year."

Dana tried to remember what she'd read, something from a drawer back on Roareim, a cutting from a newspaper. "And Jananin is the youngest person to have it?"

Ivor nodded. "Indeed, the youngest person so far to be awarded it individually, and one of not a particularly large number of women. That's of course not the fault of women. Science is just as much for women as it is for men. It's because in the past, women were discriminated against. Not that people aren't discriminated against now or that discrimination will ever go away; it's like fashion and people will just find a new one when things move on. But Jananin Blake is really a very special sort of person."

Dana considered this for a long moment. "I sort of *kind of like* Jananin Blake. I mean, before she blew up Charlie November Five and told me to poison you with cyanide. She was quite nice to talk to."

Ivor suddenly laughed. "I don't think she likes children very much."

"I don't know that I much like people who do like children." Dana frowned. "They're all high-pitched, and... *exaggerated*. And they won't tell me real answers to things I want to know, and when they do talk to me, it's like they think I'm not really a *proper* person."

"Sounds a bit like cat psychology," said Ivor. "Cats never like cat-people who approach them and try to play with them. They prefer people who ignore them."

"I suppose I like cats more than I like dogs," said Dana.

"Although I don't really like either of them much. Cats scratch and dogs lick and smell. I like plants better."

Ivor shrugged. "My aunt and uncle never wanted any children, so they never had any, but they had a smallholding in Wales with chickens and sheep. They used to have Border Collies to work the sheep, and I always loved when they had puppies. Puppies don't smell, not in any bad way at least, and if you have a puppy, by the time it grows into a dog, you've fallen in love with it, and you don't notice that it smells, then."

"Is that the same reason why some people have children?"

Ivor laughed again, and unexpectedly after he had to wipe his eyes. "I'm sorry, Dana. If things had worked out differently, if I hadn't made such a mess of everything, in a parallel universe, perhaps Blake and I might have had joint custody of you."

Dana gazed into the mist, thinking. "You know when you do a PhD and you write a thesis? Can you write a thesis about anything?"

Ivor grimaced. "Some people write theses about all kinds of rubbish these days, so I'd say the sky's the limit."

"I don't think I would want to write a thesis about the sky, but would I be able to write a thesis that is both about plants and about electrical things like fuses?"

"If that field doesn't exist, it's only because it hasn't been invented yet. You could be the one to invent it. If you invented something like Jananin's synapse, that could pass a current from a plant cell to a wire, perhaps you could make a tree charge up a battery for you."

"A power plant." Dana laughed. "Electrees."

"And then you would have invented the field of electrobotany."

Dana frowned. "No, Ivor, a wood would work better than a field. Especially if horses and sheep kept eating the grass."

Ivor smiled and shook his head very slightly. "So

how'd you know Blake's got a chair? She tell you she was a professor when you were with her?"

"No, it was in a game," Dana explained. "I think I told you about it before. It's inspired by Greek mythology, and there's a Charon the Ferryman, which is a skin you can earn by solving his puzzle, and there's a Cerberus, but it's difficult and I can't understand the code for it. There are fish inside the game that have hands instead of heads, and they've got records attached to them that are for people, and I found the records for people I know sort of by accident, and Jananin Blake's record just said she was Professor Blake."

As she had been speaking, Ivor had looked away from the boat's navigational computer to stare at her, and his mouth had fallen open. "*Dana*, Cerberus is... well, it is the name of a mythical three-headed dog, but it's also the name of an invention, a special type of computer, by a man I used to know."

"It doesn't *feel* like a computer. It's really complicated. It feels more like another player."

"It's a quantum computer; a *super*computer. He designed it so it would be able to learn, like a person does, and to solve problems autonomously. You say this is in the game you've been playing?"

"It's in the game. Eric —that's another player— says it's a puzzle. But we don't know how to solve it. I tried pushing it into the Styx, but it can swim. Who was the man, and what was his computer like?"

"His name was Steve Gideon."

"Did he not like being called Steve Gideon, and decide to call himself something else?"

Ivor glanced at the boat's navigation system briefly. "That wasn't what I meant. Unfortunately, it seems he's dead. Either that, or he wants everyone to think he's dead. The thing was, nobody ever found out what happened to Cerberus. There were a couple of computers in his house, but nothing matching its description, and all his published research on computers and the Porpoise system he developed before Cerberus mysteriously disappeared. You say you found records of real people in this game?"

"You and Jananin, and my foster family. And a teacher from school."

Ivor looked uncomfortable, like he wasn't sure he wanted to know the answer to what he asked next. "These records. What kind of information was on them?"

"On yours, not really anything much. There was a lot of data and calculations in some of the other ones. I think it was something to do with voting, and browsing history or something."

Lines formed on Ivor's forehead. He closed his eyes and passed his hand over his mouth.

"If it's a computer made by a man called Steve Gideon, and it has data about people," said Dana, "why is it online playing games?"

He looked at her, and an odd sort of smile came upon his face. "Same reason you go online and play games. You're bored. It's fun. It's a way to interact with people. If you'd seen any of Gideon's other creations, his Porpoises that were the predecessor of Cerberus, it would seem quite natural. They were curious, childlike almost. You could tell them jokes. They never understood them, but they tried their best."

"Why are they called Porpoises?" Dana asked. "I thought a porpoise was something like a dolphin?"

Ivor abruptly laughed. "It is. He called it a Porpoise because he found out that when he tried to make more and more complicated learning machines, they would just fill up with computational errors and crash, and he'd have to wipe them, and they'd lose everything they'd learned. Apparently, a porpoise can't just go to sleep in peace like you and I do, because it needs to breathe air and it'll drown. So it evolved so half its brain could sleep at a time, and that was where he got the idea from. A Porpoise was essentially two redundant computers joined together.

Only one is awake, for want of a better word, at a time. The other is defragmenting and processing the information it's assimilated. *Asleep*. When the time comes to change over, the half that's ready to sleep relays its information to the rested half to allow it to keep going. It always surprised me how much like real brains his computers ended up being, like real living things that have evolved sleep because it's necessary."

Dana sensed through GPS they were approaching the headland, although she could still make out nothing of it through the fog ahead. She could tell that Ivor was aiming the boat at a small inlet that led to a sandy cove. The first visual impression she had was the shapes of the cliff on either side taking form, in a way that reminded her of the entrance on the Styx to Cerberus's lair. The motion of the boat upon the waves calmed as it passed from the open ocean into the shelter of the natural harbour, and then the whiter crests of the waves became discernible ahead where they washed up the sand.

Ivor aimed the boat diagonally up the beach, so the water was shallower on the left-hand side to make it easier to get off. The engine dropped to idling speed. He turned to face her, and pointed to the left, where the fog revealed what looked like a road surface running down into the water, probably so people could drive up with boats and slide them straight in.

"If you follow the road, it'll take you back to civilisation. If you're at all worried about anything, just go to any house and say you're lost. Ask someone to call the police to come and get you. But don't go inside any houses, and don't accept any lifts from men, well, unless they're policemen. I know it sounds horribly sexist, but unfortunately there are some men around who are really nasty people."

Dana looked back at him, the fog surrounding them. The boat moved gently with each wave that came in. She nodded.

He laid his hand on her shoulder. "Take care, Dana.

You know where to find me, if you ever need anything. Just promise me that if you do, you'll send a message or something, and you won't go setting out in any purloined boats on your own again." He gave her shoulder a squeeze.

Dana looked down at the waves running up and down the beach. She pulled her rucksack on and climbed up onto the side of the boat, timing her jump to coincide with when a wave had run back, not wanting to have to walk however far she ended up having to go with boots wet inside with seawater. As she walked up the beach, she glanced back and Ivor waved to her, just a shape in the mist. When she looked again, the pitch of the boat's motor had changed, and she could no longer see it through the fog, and soon after that, the cold wet air swallowed even that sound.

The road led up to a rough parking area with a picnic table and a bin. Probably in summer, this was a place people liked to go. She could sense a signal here, and she recognised another of the rods pushed into the ground, of the same sort as she'd seen by the road yesterday. She stopped to study it for a moment, but she couldn't tell from the signal what the object was for, or interact with it in any way like she could a computer.

Beyond that, the road turned into a small bridge without any handrails as it went over a stream that came from a pool of water behind the beach, perhaps a saltmarsh, or a loch, or even a reservoir for the local houses. There were houses on both sides of the road ahead, but they were just featureless shapes barely visible in the mist. It was reassuring to think that if anyone looked back at her from them, the mist would grant her similar anonymity.

Dana considered Ivor's suggestion of going to a house and asking for the police to be called. She didn't want to meet people, and neither in particular did she want to go to the police. She thought of Officer Logan from yesterday, and how his car had fallen off the cliff and she and Ivor had stolen their helicopter. Ivor had meant to leave the helicopter so the police could have it back, but Jananin had blown it up.

She decided she would keep walking for now, and while she walked she could think about what to do next. Ivor had made her a potato salad in a plastic box to eat on the way, which she'd put in her bag with Jananin's computer and a change of socks and underwear. The idea of stealing a car again and trying to get back to the mainland by ferry in much the same way she'd arrived seemed less unappealing than having to speak to people. If she managed to do that, she supposed she might be able to go to a train station and just go back quietly to Pauline and Graeme's house. Maybe even, they wouldn't make too much fuss, and the police wouldn't get involved, if she came back the normal time school ended and just went to her room as usual.

She pulled up her hood before she passed through the main part of Shawbost. The houses were all set back from the road, and she saw nobody outside as she passed through. At the end, the single track joined up to a larger two-lane road. There was a bus stop on the opposite side, and she glanced about furtively, but there were no other pedestrians, and no traffic. She could tell from GPS that the road left eventually led to Tarbert, the port where the ferry went from, so she took that route, walking on the grass close to a low stone wall and keeping as far away from the houses as she was able.

GPS showed the stretch of road ahead to be clear of houses, and momentarily she relaxed. It occurred to her that she wouldn't be able to walk the whole way to Tarbert. Whether the fog lifted or not, someone was bound to notice her with the number of cars and houses she'd likely pass. Going across the open country didn't really seem feasible either, as there were walls and barbed wire fences to keep animals in that she'd be constantly having to cross.

The distant sound of an engine came into range. It was hard to tell in the fog, but it sounded more like it was coming from in front of her than behind. Dana moved as far from the edge of the road as she could on the grass, and walked along the fence line there. She wondered if perhaps it would be better to hide somewhere and try to go on once it became dark. She hoped the driver wouldn't notice her, although from the engine sound, it seemed the car had pulled over somewhere ahead before it had come into sight.

Then the engine pitch changed, and grew louder, and a shape became visible through the fog ahead. Dana put her hand up to her hood and pulled it over her face, turning her head away as the car passed.

But the car didn't pass. It halted again in the road, next to where she was walking.

Dana stopped. She slowly took her hand away from her hood to look up at the driver, who was looking straight back at her through the lowered window. It was Jananin. For a moment, neither spoke.

Then Jananin switched off the engine. She opened the car door and got out rather awkwardly, because something under her brown leather trench coat seemed to be in the way. She stared at Dana for another moment, her expression inscrutable behind her dark glasses, and she put her hand to her mouth and sort of scowled, as though she meant to say something but couldn't think of the right words.

From behind Dana, another voice. "Blake!"

They both turned to see another figure approaching from the mist, along the edge of the road. It was Ivor. His hands were held up very plainly. "Blake, we need to talk."

Jananin didn't say anything. She stared at him over the top of the car door, and then she turned and walked around the back of the car, past the other side of it. As she approached him, she broke into a run, her right hand flying to her left hip, left arm up and back out of the way, and upon her final stride the katana flew over her head, its curved blade describing a dull arc in the damp air. Dana was already on the road, running to him, and with a shout she took hold of Jananin's arm as Ivor fell to his knees in front of her. The sword struck him in the shoulder, at an angle that would have taken it into his heart had she not been in the way.

Wide-eyed, he looked to Dana, a darkness wicking into the fabric of his jacket from the blade's edge, and then back up at Jananin. It looked like a knighthood gone wrong. His voice came out in a gasp. "Blake, there are two other children in an old military base on an island. Dana knows where it is. Whatever you do to me, you need to see to it that they're okay!"

"Let go of my arm, Dana," Jananin snarled. "This ends. Now." She put her left foot on Ivor's other shoulder, and pulled the sword free. Ivor stifled a cry and pressed his hand to the spreading stain. Jananin shook her arm free, but Dana, looking up at her with grim determination, stood between them, blocking Ivor from her.

"I see you have her trained already." Jananin let out a cold, humourless bark, that might have been intended as a laugh.

"Jananin, *stop it!*" Dana sobbed at her. "He might have done horrible things, but he lives in a bunker now and he eats potatoes and weeds and whatever he can find in the sea, and he hasn't got any money or any medicine, and I won't let you kill him!"

Jananin Blake bared her teeth at Dana, her face crafty, unsettling. "You cannot even begin to understand how long I've searched, how long I've waited for this opportunity. Mark my words, I shall not have it ruined by you. Stay out of my way!"

"Jananin, she's just a child," said Ivor from behind Dana. "Don't do this in front of her."

"You try to appeal to my conscience, when I have none? The end approaches, and in your depravity you would even use this child's impressionability as a shield?"

Very distantly, Dana made out a sound through the fog. She turned her head to look behind. She saw, or fancied she saw, a flicker of blue light somewhere behind it. "The police are coming."

Jananin fixed her with a cold stare. "Dana, get in the car."

Dana did not move. She stared back up at Jananin, speechless, defying her.

Jananin gave a barely perceptible shrug with her eyebrows. "Or do not. Stay here and meet the police. They will take you home; I care not. I have what I came for."

She straightened her arm, reaching past Dana's shoulder. With the slightest rotation of her wrist, she turned the point of the blade on Ivor's throat. She leaned her weight on her back foot; set her fist on her hip under her coat, revealing the katana sheath on her left side, the knife strapped to her thigh. She looked down her nose at him, down the length of the blade. "Get up. Go to the car. We finish this elsewhere."

One hand pressed to his shoulder, the other raised in surrender, face set grimly, Ivor rose with an awkward motion to his feet and did as she ordered him.

Jananin passed the sword through something in her other hand, wiping the blood off it. She resheathed it with a meticulous precision that sent a chill crawling up Dana's spine. She went to the car behind him, pushed him roughly against the door, and tied the handcuffs he was still wearing from yesterday together behind his back. She opened the back door and shoved him into the seat.

Dana took one last look behind, in the direction of the police siren, and went back to the car and got into the passenger seat. A complicated and very heavy pair of binoculars already occupied it, so she picked them up and put them in her lap. Then Jananin was in the driver's seat and starting the car, and the car was turning and they were off down the road in the direction of Harris.

-2-

JANANIN turned the car off the road somewhere near Garrynahine, across a track over a drainage ditch that ran alongside the road and on to a parking area screened by conifers. The house there was typical of the sort on Lewis: a cottage with pale render on the outside walls and dormer windows built into the roof. The fog had begun to clear and the wind pulled the smoke that rose from the chimney diagonally into the overcast sky.

The car turned and reversed into a garage with a wooden double door which had been left open. Jananin switched off the engine and got out, slamming the door behind her, and went to the house.

Dana looked into the back of the car at Ivor. His hands were tied behind his back and he was sitting very awkwardly, looking as most men and taller women did too big for the back seat of a medium-size hatchback. The bloodstain spreading from his shoulder seemed to have slowed, but a pallor had come over his face and he shivered with each breath.

"Why did you follow me?" she said. "Why didn't you go back?"

Ivor made something of an attempt to laugh that ended with a wince and a grimace. "I was going to. I thought perhaps I ought to hang around a bit for the fog to clear, what with the navigational aids on the boat being a bit basic. Part of it was just wanting to make sure you were okay. Another part was, well, she's going to keep on hunting me now, and it's only a matter of time before she finds Roareim. I knew she was tracking you. It made sense to find her and have it out now, get it over and done with in a way that keeps Peter and Alpha and you out of it."

Dana looked down at the object in her lap. There was some writing on the casing of the binoculars, a brand name, a model number, and *AMOLED IR 10X*. Infra-red. Sometimes Dana could see things in infra-red, like at the hospital where there had been a surveillance camera she had been able to talk to. That must have been how Jananin had been able to find her in the mist, why she'd stopped on the road ahead. She realised then, that Ivor hadn't walked with her because he feared that if Jananin had seen her with him from a distance, she could have fired on him and hurt her as well.

Jananin was coming back to the car now, heading for the rear passenger door. Dana opened the door and got out.

"*Out*," Jananin ordered Ivor, opening the car door.

With some difficulty, he got his feet out the door and stood by pushing his shoulder against the side of the seat. Jananin pulled the knife out from its holster on her left leg and pointed it at him. "Go to the house."

She closed over the doors to the garage as Dana walked beside Ivor to the house. The door was open and the hallway inside looked clean and modern, not like Jananin's house in Inverness. Perhaps this was a holiday house Jananin had rented. The door to the living room had been left open, and a half-burnt fire was still going in the fireplace with a poker sticking out of the grate, as though she had lit a fire this morning and been called away suddenly, by *something*.

The front door slammed as Jananin came in. She took off her coat and threw it on the sofa. Underneath it, her katana was belted around her waist above the knife strapped to her thigh. She pulled a chair forward, feet shrieking on the stone floor.

"Sit on it."

Ivor did so by putting his tied arms over the back of it. "Will you not do this in front of Dana? And will you please at least give me your word you'll see to the rescue of other two children on Roareim?"

"You are in no position to demand bargains. The products of your unethical experiments are not my concern." Jananin went behind the chair and tied to the back the string she'd already tied between the handcuffs Officer Logan had put on him the day before. "I see you've already had a near miss with the police, unless jewellery that looks like handcuffs is now one of the fripperies known as *fashion*."

"Blake, I know I stole a helicopter and it looks bad, but I was only on Lewis because I needed medicine—"

"Shut up!" Jananin's eyes were fierce behind her dark glasses. She turned to Dana and pointed to the door. "Out." She pushed Dana back into the hall, closing the door behind her.

Dana started to say something, but Jananin interrupted forcibly. "When I am through with this, we will work out how to get you back to Coventry. That man in there." Jananin pointed at the door. "Whatever claims he has made to you, whoever you think he is, it is not true."

"You blew up Ivor's car and the helicopter! You shot bombs at the helicopter, when you saw I was in it!"

When Jananin volunteered no explanation, Dana demanded, "Why?"

Jananin made a scathing rasp in the back of her throat. "I didn't know what he was doing with you. It looked like he was brandishing you at me, like a trophy."

"He was trying to get me to find a signal and stop you from killing us! I was with him and so was Peter, and he thought you wouldn't blow it up if you knew there were children on it!" Dana considered for a moment, what Ivor had said about Jananin being able to track her, how she'd located her so quickly that morning, and the house left as though she'd been called away in the middle of lighting a fire. The things on sticks, yesterday on the road and today by the stream and the bridge.

"You planted those metal stakes. They're for tracking

me, aren't they? You didn't tell me you were going to do that. You used me to find him, and you told me something else!"

Jananin regarded Dana coolly. "I had never expected you to go through with the cyanide. If you had done, it would have been convenient, but it wasn't essential and it didn't matter if Pilgrennon did uncover it. He won't kill you. You're too useful to him alive. You are the culmination of all his research, the proof of his theory. I knew that by sending you to him, the only peril you would face was that which you brought upon yourself, by taking a boat or whatever stupid thing it was you did when I told you to wait for me. Those signal detectors, however, were a different matter. If you had knowledge of the plan, he would have found out. It's in his nature."

Jananin glanced at the closed door, and then back to Dana. "You understand computers' reactions. There are equations that govern how a computer will behave if you feed it certain information. That man in there does the same with people. Ever since he first spoke with you, he has been reading you, manipulating you, affecting the way you think, seeking out the tiny nuances in your speech and behaviour that, to him, can reveal your motives. He knows things about you that you never even told him. He could make you think white was black, if he wanted to."

"What do you mean?" Dana said angrily. "Nobody can make me do what I don't want to do."

"And therein lies the danger. He doesn't *make* you do anything. He makes you *think* what it suits him for you to think. And then you conveniently *act* on what you *think*. He somehow —and to this day I've never worked out how, exactly— managed to bribe a surgeon who was supposed to be operating on me to remove an ovarian cyst to harvest my gametes and give them to him for his research at the same time. He goes around sneaking, cajoling, making everyone think he's their friend and he's there to help, whereas everything he does is for his own interests. On this island he was keeping you; what's it called?"

"Roareim."

"Did it ever occur to you that you were being held captive?"

"No."

"But you could not open the doors, nevertheless?"

Dana stared back at Jananin for what seemed a long time. "He is not who you think he is," she said at last.

"How is he not, then? Does he deny anything I said of him?"

"No."

"And does he make claim to any extenuating circumstances?"

Dana wondered about what Ivor had said about his wife Adrienne and sister Lydia, but in the end, she supposed the answer would have to be no. "He has changed and he's sorry for what he did." Dana wanted very, very much to make Jananin understand what she knew about Ivor, but she couldn't seem to vocalise it in an ordered fashion. "There are two other children on Roareim called Peter and Alpha, and he's looking after them because Peter's got ADHD and he breaks everything and Alpha's ill from when he tried to put a device in her head like me, but it's not like that because he was trying to help her, and he's not controlling us or making us do things like slaves like you said. And there's a three-headed dog called Cerberus, from a myth, only it's not a dog, it's a computer his friend made, called after the dog in the myth..." Dana trailed off, breathless.

"Thank you, Dana. I did fear that this conversation might weaken Pilgrennon's accountability in my mind. But as it is, speaking to you has only consolidated my resolve."

She turned to the door, glancing back at Dana. "I suggest you think very carefully about what Ivor Pilgrennon has been telling you, and how it fits into what I have told you and what you have seen on Roareim."

Jananin closed the door behind her. The key scraped

in the lock. A trembling line of firelight stood out on the stone floor at the foot of the door. A dark band passed over it as Jananin paced in front of the fire. Dana could hear her voice, but the words were indistinct.

Ivor started to say something, but his voice abruptly changed pitch and volume. He shouted something and then there was a crash. Dana's heart pounded where she stood in the hallway on her own. The window to the room they were in must be around the other side of the house. Dana crept to the front door and slipped out, trying to walk as quietly as possible on the gravel. She fled to the back of the house and crouched under the window. A freezing wind blew from the mountains. She pulled her knees in close and gripped her coat around herself. Peering through the glass at the corner, only the bright fire showed, the darkness of the room eclipsing everything else.

Her eyes adjusted after a moment. Jananin stood in front of the fire. Did she have a computer or something Dana could hear through with her — yes, her mobile phone. It was in her coat pocket on the sofa.

As Dana watched, Jananin took hold of the poker, a few glowing motes drifting from the pile and rising up the chimney. When she pulled it out, it scattered sparks onto the hearth and made a horrible noise on the grate that the phone recorded as an unrealistic rasp. The shaft glowed a dull red halfway down from the handle that left neon-blue ghosts in Dana's eyes.

She could make out Ivor behind her, lying on the floor entangled with the overturned chair. Jananin pointed the poker at his face, moving it closer until he went cross-eyed. Ivor bent his knee and shuffled his shoulder along the ground, trying to manoeuvre away from the poker. His lips moved.

His voice came muffled and distorted through the material of the coat around the mobile phone. "If you kill me here, you will cover this house with indelible evidence."

"I'll think of something. It's not as though you'll

be missed." Jananin delicately touched the tip of the poker against the inside of his arm. Ivor screamed and convulsed on the floor. Why couldn't Ivor *explain*? When Ivor explained things, they always seemed to make sense. Even what he had said to her last night, although it had made her angry and upset, had made sense. Why wouldn't Jananin listen either to him or to Dana?

A siren had just become audible in the distance. On the lawn under the window where she crouched there were some garden ornaments: a stone birdbath and some garden gnomes and things. With both hand she picked up a heavy sculpture of a fantastic-looking horned creature on a plinth bearing lettering that identified it as a *Wild Hairy Haggis*, and heaved it through the window. "The police are coming!"

Jananin had turned at the interruption, the poker still in her hand. As Dana climbed onto the windowsill and stepped over the broken glass and the Wild Hairy Haggis lying on the floor, Jananin demanded, "Did you summon the police?"

"No," said Dana.

There came the sound of tyres on the gravel outside. Jananin drew her knife and bent over Ivor to cut the string tying his hands. Dana went to the door, finding the key still in it, and unlocked it. In the hallway, the only light came from a window on the landing above. The door was solid. Jananin stood with her coat under one arm, the knife in her other hand pointed at Ivor.

Footsteps on gravel outside, and a knock on the door.

The police were outside. Dana looked at Ivor and Jananin. She could call out to them, stop this, have both Ivor and Jananin arrested and tell the police where to find Peter and Alpha. Her mind raced with conflicting memories: Beatrix striking Millie across the face with the flat of her hand, Miss Robinson and Abigail at school, the doctors in the hospital, Officer Logan yesterday.

Dana was breathing hard and Ivor must have noticed,

because he put his hand on her shoulder to try to calm her. She looked at it, at the handcuff still fixed around his wrist like a bracelet.

A bang on the pane of the window in the room to the front of the house, and a man's voice. "Can't see anyone. What's this call about."

"Enquiry about a missing kid from England," said another.

The letterbox rattled, and the voice called, "Hello?" but the letterbox had a draught excluder fitted to it made from thick nylon fibres like on a vacuum cleaner brush, and the policeman couldn't see in.

"Someone's been here recently," said one of the policemen. "There's smoke."

"They're not answering," said the other. "Go and have a look round the back, see if there's a door open. We've not been given much information, but if they want us to look into this we're probably going to have to go back for a warrant."

The scrunch of footsteps on gravel again, receding around the side of the house, and then a shout. "The window back here's been broken!"

The footsteps of the other man in hurried pursuit. Jananin looked fiercely at Dana, before throwing open the front door. An unoccupied police car was pulled over lopsidedly in front of the house. The three of them ran for the garage. Jananin and Ivor threw open the doors and they got into the car, Jananin pulling away before either Dana or Ivor had a chance to put on their seatbelts, tearing down the track and turning out onto the road.

"You are telling me you haven't called the police?" Jananin demanded. "I rented that house under a false name. This car is registered under a false name, which I used when I boarded the ferry. I have been using an anonymous mobile phone ever since Rupert Osric informed me you were at Coventry General. This was very carefully planned. There is nothing to connect any of what is going on here to your missing person's case. It must have been you."

"It wasn't me!" Dana protested.

From the back seat, Ivor backed her up. "She can only transmit short-range radio signals."

"Do you think if I could make phone calls just by thinking, you'd have got away with putting me in your car at the hospital?" In the passenger seat with the heavy binoculars in her lap, something uncomfortable was starting to dawn on Dana. "I think it might have been Cerberus."

"Who or what is Cerberus?"

"It's a three-headed dog in a myth," Dana began.

"I know *that*," said Jananin, "but it obviously *isn't* that, is it now?"

"It's a computer," said Ivor from the back. "Did you ever hear of Steve Gideon?"

"Did I ever hear of him? He was one of the other Nobel nominees the year I won it, for his Porpoise system design. He was very magnanimous about it, sent me a letter of congratulations wishing me the best. The last I heard of him, he killed himself after being accused of murdering his own partner."

"Someone's got hold of one of his computers," Ivor said. "I'm not sure who, but it's potentially someone in government, or the civil service. We've had the same party in power for more than ten years; since Gideon disappeared, in fact. Cerberus is possibly the only computer ever invented that can number-crunch that volume of data, the political leanings and voting patterns of the entire electorate. I'd not be surprised if someone has been using it to manipulate and rig the general election results."

They were passing an empty stretch of road, and as a layby approached, Jananin indicated and pulled into it. With the car stopped, she turned back to face Ivor. "And I suppose you have put her up to some mischief, because you want this computer for yourself?"

Dana interrupted. "It wasn't him. I just found it online. I thought it was a multiplayer online game!"

"And I suppose, by some great coincidence, you just *happened* to stumble across this when you were with him, and not ever before then? Pilgrennon, you want this computer, made by probably the most brilliant scientist in his field since Turing, so you can use it to wipe any incriminating information the authorities might have about yourself. So you can exonerate yourself. So, I suppose, you can make yourself Master of the World. And you set Dana onto it, exploiting her like a pawn in a game; something of no consequence for you to waste in a gambit!"

"It wasn't me that shot explosives at her!" Ivor took his bloodstained hand away from his shoulder, and passed it over his face. "I didn't realise it was embedded in the electoral system until Dana found that out. If you'd ever seen Gideon's porpoises, you wouldn't have seen any harm in it. They were just cute little things that played chess with you. They interacted with people and solved puzzles." He frowned, breathing roughly for a few moments. "Can I suggest something?"

"No." Jananin reached to the car's stereo, switched on the radio, and began flipping rapidly between channels.

"If it's Cerberus," Dana said, "how is it it can tell where I am? Is it through GPS?"

"No," said Ivor. "You can receive radio signals of various sorts, but you can only transmit short-range high-frequency signals, like WiFi and Bluetooth. You're not detectable unless you're in range of one of those."

Police are searching Lewis and Harris for two suspects in connection with the murder of a missing child. Remains discovered in the boot of a burnt-out car abandoned near Miavaig yesterday have tragically been identified as Dana Provine, who was abducted from Coventry General Hospital in England two weeks ago. The two suspects are Ivor Pilgrennon, male, 41, who is described as white and around six foot one, and Jananin Blake, female, 38, white and around five foot eight who is... the radio reporter's voice faltered, as though she didn't quite believe what she was reading, *a professor of Cambridge University and a Nobel laureate. The suspects are believed to be dangerous and police request that anyone sighting them not approach and dial 999.*

The news changed to a weather forecast, and for a moment nobody said anything. Jananin stared at Ivor, her expression becoming increasingly distorted with disgust.

"What do they mean, saying I was dead and there are remains in the boot of a car?" Dana burst out. There were no signals in Jananin's car, apart from her mobile phone, and for a moment Dana felt a surreal sort of horror that she might in fact be dead, or dreaming. "Why is it saying that?"

A look of horrified realisation had come over Ivor. "Whoever took Cerberus must have framed Gideon for the murder of his partner. Now it looks like that same person is trying to frame us, for the worst crime imaginable."

Jananin looked at Dana, and then back at Ivor. "So now I am being framed for murdering a child who is in fact alive, because of your incessant meddling in everything you can get your hands on. Yet somehow what is more offensive is that I am being framed in a way that implies I am some sort of *accomplice* of yours."

"It's your mobile phone! That's how it's tracking us!" Dana realised. "Jananin, I didn't mean to, but last night, when I was playing the game, I was upset about something, and I found all these records. From, like, voting, or something; I don't know. And I didn't do it on purpose, but there was one with your name on it. And one of Ivor. And my foster family, and my brother, and a teacher from my school! They were full of phone numbers and IP addresses!"

Jananin put both her hands on the steering wheel and gripped it until her knuckles turned white. She cast about, at Ivor, at Dana, at the scenery outside, and all the dials and switches on the dashboard. She said an extremely rude word, very loudly.

"Jananin, I'm sorry." Dana breathed in hard and put her hands to her face, trying not to cry and not to let Ivor and Jananin see it.

"Dana," said Ivor, and he must have leaned forward, because when Dana took her hands away, Jananin had drawn her knife again and was pointing it into the back at him.

"This car is a Faraday cage. Nothing in it can be detected with the windows shut. I can turn my mobile phone off, but as soon as Dana comes in range of a wLAN or a mobile phone, it will trigger an alert, and there is no way we can get off the island. You just said you wanted to suggest something. What is it?"

Ivor breathed for a moment, composing his answer. "If you go to the beach at Shawbost back where you found Dana, my boat should hopefully still be there. If we go back to Roareim, it's an island and there are no other people and nothing that can detect signals. I have an Internet connection set up with a VPN. We go back there, Dana goes back into the game and puts right whatever she did wrong, and we just stay there until she's done it. This is a misunderstanding, a mistake. She can use Cerberus to countermand whatever she unintentionally set in motion last time."

Dana wasn't at all sure she would be able to do this, but at least back on Roareim they'd be away from other people, and things that could reveal to Cerberus where she was. And perhaps Jananin would calm down.

Jananin turned away from him, staring at the road ahead. "And this remote island. After we do this, nobody will find your corpse there."

Ivor closed his eyes for a moment. "Just give me your word. Dana and Peter and Alpha go back on the boat with you, and you leave them somewhere safe for the authorities to find once you're done with me."

Jananin turned the key to restart the car. "Your terms are acceptable."

-3-

IT was starting to get dark by the time they reached the beach at Shawbost. Dana hadn't had any lunch, and now the stress of what had happened had died down a bit, she was starting to feel very hungry and thirsty. The boat was still there on the beach, although the tide had gone out and stranded it, and fortunately the only person they saw was a woman some distance away on the moor, out walking with a dog.

Jananin switched off her mobile phone before opening the door. She told Dana to bring the binoculars, and got some other equipment out of the boot. They had parked up at the picnic table. Ivor said it was quite common for strange cars to park in such places when people went off to sea, and as Jananin had told him the car was registered in a fake name, probably it wouldn't be seen as anything remarkable. He had some trouble pushing the boat down the beach to the water with his shoulder injury, and couldn't pick Dana up to help her in.

By the time they and Jananin's equipment were aboard, and Ivor had started the engine and turned the boat around to head west, the sun had already set behind the shroud of the overcast sky.

Jananin spoke very little on the journey. She sat behind Ivor as he piloted the boat, watching him intently, her hand on the hilt of her knife the whole way. Ivor himself seemed pale and exhausted.

The lighthouse on Eilean Mór began to flash as they rounded the north side of Roareim, and as the shape of the rock stacks came into view, Jananin at last broke the silence. "Have you really been *here* all these years?"

"There's an old military base inside it," Ivor explained.

"Probably started off as a natural cave which they enlarged. I've never found out what exactly its purpose was."

The boat slowed to a crawl as he turned it into the submarine bay. Jananin frowned up at the cliff above as it swallowed the sky.

The door in the submarine bay had an electronic lock on the outside, the same as the other external door. Dana told it to unlock and went in, intending to go to the kitchen and get a drink. A bad smell of excrement was immediately apparent when she went in, which got stronger as she made her way to the kitchen. Alpha was sat at the chess table, where Ivor had left her, and there was a puddle beneath her chair. The cogs inside the tape player Ivor had left running on the table in front of her had stopped.

Ivor appeared behind her. "Oh, *Peter*," he said, upon seeing Alpha. "I asked him to do one thing. I expect he's fallen asleep."

As he went to Alpha, taking her shoulder and telling her to stand up, Jananin came into the doorway behind him, her nose wrinkled in disgust. She stared at Alpha, where she stood in front of the chess table, staring gormlessly into space in clothing soaked with urine and faeces.

"Pilgrennon!" she exclaimed. "If you were caught keeping a dog alive in this state, you would be arrested for an animal welfare offence!"

Ivor turned to her, apparently as much appalled by her words as she was by Alpha's condition. "She's not a dog, Blake! She's a human being! She's just had an accident."

"What is the matter with this child?" Jananin stared into Alpha's face. "Braindamaged, no doubt. And I'll vouch it's as a result of something you did."

Alpha tended to collapse her shoulders and slump forward when she stood, but seeing her standing beside Jananin made Dana realise that if Alpha stood straight, she would be quite tall, probably coming up to Jananin's shoulder. Alpha stood, oblivious to the argument occurring in front of her, the stranger in the room who scrutinised her vacuous stare, taking in the scar on her forehead, stepping back to look her up and down. "How old is she?"

"Blake, this really isn't the priority right now. Just let me get her cleaned up."

"*How old is she?*"

"She's fifteen. She's not —*yours*— if that's what you want to know. There are only five of them, and only Dana and her brother were from you." After a long pause, Ivor said: "The device in Alpha's head has taught her to respond to my commands." He licked his lips and swallowed. "She's only —*stinking*— and in this state because I've been away and there's been no-one to tell her when to do things."

"You kept her alive... like a *robot*?"

Ivor shook his head. He ran his hand over his forehead, untidying his hair. "I was trying to help her. She was mute. She was completely disengaged. Her mother signed her up for residential care, and just stopped visiting. But she always used to smile at computers." He shook his head. "It just didn't work out."

Jananin surveyed the room, taking several heavy breaths, her face completely expressionless. "Dana, come back to the boat with me."

"No!" Dana shouted out. "I'm sick of you arguing! I'm tired and hungry, and I want a drink, and you said you'd come back and wait here until I'd sorted out what I'd done with Cerberus."

"I'm going to find all the entrances to this place and blow them up. He can stay here and die in the cave-in with his failed experiments. Then we are going to the police, so they can see you are not dead in the boot of a burnt-out car, and you are going to tell them the truth, and I am getting the solicitor who defended me when my employer tried to sue me, and I will tell the police whatever she tells me to say to them."

Ivor raised his hands, his eyes wide. "We need to stop this, Blake. It's looking increasingly like whoever has Cerberus acquired it by framing Gideon for the murder of his partner, and possibly that same person was responsible for both their deaths. That person is likely intending on doing the same thing to Dana and both of us because they've decided we're a risk because we're on the brink of discovering this and the reason for it, and they will use whatever power they can exert through Cerberus over the police or any other authorities to do so. You take her back out there, you'll get both of you killed."

Jananin stared at the three of them, standing together by the chess table. "Then stay here and die with him in this maggot-holed pile of gneiss stinking like a sewer." She turned and left the room.

Ivor's forehead gleamed with sweat in the kitchen light. "Dana, get yourself a drink, and then go and find Peter. He's probably asleep in his bedroom; bring him back here."

Peter was asleep on the least broken bed amongst several trashed bunks in his room when Dana went to look for him, but he stirred when the door opened. He looked to have been quite deeply asleep, but he came along cheerfully when Dana asked him to.

"Peter, what happened while Dana and I were out?" Ivor asked him in the kitchen.

"Alpha poo'd herself," said Peter.

"So, what did you do?"

Peter grinned. "I went to my bedroom, and shut the door, to get away from the smell."

"Do you remember what I asked you to do?"

Peter shrugged. "Feed the fish?"

"To turn the tape over, when it stopped, so that Alpha would go to the toilet at the right time?"

Peter's face fell.

Jananin had by now come back, and Peter looked at her, and said, "Hello." He turned back to Ivor. "Has she come to live here, too?"

Jananin ignored him. "That door needs a key to open it."

"I see," said Ivor, "that the years have not tarnished or rusted a mind like a steel trap." There was an exhausted desperation to his manner.

"Where is it?"

Ivor's expression changed. "Oh, it's safe."

Jananin drew her knife. "*Where is it?*"

"Calm down, Blake. You won't find it if you kill me."

Jananin stared at him for a moment. She turned and started pulling the drawers out on the kitchen units, rifling about in them. She slammed each of them shut with increasing violence, before turning her attention to the fish tank. Peter shouted.

"It's not in there," said Ivor as she knocked the hood out the way and pulled her sleeve up. "This place isn't big, but it's neither simple. Conceivably, one might run out of food before finding the key." He raised his eyebrows.

Jananin pointed her knife at his neck, the tip of the blade quivering madly. "Where is the key?"

Ivor's position did not change. He calmly reached up and held the blade between his thumb and forefinger, and pushed it out of the way. When he spoke it was with a sardonic smile, and an even, almost jocular tone. "You've had your pint of blood and your pound of flesh. Now it's my turn." He suddenly drew himself up to his full height. Although Jananin wasn't short, he was several inches taller, and even with her heavy-collared coat on he was nearly twice her breadth across the shoulders and chest. "You're smart, Blake. You've done great things. You've brought along poisons, knives, explosives, your martial arts skills, all manner of ingenious stuff. I don't have any weapons. The only weapons I need are up here." He tapped his right temple with his index finger, his voice changing to an unkind tone Dana hadn't heard him use before. "Don't you forget that. And don't you forget that I can *read* you."

At the same time as he said *you*, he took hold of Jananin's coat collar. In an instant, she pivoted against his grip, ducking under his arm. As he turned after her, her fist sprang back in his face. He'd been flinching away as she hit him, but when he staggered back against the wall, blood streamed from his nostrils and down his chin like it had out of Abigail when Dana had hit *her*.

He pulled a piece of cloth from his pocket and swabbed at his face with it, groping for the back of the chair to steady himself. He sat and leaned his elbows on the table, clenching his nose in one hand and trying to wipe the blood off the rest of his face with the tail of the cloth in the other.

Jananin put her knife back in its sheath. She glared sideways at him, rubbing the knuckles of her right hand briskly. She took a few steps forward, flexing her shoulders, and kicked the door so hard that it swung 180 degrees, rebounded off the wall, and slammed shut inches before her nose.

"Do not put your hands on me again, unless you would prefer them detached from your arms!"

Ivor sniffed, swallowing blood.

She stormed out of the room without another word.

Peter moved cautiously towards the door, his face pale, eyes wide under the rim of his Viking helmet. Ivor leaned forward, still holding his nose. "Peter, don't antagonise her!" he hissed, his voice nasal and muffled. "Take Alpha to the showers. I'll sort her out in a minute. Alpha, go with Peter to the showers."

Dana sat down at the chess table opposite Ivor. "You hid the key? While I was getting Peter?"

He raised his eyebrows, snuffling. "You know I can't tell you where. I've bought myself a stay of execution, but it's made her even more mad at me, because I've won, at least for now. She'll probably tell you I masterminded it this way all along, but in truth there's no grand plan, not any more. It's just the will to survive, day to day."

He gave his nose a few cautious, tender rubs, and sniffed experimentally. The bleeding seemed staunched. Stiffly and cautiously, he slid his jacket off his shoulders, wincing at the sensation, the shirt he wore beneath stained brown with dry blood. "Well, I suppose it can't be too horrendous, as I think it's stopped bleeding. I'd better go and clean up myself as well as Alpha, and make the dinner."

With that he rose and left the kitchen.

Dana remembered there were three lobsters hanging in the cloth bag by the stove. Ivor had found them in the traps that morning, and put them there for tonight's meal. In spite of her tiredness, her aching legs, and the bruises from yesterday, she got up and put some water in the pans and set the bag of lobsters down on the table for when he came back. A great many things had gone wrong, but at the moment, all she could feel was relief that Jananin wasn't going to kill Ivor for the time being and that she didn't have to go back to Pauline and Graeme's house. She no longer cared what Ivor had done, and wished it could just stay like this and she could live on the island and fall back into his routine. Perhaps if she could sort out whatever she'd done in Cerberus's game, Jananin would agree to go away in peace in exchange for Ivor opening the door.

When he came back, Alpha was with him and was clean, and he'd put on a fresh shirt, although the white gauze of a dressing showed through where the top button was unfastened.

Dana went back to her bedroom to put her bag away, but Jananin was there, and seemed to have claimed the room. "Do you know where the key is?" she asked when she saw Dana.

"No." Dana waited, a cocktail of aching dread swirling about her intestines, but Jananin didn't say anything more to her. She went back to the kitchen to help Ivor make the dinner.

He kept asking her to hold things that didn't need holding: banal anythings to occupy her mind. He kept telling Alpha to fetch things and tripping over her whenever he turned round. And he wept into the dinner.

He put Prokofiev on the CD player and tried to keep his back turned so Dana wouldn't see him doing it, but she could hear his faltering breathing and see his shoulders trembling.

Peter set an extra place at the dinner table, and when the food was ready, Ivor wiped his nose and his spectacles, and put his hand over the wound on his shoulder with a slight grimace, and went to ask Jananin if she would come and eat with them.

She came in after he had returned and sat down, and ignored the place set for her, and took Ivor's meal from in front of him. "Oh, come on!" he said as she left with it the same way she'd come. "That's your speciality, not mine!"

Peter seemed to find this amusing, and he took Dana's plate from in front of her instead of his own, and then Ivor told him to stop it, and took his plate and gave it back to Dana, and all the time Alpha sat in front of her plate, staring ahead and waiting for Ivor's instruction for her to eat. Dana was ravenous and lobster and potato never tasted as good as it did tonight. She even did what Peter did and picked at the legs and the crevices in the carapace to get the last scraps of meat.

After dinner, Ivor tried to talk to Jananin again, and Dana listened from the dining room.

"Will you come to the kitchen and talk to me?"

"What, you want me to do therapy with you? You think you can give me Stockholm Syndrome? Steel and Flame will not be corrupted."

"I think my answer to that, in the capacity of a therapist, is that you have to want an outcome as the patient in order to start moving towards it. I was rather hoping you'd talk to me about Dana, and what we are going to do to resolve this situation and make it safe for her. I was also rather hoping to talk to you, because it's a long time since I've been able to have a real conversation with another adult, let alone a Nobel laureate."

"I thought your plan was to get Dana to go back into

this program and correct whatever she did with this computer to cause someone in a position of authority with the police to attempt to frame both of us for her murder? I suggest you concentrate on facilitating that."

Dana could see Ivor standing before the threshold to the room, through the corridor. "I'm sorry. For everything." He closed the door and came back, and sat on one of the dining chairs facing her.

"I don't really want to ask you this after everything that's gone on today, but do you think you could have another go at that game? There's a VPN on the Internet connection, so Cerberus has never been able to tell where you're connected from."

Dana didn't really want to, but she nodded and went back through Ivor's bedroom to the computer room, and put the bag with Jananin's laptop away there. She sat on the floor, leaning against the wall as usual, and closed her eyes and concentrated until she slipped into the game. She didn't think she could stand being there alone if Eric wasn't there, but he was, and they found each other in the desert by the waterfall.

"There you are, at last!" he said. "I was beginning to wonder whether you'd be on tonight at all. How is stuff going, with your dad and you going back to your mum?"

Dana considered. "They kind of got back together."

"Well, that's something, isn't it?"

"I dunno," said Dana. "She wants to kill him."

Eric picked up a stone and flung it down the gully into the river below, which looked much larger than Dana remembered it, filling up the bottom and flowing swiftly instead of the meandering trickle it had once been. "If she wants to kill him, there's still hope. It was when my mum *stopped* wanting to kill my dad that I knew it was over between them."

Dana pretended to laugh.

Eric pointed at the waterfall. "Whatever we did last time, it must have worked, because the puzzle has changed again. The water is flowing too fast. It's impossible to climb in that way now."

The waterfall had once been a cascade wreathed in mist and refracted rainbows, but now it was a torrent, looking more like a burst mains.

"Do you think there's a way of resetting it?" Dana said. "Could we make it go back the way it was before?"

"I dunno. I've never seen a server reset happen in this game. It's very sandbox-like. It just evolves over time."

Dana tried cutting and pasting hers and Eric's code into the place Cerberus had last been, but they found themselves in an empty pocket of air inside rock, with no light or water, and she had to cut and paste them back into the desert. They walked around for a bit, and then Eric said he had to go to bed as he was supposed to be going to visit his grandmother tomorrow, and that Dana should probably talk to her family if she was upset.

Dana came out of the Cerberus game, but she didn't leave the computer room, yet. She went to Pauline and Graeme's IP address, and saw that Duncan was playing *Pillage and Burn* online.

Dana closed her eyes, and slipped into the game code just as she had with the Cerberus game, just as she did when she'd played with Duncan. Now she was the dwarf wizard, and Duncan was here, somewhere, the giantess warrior.

Dana had materialised in a forest, and she wandered around the paths between the pixellated trees until she saw a group of players in a clearing, killing a dragon that slashed those behind it with its tail, and breathed fire over those in front of it. She decided to join in and started to heal the players and cast spells on the dragon. When the dragon fell down dead, everyone looted it and wrote thanks and farewells in the game chat, and the crowd began to disperse.

Dana identified the giantess, and she targeted Duncan's character and sent a private message to him.

Duncan.

Most of the others had gone now, and Duncan ran back and forward, his character disappearing inside the bulk of the dead dragon and reappearing. After a moment his reply came back.

Dana?

It is Dana. Someone on the news said I was dead, and it's a lie.

Is that really you? Mum and Dad were really upset. They announced that on the news and they're supposed to tell people's family first. Mum and Dad said they were being discriminated against because they're foster parents, and then they asked for arrangements to be made for the body to be returned, and the police in Scotland said they'd lost it, and they're waiting to hear back from a solicitor. And something about how ridiculous it is that they're saying some bloke did it who disappeared ten years ago or so and his wife had him declared legally dead so she could have his money, and a woman who's a respected scientist and has won an award for her work.

I can't stay long, said Dana, worried that anything she did might risk drawing Cerberus's attention to Duncan, and something happening to him, or to Cale, or Pauline and Graeme. *I wanted you to know I'm OK. But something's gone wrong, and the people I'm with are trying to fix it. If you tell the police, it will make it worse.*

I dunno if I should tell Mum and Dad even, said Duncan. *It was hard enough to get them to let me play games online. I said I was miserable without you to play with. I don't think they'd believe me if I said I'd talked to you online anyway. They'd think I was being trolled. Hey, have you learned the spell to summon a wizard familiar?*

A wizard familiar?

The crow.

Dana looked to see an enormous black crow standing next to her in the game. It was hugely detailed with realistic shiny eyes and a thick grey beak, and it looked at her intelligently. Immediately she realised it didn't match with the blocky, low-polygon, pixellated art of *Pillage and Burn*. It was Cale. Cale had made an avatar and come into a game. It was such a relief and a reassurance to feel his signal again, even if it was over a great distance and through a game.

Is Cale there with you?

He's here. He was watching, but I think he's fallen asleep.

Tell him I'm OK.

Will do. Thanks for coming and letting me know you're all right.

I'll come and see you, when I can. Dana faced Cale's crow once again, thinking to him that it would be all right.

When Dana came out of the game, she got up off the floor in the computer room and opened the door, to find Ivor sitting in the bedroom with Alpha. It appeared he had been reading her a children's picture book, although she showed no interest in it or anything else, and there was snot hanging out of her nose.

Ivor closed the book and set it down on his lap, looking expectantly to Dana as she emerged.

"I couldn't. The game's changed. I found the other player who helps me, but we couldn't get anywhere."

Ivor exhaled. "It's okay. You're tired and it's been a hard day for all of us. It'll come to you."

A shadow passed over the doorway between the bedroom and the corridor. Jananin had emerged. "Have you fixed this Cerberus computer... thing?"

"No," said Dana.

Jananin gave an impatient sigh. "In Greek mythology, there are a great many characters in addition to Cerberus, such as Pandora, who was given a box which she was told under no circumstances should she open. When she ignored the instructions and opened it, all manner of evil was unleashed upon the world."

"Sorry," Dana mumbled.

Jananin turned to Ivor. "There isn't any toilet paper."

"You're right," he said. "There's no toilet paper. There's

no shampoo or conditioner either, and no tins of food. They were all in my car, along with my Rachmaninov CD, and you blew them all to Kingdom Come with that missile launcher or whatever it was you were running around Lewis with."

Jananin glowered and went away.

Ivor picked up half a plastic comb from a shelf and handed it to Dana. "That reminds me. I did buy you a comb. You'd better have mine now. I don't know where the other half's gone."

Alpha turned her head. Instead of staring blankly ahead as she usually did, her gaze had been drawn to the open door behind Dana. She stood up from where she'd been sitting on the bed next to Ivor, and looked down at her hands, and then she raised her arm to wipe her nose on the back of her wrist.

Ivor was transfixed upon her, his mouth slack with surprise. He glanced at Dana for a second and got to his feet, the book falling from his knee to the floor.

Alpha took a faltering step towards the computer room, elbows bent and hands limp before her, head leaned forward so her eyes looked up through the hair overhanging her forehead. An inflexible smile passed over her face.

"She's thinking for herself!" Ivor's voice was somewhere between a gasp and a whisper. "She's not done this since —the computers— she always used to smile at computers!"

Alpha took a couple more steps to stand in the doorway beside Dana and look at the computers, but after a few minutes, her odd, stiff smile faded, and her arms dropped to her sides, and she became passive once more.

"Alpha?" Ivor put a hand on her shoulder, but she didn't respond.

"I suppose I can't ask for miracles, but that's hope. If it happens once, chances are it'll happen again. Pity I can't leave the door open for her with Peter running amok." He closed and locked the door. "Come on, Alpha."

In the kitchen, Ivor made Alpha sit down on one of the floor cushions.

"Doesn't she have a bed to sleep in?" Dana asked.

"She doesn't sleep, because she's always asleep," said Peter, who was looking at his fish tank.

"Steve Gideon's computers sleep." Dana thought of what Ivor had said about the porpoises, and how Cerberus in the game would sleep with one or two heads at a time. "But Alpha doesn't sleep?"

"We did try to find out what had gone wrong with her implant." Ivor stroked his hand over Alpha's lank, straight hair. "She was in a coma for a fortnight after the surgery. We did a lot of MRI scans of her brain, before you were born, before Jananin... found out and my research got broken up. She's not braindamaged like Jananin thinks. There's nothing wrong with her brain, it's just she's not using it, apart from a small part that's learnt to respond to signals and simple spoken instructions. Medically, it's what we call a disorder of consciousness. It's not quite a coma, but not quite awake. She does have brain activity that resembles REM sleep, so I think she does dream."

Ivor turned to Peter. "Peter, time for bed. Remind me, what did I tell you before, about when you wake up?"

Under his helmet, Peter's face twisted in concentration. "Not to go into Dana's bedroom, because of the lady."

"Good. And?"

"And knock hard on the door to the loo, and not go in unless nobody answers after ten seconds."

"Well done." Ivor hugged Peter. "Goodnight." He gestured to Dana. "Let's sort you out somewhere to sleep. I've put a mattress for you in the old control room."

He switched off the kitchen light as they left. In the room with the dead consoles of switches and lights, there was a mattress on the floor with a blanket and a cushion to use for a pillow, and a dressing-gown and an old shirt to do for pyjamas.

"Is this really how computers used to be?" Dana asked.

"In the Second World War. Probably to do with a radar station or something up on the island that's since been dismantled. Pity they don't work any more. Doubt even Peter would be able to break something so primitive."

Dana sat on the mattress and started pulling her boots off. "Ivor, what if I can't undo whatever I did to Cerberus?"

He sat down beside her, and put his arm around her. "You will. Some problems take time to solve. You ask Jananin. She didn't invent her synapse in a single evening."

Dana sniffed and wiped her eyes. "But what if I *don't*?"

"Well, we'll just have to work out something else."

"Ivor, what if Jananin finds the key in the night, and murders you while you're asleep?"

He looked a bit shocked when she said this, and didn't reply at once. Dana leaned her head against his chest miserably, listening to his heartbeat and the pulse of his watch.

"She's very angry with me, and to be honest she's got every right to be. I had rather hoped she might have calmed down a bit, with all the time I've been away and us both being so much older. I am trying my best with her."

Dana's next breath came out as a sob, and he added in a hurry, "I don't think she will kill me now. It takes a lot, psychologically, for a normal person to be able to kill someone. You have to be very angry, or make yourself stop seeing your victim as another person. She would have done it back there on the road, but she didn't, and it's likely the momentum has run out."

"But Jananin and I aren't normal people. We both have autism."

"I'm sorry, Dana, that's not what I meant at all. People who have autism are not, *not normal*, and they have just the same inhibitions about doing awful things to other people as does anyone else. The kind of not normal people I mean are psychopaths, and psychopathy is very different to autism."

Dana put her hand into her pocket and fiddled with the fuses in it. "Did you go looking for Cerberus, thinking you could steal it or control it, like Jananin said?"

"Well, I..." Ivor sighed and shifted a bit where he sat, squeezing her more firmly with his arm. "I was looking for it. I didn't realise up until you told me about it that it was embedded in the civil service, or exerting influence on the voting system. I tried to hack into it manually, and I tried to get Alpha to interact with it, but nothing I did worked. Obviously if I could have controlled it and used it to give myself a new identity, I could have taken Peter and Alpha and we could have gone and lived quietly somewhere out the way, and they would have had more medical support, and Peter would have a better education."

"Peter is lucky that he doesn't have to go to a school," Dana countered.

"I don't think I would send Peter to school, but it would be easier if I could take him to the library and other places he can learn and interact with other people. And homeschooled children with official identities have rights to sit exams when they're ready for them, and get qualifications."

Dana looked up at him, noticing again the dressing through the collar of his shirt. "Is where you got cut going to be okay?"

"I think so. It's long, but not deep. She ruined a decent jacket and a good shirt, though. As long as the sword didn't have anything unhygienic on it, it shouldn't get infected. I don't think Jananin is the sort of person to keep dirty swords about her, do you? She seems quite a tidy sort of person."

"She is." Dana laughed. "She doesn't like people spilling Chinese takeaway in her car, or farting in it!"

Ivor wrapped both arms firmly around Dana as they both laughed.

Dana said, "I wish I could go with you, and Peter and Alpha, and not go to school. But I'd want Cale to come, too."

Ivor loosened his grip on her a bit, leaning back to see her face. "Tell me more about Cale. I wish I could meet him."

"Well, he doesn't talk if he can avoid it. People think he's stupid. I once heard a specialist say he is *low functioning*." Dana frowned.

"That used to be said about Alpha," said Ivor. "I preferred to think of it as her just not interacting with the world because she didn't see it as terribly relevant to her."

"I can feel Cale thinking, and he can feel me thinking. He's not stupid and he can think just as well as I can. He knows all sorts of things about beetles, but he just won't tell anyone, because it's nobody else's business. He can read and write, but he won't read out loud or write what people tell him to. He can play the keyboard, but he won't play music someone else has written, like Rackman that you listen to..."

"Rachmaninov."

"He is working out the number Pi and writing all the numbers down in a book as he goes. And he converts the numbers into music notes and plays them, a bit like how bits on computers translate into pictures and words."

"He sounds like a lovely brother," said Ivor. "And he's probably quite right about it not being anyone else's business!"

Although his words and his closeness comforted her, Dana could not escape the ominous pressure inside her, the feeling that everything was really, *really* broken and things would never be right, and that it was all because of her.

-4-

DANA must have fallen asleep, for now it was dark, and Ivor had gone, leaving the blanket over her and the cushion tucked under her head. She'd gone to sleep in her clothes, discomfort and confusion penetrating her dream, a dream she only remembered the ending and the shock of waking from: Jananin's katana coming down on Ivor.

She sensed a signal, and although the room was still dark, she made out a figure standing in the doorway, the corridor behind dim with the blue-tinged lights that always stayed on. "Alpha?"

Alpha didn't sleep, Ivor had told her. Someone who doesn't sleep, presumably can't sleepwalk, so she must be awake. Alpha, even though she was awake, didn't walk around or do things by herself without Ivor prompting her. When Dana tried to recall seeing Alpha walking previously, she could only remember her doing so with him holding her hand to guide her, or telling her where to go. How, then, had she walked from the kitchen to the corridor in the dark, without him there?

She made out motion from the dim silhouette, and sensed Alpha's signal coming closer. Dana pulled the blanket away from her face and sat up. Alpha's hands reached out in front of her, blindly almost, closing in on Dana with clumsy, deliberate steps. She reminded Dana of one of the zombies from the game she played with Duncan.

Dana called out, "Ivor!" as she got to her feet. She flung the blanket over Alpha's head, realising as she did so that Alpha must be targeting her not through sight in the dark, but by Dana's own signal that she gave out. She backed away, trying to avoid the clutching hands, finding the edge of one of the sloping consoles. She leaned back against it, feeling switches and dials press into her back, and raised her knee. At the same time her hand found a forgotten mug of tea that had gone cold. She uncoiled her leg, hitting the bigger girl hard in the ribs and knocking her to the floor. Dana hurled the mug at her dark shape; hearing it smash on the concrete and splash its contents. "Ivor! Jananin!"

She looked to the rectangle of dim light that led to the corridor, and in panic she tried to jump over Alpha where she sprawled on the floor to get to it, but hands caught her leg and she fell on the concrete. She tried to roll out of the way as Alpha came at her again, but she couldn't move fast enough. Alpha was on top of her, pinning her down, and from the scant light the corridor offered she could just make out her eyes, vacant, unseeing. Fingers closed around her throat.

The light came on. Alpha's head jerked back on her neck. Her arms straightened as something pulled her back by the hair, and over the sensation of blood building up in her head and the buzzing in her ears, Jananin's voice was shouting something. Dana sensed she was being dragged about the room, but Alpha wasn't letting go. She reached for the girl's wrists, digging her thumbnails into the tendons and blood vessels, but Alpha seemed to feel no pain.

The room spun. A sickening thud of some body part striking concrete. Alpha's grip loosed and Dana was finally able to throw her hands away from her neck and scoot away from her, under the console, gulping down air that didn't seem able to fit inside her in sufficient quantity.

Alpha staggered, reeling. It looked as though Jananin had driven her head into the doorframe. Jananin was standing there now, her hair messed up, but still wearing her clothes, and her boots, and her knife. She looked like she'd fallen asleep same as Dana had.

Now Alpha had recovered, but she sought Dana at

once, advancing towards her and reaching out. Jananin, incomprehension and disgust on her face, kicked her forcibly in the stomach, at which she staggered, fell down on one knee, and then rose, gasping and wheezing, but undeterred. Jananin grabbed her arm and hurled her over her shoulder in a judo throw that landed her flat on her back on the concrete floor in a way that couldn't possibly not hurt, but she got up again and kept coming at Dana.

"Don't hurt her!" Dana cried out as Jananin drew her knife, but Alpha was upon her again, her hands reaching for Dana's neck.

If Dana focused on Alpha's signal, in much the way she could do to Cale, and that she and Peter could do to each other, she could feel what felt like a closed door, almost a blockage. The door was locked, but Dana sensed the lock was weak, and if she pushed hard enough, the lock would break. She did her best to ignore the grip that had fastened once more around her neck, and the static snow that filled her vision or the buzzing in her ears, or that Jananin was dragging both of them about the room in her attempts to get Alpha off her. She concentrated all her mental strength on that point. *Alpha I'll break you if you won't stop...*

A thin, strangulated cry escaped from Alpha. The grip on Dana's neck abated, and she opened her eyes to see Jananin throw Alpha sprawling upon the floor, Ivor standing in the door behind them, his dressing-gown pulled on over his pyjamas, his eyes wide.

Alpha got up off the floor and screamed with the full force of her lungs. She put her hands up to her face and screamed again, and again, and the scream became an ululating cry that segued into vocal sobs of the sort a young child that has hurt itself makes. Ivor went to her, taking hold of her, and when he saw the state she was in and the bruise on her scarred forehead, he shouted, "What have you done to her?" He seemed distant, somehow, and his voice seemed to echo.

Dana tried to speak. She put her hand to her throat,

but the words wouldn't come.

"You've got a screw loose!" Ivor was speaking to Jananin, who faced him, knife in hand. "Don't you bring her into this! Don't you bring any of them into it. This is between you and me, Blake, and you've crossed a line!"

"Your *pet vegetable* just tried to kill Dana!" Jananin shouted back at him. "She was strangling her!"

Ivor shook his head, indignant, disbelieving. "She'd never do that!"

"Cerberus made her do it!" Dana managed to get out. Her voice didn't sound like her own.

"Dana, she only follows simple instructions, only from me."

"She can follow your instructions when you're not there, on the tapes you make," Dana said. "Last night, in the computer room."

Ivor's expression changed.

"Ivor, what if—" A coughing fit overcame Dana, and for a few seconds she couldn't speak. "What if I went into Cerberus's world, and treated it as a game, and tried to defeat it, and now it's doing the same back to me?"

Ivor stared at her, and then he turned back to Alpha, who continued to scream and cry. "I have to deal with this first. Dana, did you do this to her?"

Dana nodded.

"It was the only way to stop her!" Jananin interjected. "Asides from the alternative." She pushed her knife pointedly back into the sheath on her thigh.

Ivor held up his hand, not looking at Jananin. "Dana, I'm not blaming you, and this is potentially very good news, but is there any chance you could undo it and then redo it once we have resolved things to a slightly more conducive situation?"

Dana shook her head. "The *thing* you said she had, that happened because of what you did?"

"A disorder of consciousness?"

Dana nodded. "I fixed it."

Peter had now been roused from his bed, and as he came into the room, a grin sprang upon his face beneath his helmet. "Alpha, you're awake at last!"

As Ivor led Alpha away, Peter went with them, bombarding Ivor with suggestions to calm her down: *Perhaps we should show her the fish tank? Perhaps she could draw a picture, or read a book?* To which Ivor replied variously, *Let's see. We should try to get her to sleep. Perhaps tomorrow.*

Jananin took hold of Dana's arm. "Sit on your mattress."

Dana half sat, half lay, and let Jananin look at her neck. "Am I all right?"

"I'm no medical expert, but I expect so."

Dana coughed experimentally. Jananin stepped in the cold tea splattered across the floor and, seeing no other means to clear it up, began to push the broken pieces of the mug into a corner with the toe of her boot.

"Jananin... what you said... I'm Pandora, aren't I?"

Jananin exhaled loudly. She cast about the room for a chair that was not broken, and found a swivel chair with the back missing and the cloth on the seat all ripped and showing yellow foam. "I said that to you in anger, and the anger was at Pilgrennon, not at you. What it means, is not really how I said it. Have you heard of it before?"

Dana shook her head.

"Pandora means 'all gifts'. Pandora in the story was the first woman, a gift to the first men. The harmful gifts inside the box came with the beneficial gifts embodied in its bearer, Pandora herself. Pandora opened the box because of curiosity, the same curiosity that drives scientific advance, the very thing that makes us human instead of being mere animals. The point of the story is that no light can exist without darkness, and the good and bad things we experience and are can't be experienced independent of each other."

Dana sniffed. "What Ivor did to you, the bad thing

that made me, I wish it hadn't happened. But if it hadn't happened, I wouldn't be here to wish that or anything else, so it sort of doesn't make sense."

"It's a paradox. Possibly it is a variant of the anthropic principle, although I am no philosopher. I could wish that, logically. I did wish that. But when I met you, I did not wish that."

"I wish it had happened differently. Like when people are born the usual way."

"I see that you suffer. I remember what it was like to have to grow up, like having to fight my way out of a pit of snakes."

Dana looked up, astonished by her words. "But you're a genius!"

Jananin arched her eyebrows in a humourless smile. "Tell me, if you can, what is the difference between a genius and a fool?"

"I should have thought that was obvious. A genius is clever and makes things. A fool just says silly things."

"*Makes things*," Jananin considered. "I suppose, fools do not usually make things, or if they do, the things do not service any human need. However, fools do not have a monopoly on saying silly things. People have not always called me a genius, and before I was a genius, I was a fool. Both of them are peerless. Nobody understands either of them."

"When you invented your..." Dana waved her hand inarticulately at her own head.

"My bioelectronic synapse."

"Why did you not let the people who offered you money for it use it?"

"I was young. I was perhaps idealistic, and probably paranoid. At the time I thought perhaps it was a fluke, that I had lightning in a bottle, and that I'd have no leverage in my career if I didn't hold on to the rights. You see, when I did that work, I did it in rather an odd way, in a laboratory I set up at home. At the time I was a postdoctoral fellow at Bristol University, and the person in charge of my work there did not like me, and had deliberately omitted my name from a number of research papers I contributed to, and was threatening not to renew my contract. Until I got tenure at Cambridge on the basis of my work on the synapse and my proposal to develop polymer alloys there, it was looking rather like my career could have been ended very unceremoniously. I did sell the rights to my synapse, for various purposes in the end, but that was after Pilgrennon stole it."

"You didn't like going to school, then?"

"I liked studying science there, but that was it. I wish you did not have to experience the same thing. But the two are inseparable, like Pandora and the box, and to live is to suffer."

"I think this thing in my head perhaps helps me." Dana raised her hand to touch her forehead. "I think I would rather have it than not."

"Again, you have no experience of not having it to compare it to."

"But what if Cerberus won't stop? Graeme said the doctors probably wouldn't remove it."

"I expect there would be a very skilled surgeon, who could be found somewhere in the world, who would be able to do it, if you wanted that."

"I don't think I want that."

After neither spoke for a few minutes, Dana said, "That Ivor did this thing was wrong, but it's done now, and it can't be undone, and I don't expect he will do it again, and I don't think he would actually *hurt* anyone."

"Not physically."

Dana looked up at Jananin, her eyes burning, and felt a tear spill over. "Could you not hurt him, please?"

Jananin beheld her for a moment, her face grim. "Just because I express sympathy for your situation, that does not give you licence to comment on mine. It's not your concern." She stood up. "You have tea splattered all over your clothes. You should change them and go to sleep. It's 3 AM."

*

Dana woke to a wailing sound in another room. It was the sort of noise only one with no skill to express needs such as hunger, or exhaustion, or boredom, would make. A childish sound, *grizzling*, adults she had heard speak about young children called it, but the voice that made it was incongruously older.

The light was on in the corridor. She got up and put on her dressing gown and slippers, and went into the dining area. Peter and Alpha were sitting at the table and Ivor was setting plates of food in front of them. "Breakfast is ready," he said, noticing Dana.

Alpha, who had been making the noise, quietened and put her elbows on the table and her hands on her plate. Her fingers squeezed and groped at the grated potato fritters and oily seagull meat Ivor had put in front of her. When she tried putting the food in her mouth, she made a choking sound and opened her mouth and stuck out her tongue until the food fell back onto her plate.

"She never liked food with funny textures or strong flavours," Ivor said.

"Cale is a bit like that." Dana considered. "Cale likes tapioca."

"Unfortunately, I haven't got any tapioca."

"If you squashed a potato, like when you make mashed potatoes, and you put a lot of milk in it, it might come out like something that Cale would eat," Dana suggested.

"Squash a potato!" Peter shouted with glee. He picked up his potato fritter from his plate, dropped it on the floor, and deliberately trod on it.

"Oh, Peter, *really*," said Ivor.

Alpha started wailing again. He took hold of her arm. "Come back into the kitchen before you wake Jananin. I wonder..."

In the kitchen, Ivor started opening all the drawers

and looking through them. "I'm looking for a thing... a silly little thing. Called a Tamagotchi. A Japanese toy from the 1990s. I can't think I'd have thrown it away. She used to love it."

Dana glanced around the kitchen units, the chess table, the bookcase. "What does it look like?"

"It's on a keyring, a little oval plastic thing with a screen on it."

Dana tried to remember if she'd seen anything about the place matching that description as Ivor rifled through drawers. "Aha!" he exclaimed upon opening a metal box from one of the bookcase shelves, and he brought out a thing on a keyring, as he'd said, made from old, discoloured plastic.

Alpha quieted upon seeing it, and snatched it from his hand. When she saw the screen on it was blank, a rictus of anger contorted her face, as though she thought he'd played a mean joke on her. She let off an ear-rending shriek and flung the Tamagotchi across the kitchen.

"I must have taken the battery out of it." Ivor grabbed a toolbox from the bottom of the bookcase, and hefted it up onto the chess table. It opened into lots of little compartments that cantilevered from the lid, containing batteries and components all sorted into their own type, rather unlike the way Ivor kept most things with odds and ends in boxes and all mixed in with the cutlery in the kitchen drawers. He selected a disc-shaped battery of the kind that goes in watches, but when he turned to search the floor for the Tamagotchi, Alpha with a roar of rage took hold of his nicely organised box of components and overturned it onto the floor with a sound like a metal avalanche.

Peter laughed, and then he took hold of a laundry basket containing Ivor's bloodstained shirt bundled up with various other items, and flung the contents of that on top of the mess Alpha had made.

"*Peter* for goodness' sake!" Ivor shouted at him,

standing amidst the carnage, the watch battery in one hand and the Tamagotchi in the other, but Peter had already run off down the corridor, laughing loudly as he went.

Ivor picked up a screwdriver from the floor, set the toy down on the kitchen worktop, and hurriedly took the compartment off the back of it and fitted the battery in.

When he handed it back to Alpha, the tiny LCD screen had a very basic animated picture on it, made up of black pixels. A circle with two eyes and a line for a mouth, that moved back and forth between two positions.

Alpha stopped wailing. She stared at the toy and smiled her odd, stiff, smile. She started to press buttons that beeped, changing the animations on the screen.

In the abrupt, welcome silence, Ivor sighed and wiped the back of his hand across his forehead. "Let's see what we can do to make it so she doesn't lose it, now."

He searched in the drawers until he found a grubby tartan ribbon, and without interrupting Alpha, he looped it through the keyring and tied it like a lanyard around her neck.

Running footsteps approached, and Peter irrupted into the kitchen once more, out of breath and giggling. "Look what I made," he said, holding up a piece of paper folded up like origami. "It's a Viking ship!"

"Peter," Ivor admonished him, "that Tamagotchi is Alpha's, not yours, and we can't have it broken or she'll get upset, so I don't want you to play with it or touch it."

"But look." Peter waved his boat in Ivor's face.

"*Peter*." Ivor took hold of him by the shoulders and made him sit down. "This is very important. What did I just say?"

"Don't remember." said Peter.

"I said that Alpha's Tamagotchi is hers, and you mustn't touch it. Say it back to me."

"I mustn't touch Alpha's Tamagotchi, because it's hers."

"Good, and now, before you run off again, you will put that ship you have made on the bookcase and you can show it to me later, and then you can help me clear up this mess that you helped make."

Peter nodded. "Okay."

Dana went to help as Peter and Ivor started to clear up, but Ivor told her, "Dana, no, you've got enough on your shoulders. Go and have your breakfast."

In the dining room, Dana poured herself some tea from the pot, and ate the fritters and seagull meat that Peter hadn't thrown on the floor and Alpha hadn't mauled. She found some clean clothes from the cupboard and went to use the shower.

When she was dressed and had combed her hair with Ivor's broken comb, she went to look for him, meaning to give it back, but as she approached the dining room, she heard both his and Jananin's voices.

What surprised her most was that they were not arguing. They were having a discussion about what to do.

"There's no chance of us getting back to the mainland via the ferry without being noticed," Ivor was saying, "but if I fill up the tank on the boat, I can get us to Skye."

"I will have to arrange for someone else to recover my car, bring it back on the ferry, and leave it at a rendezvous point on Skye, amongst other things," Jananin said. "The issue is, it seems if I switch my mobile phone on, its location and anything I use it for will be noticed."

"I have a mobile for emergencies. I keep it charged but switched off."

"Have you ever switched it on in front of Dana?"

"No. If I take you out on the boat, far from the island, and we use it, it's unlikely to be recognised as anything of importance."

"To do that, you would have to unlock the door."

"I could give you the key for you to keep. You'd have control over me, if you want. But we need to make an agreement. We need to put what's gone on between us aside until we've made things safe for Dana and Peter and Alpha."

There was a long pause, and then Jananin said, "Agreed."

Dana had stopped in the corridor outside the toilet, listening in on the conversation. She took a step forwards to look through the door.

While she had been living with Pauline and Graeme, Dana had been going once a fortnight to see a psychologist or a behaviourist or some kind of specialist who would ask her questions about herself, and give her advice. One of the things they had been talking about before Abigail and the toilets and the hospital was about 'body language' a code used by people who are not autistic to send secret messages to each other. This specialist had said that it would help Dana if she could try to look at people's faces more, instead of people's ties or collars. She was a nice lady, but she was quite a large lady with a big bosom, and she wore a low-cut top and a bra of the sort that made a huge sweaty cleavage that looked more like something belonging on a person's lower back than their upper front, and Dana had found it difficult not to look at that.

The woman had also said about something called *mirroring*, and that people like you more if you can sit in a position that copies theirs.

When Dana saw how Jananin was sitting by the table facing Ivor, she was pretty sure she didn't understand body language either. She was leaning forward, staring fiercely at him, her whole body tensed. Her hands were folded in her lap, close to the handle of her knife.

Ivor, on the other hand, was sitting in the most indolent way imaginable. He was leaning back on his chair so only the two rear feet were in contact with the floor, his arms were folded behind his head, and his left foot was up on his right knee. Dana had never known him to sit like this before, and she wondered if he did perhaps understand body language and was trying to use it to look unthreatening to Jananin, like a dog rolling onto its back in front of someone it liked.

Ivor glanced to the door, and suddenly he noticed her standing there, and he lost his balance and the chair tipped backwards and he fell with a shout and a crash. At the instant it happened, Jananin sprang to her feet, her left hand flying to her knife, and pressed herself back against the table. She stared at him sprawling on the floor, bewildered for a moment, and then she started to laugh.

Ivor looked about himself, appearing to realise he wasn't hurt, and then he laughed too.

Dana came into the room and Ivor got up off the floor and righted the chair. Suddenly, it seemed to Dana that an obstacle had been surpassed, and that perhaps things between Jananin and Ivor might get easier. After everything that had happened in the night and the previous day, it was as though some semblance of normality had come back.

A computer lay on the table, and on the screen, Jananin had drawn something: a leafless tree, bearing three white flowers, with a huge owl sitting in the fork of its branches in the centre. Dana frowned. "Is that the message you want to send?"

"It is an encrypted message. The intended recipients will understand perfectly well what it means. But not," Jananin glanced critically at Dana, "anyone else who might be eavesdropping."

"If you need to go and send a message," Dana began, "and you don't want Cerberus to notice, perhaps I could go into the game, so if Cerberus is busy watching me, it won't notice you?"

Ivor held up his hands. "I'm not sure it works like that. If Cerberus is what we think it is, it's a triply-redundant supercomputer that's being used to number-crunch the Internet browsing behaviour of the entire electorate so it can predict the voting outcome and manipulate the results. It multitasks to the extreme, and you can't exactly distract it."

"Nevertheless, she may have a valid point," Jananin said. "It's been alerted specifically by Dana's signal. If it knows she's in a separate location at the time the communications are sent, the device that sends them will look less suspicious. If we are to take advantage of the opportunity, I should send several messages, to recover the car and arrange somewhere for us to hide once we get back to the mainland. If as we suspect Cerberus is embedded in the political infrastructure, I have some contacts who may be able to help, and may be able to reach onward contacts in a position to find out who is controlling it, and how we can remove it and that person."

Ivor folded his arms. "I'm very wary of letting her go back on there, after what happened last night."

"I won't let Alpha or Peter go in there. And what about if I just went in the game, and I played with Eric and explored other parts of it, and didn't go looking for Cerberus or try to fight with it? Then it would know I was in the game at the time you send the messages, and it wouldn't think them suspicious. Actually, what day is it?"

"Sunday," said Jananin.

"Then Eric will be not at school, and Duncan too. Perhaps I could show it to him and see if he wants to play too."

"I can't say I like this," Ivor said. "But if it's what you want to do, and you promise to be careful. And anyone else who plays this game with you should be using a VPN just in case Cerberus traces their locations and someone tries to do something to them like they are to Jananin and me."

Dana nodded. "Okay. A VPN. I'll tell them."

Ivor turned to Jananin. "You'd better prepare what you're going to send. And I'd better get the boat ready."

In the kitchen, Peter and Alpha were sitting at the chess table, which was covered with sheets of paper upon which Peter was drawing. His helmet was on the floor beside his chair, and he frowned as if concentrating intensely.

Dana looked at the pictures Peter had drawn, of Vikings with shields and swords, and boats and funny dragons. She found a green pencil and drew a picture of a plant, one of the cacti she had on her windowsill at Pauline and Graeme's house.

Peter held out a blue pencil to Alpha. She looked at it for a moment, squinting as though she had trouble focusing her eyes, and then she took it. With a slightly shaky hand and in a way that made it look as though she'd not done it for a long time, she drew on the paper a circle, with two circles within it for eyes, and a horizontal line for a mouth. The character from the screen of her Tamagotchi toy.

Ivor and Jananin came into the kitchen, and Ivor announced, "I am going to put Shostakovitch on the CD player to help keep Alpha calm, and then Jananin and I are going out in the boat, so Jananin can send some messages to some friends of hers, who are going to help us." He noticed Peter's helmet on the floor. "Peter, why aren't you wearing your helmet?"

"Because," said Peter, rather eloquently, "I am showing Alpha how to do some things, and if I wear my helmet, she can't hear what I am thinking, and it makes it harder to explain."

Ivor made a face at Dana. She didn't know what it meant, but it was the sort of expression a comedian playing an eccentric person in a sitcom might make if another character said something shocking. "That's jolly considerate of you. Especially as before today, you've always thought things at her that hurt her."

Peter shrugged. "Well, Dana has woken her up, so now I don't have to keep on doing that."

Jananin said, "I do not understand why you seem so concerned about leaving this boy here for a couple of hours. He seems a perfectly personable and creative young man."

Ivor looked at Dana again, and made an even more

exaggerated version of the face he'd made before.

"Peter, are you okay to stay here and show things to Alpha until we come back for dinner? She should go to the toilet by herself, but you might have to remind her if she gets engrossed in what you're doing."

"Yes," said Peter, busy colouring in a Viking.

"In fact, if you can feel what she's thinking, you'll know when to remind her, and there'll be no excuse for you not to."

"Maybe."

"Peter, repeat back to me what I just asked you to do."

Peter turned his head and burped derisively in Ivor's direction.

Ivor pushed out his chest and tipped up his chin, spreading one hand over his chest and gesticulating expansively with the other, as though impersonating a seasoned tenor. He let off a thunderous belch that sent Peter into peals of laughter.

"I think I win."

-5-

DANA found Duncan slaying dragons in *Pillage and Burn.*

Do you know how to use a VPN? she interrupted him.

Yes. It's something people use if they don't want people to be able to trace their connection back to their location. It's what you use if you're up to no good, not for gaming, because it slows your connection down.

There's a really cool game I want to show you, but you have to use a VPN.

Why?

It's a leaked beta test or something I think. It's nothing illegal, but it's kind of like hacking in. Can you just get one and I'll show you?

All right.

Duncan logged out of the game. While he was finding and downloading a VPN, Dana hashed together an executable program by combining the IP address of the Cerberus game with the base code of *Pillage and Burn.* Duncan didn't have a VR headset like she assumed Eric did, but she could translate the code into a form Duncan's computer could navigate.

Dana sent him a message through *Pillage and Burn. I've sent you a program. It's on your desktop.*

Dana, are you sure this is safe? This is an exe file and the antivirus software doesn't like it. Dad will...

Please, it's not a virus. It's a really cool game I want to show you.

Dana ported herself back into the Cerberus game. She anxiously put her hand in her pocket and held her fuse. Or rather, she held an imagined fuse in what she imagined was her hand, in a virtual simulation into which she had projected an imagination of herself. This caused her to wonder: if she could control her own appearance, and affect gravity, and the appearance of fish-hands relating to the records of people she knew, where was the limit in the influence she could exert in this world? And where was Cerberus's? If the fish-hands were in fact just the manifestations of records from the electoral roll, were other things in the game also derived from information that had a real-life basis? She looked again at the plants and animals in the desert simulation, wondering if perhaps a tortoise might be the red briefcase the Chancellor of the Exchequer carried, or if the pumas contained within their code the launch codes for Trident missiles.

She glanced down at the leggings, skirt, and jersey she'd generated her avatar from, the same outfit she'd run away from the hospital wearing, but she also had on the sleeveless fur jacket that she'd received as the reward for solving a puzzle in the desert. Now she took it off to examine it, and found in the back of the neck a white polyester label, the sort she'd usually ask Pauline or Graeme to cut out of her clothes because they itched.

Printed on the front of the label were characters in a language Dana couldn't read. They looked a little like very complicated versions of the hash key on a computer, with lines all going in different directions and intersecting each other:

浮遊都市

She turned as the air to her left blurred. A shadow appeared on the ground, and a human shape slowly began to congeal out of the code that made up the simulation of the desert. She made out clothing first, shorts and hiking boots, a shirt and a wide-brimmed hat. He was well-rendered, but quite a generic sort of man, a stock explorer character.

"Duncan?"

"Dana! How did you make an avatar that looks so much like you? The options I got on the creation screen were really limited." Duncan's character looked about himself. "Blimey! This is some high-end stuff!"

Dana looked the other way to see Eric approaching, his hand up and waving.

"Who's he? Is he a boss we can kill?"

"He's another player," Dana explained. "But I like to RP with him, so you have to call me Epsilon and not Dana."

"OK, cool," said Duncan. "My gaming handle that I use online is Falfreund."

"Hi," said Eric. "I'm Charon. Have you just found the game?"

"I'm Falfreund," said Duncan. "She just invited me."

"He's my foster brother," Dana explained.

"Does he live with your dad too?"

"I've lived with lots of people. All over the place. Never mind about that." Anxious to get away from the subject of her family to avoid giving Duncan questions to ask, Dana held up her puma-skin gilet. "What does this say?"

Eric and Duncan looked at the label.

"Looks like Chinese," said Duncan.

"Probably it says, *Made in China*, then," said Eric, and both of them laughed. Eric turned over the gilet in his hands. "It's from the cave puzzle, fairly easy game. I've got one too." He handed it back. "We can show it to Fal if he's new, as an intro."

"I'm not really mad keen on puzzles," said Duncan.

"What's that bird doing here?" Eric asked. "I've never seen one of those before."

Dana turned to see a large crow sitting on a boulder. Cale had come into a game again.

"That's... that's just me. It's like a wizard familiar. Actually, it was from another puzzle I found when you weren't here."

"What puzzle's that?" Eric looked at Cale's avatar enviously. "And that reminds me, where's the puzzle you got that skin from?"

"Falfreund, what kind of game do you want to play?" Dana tried to steer the conversation away from this subject.

"I'd like to play a pirate game!" Duncan enthused. "You know something of a similar theme to *The Goonies*, or *Pirates of the Caribbean!*"

"But this game is set in a desert," said Eric. "Where'd you find this guy, Epsilon? He's a total noob."

Dana said, "There's a river here, isn't there? And all rivers lead to the sea. And the sea is where pirates are. I mean traditionally, at least. Some games are about space pirates."

"But I've tried to get out of the desert before," Eric objected. "It just goes on and on, endlessly."

Cale suddenly launched himself from his boulder and flapped laboriously up into the sky. He hovered over the chasm where the river flowed. When Dana went to look down to the river, which was already much deeper owing to the greater flow of water from the Styx since she and Eric last confronted Cerberus, she saw a rowing boat set aground beside it. She glanced up to Cale's crow in the sky. Cale was very good at drawing things. Could he have drawn this boat from his imagination when Duncan had requested a pirate game?

"That's a bit of a noob thing to say," Duncan was saying back to Eric as the three of them gazed down upon the boat. "Games often do things like that so as not to make things too easy. I bet if we take this boat, the way the game designers intended for it to be done, we can travel to the sea."

The sides of the river's gorge were near vertical, but a winding path broken by gaps with handholds in the rock led down. As they began the descent, Eric first, followed by Dana and Duncan last, Cale flew down to the boat and perched on its prow, shifting from foot to foot impatiently.

They boarded the boat and pushed off from the shore.

Eric took up the oars and Dana sat in the front with Cale, watching the journey, and knowing that although Cale never spoke or even squawked, he was as happy to be here and to be going on an adventure with Dana as she was to be with him. The clear waters of the river sparkled in the sun and the ochre rocks were hung with exotic plants and clambered over by tiny lizards, and it didn't even matter so much that Eric and Duncan argued most of the way.

"Do you think we're pirates, or something else?"

"I should think we are pirates, and that's a good thing, because in the days when they were pirates, the people on the seas who weren't pirates were like princes and dukes and stinking aristos; bad men who treated women wrong, and let the peasants and serfs they were supposed to be responsible for at home live in poverty and starve in famines, while they went off to other countries and kidnapped the native people to use as slaves!"

"Is she really a girl? Like IRL I mean?"

"Yes, OFC she's a girl. Just because you've never had a girlfriend and you don't know any girls, and you're sexist and think they don't play games."

"I never had a sister! I've only got a mum and a grandma, and neither of them play games!"

As they passed farther downstream, the river widened as tributaries joined together. Soon Eric rowed the boat upon a broad delta bordered on either side by promontories of greyish indistinct land, and the desert was far behind. The atmosphere of the game changed from sunny to overcast, and the water became grey and salty smelling, the air slightly misty. Ahead of them, somewhere between river and sea, a great pirate galleon lay at anchor, rocking gently in the water.

A rope ladder hung down the side of the ship to the water, and Eric rowed the boat and turned it about to bring it in line. A real ship, Dana supposed, would have something with a funny nautical name, a *jib*, she thought it might be, to stow the rowing boat back onboard, but none of them could see one on this virtual ship, so they left the boat drifting in the water and climbed the ladder one by one up to the poop deck.

An exploration of the ship by the three of them revealed it to be empty, with no crew and no cargo aboard. The only things they found were some pirate accoutrements that could be equipped to their in-game characters, and several cannons and plenty of cannonballs.

"Does this ship have a name?" Duncan speculated. He had donned a pirate hat, a pair of boots, and a cutlass. "Perhaps the *Mary Celeste*?"

"The puzzles adapt to get harder, once they've been solved. I couldn't get any further on the Cerberus puzzle until Epsilon joined the game, so perhaps the harder levels need more people. Maybe we need some more players to make up a crew." Eric had replaced his blond mohawk with a red head-rag, and his jeans and trainers with pirate trousers and boots.

Cale alighted on the balustrade up on the open bridge before the ship's wooden steering wheel. He fidgeted back and forth along it, bobbing his head, crow feet moving up and down nimbly.

"Perhaps we could make a crew," Dana suggested. "But not from people." She didn't want to try to imagine people, in case she imagined real people and bad things happened to them.

"Like walking skeletons for crew," Duncan said, "or ghosts, or people with squids for faces."

None of those sounded very pleasant to have as crewmates to Dana. "We need sailors who can climb the rigging."

Eric shrugged. "Cats can climb. We could have a cat crew."

As soon as he said it, Cale imagined a crew of cats dressed as sailors, and they appeared on the ship before them. "Oh," said Dana. "*Oh*." For although the cats were quite realistic, they were uncanny and a bit grotesque.

Some of them sprawled about, trying to lick themselves under their pirate clothing, while others just sat looking at her with the contemptuous expression cats tend to have, but with an eerily human something to them. Cale wasn't much of a cat person, and he'd made the cats look somewhere in between domestic cats and big cats, some more like pumas and lynx, and others like leopards and tigers.

"Nice idea, Charon," Duncan said. "Sooner or later one of them's going to scale the main mast and not be able to work out how to get down, and we'll have to call the fire brigade."

"It was only a suggestion! I didn't realise they'd automatically come into existence by me saying it!"

"They're here, now," Dana said. "Don't you think we should give them an order?"

Duncan's character stood upright and addressed the cats. "Weigh anchor, and set sail!"

The crew of cats scrambled to obey Duncan's command, and soon the wind was in the sails and the galleon was heading out to sea. With the land dwindling behind and the grey, sullen ocean, it reminded Dana disconcertingly of the sea around Lewis. In the distance, shattered rocks protruded from the water, the only indication of a deadly reef below. Farther away were broken archipelagos, skerries, the last remnants of land, and then a craggy grouping, topped with a single tower, caught her attention. With a rising sensation of dread, she recognised it as the Flannan Isles.

The lighthouse flashed once, as though to acknowledge her recognition, and then someone shouted. On the other side of the ship, another galleon had come into view. Duncan gave the order for the cats to man the cannons, and Eric was turning the great wheel to bring the pirate ship about, broadside to the stricken vessel.

Gunports in the flank of the other ship burst open, revealing the ominous apertures of cannons within.

"Fire!" Duncan shouted, raising his cutlass.

The ship shook with the noise and tremors of the firing cannons, and the other ship answered with its own fire. Wood splintered as cannonballs ripped through the hull, and the screams of injured cats rose from the decks below.

"Call the vet!" Eric shouted.

"You're steering too close!" Dana shouted at Eric, but it was too late, and the ships struck, port against starboard, the impact knocking Dana off her feet. Cale took off and flew to the other ship.

"Prepare to board!" Duncan ordered.

Cats appeared, hefting grappling irons. The ships quickly became tethered together, the cats arranging rope ladders and planks between them. Once aboard the other ship, they had to fight the crew, all generic navy men in uniforms probably something from the time of Admiral Nelson. The cats pounced on them, mauling them and biting at their throats, but as often happened in games, there was no blood, and when either the cats or the sailors had been injured enough times to count as being dead in the algorithm, they just fell to the decks and lay still. Finally, all the cats and sailors were dead, and their bodies despawned, leaving the decks clean.

Dana looked up at Cale, where he clung to the rigging. "What now?"

"We haven't killed the captain!" Duncan waved his cutlass. "He must be hiding below deck, making his crew fight for him, the coward!"

Below decks they went, kicking open all the doors, until they found a single NPC in a luxuriously appointed room at the stern of the ship with windows looking out. Duncan and Eric fought him, Duncan striking him with a cutlass and Eric with a pirate pistol that he had to stop to reload each time, and Dana healed them, until the captain too fell unmoving over his desk.

"Looks like he was the boss," said Duncan breathlessly. "Let's see if he dropped any loot."

They searched the captain's pockets, and found a compass and another instrument inside a box, which Duncan thought was called a sextant.

Dana turned her attention to the captain's quarters. There was a bookcase, a treasure chest, and beside the desk, a straight-sided barrel with large rolled-up maps stuffed into it. She began taking out the maps and unrolling them on the desk, one on top of the other. Most of them appeared to be maritime maps of islands. One was a map of the world. The next one she opened was very different to the others. It showed several views of what looked like an architectural plan, of a hexagon within a hexagon. Immediately she knew this was something that didn't belong in this world, that it was a clue. As she pored over the map, trying to make sense of what it showed, there came a great tearing sound of splintering wood, and the ship shook. Dana hurriedly rolled up the map and held it close to her, and followed Duncan and Eric out of the captain's cabin.

Eric let out a shout, for before him was a stairway leading down, and seawater was pouring into the ship's bilge section. They charged up the other stairs, but the ship was taking on water fast, and already every horizontal surface was listing to one side. They emerged on deck to find enormous muscular black tentacles covered with glistening violet suckers wrapped around both the ship they were on and the pirate ship they'd come in.

"To the rowboats!" said Duncan.

Eric grabbed the oars and tried to push the boat off as water spilled onto the deck. Dana clutched the rolled map to her, but as the ships were pulled down by the kraken, trapped air and pieces of debris were bursting to the surface, making the water roil. As the rowing boat spun out of control, she closed her eyes and collected all the code she could sense from the map. She compiled it into a PDF and transferred it to Ivor's computer.

When she opened her eyes, a great bubble of gas

rose from the depths and flung the boat sideways, and then a wave crashed over it from another direction, and it capsized. She was sinking in the water amidst all the flotsam and the vast, confusing body of the kraken, and the timer had started and the map was gone. Yet when she looked to the surface of the water, she saw not the overcast sky above the sullen sea, but the shapes of Big Ben and the Houses of Parliament, and the other strange buildings she'd seen in the Styx, through the turbulent surface.

Then she was back in the computer room, sitting on the floor, and she got up at once to look at Ivor's computer and see if the file she'd tried to send it had transferred. It had, and when she opened it, all the schemata were there as she remembered seeing them, all the writing on them legible.

How long had she been in the game? A few hours. She unlocked the door and went out, locking it behind her. Were Ivor and Jananin back, both of them, together, safe?

As she approached the door to the submarine bay, it opened, and in came Ivor to Dana's great relief, followed by Jananin.

"Did you send the messages?" Dana asked breathlessly.

"Yes."

"I think I've found something. Come and look."

Dana showed Ivor and Jananin the file she'd saved on Ivor's computer.

"It's a technical diagram," said Ivor after looking at it for a little while. "Blueprints to build something."

"It looks like an underground bomb shelter," said Jananin. "With two sections, one inside the other, reinforced concrete walls and blast-proof doors." She studied the schemata further. "The central section seems designed to accommodate a computer system that has extremely high demands for power and data consumption. This is a Faraday bunker."

"Oh?" Dana looked at her, not sure if this was a good or bad thing.

Jananin studied the screen a little longer. "Dana, whoever has Cerberus, and wherever that may be, what you have found suggests that place must be of this design, or a very similar one."

Ivor put his hand on Dana's shoulder, and a delighted grin spread across his face. "Well done, Dana!"

-6-

MOST of the following day passed fairly uneventfully. Jananin and Ivor kept out of each other's way, as Ivor was preoccupied with organising his and Peter's and Alpha's possessions ready for departure, and Jananin worked on something in the privacy of Dana's old bedroom. Alpha entertained herself with her Tamagotchi, or Peter would show her things or read books to her.

The problem remained with getting Alpha to eat food. She had eaten some of the potatoes and milk Dana had suggested for breakfast and lunch, but Ivor was concerned that it didn't have enough protein and nutrients in it, and had prepared mussels and salad for dinner. Alpha had spat out the mussels, and this seemed to have set Peter off.

"Of course she doesn't like them!" he shouted, tilting his spoon so the mussels dropped on his plate from on high and spattered sauce onto everything around it. "I hate mussels, they're disgusting, especially they way you do them; they're like *turds* cooked in *snot*!"

Ivor slapped his hand down hard on the table. "Peter, that's enough. And you've never had turds cooked in snot, so you can't know what it tastes like for comparison!"

Jananin came in, and having heard Peter's comment and taken up her place, took his plate from him and scraped the mussels onto her own plate, before setting it back before him.

"You took my food!" Peter's voice was indignant.

"You said you didn't want it." Jananin shrugged and started eating Peter's mussels as well as her own.

Peter gestured to his plate. "But now I haven't got anything to eat."

"Tough."

Since Jananin had arrived on Roareim, Peter it seemed had regarded this tall, terse, quick-reflexed female stranger with awe and not an insignificant degree of intimidation. The glower she gave him with her single-word reply silenced him, and Ivor put his hand to his face as he ate in an attempt to stop Peter noticing his amusement at the situation.

Rather than challenge Jananin, Peter reached for Dana's plate where she sat next to him. Dana exclaimed, "But I never said I didn't want mine!" and Ivor, who sat on her other side, put his hand out to stop him. "Peter, no. You've made your bed, so now you're going to have to lie in it. So you can either stop whinging, or you can literally go to bed so the rest of us can eat dinner in peace."

A great wailing racket started up from something embedded in the roof, and the room filled with panic, Ivor pushing back his chair and Alpha clapping her hands to her ears and screaming. It took a moment for Dana to realise it was the proximity siren that Ivor had set up, connected to a radar or something up on the island, the same one that had warned them when the police sent helicopters to search after Jananin blew up Charlie November Five. In a hurry, Ivor barked something to Jananin about a possible attack, and she acknowledged it and went to her room without speaking. He told Alpha and Peter to stay put, and then he asked Dana to come outside with him.

As she went with Ivor up the steps to the main door, Jananin was already there, carrying a large and awkwardly shaped bag, for she had the key now. Once the door was open, she put the bag down in the entrance to the cave outside and set about unzipping it and taking something out.

Dana felt for signals, moving out past Jananin where the roof of the rock gave way to sky. "I think there's two of them," she told Ivor.

Jananin dropped the front end of a cumbersome

object to the floor, a butt and a trigger like a shotgun, but a broad crescent shape at the front. She unfolded a metal stirrup and braced her foot against it, taking hold of a thick tensile cord with both hands and straightening her back against it until it clicked into position. Dana realised she was looking at the same weapon that she had fired upon the helicopter with, the one that had broken when she'd tried to shoot it at her and Ivor and Peter when they had fallen defenceless on the sand. It was a crossbow. Jananin fitted a heavy-looking silver cylinder with a blunt nose and fins at the rear end into the slot intended for the crossbolt.

A tremendous noise. Overhead, flames ripped across the crack of sky visible from the cave where they hid, and fragments of soil and rock rained down from above. A signal had disappeared, and with a rising horror, Dana recognised what it was, the signal she'd followed all the way here, that Jananin had told her would lead her to Ivor.

"The beacon's been destroyed!"

"Where are they?" Jananin lifted up the crossbow, something like a tiny light bulb filled with bright pink fluid in her right hand.

Dana felt again, interpreting the signals that remained, listening to the throb of helicopter blades. "I think there's one coming around the side of the island now."

"Can you tell me exactly when? It's important you be precise."

Dana shook her head. "Any moment now, I think."

Jananin screwed the pink bulb into a port on the crossbow. The magenta colour disappeared, but a pinkish flush suffused the centre of the crescent to the tips of the limbs where the string attacked. Jananin lifted the crossbow to her shoulder and took a step out into the entrance of the cave, dropping to one knee and looking through a telescope mounted on the bow. A loud snap drove the butt of the weapon hard into her shoulder, and the missile mounted on it was gone. Out over the ocean visible from the cave, the helicopter came into view, details on it indistinct against the setting sun, and immediately it blossomed into a marigold of fire.

The explosion was disarmingly silent, and it was only after the expanding shell of flame spent itself and broke into burning debris that the earsplitting crack of the explosion reached where they stood on the island and a hot wind blew in from the sea.

"Another one, you say?"

Dana nodded. "One more, only one, I think. Around the other side."

Ivor stared out upon the wreck flaming upon the surface of the ocean. "These are military helicopters. They're armed. Their weapons systems should have some electronic component, and if you're doing this, Dana, you'll need to find them and jam them before they can fire."

"I'll try," Dana said.

Ivor looked to Jananin. "Is it worth trying to surrender? For her sake?"

"You said it yourself. It may be her whoever is doing this means to kill. You want to help, carry the bag."

Jananin cocked the crossbow again, and Dana started up the path that led to the top of the island, Jananin close behind her.

As she came up cautiously over the steep incline, the mast with the beacon and the wind turbine and the photovoltaics were gone. A blackened area showed where the grass and topsoil had been scorched away, and all that remained was a tangle of rent metal hanging over the cliff and jutting out to sea, swaying back and forth in the wind. She couldn't see the helicopter yet but she could hear it and feel its signal. It must be low over the sea, searching the cliffs for the entrance.

Dana could hear a high-pitched whistling. She put her hands over her ears, but the noise continued. When she took her hands away, Jananin's lips were moving, but she heard no words. The noise burned her ears, and her head ached with a heavy heat. With it came a vertigo that made

Roareim lurch and spin in her vision, and a sensation of the utmost dread and despair. Cold weighed down her limbs like waterlogged clothing. Her mouth seemed filled with something heavy and rank, and as she felt the stony ground rise up to hit her knees and the spasms of vomiting started, she made out, blurred and distorted, the slow ascent of the hideous grey-green helicopter up over the cliff, like some monstrous hornet.

Jananin was shaking her and shouting something, and Dana tried to reply and point to the helicopter, but all she could sense now was a spiky, prickly texture filled with burning neon colours, and the pressure in her head. The evening sky above was an unfathomable chasm, and beyond it an infinity filled with radiation and dust and heat and cold. Suspended there in the roaring silence, between the outer limits of the Earth's atmosphere and the vast emptiness of space, there was something with eyes that didn't see, yet looked down on the unfathomable vastness of the world, something that was all crystal knives gleaming with savage albedo, and it was driving stakes of raw pain into her.

Ivor shouted something, his voice distorted and basso. She was on the floor, convulsing, a rock digging into her face, feeling sick running from her mouth, unable to respond. The sky was a wall of thunder.

Something came down over her head with a blow. Dana managed to stop retching and breathe in, although the air was like broken glass. When she opened her eyes, she saw two horizons, one up, one down, with the helicopter suspended between them. Into this panorama strode a skinny boy with curly ginger hair. Dana put her hands up to her head. Peter's helmet.

Peter must have managed to break the weapons system on the helicopter, because it hadn't fired, but he must also have broken something to do with its flight and navigation systems, because the pitch of the engine changed, and the helicopter started to drift around, its tail turning around its front axis like a sycamore seed. The horrible signal had also started to affect Peter, and as he tried to control the helicopter, he staggered and swayed like a drunk, dangerously close to a cliff edge that fell to a steep drop into deep water. The helicopter careered over the island in a great arc, out of control.

Jananin fought to screw the bulb into her crossbow. On one knee, she struggled to aim through the telescope as the helicopter tumbled in the air over their heads, and Dana got behind her, clinging with her arms about her waist and pressing her face into the woman's back.

The crossbow discharged with a snap and the fuselage of the helicopter above them blew into pieces, thrown upwards and outwards on a bubble of fire. Jananin threw the crossbow away from her and flung herself down on top of Dana as the noise and the hot wind tore over them. When Dana opened her eyes again, everything had fallen silent, save for the keening of the wind and the sound of pieces of debris falling in to the water.

Jananin was up off her, and she shouted to Ivor, her voice hoarse, "I can't find Peter! I think he was blown off the cliff!"

Dana sat up. Ivor was running down the path already. He reached the shore and jumped straight into the sea. Dana got to her feet, meaning to make for the cliff edge where she'd last seen Peter to look over and search for him in the water, but something black and shiny lay amongst the dandelion leaves: a boot. At first it seemed the most mundane thing, like Peter had brought it up here and been throwing it around like a toy, but then she noticed blood staining the grass, and wet gobbets of red stuff around the rim. "*Urh*!"

At her exclamation, Jananin seized her arm and pulled her away, back down the path to the cave. The boot could only have come from the helicopter, Dana realised. There had been people on those helicopters, soldiers or airmen or something, and now they weren't any more. That boot had been worn by someone's son, someone's partner or dad, perhaps.

Dana looked out to the sea where Ivor had jumped in. "Ivor!" she shouted, seeing nothing of him, pulling against Jananin's grip.

"No! The more of us go into the sea, the greater the risk some of us won't come out. Wait and give him time!"

As they watched, something in the water came into view around the rock bordering the cave. She strained her eyes to see, dreading it might be a sea bird or a marine mammal, or some other thing from nature, but then she made out two heads and an arm. Ivor had Peter.

Jananin went down to the sea as he came closer, struggling to keep Peter's head clear of the water. She waded in to meet them, catching hold of Peter's arm so the two of them could lift him between them. Water ran from their clothes, Ivor staggering barefoot on the rocks, up to the rock that would hide Peter safely from the awful signal. Ivor sat heavily, Peter collapsing next to him, his hands reaching up for his face, great shivers racking his body, their breathing very close and loud in the narrow entrance to the cave outside of the door.

Ivor held Peter to stop him from falling down. "What's happened to him? He's usually a strong swimmer. It's like he's having a seizure."

"There's something in the sky," Dana said. "Much farther away than the helicopters, making a horrible signal."

"A satellite?" Jananin suggested. Dana thought again of that hard, spiky thing, hurting her from distances too great for her to fathom.

After some time, Ivor spoke. "The power supply's gone. The panels, the wind turbine, charge up a battery. After a few hours, it'll run out of power, and the lights and the ventilation will stop working."

"That's immaterial," Jananin replied. "They will send more, better armed. We cannot stay. We have to set out tonight."

Frowning, Ivor took a few heavy breaths. "What is that thing, anyway?"

Jananin glanced at the crossbow in her hand. "The ballistics are just old-school trinitrotoluene. The limbs are a polymer alloy idea I've been testing out. Applying an enhancer solution to it initiates a chemical change that causes it to release with a far greater magnitude of force than is needed to load it. Forty-pound draw weight, shoots like 400 pounds. Only difficulty is, it makes the material unstable, and it has to be fired immediately after the solution is applied to it."

Ivor considered this for a moment. "And that's why it shattered, on Lewis? You hesitated too long. Perhaps your loose screw isn't as loose as it looks."

"That is a rather outlandish hypothesis you have there, Pilgrennon, and something you should not take for granted."

Standing at the entrance to the cave, the crossbow in her hand and the knife strapped about her leg, the sunset upon the sea behind her and the wind in her hair, she did look wild and perhaps a bit mad.

Peter said, "Why do you always call him Pilgrennon? He's called Ivor. Pilgrennon's his last name." He abruptly coughed and spat up a mouthful of vomit, and Ivor patted him on the back.

Jananin regarded him and his act of regurgitation impassively. "I'm not on first-name terms with him."

"Why are there carrots in it?" Peter turned to Ivor frustratedly. "I've not eaten carrots! There aren't any here! Now I'm afraid I've been asleep, but not asleep, like Alpha was, and you gave me carrots to eat in secret!"

Ivor smiled and ran a hand over Peter's damp curls. "You did well, Peter. But I'm afraid now we need to go back inside and get everything we need into the boat and go."

Dana took off Peter's Viking helmet and handed it back to him. "If you make me and Alpha helmets like you did for Peter, then if we go near anything that can detect our signals, Cerberus will not be able to find us."

"Well, I don't know if I can make them as nice as Peter's in the time we've got, but I can certainly work out something." Ivor got to his feet. "Come on. Peter, I need you to listen to me. Because of that horrible signal you and Dana just felt, that made you fall in the sea and throw up, we have to go away from here, and I don't know when, if ever, we'll be able to come back. So we need to decide what things you need to take and get them into the boat, and we need to take your tompot blenny and all the other fish out of the fish tank, and bring them outside and put them back in the sea, so they can go."

Peter nodded.

"Did you understand what I said? Repeat it back to me."

"We need to get Susan and the other fish and put them in the sea, and I need to put the things I want to take into the boat."

"Perfect. Dana, those blueprints you found. Let's get them printed out before we forget them."

When Dana went into the computer room, Ivor pushed the door to behind her, muttering an apology about there being nowhere else to get changed.

When he came back, she was printing out the diagrams. He'd changed his trousers but he had a towel draped round his neck and no shirt on, and as he hadn't had a shower he smelt musky and seawatery. Dana tried not to look at him, because she didn't like how anyone looked without clothes over the parts that were usually covered, and how they tended to have moles and hair and rolls of fat everywhere. As she gathered the papers together, Peter came in, and even though he was less hairy and moley, he was almost as bad as he had on only a pair of wet pants.

"Peter, what have I told you about this room?" Ivor said as Dana tried to get past them to the door without looking at them.

"That I'm not allowed in it, and I'm especially not allowed in it without my helmet on, because I'll break the computer."

"Then why are you in here, without your helmet on, and why does the computer still work?"

Peter considered this for a moment. "I think, since I was practising with Alpha while you were out, I got better at not breaking things."

Ivor reflected upon this. "Either this is a testament to the benefits of having a sibling, or the person who invented that new medicine deserves a Nobel prize. Peter, because we are going away, and because we may not be coming back, and because bad people may come here looking for evidence of us, I'd actually prefer it if you were to break this computer, so nothing can be found on it."

As soon as Peter understood what was being asked of him, he grinned maniacally, and then the computer went off with a flash and a bang that made Dana start, followed by a sputtering of sparks under its casing and an acrid, burnt smell.

-7-

DANA remembered that night in the boat as a constant cycle of falling asleep only to wake again to the noise of the engine and the motion of the sea. Occasionally Ivor had spoken as he steered at the front, to point out flickers of light against the starry night sky to her, the Aurora Borealis.

"This clear sky may be very picturesque," Jananin had said, "but it increases the risk that satellite surveillance may be tracking us."

Dana had worried about this, and something else worried her too. As it began to get light, she put her hand in her pocket, but found it empty.

"Ivor, I think I've forgotten my fuses. They must have been in the pocket of my other clothes."

Jananin frowned. "Why do you need fuses in your pocket?" She was sitting directly behind Ivor, next to Dana, and all the time Dana had been awake she'd been watching him, her fingers wandering across the handle of the knife belted to her thigh. Every so often, she would slide it out of its sheath an inch or so, before snapping it back in. The woven leather of the handle showed a shiny polish in areas from this habit.

"I like to hold them. They feel calming, when it's stressful."

Ivor sighed. "Why are you stressed, Dana?"

"In the Cerberus game, I played with my brother and my foster brother. We went to a different part of the game and we were pirates and we raided a ship. That's how I found those diagrams we printed out. But the sea where the ships were looked like the sea around Lewis, and I saw the Flannan Isles in the game, and I think that's how

Cerberus managed to work out where we were, and sent those helicopters. I was thinking, what if Cerberus finds out where my brother and my foster family live, and does something to them?"

"If they used a VPN like I said, hopefully they'll be okay. If your fuses were in your spare clothes, they probably got left behind. I'll give you some more fuses when we get where we're going."

"If we listen to the radio when we get to the car," Jananin snapped her knife back into its holster, "it should say if anything untoward has happened in Coventry."

"Dana," Ivor glanced over his shoulder, "Don't go into that game again, you understand me?"

Peter, sitting beside Ivor in the front, turned to him and said, "Dana should not go into the game, because a horrible signal and helicopters came, and now we can't go back to Roareim."

"Peter I was talking to Dana!" said Ivor irritably. "I don't need you to repeat it back to me." He sighed. "I'm sorry, Peter. I guess all of us are a bit stressed right now."

As the light on the horizon grew, the sound of a helicopter became audible in the distance, and shortly after, one passed slowly over the boat. Dana pulled the woolly hat lined with tin foil that Ivor had given her to wear down over her head as far as it would go, hating every second of that noise in the sky and dreading that they had been recognised, but the helicopter moved on.

"If they were after us, they were probably searching for signals," Jananin said. "And they found none."

Presently the sky clouded over, which came as a relief from satellites, but with the cloud came a thin rain, and as the boat had no roof, it fell over them and on the blankets and luggage and got everything wet. Alpha began to cry, and Peter began to complain. "Ivor, I need a wee!"

"We're nearly there!" Ivor looked exhausted. Through the rain, the coast of Skye was coming into view, a mass of land edged with sparse, tall conifers, although Dana couldn't tell that it was Skye at all, as she could feel nothing of GPS with the silver foil inside her hat blocking her signal from anyone who might be searching for it.

Ivor landed the boat on a beach. While Jananin and Dana searched for the car and Peter and Alpha searched for a secluded area amongst the conifers to use for a toilet, Ivor turned the boat so that it pointed back to sea, and set the engine in gear and jumped off, sending it out to sea alone so no-one would find it here.

They found the car, at last, in a sightseeing layby beside a lonely stretch of road. Jananin unlocked it, and Ivor rounded up Peter and Alpha and they loaded the things they'd brought from Roareim into the boot: Ivor's box of tools and parts, the few bags of clothing and possessions Dana, Peter, and Alpha had amongst them, and Jananin's crossbow bag and other luggage. Then at last they were in the car, Ivor and Peter and Alpha on the back seat and Dana in the front next to Jananin, and with the doors shut, Dana could finally take off her damp hat.

Jananin started the engine and switched on the radio.

An internal investigation into Police Scotland has been announced after a statement was released concerning missing schoolgirl Dana Provine, who disappeared from Coventry in England. The report concerned the identification of a body, and after complaints were raised, it seems this report may have been made in error. Meanwhile, explosions heard off the coast of Lewis have been reported by the MOD to be the result of a terrorist attack on the base at Cape Wrath.

"Cape Wrath is on mainland Scotland, nowhere near the west coast of Lewis," Jananin said. "They don't want people to know what's been going on."

"I wish they would not say, *school girl*," said Dana at length. "Like it was something important to who I am. I hated the school, and I only went because they made me."

Ivor gave an ironic laugh. "A bit like Blake here, saying it bothered her more that she'd been framed as being in league with me than that the framing was for a murder!"

"And is it right to say I am English, when my DNA is 49% you, and you are half Scottish?"

Ivor considered this. "The other half's Welsh, as well. Jananin is probably English. Although I wouldn't be surprised if there was a bit of Irish in there as well, going by her temper."

Jananin scowled, but didn't reply.

"Do you think we should write the radio producers a letter?" Ivor suggested. "That you don't mind if they want to pretend you're dead when you're not, but they have to call you an Electrobotanist girl?"

Dana nodded. "And that I am 24.5% Scottish, 24.5 Welsh, and the rest English but might be Irish as well, because Jananin won't say."

"Have you ever considered," Jananin said, "that if you behaved like a violent lunatic at school, such that you were a menace to the teachers and other pupils, they would have to expel you, and then you wouldn't have to go?"

"Don't give her ideas like that!" Ivor laughed. "You might have been able to pull that off, but your parents were educated and well off."

Jananin reached across and opened the glove compartment. Inside, there was a mobile phone and a paper envelope. Jananin took the phone, and spent a moment scanning through the messages on it.

"I've received some information from a contact with political connections. The leader of the opposition won't speak to us, but it seems someone from a fringe party has been noticing discrepancies and anomalies in the claims made in the news about us and has offered his help. He is," Jananin paused to read the details from her phone, "Colin Antrobus, leader of the Meritocratic Party. I will arrange to meet him. Dana, there should be keys and information on where we are to go in there."

Dana opened the envelope. Inside was a set of keys and a handwritten letter, stating briefly an address and a postcode in the vicinity of Edinburgh, and beneath, *hope you like the laboratory, love Rupert. X*

"Is Rupert Osric your boyfriend?"

"No." Jananin took the piece of paper, frowning as she read it. "Perhaps he is, in his own head."

For some unknown reason, Ivor seemed to find this amusing.

Despite everything that had happened, the drive to Edinburgh was uneventful, and Dana fell asleep in the passenger seat, waking to find they'd arrived at the house that Jananin's friend had arranged for them. It was rather an old house, and cold and not particularly clean or tidy, but the electricity and the plumbing worked, and it had a television and a stereo. There was a very large and overgrown garden, with a shed within it that had been repurposed as a laboratory.

Alpha paid little heed to the house, and settled herself in a chair, engrossed in her Tamagotchi. Peter thought it was luxury, and declared it to be a millionaire's house, a mansion. He wanted to know how the stereo worked, so Ivor showed him how to use a pair of the headphones that you put inside your ears, so he could wear them under his helmet, and everyone else could listen to the news when it came on the television.

"A photograph purporting to show Professor of Chemistry at Cambridge University, Jananin Blake, engaged in an act of terrorism at Cape Wrath, has been widely scrutinised online. Initial examination of the photograph showed discrepancies in the image where something seems to have been edited out, and further analysis has raised concerns that the blurring of the image is an attempt to disguise an original that is inauthentic, a *deepfake*."

The image changed, to show two pictures side-by-side. The first was of Jananin, squinting up the scope of her crossbow, quite possibly the last image sent from the helicopter before it was destroyed. She wasn't wearing her coat or her dark glasses, and the picture was quite indistinct from the blur and the angle. The second was the same image, but with pink markings around Jananin's waist and the scenery behind her to highlight where the code suggested the image had been tampered with. *She'd* been airbrushed out of the picture, Dana realised. When Jananin had been standing like that, Dana had been standing behind her, clutching her about the middle with both arms.

"Speculation has arisen online that the form of a child has been edited out of the picture. The police are asking people not to speculate online about the whereabouts of a child reported missing from England, and in the interests of privacy of this child and her family, the child's name has been publicly withdrawn."

The other newsreader interrupted, whispering, "We're not supposed to reveal *any* details about the child."

"I apologise for referring to the child as *her*. Meanwhile, the University of Cambridge has released a statement saying that Professor Jananin Blake is away on a pre-arranged absence and refusing to comment on speculation. It is believed Blake is currently out of the country on business to do with her work, and we understand the authorities have been unable to contact her thus far. The other named individual, Ivor Pilgrennon, went missing more than ten years ago and was believed to be dead, but the police earlier issued a statement that some evidence has arisen suggesting he may still be alive and fraudulently using a charity to fund his lifestyle. The charity Lydia's Trust was set up by Pilgrennon around the same time as he founded a private hospital called the Institute of Neurodivergence. At the time of setting up both, Pilgrennon claimed to have a BSc and a PhD from Oxford University and to have published research papers in respected journals, both claims which were later discovered to be false. The Charities Commission entry on Lydia's Trust claims its objectives are to fund research and technology to improving the outcomes for young people on the autistic spectrum, however the charity is now under investigation."

Ivor had been staring at the screen, speechless, and now he burst out. "That's a lie! I set up that charity in honour of my sister! *Lydia's Trust!* Like I'd do such a thing!"

"Pilgrennon, no depravity you have committed can surprise me any more. I am beyond disgust. Besides, I need to attend a meeting with this politician, Antrobus or whoever he is." Jananin went into the hallway of the house and pulled on her coat. Ivor followed her, and Dana stood in the doorway behind him.

"Over Lydia's dead body! On my aunt's life! I swear I have never stolen money from my own charity or any other!"

Jananin was shaking her head.

"Jananin, this is lies! You know all of this is lies! You *know* I was qualified and I published my research! And now they're saying I'm not and I didn't, same as they're saying Dana's dead and we're terrorists and that I robbed my own charity!"

"Ah. I can explain that."

Some of the anger fell from Ivor's face, to be replaced by something that was, possibly, dismay. When he spoke, his voice was very quiet. "Blake, what have you done?"

"After you destroyed your research institute and disappeared, the police refused to take my complaint further, so I took all the evidence I had amassed to the ethics committee which oversees all scientific research. I petitioned them to revoke your qualifications and rescind all your papers, because the evidence pointed to your research being illegal and motivated by eugenics. They agreed with me."

Ivor could not speak for a moment. "You did *what*? You accused me of *eugenics*?"

"In your paper about the genetic factors responsible for autism, if you read the conclusions carefully, although it is not said outright, it appears you discovered that the more genetically complete variant of autism corresponded with the high-functioning phenotype of the condition. The low-functioning forms, you discovered, resulted from genotypes intermediate of the autistic complement and the neurotypical wild type. Their developmental disabilities, you concluded, were the result of outbreeding depression, latent genetic incompatibility between the autistic and the neurotypical."

Ivor raised his hand, levelling his index finger at Jananin, a rigid fury overtaking his body. "I took the utmost care that it would not be construed in that way. And the data was the data and that was what the results said and the conclusion to which they pointed. Only someone who insists on seeing those with developmental disabilities, people like Alpha, as lesser, as *unwanted*, would have a problem with it!"

Jananin had raised her finger back at him now, a ferocious stillness upon her, and Dana wondered if they were *mirroring*, although if they were, it didn't seem to be putting them more at ease with each other like it was supposed to. "There is some research that cannot be published and discussed, the kind of research that was done in Germany in the 1940s. The ethics committee agreed with my interpretation of your paper; and the confession before a court of law, of the gynaecologist who harvested my ova and sold them to you, sealed your fate! This is how posterity will remember you, Pilgrennon, if it remembers you at all." Jananin's voice had lowered now, but there was no disguising the triumph on her face, how she exulted in telling him this. "As a charlatan who masqueraded as a doctor, who feigned his own death to avoid his lie being exposed and to stop his wife from claiming half of his deceitfully acquired money in a divorce settlement, and who fraudulently abused a charity set up in his dead sister's name."

For a moment, Ivor's breathing came very fast and loud in the hallway, a shudder starting in his throat and spreading across him. Then he turned and wrenched open a door, slamming it behind him, and there came a roar of fury and the thud of something kicked or thrown. It sounded very much like at Pauline and Graeme's house, when Duncan would lose his temper because Pauline wouldn't let him have a motorbike, and he would go to his bedroom to rage and enact violence on some inanimate object.

In the sudden silence of the hallway, Jananin said to Dana, "Do you know, I almost do not regret that you got in my way and I failed to kill him when I had the opportunity. That way, I would have never have had the satisfaction of seeing him see himself destroyed." She turned and said nothing more as she left, and the front door slammed behind her.

Dana went back into the sitting-room where Alpha was still engrossed in her Tamagotchi and Peter sat drawing with the headphones on. The television was now displaying a wanted person's information bulletin on Ivor, showing an old picture that must have been dredged from a defunct website. It showed Ivor as a younger man, his hair brighter, his face plumper, the white collar of a lab coat visible where the photograph included his shoulders. He looked every bit the arrogant young doctor he'd admitted to Dana he once had been.

Dana tried to switch off the television, but because of the tin foil lining her hat, it didn't work. She went up to it and found the button to turn it off.

Not long later, Ivor came back in, looking tired. "Dana and Peter, I want to see if we can find some metal sheets about the place, that we can use to adapt the beds so you three have all got somewhere to sleep where you don't need to wear hats. Alpha, do you need the toilet? Alpha?"

Alpha looked up at him. "Alpha, do you need a wee?"

Alpha shook her head, smiled her odd, stiff smile, and went back to her Tamagotchi.

In the garden, Peter helped Ivor sort into a pile some

old sheets of tin roofing and some mesh panels.

"But that's got holes in it," Dana said.

"Signals can't get through holes that small," Ivor explained.

"Really?"

"You can't see the signals that make wLANs and radios and that you send out. They're waves, and they have an amplitude and a wavelength, and whichever one determines it, I forget, is too big to go through a mesh like that."

Peter chose a bedroom upstairs with a desk and a bunk bed. "This is a rich person's bed," he said, looking at the cheap matching covers on the duvet and pillowcase. "A prince must have slept in it."

"You were always a prince to me, Peter." Ivor set about fixing a piece of tin to the back of the bed with some nails and a hammer, pushing his spectacles higher up his nose to see them.

Peter laughed. "I'm not a prince. I'm a Viking!"

"Fine, you're a Viking. Dana's an electrobotanist, and Alpha's my princess." He set down the hammer for a moment to put one arm each around Peter and Dana. "I am a poor man, but as long as I know you three are all happy, that makes me a rich man."

"Were you arguing with the lady, Ivor?" Peter asked. "Something about your *paper*?"

"Yes, just about some pieces of paper, that I used to write some ideas down I'd had, a long time ago, and they got lost. I suppose it shouldn't matter, in the grander scheme of things. Hell hath no fury, like a woman scorned." He glanced at Dana. "Forgive me. I shouldn't have said that. It was sexist of me."

*

By the time Jananin returned, it was nearly ten o'clock. After eating a meagre dinner of porridge made with milk someone, presumably Rupert Osric, had left in the fridge, as this was the only food in the house, Peter was asleep in his bunk bed, with metal sheets under the mattresses of both bunks and tin roofing and mesh surrounding the sides to keep signals out. Alpha, who had managed to eat the porridge, slept in a bed similarly ensconced, in the same room as Ivor would have, so he could keep an eye on her in case she wandered around at night. Dana had found a box room over the stairs, where it seemed a large steel girder already shielded it from electromagnetic radiation to an extent, and she and Ivor had put a sheet of mesh over the window so light could still come in, and stuck tin foil wallpaper on all the walls and the back of the door. Dana wasn't in bed because Ivor had said she could stay up and watch the ten o'clock news.

"Why hasn't it started yet?" Janain dumped a bag filled with Indian takeaway on the coffee table. Ivor and Dana set upon it like starving vultures.

"They say they're having technical faults." Ivor ripped open a bag of poppadoms.

"He said he would be on at ten."

Ten minutes later, the news came online. "We apologise for the delay in bringing you the news, and in the quality of the upcoming broadcast, as we have had some problems with our equipment, and are having to resort to using old equipment to film and broadcast it."

Dana looked at Ivor. "Cerberus tried to stop the news?"

"The BBC has been around longer than the Internet, and it looks like Cerberus doesn't have such a firm grip on it." Ivor suggested as the news began and the reporters went through the headlines, and the first article began.

"We are joined here today by the leader of the Meritocratic Party, Mr Colin Antrobus."

"It's actually Dr Antrobus," said Colin Antrobus, who was sitting on a luridly green sofa in the studio opposite the interviewer, dressed in a brown suit, hands clasped in his lap, between two very burly men wearing sunglasses and dark suits. "But you can address me as Citizen Antrobus if you prefer. We advocate having the same salutation for men and women, to stress that we are all born equal and have equal opportunities."

"Very well, Dr Antrobus. Would you like to explain to our viewers the information you have about the claims about terrorists?"

"Well, first of all," began Colin Antrobus, "Part of the reason this interview was delayed, and the reason I need security here with me, is that as I was arriving at the studio this afternoon, an assassination attempt was made against me, no doubt to try to prevent me from disseminating the information I'm about to give you. The information we have been given about these so-called terrorists is of an extremely dubious nature, and when you consider it together, it isn't even internally consistent. This girl who is missing, who was claimed to be dead—"

"I must interrupt to remind you that the media has decided not to use the name or the image of this missing child, to provide privacy to the child's family in light of the concerning nature of these reports."

Antrobus nodded. "There's no evidence that this child is dead. It was claimed there was a body found; and now it's been confirmed there's no body. And these claims about Professor Jananin Blake. The evidence suggests she's out of the country at the moment. She's a Nobel laureate and a highly respected figure in the scientific community, with no criminal record. There's absolutely no evidence of any involvement. And this other fellow, Pilgrennon, if he is still alive after all this time, again there's no evidence for his involvement, and it seems completely out of character. It sounds like when he was in business he was a bit of a shady sort of quack, never published any research papers, so it's more probable he's just a common crook who's staged his own death in order to rob the charity he set up to stop his wife divorcing him and taking half of it."

From where he watched on the sofa, Ivor was clenching his fists and shaking his head. He looked away from the screen to stare fiercely at Jananin, who glared back at him defiantly. Dana licked mango chutney off a poppadom.

"And what's this information you have uncovered about a computer?"

"We have compelling evidence, and we intend to publish it on our website and in other venues soon, that there is a very powerful computer embedded in the civil service. We're not sure exactly who is controlling it, but it is being used to predict and manipulate the results of elections. It calculates how many seats short the incumbent government's candidates are likely to be in key constituencies needed to win by analysing people's voting records and Internet browsing behaviour. Then it identifies those members of the electorate in those constituencies who rarely vote, and uses mail redirection to exploit a loophole through the postal voting system with their votes to make up the shortfall."

"Dr Antrobus, as the leader of a political party yourself, you can hardly be described as neutral in this process."

"Well, no, but it is not the job of a political candidate to be neutral in anything."

"Can you tell me more about your political party, the Meritocratic Party?"

"Well now, the principle behind it is that there needs to be much less politics, and fewer politicians and political personalities, fewer civil servants, and much more accountability to the electorate in the decisions we make. We advocate on nominating and holding public referenda on all decisions that matter to the people, rather than having them decided in Parliament."

"Dr Antrobus, some people would describe the situation you just illustrated as utter chaos, bedlam even, with people voting blindly on topics they have no understanding of."

"Well, yes, and that's why we've worked out the system we have, and why we're called the Meritocratic Party. We believe that those who contribute the most to society, deserve the most say." Antrobus held up his hands to quell any objections. "There are many varied ways people can contribute to society. Some dedicate their life to scientific discovery and making the lives of everyone better. Some dedicate themselves to parenthood and raising the next generation. Others simply work hard and pay their taxes, and the products of their labour enrich society. So we propose a weighted voting system, with the votes of those who contribute the most being given the greatest weight."

"Dr Antrobus, your party's proposal of giving different weights to the votes of different people would mean that some people, the null tier, as they are described in your manifesto, would have no say at all."

"That is true, but the null tier is intended as a temporary safety net for people who are unable to support themselves for whatever reason. It's there as an incentive to help people get out of that rut, and make their lives better, and we will do everything to try to avoid people becoming stuck as null tier. There is more information on how we will help the null tier on our website."

"On the other hand, some commentators have said that using such a voting system would mean that the UK is no longer considered a democracy by important international bodies such as the EU and the ECHR. We would have to withdraw from them if this policy were to be enacted."

"If that is so, it should be taken as a sign that those institutions are no longer fit for purpose, and that to leave them is the right thing to do, so we can create new systems that work for this country and its people. Likewise we should dispose of outdated national institutions such as the monarchy and the House of Lords if the citizens of this country wish it so; indeed we intend to hold referenda on these very matters as soon as possible should we be voted in at the next general election."

Then the same two men who were always interviewed on television whenever anything important happened were asked for their opinions. Dana knew one of them was the Prime Minister and the other was the leader of the opposition, but she could never remember which was which. They had the same hairstyle, they spoke the same way, and one of them had brown skin and the other had light skin, but in all other ways they were as alike as two brothers who had fallen out. Neither of them talked about anything to do with Ivor and Jananin being framed, or the attempt to assassinate Colin Antrobus. Instead they began to discuss the character and motives of the leader of the Meritocratic Party, using long strings of jargon and esoteric insults. One of them said he was an elitist who stood for the wealthy and educated, and sought to disenfranchise the poorest and most deprived people in the country; the other said he was a populist who would only appeal to stupid people with no education, and that he would destroy the economy and stultify science and business in the country.

As Ivor shovelled prawn korma and rice into his mouth, watching the men arguing on the television, an irascibility came over him of the kind that Dana had never known, even when Peter behaved at his worst; not even when he'd discovered Jananin had destroyed all evidence of his work. "I've not watched television for more than ten years," he said. "Nothing has improved! It's still Tweedledum and Tweedledee agreeing to have a battle!"

-8-

DANA remembered the next morning to put on her hat with the foil inside it before she left her bedroom. She found Ivor downstairs, dividing the cold remains of the curries from last night between plates. "Ah," he said, and gestured to a seat for her. Alpha was already sitting at the table, her hat pulled down over the scar on her forehead, her concentration focused on her Tamagotchi.

Peter came bouncing downstairs, fully dressed and wearing his Viking helmet. "Did you enjoy your shower?" Ivor asked him.

"I had an amazing shower," Peter announced dramatically. "I had a shower worthy of Neptune, who is the god under the sea, in a shower-room with shiny walls, like mother-of-pearl, so it was like having a shower in a seashell."

Ivor smiled. He'd been up rather late last night, sticking tin foil to the walls, ceiling, and door of the bathroom, after realising he'd overlooked that people wouldn't be able to wash their hair if they had to wear hats in there.

"And I found you some paper, in the drawer of the desk in my bedroom." Peter thrust a wad of A4 paper into Ivor's hands. "I was going to draw on it, but then I thought you might like it better to write your ideas on, since you lost the other papers with your ideas written on them."

"Thank you, Peter!" Ivor took the paper, and he suddenly had to wipe his eyes, and tried to turn away so Peter wouldn't see. But Peter had already moved on, and as Jananin entered the kitchen, he greeted her with a salute, and said, "Good morning. I am a perfectly personable and creative young man." With that, he ran off up the stairs.

"Peter, come back and have some breakfast!" Ivor shouted after him.

Jananin sat at the table and Ivor passed her a plate. When Peter came back and sat down, Jananin took Ivor's plate and replaced it with hers. Peter giggled and tried to take Alpha's plate, but Ivor put his hand on top of his, and told him no.

"Oo, this must be rich people's food," said Peter, shovelling curry into his mouth. Suddenly he started to cough. "How can it be hot and cold both at once?" he gasped.

"One of us is going to have to go out and get some proper food," Ivor said to Jananin.

"I have a very good alibi for where I am at the moment, and I do not intend to risk compromising it. I don't want to go out any more than necessary."

"Then give me some cash and let me borrow your car. The only photograph they've got of me is old. It's unlikely I'd be recognised."

"Give you money and my car? I wouldn't trust you with tuppence and a bicycle!"

Jananin had already had a shower, because Ivor and Dana had decided the day before it was probably polite to let her have the only room with the ensuite, since her friend had arranged the house for them to stay in. So after breakfast, Dana had the shower to herself, and stood letting the hot water run over her, trying to imagine like Peter had that the walls Ivor had stuck foil to were mother-of-pearl.

She had searched through the drawers of the house and found some clothing left behind, that had probably belonged to a small woman. It was old but it was clean and comfortable: a pair of jeans, that were too big so she had to roll up the legs and wear a belt with them, a turtleneck top, and a T-shirt with a band name on the front to wear over it. She dried her hair as best as she could on a towel before putting on her woolly hat that Ivor had sewn foil into the lining of.

Downstairs, the breakfast plates had been cleared away, and the blueprints Dana had recovered from the Cerberus game had been spread out on the dining-room table.

"You look very cool, Dana. Grungy and retro. Very 1990s." Ivor said.

"Now you're here," began Jananin. "When I met with Antrobus, I asked him if he knew of anything to do with a bunker being built somewhere in the past fifteen years, anything he thought might be to do with the government or the civil service. He had one suggestion. The Amethyst building in central London. Apparently, during the construction of its foundations, there was a great deal of delay, and a lot of screening around the site, and an excessive amount of complex plant and materials for the task in hand, which raised suspicion amongst those who took an interest in such things. Subsequent investigations tracked down a number of German labourers who had been brought in and shipped out, under the condition of not discussing the project they worked on."

Jananin spread some more plans out on the table. "These are its official architectural plans. Permission was granted for its construction in London shortly after Steve Gideon's death. It was completed eleven years ago."

"So, what is it?" Ivor asked.

"Officially, and apparently, it is a public library." Jananin positioned the blueprints of the bunker next to the plans detailing the bottom of the Amethyst building's structure. "See how the shape and dimensions of the Faraday bunker match up with those of the foundations for the building precisely?"

"Is central London where Big Ben and the Houses of Parliament are?" Dana asked.

Ivor looked at her. "Yes."

"I keep seeing them in the game. Some other buildings as well, and always if I die by falling into water."

Jananin considered. "The Amethyst building is across the Thames, opposite those buildings. It could be that there are cameras on the outside of the building, and you are seeing Cerberus's view of the city."

Ivor took a seat at the table and scrutinised the blueprints closely. "These plans, you say this bunker is reinforced concrete. Blastproof?"

"It's not large, but it's substantial, and deep enough that probably nothing short of a direct hit from a military-grade warhead or something with similar explosive force would achieve penetration. You'll also notice that it's designed from the ground up as a Faraday cage within a Faraday cage, each with its own independent power supply. If an electromagnetic disturbance like the one you committed in Oxford were to take place in London, it would be protected."

A wry smile spread across Ivor's face. "You're talking about an external attack. How about internally? You say it's blast proof. Do you just mean deflagration, or can it take a detonation without the roof coming down?"

"Possibly. It depends on the explosive and the amount of it. I would have to calculate the forces involved."

"How about your old school TNT? Can you get any more of it."

"No," Jananin said quietly. "One does not just go out and *buy* trinitrotoluene. I can, however, *synthesise* it."

A nervous sort of passion had come over Ivor. "If you can make TNT, and I can make a flux compression generator, and we can get a Compton bomb into that central structure that'll work without bringing the whole thing down..."

"A Compton bomb?" Dana exclaimed.

Ivor turned to her, holding up his hands in an explanatory sort of way. "A Compton bomb is an explosion, like any bomb, but that generates an electromagnetic pulse."

"Jananin told me. It destroys anything electronic.

Including me and Peter and Alpha!"

"But not if those things are protected by a Faraday cage! Do you remember what I told you about the metal I put round the beds, and whatever Jananin put on her car, to make it so that radio waves and other electromagnetic signals can't get into it?"

"So if I was in bed, and you set off a Compton bomb, I would be OK?"

"I would perhaps want to use something I'd put more care into than a foil-lined bedroom, but in principle, yes. And it works both ways, so if I set off a Compton bomb in a Faraday cage and you weren't in it, you wouldn't be harmed either, as long as the Faraday cage was strong enough not to break during the explosion." Ivor widened his eyes. "And that also means that if Cerberus is in a Faraday cage, with a Compton bomb and *nothing else anyone cares about*, Cerberus gets destroyed and nothing else gets damaged!"

Jananin cast her eye over the plans spread on the table. "How would we get into the bunker? How would we even be able to approach the Amethyst building without being recognised?"

"We'll have to think on it. These sorts of things take a while to plan." Ivor closed his eyes and rubbed his forehead, and after a little while he suggested that, if Jananin could manage and did not mind, he would go upstairs and lie in the bath for an hour, to see if that would help him have an idea.

Things were quiet for about ten minutes, with Jananin pondering the architectural diagrams spread on the table and Dana looking on, uncomprehending. Then Peter ran upstairs and hammered on the bathroom door, demanding to know if Ivor had finished doing his idea, as he was minded to have an idea too, and didn't want to have it in his pants.

Ivor came downstairs soon after, wearing his RAF jacket. He'd sewn up the cut Jananin had made in the shoulder of it with her katana, but he'd used orange thread that didn't match, and he had a cardboard box with a picture on it under his arm. "Can you give me some money to go out and get us some food?"

Jananin produced a wallet from her trouser pocket, and threw some notes on the table for him.

"Can I have more than that? If I can get the children some books, it'll help occupy them."

Jananin sighed and threw some more notes at him.

"Keep an eye on them for me, would you? Alpha shouldn't be a problem to anyone. Peter's a bright enough boy, but he doesn't always pay attention. I find it helps to get him to repeat it back to me when I ask him to do something, then you'll know he's heard it." Ivor turned and spoke loudly over his shoulder. "Peter, can you come in here please?"

Peter came obediently, looking cheerful.

"I'm going to go out, to get some food and some books. Professor Blake has said she will keep an eye on you for me, so you need to be on your best behaviour."

Peter nodded.

Ivor rattled the box under his arm. "I've found this jigsaw. Perhaps you could try to do it for me, see if all the pieces are there."

Peter took the box with interest, and sat at the table.

"Tell me what you're going to do? *Peter*?" Peter had taken the lid off the box and wasn't listening.

"I'm going to stay here, and be on my best behaviour with Jininan."

Ivor crouched down, hands on his knees, so his face was level with Peter's. "*Ja-na-nin*. Or preferably Professor Blake, as it's very kind of her to do that for us."

"He can call me Jininan if he wants," said Jananin.

Ivor straightened up, shrugged, and quietly left the room. A few minutes later, Dana looked out the window and saw him going into one of the sheds in the back garden. He emerged pushing an ancient bicycle, and turned it down the path, but had to stop and bend over because the chain had fallen off.

Jananin got up from the table with a noise of exasperation. Then she was outside with him, and it looked as though she'd agreed to lend him her car.

When she came back, Peter had found the four corner pieces of jigsaw that each had two straight edges. "Are you going to stay with us?"

He asked it in such an earnest, direct way that Jananin set down her pen and looked up at him over the table. "I am going to stay with you until we find and stop whoever it was who is controlling the computer that sent helicopters and the signal that hurt you and Dana. Then I need to go back to my work, but I will make sure that you and Dana and Alpha are safe."

"Why's that?" Peter asked.

"Because I gave Ivor my word that I would see to it, and I do not lie, and I do not renege on my word, and the world would be a better place and we wouldn't have all the problems we have now, if everyone else did the same."

Jananin picked up her pen again. Dana was sitting at the table with a blank piece of paper in front of her, and she began to worry again about what Jananin might do to Ivor, and about Duncan and Cale and the game, and the helicopter attack.

After a moment, Peter said, "Ivor says you are cross with him. Is it because the food he cooks is horrible? If it's because of that, I don't think he does it on purpose. He's trying to get better."

"It's not because of that," said Jananin. "It's because of something he did a long time ago, before you were born."

"Ivor says you are a very clever person, and that you invent things." Peter said, arranging his jigsaw pieces. "Did you invent helicopters?"

"No."

"That's good, then, because I don't think helicopters are a very good invention, and probably the person who invented them wasn't very clever. Ivor borrowed one and that blew up as well. We had to jump out of it."

Dana wondered, nervously, if Jananin was wondering if Ivor had told Peter to say this to her deliberately. After Jananin had returned to her calculation, and Peter had focused all his attention on turning his jigsaw pieces the right way up, and Dana had sat, with nothing to do, she asked Jananin, "What is this thing, *tri-nifo...*"

"Tri-nitro-toluene. TNT. Look it up."

"I can't." Dana put her hand up to her woolly hat.

Jananin pushed her laptop, rotating it so Dana could reach it. Dana looked at the keyboard and screen, a slow panic starting to rise inside her. The computer was clearly on, but she could sense no signal from it, and the screen and the keyboard suddenly looked completely foreign to her. There were too many keys, and most of them had three or more different letters or symbols on them. When she'd had to use a computer at school, she'd put her hands over the keyboard to make it look like how everyone else was doing it, but if she'd pressed the keys at all she'd overridden it with her thoughts. She couldn't understand the computer at all, and hadn't the faintest idea of how she could go about making it search on the Internet for what TNT was.

"It's routed through a VPN," Jananin said, noticing Dana hadn't touched the computer, but with her attention still on her writing. Dana saw what she'd written and it made absolutely no sense either. She'd filled a piece of paper with numbers and letters and lines going this way and that. The panic was rising, and without any signals, it was starting to feel like it had in Miss Robinson's class, when the wLAN broke. Dana put her hand in her pocket, but found it empty.

"Jananin, I don't know how to work your computer!" Dana burst out. "I can't find any signals and everything feels wrong!"

Jananin's response to this was to shout at Dana, much like she had when Dana had used a computer to make a phone call from Lewis in a panic because she couldn't get to the beacon. "Pull yourself together! It's a perfectly ordinary computer! Can I not have half an hour's peace and quiet to do a calculation?"

The anger in her voice made the panic worse, and Dana started to cry despite herself. "I think I would be all right, if I could have a fuse, but I left them behind!"

Jananin got up and ripped the plug from a lamp out of a wall socket. "Just a normal fuse, from an appliance?"

"Yes, like in that."

Jananin couldn't find a screwdriver to take the plug apart. She went through the kitchen drawers and the ones in the dining-room sideboard. She tried to use the point of her knife as a screwdriver, but it didn't work. She lost her temper and swore, and thrashed the plug against the wall. All of this made Dana feel worse. She started breathing too fast again and feeling dizzy, and a horrible buzzing sensation spread from her fingers up her arms and legs.

"I can't have this hat on!"

"You can't take it off! Sit there and calm down!" Jananin yelled at her, and because she had, Peter shouted something at Dana as well which made things even worse, and that moment Ivor came in through the kitchen door with the shopping. He dropped it all over the floor as soon as he saw Dana.

"Dana, I need you to shut your mouth and concentrate on breathing through your nose. Has anyone got a paper bag?" Ivor made her stand up, and he pressed the lid of the computer down to switch it off, and put his arms around her and hugged her very tightly against him. Dana's vision had gone like a television that wasn't tuned properly, filled with white static, and she couldn't see anything. Everyone's voices sounded distant and weird.

"She just went off completely unprovoked, something about the computer and that bloody fuse you told her you'd replace!"

"Dana threw a wobbly!" Peter shouted. "We didn't do

anything!"

"Peter, sit down and do your jigsaw. Blake, we need to have a conversation later about how you can better manage your temper, because this isn't helping. Sit down and do your calculation! Dana, I'm so sorry I forgot to give you some more fuses. I'll get you them, but you need to listen to me and to calm your breathing down first. I need you to breathe out and hold your breath, and then we're going to count four potatoes. Ready?" He squeezed her tightly, but, oddly, it did make her feel a bit calmer, and she pressed her head against his chest and breathed out. "One potato, two potato, three potato, four potato, OK?"

He must have shepherded her into the kitchen, where it was darker, and her vision was starting to clear as he counted and told her when to breathe in and out.

And then Alpha walked into the kitchen, in a state of agitation from their raised voices. She took one of the cartons of milk out of Ivor's shopping, threw it on the floor, and stamped on it, sending an explosion of white spraying all over the tiles. "No!"

Peter began laughing hysterically.

"She said something," Ivor was saying. He steered Dana back into the dining room, sat her down, calmly picked up the toolbox with all the components that he'd brought from Roareim from beside the sideboard, and set it down on the table. "What size fuses have you lost?"

Dana took a deep, slow breath. "13A, 2A, 3A."

He quickly and calmly sorted them out, put them in her hand, and put the box away. "Help Peter do his jigsaw."

As Dana turned the fuses over in both hands, feeling their reassuring shapes, and arranged them standing on end in ascending order on the table in front of her, Ivor went back into the kitchen, bade Alpha sit on a chair there, and said, "Would you like to try a strawberry?"

Alpha looked down at the plastic container he was offering her with red and green things in it, and she went, "Urh!" and picked up the Tamagotchi from where it hung on the ribbon around her neck.

Ivor got down on his hands and knees on the kitchen floor with a cloth and began to clean up the milk. Jananin made savage strokes with her pen as she wrote. The Tamagotchi made a few random beeps from the kitchen. Dana put the fuses safely back in her pocket and found a piece of jigsaw that fitted into what Peter had already assembled, and slowly things began to feel normal again.

Jananin raised her pen, circled something twice at the bottom of her piece of paper, and drew a line underscoring it. She cast her pen down on the table and leaned back on her chair, folding her arms. "The mass of TNT that can safely be deployed without compromising the structural integrity of the walls. I calculated sufficient to break the door, as it's the weakest point and the schemata indicate it won't open unless it has power on both sides."

Ivor came and stood by the table to look at Jananin's calculation. Some of her pen strokes had torn the surface of the paper, gouging the sheet below.

"Can you give me some indication of what that is in terms of volume?"

Jananin rose from her seat and cast about the dining room and the kitchen. She picked up a packet of toilet rolls from Ivor's shopping, and pointed to the hole in the middle of one. "Approximately that."

*

Dinner was sausages, mashed potato, and broccoli, with tapioca for dessert that Ivor had bought and cooked up on Dana's suggestion. Although it would have been a very ordinary meal at Pauline and Graeme's house, Peter said it must be what kings and queens eat, and expressed disbelief that Ivor had in fact prepared it. Alpha licked her sausage, and went *urh*, and wouldn't try any more. But she did eat the tapioca, to Dana's delight.

"This is a breakthrough," Ivor said, meaning Alpha's behaviour. "She's always been nonverbal, yet today she said two words."

"I hardly think *urh* counts as a word," said Jananin.

"I'm sure *urh* is a perfectly good old Anglo-Saxon word," Ivor countered, "with a venerable history, the same as most words that shouldn't be used in polite conversation."

Jananin made a trenchant expression. "I do not see much of a future for someone who has the body of a fifteen-year-old and the mind of a four-year-old, who can say, *urh* and *no*, and has scurvy from refusing to eat anything other than tapioca pudding. I expect she will end up in an institution, as one of Colin Antrobus's null tier."

"If a nutcase like Antrobus and his crackpot party ever get elected to power, I'd hope there'd be enough compassionate voters to take care of her and everyone else who needs social housing and specialist care. And besides, she's improving. She'll probably continue to improve. Who knows where she might end up?"

Peter said, "It would be better if we didn't have to wear hats. Then she would know the food isn't *urh*, because she would be able to feel us eating it!" After a moment, he added, "And who's Colin Antrobus?"

"Colin Antrobus is nobody," said Ivor. "He's just some idiot on the tellybox."

After dinner, Ivor sat on the sofa with Alpha next to him, and read to her *The Three Billy Goats Gruff*. She looked at it some of the time, but she mostly looked at her Tamagotchi, and Ivor kept stopping to say, *not now*, or *play with it later*. Halfway through, Peter came to sit on Ivor's other side to look, and he sniffed very loudly, rattling it about in the back of his throat.

"Beam me up, Snotty," said Ivor, but after he'd gone back to reading and Peter had done it again, he stopped. "Peter, you're very welcome to listen, but can you wipe your nose or do something so you're not sniffing like that, right in my ear?"

"Are you having an idea?" Peter said loudly to Jananin, who was sitting in an armchair, drawing diagrams and writing numbers and letters on a notepad. She was so engrossed in it that she didn't hear him.

"If she is," Ivor said, "it would probably help her if you could be a bit quieter."

Dana was sitting in the other armchair. She held her fuses in her lap and closed her eyes.

After Ivor had told Peter and Alpha to go to bed, he came back, beckoning to Dana from the door. "Dana? You want to talk about what happened today?"

They sat down at the bottom of the stairs. "I'm sorry I threw a wobbly like Peter said when you went out. It was because I couldn't understand the computer without any signals, and I was worried about my brother, and..."

"Dana, there's nothing to be sorry about!" Ivor put his arms around her and held her close. "These things happen. And when I get my hands on that Cerberus, it'll wish Steve Gideon had never had the idea of it!"

Dana laughed a bit. Ivor put his chin on top of her head. "Don't you worry about Cerberus. Blake and I are going to do Cerberus in."

Dana tensed in his embrace. "What about afterwards? What about you?"

"Perhaps if I just let Jananin tar and feather me, and make even more of a fool of myself than she's already made of me, she'll content herself with handing me over to the police and cut her losses. And you'll have to ask your foster parents if they'll let you come and visit me in jail."

Dana shuddered. "What if I'm actually really stupid, and I can only understand things because of the device in my head?"

"Of course you're not stupid! What things can you not understand?"

"Computers." Dana looked down, noticing his watch on his wrist. "That."

"*That*?" He took it off. "You don't need a device in your head to understand that." He held it up and swung the face of it back and forth in front of her eyes, like a hypnotist. "It's wind-up. Entirely clockwork. If I have a digital watch or a watch with a battery in it, sooner or later Peter breaks it. This one's immune."

Dana took the watch. She turned it the other way up, but it didn't make any more sense like that. She pressed the face of it against her forehead, trying to sense the signal it made through the hat she was wearing.

"OK, well, maybe it's just because it's got Roman numerals on it instead of proper numbers. Maybe you've never really looked at clocks before, since you could always tell what time it was from some other signal." Ivor took it back. "Can you read that clock there?"

On the table in the hallway stood a radio, showing 21:15.

"I can read that!" Dana realised. "It means it's quarter past nine!"

"Well, there you go then!" Ivor patted her on the shoulder. "You're perhaps just a digital native. Perhaps we should go through how to read a clock some other time, but for now, just try not to worry about it too much. It's time you went to bed now, anyway."

"Okay, then."

"Goodnight." Ivor hugged her again, and kissed her hat.

After cleaning her teeth, Dana went to her bedroom, shut the door, took her hat off, changed into her pyjamas, and got into bed and tried to sleep. But she wasn't very tired, probably because she hadn't done very much that day, and Ivor had asked her to go to bed early because he wanted to talk to Jananin without her there. She also did not like how it felt to not be able to feel GPS or any other signals from anything, and she worried about what Ivor and Jananin might be talking about. After a while she got up and put her hat back on, and crept downstairs into the hall to see if she could hear them talking. She sat against the wall with her legs bent up and her arms wrapped around them.

A loud hiss from the seal on a fizzy drink being broken.

Ivor said, "Do you want me to get you anything?"

"No."

"Suit yourself." The sound of liquid being poured into a glass, the protesting creak of furniture sat down on too hard. "That's the stuff." Ivor followed this with a loud appreciative groan and an even louder burp.

Dana tried to imagine how Jananin might look in response to this, but couldn't. After a moment, she said, "Can you imagine, if the police turned up here tonight, and we had to flee, and you were blind drunk, what would happen?"

"I'm not getting blind drunk. I'm only having one. Not that I have much to be sober for. Not now your Machiavellian machinations with the ethics committee are through with me."

"I can't see how we are going to get access to this bunker without creating some sort of disruption in the vicinity of the Amethyst Building. A Compton bomb in central London is not an appealing prospect."

"It's doable. There's always building works going on in London somewhere. If we plan it for a Sunday, and find some project under construction or building empty for refurbishments, we should be able to avoid hurting anyone in the blast. The area that can be affected is limited, though. We'd have to build it as big as possible. Detonating it from a high point would help. My worry's the children. I can't leave them behind. Have you tested that car of yours? I mean, tested the as a complete Faraday cage, not just the shielding?"

"Yes, I've tested it."

"The other issue is, the most effective solution is to get the device into that central bunker and detonate it without damaging the outer level of security. It's potentially feasible with two devices to take out the system in the outer bunker first, but it's a lot harder. That's why it's been designed that way. If we cut the power to the outer shell, the lift won't work, and we'd have to climb back up the shaft. The door connecting the two levels is designed to lock in the event of power failure on either side. And we've no idea what sort of security there is down there."

"No doubt personnel. I may be able to do something about that."

"Blake, please, these guards, whoever they are, are just people doing a job. Can we find some alternative to lethal force? And while we're on the subject, I wish you wouldn't carry that knife openly in front of Peter. You've seen how impressionable he is."

"If we can take out the personnel, lethally or non lethally, we will be left with whatever electronic security systems they have down there to contend with. They're not on the plans. We won't know what we're dealing with until we get down there."

"Hopefully largely isolated if we set off a Compton bomb outside. Dana should be able to hack in to anything that's left."

Dana tensed where she sat in the hall, eavesdropping.

"You are suggesting taking her, on a raid on government property which may be patrolled by armed guards?"

"Well, she's a better prospect than either of the other two! This is as much of a problem for her as it is for us. She has no future while whoever's doing this still has control of that thing."

After a moment in which neither spoke, Jananin said, "There is a small blast wall in front of the door to the inner chamber. If we can set off the device behind the door, the electromagnetic pulse should still work, but whatever is behind that blast wall likely won't be physically destroyed. We would have to go back, smash it up, so it can't be repaired or copied."

"If the door can't withstand the detonation, that should make it easier. The layout of the corridor should screen us from anything that gets out if we go back to the start."

The conversation seemed to have moved on to

technical details now, and Dana was relieved that they were discussing and not arguing. Even the argument they'd had the day before, in which Jananin had told him about the research papers, had been of a far different calibre to the confrontation on Lewis, or in Roareim. Dana had once walked in on Pauline and Graeme having an argument because Graeme had dug up a shrub and thrown it on a bonfire because he thought it was dead when it wasn't. It had felt like a more intense version of the arguments normal people had.

She crept back upstairs and went to sleep.

*

When Dana woke the next morning, she had no way of telling what time it was, and when she put on her hat and went downstairs, it seemed everyone else was already up. Ivor sat at the dining table, trying to wrap a long piece of copper wire around a toilet roll tube, his brow furrowed, bottom lip jutting out. The box with the batteries and other components was open next to him. He noticed Dana watching him, and put it down and took his spectacles off.

"Are you making a Compton bomb?"

"I'm afraid I am. Are you okay getting your own breakfast and getting ready?"

Dana nodded.

She couldn't find Jananin in the house that morning, and that turned out to be because Jananin was in the large outbuilding in the back garden, which had been converted to a laboratory, because she was synthesising TNT.

"Can I look?" Dana asked. "Or will it just explode if it's looked at?"

"Come in and shut the door. And put these on." Jananin handed Dana a pair or large plastic glasses. "It won't explode, because it's very stable and it needs a detonator to make it explode, but making it involves using strong acids."

Jananin drew a picture on a piece of paper, of a hexagon with a circle inside of it, and a line coming off the top of it, with 'CH_3'. "Trinitrotoluene is toluene with NO_2 groups in the para and meta positions." Jananin wrote 'NO_2' on three more lines coming off the hexagon.

"It looks like the bunker where Cerberus is," Dana said.

Jananin frowned. "I suppose it does rather. So we have toluene, and we have nitric and sulphuric acid to nitrate it with."

Dana watched with interest as Jananin prepared a large spherical flask with a Teflon magnet in the bottom that spun around when it was put over a magnetic plate. She got Dana to help by taking a basin to the kitchen in the house and filling it with water and ice cubes from the freezer.

Jananin had just finished measuring out the toluene and the horrible smelly acids when Peter came banging on the door, all out of breath, and shouted something that started with 'Dana and Jananin' but the rest was difficult to understand.

"What did he say?" Jananin said.

"Something about lunch being ready."

"I thought so. But then it sounded like something about a puffin having hurt its bottom."

"Probably," said Dana. "Peter is a bit like that. He talks a lot about things to do with the toilet. But I quite like him."

Jananin raised her eyebrows. "Yes."

Back in the house, it turned out that Peter's excitement was because Ivor had made egg sandwiches, and Peter had never seen eggs so big. Despite Ivor's attempts to explain that the eggs had been laid by a chicken hen and not a puffin hen, Peter was convinced there must be a puffin somewhere who had badly injured herself through her Herculean effort.

Jananin took Ivor's plate of sandwiches from in front of him, and Peter laughed.

"Come on, Peter, it's not a game. You want to know why Jananin keeps taking my food? It's because she thinks

I might play nasty jokes on her, by putting things in her food to make it taste bad."

"That's not a nice joke," said Peter. "You should only play nice jokes that don't hurt people. Like whoopee cushions. Or that time when I put a sea cucumber in your pocket without you noticing."

"I don't think the sea cucumber thought that joke was very funny." Ivor made an exaggerated, morose expression. "And besides, Jananin does this with such consistency, that if I did want to poison her, all I'd have to do is put it in my own food!"

"Have you worked out if you can make a flux compression generator from what's here yet?" Jananin asked.

"I might need to get hold of a few more things."

By the end of the week, Jananin had finished making all the TNT she had materials for. It sat in the laboratory inside a big plastic bucket, pale yellowish-brown powdery chunks of it.

"It looks like fudge," Dana said, a morbid horror coming over her. "What would happen if someone ate it?"

"It wouldn't explode," Jananin said. "But you would be horribly ill and probably turn yellow."

Then Jananin heated up the TNT in a water bath until it melted, and it had to be poured into lots of moulds inside buckets of wet sand. By this time Ivor had assembled in the dining room an old suitcase and two briefcases filled with huge batteries and electrical components. In each there was a coil of copper wire into which each assembled TNT shape fitted perfectly. All that remained to add was the detonators: small metal objects with pins that allowed them to be pressed into the TNT and wired up to an egg timer in each case. Jananin kept these in a small padded box and intended to transport them in her coat pocket.

Ivor and Jananin had gone through the plans of the bunker under the Amethyst Building several times and tried to explain what they intended to do. First, they would set the large Compton bomb in the suitcase in an open place in London. Then, they would return to the car so they would be safe when the bomb went off. Once this was done, they would go to the Amethyst Building and try to get down into the bunker, which would have some sort of security system that Dana would have to help with once they got there and found out what they were dealing with. Once they were there, they would ideally try to get one of the briefcase bombs into the shielded inner chamber where Cerberus was, and set it off there.

Dana studied the plans with a nervous fear, the narrow corridor that led around the perimeter of the hexagon to the entrance to Cerberus's central lair, just above the first entrance but blocked by a thick blast wall. The corridor, while not exactly a maze, was a gauntlet to run, and there was no telling what might be down there. She imagined robots with glowing lights for eyes and laser guns, and unspeakable emitters that made painful signals.

That evening, everyone sat down at the table and Ivor tried to explain what they were going to do to Peter.

"We are going to London, which is where this computer is that's been causing all these problems."

"London is where Oliver Twits in a book I'm reading lives," said Peter.

"If you read it more carefully, you'll see he's called Oliver Twist, and not Oliver Twits. Although Twits is as good a name for him. And I don't think he lives there any more. Now, while I go with Jananin and Dana to do this, you and Alpha are going to have to stay in Jananin's car. You remember Jananin's car, where it's safe, and the bad signals can't find us?"

Peter nodded.

"I want you to stay there, and make sure Alpha stays there too. On no account must you leave the car or open the doors or windows until we come back. Can you do that for me?"

"I will stay in the car, and make sure Alpha stays in the

car, and not open the doors and windows, until you come back."

Ivor nodded vigorously. "Excellent."

-9-

"**O**H, Peter, stop sniffing!"

Peter snorted, rattling it about in the back of his throat and swallowing emphatically. "Are we in London yet."

"Yes, we're in London." Ivor looked around the multi-storey car park, twisting the gold ring on the finger of his left hand. "It's too early in the year for hayfever. I hope you're not coming down with the lurgy."

Jananin was behind the car, opening the boot. A sensation of dread rose in Dana's chest when she lifted out the big suitcase.

Ivor got out and opened the back door. "Dana, you ready?"

Dana unfastened her seatbelt and got out. She nodded without speaking, standing stiffly before him from sitting in the car with her feet on the toolbox stowed down there as there was no room in the boot because of the cases. They'd driven down and stayed overnight in one of the motorway lodges, with her having to wear her hat in bed. She'd had upset guts that morning, and had eaten scant breakfast with the apprehension about what they intended to do today. He put his hand on her shoulder. "It's going to be OK. Let's get this over and done with." He pressed a button on his watch to start a timer.

He turned to Peter, leaning into the back seat to speak to him. "Peter, do you remember what we talked about, and what you're going to do?"

Peter nodded. "I'm going to stay in the car and read my book until you come back, and wear my helmet all the time, and Alpha's going to wear her hat, and we are not either of us to get out of the car, under any circumstances."

Alpha, in a moment of lucidity, turned her head from her Tamagotchi to look at him.

"That's great. Peter, I want you to promise to me and to Jananin, that you'll stay in the car. You mustn't open the windows or the doors or get out for any reason. Can you promise that?"

"I promise, Ivor, to stay in the car." Peter's voice became high pitched and melodramatic. "I promise it from the heart of my bottom!"

"Good!" Ivor grinned, squeezed Peter's shoulder, and closed the door. Jananin locked the car.

Dana walked between Ivor and Jananin out of the car park, Ivor towing the case on its corner castors. Over the other side of the Thames was an enormous building with an almost Aztec look to it, of yellowish concrete and green glass, gleaming in the winter sun.

"What's that?" she asked Ivor.

"That's MI6, where the spies work." He'd found a leftover jelly bean in his jacket pocket, and he gave it to Dana.

They followed a path beside the river. People on bicycles passed quickly, ignoring them. It was Sunday morning, and only just light, but it still seemed very busy compared to the suburb in Coventry where Pauline and Graeme lived. The sound of traffic up on the bridge behind them was a constant low hum, the upper decks of occasional red buses visible as they moved back and forth slowly behind its rail.

Jananin pointed to a tower that gleamed like black obsidian beyond the waterfront buildings. "That's the Amethyst Building, or so I believe."

"I don't understand it," said Dana. "Why is it a library? If it belongs to the government, why aren't there fences round it and things to protect it, like the MoD base on Gallan Head?"

"Because Cerberus uses the very same mode of defence for its corporeal self as it uses for its manifestation on the

Internet." Jananin tilted her head up to take in the full perspective of the tower. "If this place was swarming with guards and military personnel, people would realise there was something here. So long as no-one knows about it and it does nothing to draw attention to itself, it's safe."

They walked away from the path along the river, the suitcase bumping along behind, up a street to where the road had been blocked with wire fencing panels covered with hazard signs and 'NO ENTRY', and scaffolding had been set up around a building under construction. Ivor found a corner point where the panels could be lifted out, and he passed the suitcase through, squeezing himself through the gap behind it. Jananin took from her inside coat pocket the case made from thick plastic, opening it to reveal the detonation charges packed tightly inside dense insulating foam. She pulled one out and passed it to him through the mesh. Very carefully, he wrapped it inside his handkerchief and put it into his jacket pocket. "I'll see if I can climb to the top with it."

He moved quickly out of sight, and Dana couldn't tell where he was, because the scaffolding was covered with orange safety netting and sheets that flapped in the wind. All Dana and Jananin could do was wait.

After an interminable time, Ivor re-emerged and hurried to the corner of the fencing, which Jananin lifted for him to get out. "It's right on the top, nothing to confine it, maximum exposure, let's hope minimum risk to human life. We've got just under twenty minutes to get back to the car."

They hurried back the way they'd come, Big Ben striking half past eight from its outpost on the far bank of the Thames, rather faster without the suitcase to pull along. Then the car park was in sight, and they were making their way up to the level, and with a pang of relief, there was the car, still parked where they'd left it...

Ivor skidded to a halt ahead of Jananin and Dana, and stared at the car, breathing heavily from the exertion of running. The front passenger window had been smashed. Tiny cubes of broken glass lay on the surface of the car park beneath the door and clung to the edges of the frame where the window had been. Ivor covered the last few strides to the car in a dash, thrusting his head and shoulders through the window. "Peter! Alpha!" He pulled back from the car, his hands rising in panic. "They're gone! I told Peter to stay in the car!"

Jananin went around to the other side of the car. She pulled a yellow sticky note off the driver's door. "Dear Sir or Madam," she read. "You should not leave children unattended in the car. They were clearly very distressed and we have taken them to the police station." She closed her fist, crushing the note, and threw it on the tarmac. "The idiots vandalised my car!"

Dana stared at her. "Will the car not work now?"

"It'll work, as a car. Not as a Faraday cage!"

Ivor looked frantically at his watch. "I have to go back and stop it!"

"There's not time. We have to get Dana somewhere she'll be shielded!"

"But what about Peter and Alpha?"

"I can't do anything about them!" Jananin went to the back of the car and opened the boot. The two briefcases containing the smaller Compton bombs lay within. "With the car compromised, it's possible these may not be shielded if they are left here as planned. If the blast disables them, we lose what chance we have left to take out Cerberus." Jananin seized one of the cases, a tatty leather thing with a strap, and pulled it over her shoulder. "Dana, come with me. We need to find a tall building. Regulations mean that lifts and shafts for high rises have to be built to a more robust standard. That's our best bet as a makeshift Faraday cage. Pilgrennon?"

"I can't. I have to try to stop the bomb." With that, he turned and ran, back the way they'd come.

"*Idiot.*" Jananin slammed the boot door over the

remaining case.

"Look after her!" he shouted over his shoulder at Jananin.

Half frozen with fear, Dana fell, unable to keep up, as Jananin dragged her down a street, up some steps, and into the foyer of a tall building. "Excuse me!" shouted whoever was behind the desk there, indignantly, but Jananin ignored her, steering Dana straight across the entrance lobby and to an open lift door, and smacked the heel of her hand down on the button for the highest floor. The lift lurched up as it began its ascent, and then suddenly stalled. The lights went out and the ventilator fan stopped.

In the darkness Dana's breathing seemed to fill up the place. In the instant the lift had failed, she'd grabbed hold of Jananin's arm, and now she clung to it in the dark.

"Are you all right?" Jananin asked.

"I think so."

"Can you please stop touching me, in that case?"

Dana released Jananin's arm. "Does this mean the bomb's gone off? What about Ivor, and Peter and Alpha?"

"Going by the time remaining, and Pilgrennon being middle-aged, probably of slightly higher weight than is optimum, and not having an especially high fitness level, it's unlikely he got anywhere near the building before the bomb went off, and hence is likely unharmed. Peter and Alpha, unless they managed to get out of range or into something that would have served as a Faraday cage, are likely dead." Jananin had been fumbling with something as she spoke, and now a light came on. It was fixed to a strap, which she fitted around her head. The inside of the metal box was cramped and claustrophobic in the torch's weak light. "Now, to get this door open."

A silence followed as Jananin examined the panel with the buttons for the floors on it. Dana sneezed and it echoed around the lift. When Jananin didn't get anywhere with that, she turned her attention to a hatch on the ceiling, which she managed to get open.

"You're going to have to climb up." She picked Dana up under the arms. Dana got hold of the edge and scrambled out through the square hole and onto the top of the lift.

"Here, have this torch."

Dana took the torch and shone it about. The lift shaft stretched up so far the torch didn't seem to be able to reach its end. Two thick cables on either side of the lift appeared to be part of the mechanism that moved it up and down.

Jananin jumped a few times, grasping at the edge of the hatch and cursing, and then her arm came up through the hole to the elbow, and she levered herself up into the shaft.

"Can you find where the door is?"

Dana ran her hands over the wall at the front of the lift and felt the indentation where the doors met in the middle. "Yes!"

Jananin was fumbling about the passage. "There should be something for opening the doors manually in an emergency to one side."

"I can't find anything!"

"Then keep looking!"

Jananin found a wheel on the right side of the door and began to turn it. The doors creaked apart slowly, and daylight penetrated the shaft. Once it was wide enough, Jananin lay down so she could see under it. There wasn't a great deal of room, as the lift had come to a halt a couple of feet below where it was supposed to be to line up with the outer doors. Dana slid through the gap and dropped to the door. Jananin, being bigger than her, had more trouble. First she threw the briefcase with the Compton bomb in it down, followed by her coat, and then her katana, and then she slid through feet first, at an instant that coincided with a businessman coming into the corridor. He took one look at the things on the floor, and at Jananin with her knife strapped to her thigh and a lot of cylinders and other strange things strapped about her body, and he turned and hurried back the way he'd come.

Jananin shoved through a door marked *Fire Exit*. Dana threaded the torch onto her wrist by its rubber strap as they hurried through the door and down a stairwell at the side of the tower. Looking out the windows she saw unlit buildings surrounded by roads of motionless traffic, like rivers that had suddenly become glaciers.

They burst through a fire escape door and out onto a metal staircase leading down into a rubbish-strewn alley. The stairs rattled and shook as they descended, and big rats with bedraggled fur scuttled and darted away as they ran through the alley towards the street.

Jananin looked left and right at the end of the alley. "We're on the wrong side of the building."

A large crowd was beginning to congregate in the street, in the direction they needed to go to get to the Amethyst Building. Opposite where they stood, over the roof of a stalled car, Dana could see an unlit shop window displaying blank-screened televisions. She was still wearing her foil-lined woolly hat, and wouldn't have been able to sense any signals even had things still been working.

Jananin and Dana moved into a different alley, away from the throng. A noise of smashing glass and a piercing scream cut through the background murmur of many voices. People scattered as two youths charged from a shop into the alley, one with a DVD player and a laptop under his arm and the other with several ladies' handbags.

"You! Giz your wallet!" the first boy demanded in a Cockney accent, his face a distorted rictus of hate. His free hand pointed a knife with an upcurved tip towards Jananin as he advanced on her. Jananin pushed Dana back as the other boy leered down at her.

Jananin's right hand shot up from her left hip, and steel flashed before the first boy, her left hand striking out an instant after with the knife in it, its point hitting close to the second boy into a piece of chip-board covering a window with a jarring thump. The first boy's knife was lying on the floor along with a couple of what looked like sliced sausages, which turned out in fact to be some of his fingers.

The boy stared at Jananin, the katana in her hand, and the things on the floor, and then at the blood running from his hand down his arm. His face contorted in horrified disbelief, and he started to scream, over and over again. Jananin's teeth were bared, her eyes fierce behind her dark glasses. The other boy stumbled and flailed, unable to get away, pinned by the material under the arm of his hoodie to the board by the knife. Eventually he wriggled out of it, tumbled over on the pavement, shouted, "Batshit bitch!" and got up and fled.

Jananin pulled the knife away from the board with a savage twist of her shoulder, and pushed it back into its sheath. She picked up the hoodie the boy had left behind and used it to wipe the blood off her katana, before throwing it on the ground and resheathing the sword. "With me," she told Dana, setting off at a brisk pace towards the place where the Amethyst Building's dark tower rose over the roofs of the surrounding buildings.

Skeletal leaves whirled around their ankles as they fled past a park. They reached the plaza before the building, but a crowd had gathered there, and up the steps by the entrance, guards blocked the entrance door.

A man in a dark green boiler suit with *paramedic* written in bold yellow letters on the back stood waving his arms in the midst of it, ordering the people to stand back. A woman in an identical outfit crouched on the ground, and through numerous legs and coats and umbrellas Dana could see boxes and wires lying around. As the man waved the people away, she saw a pair of thin legs sticking out where someone lay on the pavement, wearing army boots. On the ground at the edge of the worried crowd lay a small plastic object on a broken piece of grubby tartan ribbon, and although the outside of the Tamagotchi showed no sign of damage, its screen was blank, with no pixellated character moving to and fro.

There came a whine like an electric guinea pig. "Please, keep back and let us do our job!" the man exhorted the crowd. The increasing pitch stopped with a *thunk*. The legs gave a mechanical jerk.

It was then Dana saw Ivor amongst the concerned bystanders, sitting on the steps that led up from the plaza to the Amethyst Building. His elbows were on his knees, his hands over his face, and his shoulders shook. When she went to him, her head swam and her knees felt weak, so she sat beside him on the step.

"Oh Dana, thank goodness you're all right," he said. "But Alpha..."

Over the silent city, Big Ben began to strike, a funeral bell that tolled for Alpha and the crowd of black-clad business mourners. A dirge to the death of computers. The sight of them blurred before Dana's eyes.

"All this time, I never lost hope in her." Ivor's voice was feeble and plaintive. "Just as things were looking up for her, and now..."

"We need to go, now." Jananin had moved to stand on Ivor's other side.

Ivor's shoulders shook harder, and his breath came out in a gasp. "What about Peter?"

To Dana's surprise, Jananin spoke rather optimistically. "We haven't seen any other commotions like this to suggest he's dead, so if he wasn't with her, it's likely he got away. If he was still wearing his helmet, that would have given him more protection than a hat with foil in it, and if he was running away, the radius it can affect is limited, and so he may have got far enough out of range to have been all right."

"Peter understood he had to stay in the car," Dana realised. "If someone forced him to get out, he wouldn't have been happy, and he wouldn't have done as he was told. I think he would have thrown a wobbly."

Ivor looked at Dana and took a few shaky breaths.

Jananin said, "He knew what was expected of him. He likely got out of that car under duress, and Dana is right."

Ivor wiped his face with the heel of his hand. "I have to go to Alpha, to say goodbye."

"You'll do no such thing." Jananin said. "If she'd dead, she's very much dead, and nothing you or anyone else can do will make any difference. I agreed to help sort out this mess, which you created, and we need to get on with what we intended to do for the sake of Dana and Peter. Your skill is lying and cheating and persuading people to think and do whatever you want, so you had better get up now and use it to get us into that library."

Ivor stood up slowly. He took a few deep breaths, and he adjusted his jacket, rolling his shoulders to settle it into position and fumbling with the sleeves so the handcuffs still attached to his wrists didn't show, and he straightened his back. When he turned and began to mount the steps, he had assumed an attitude of grim professionalism, and he moved in a hurry to the guards blocking the doors to the Amethyst Building.

"I'm a doctor," he introduced himself gravely. "A child has suffered a cardiac arrest. We are all doing the best we can for her, but whatever has happened has affected the paramedics' defibrillator and it's not working effectively. I wondered if we might have access to the library to see if we can find any working defibrillators at your first-aid points?"

The two men glanced at each other, and then they stepped aside to let the three of them through without question.

In the foyer, a board on the wall referenced the floor locations of books on various subjects and advised that the viewing tower was closed for the winter. The foyer itself was plain in appearance, and unfurnished. One door led to the library, and another was clearly marked *No Admittance*.

Ivor went to this door and pushed it open. Inside, a security guard with a taser holstered at his hip turned to behold them. "There's no entrance for the general public to this part of the library."

"I'm a doctor." Ivor pointed to the first aid point marked out in green on the wall behind the guard. "We're trying to find a working defibrillator."

At the instant the guard looked where Ivor was pointing, Jananin sprang forward and engaged him with a judo grab. Ivor shouted at her not to use lethal force, and the taser discharged with a sudden pop. Jananin heaved the man over her shoulder and down hard on to the floor, thin silvery wires entangling everything. Ivor pinned the man face down, holding his hands behind his back, while Jananin broke open the first aid point and pulled out some bandages to bind him with.

They left the guard trussed up facing the wall. Ivor searched his pockets and found a key, while Jananin disentangled herself from the taser wire and pulled barbed prongs out of her clothing, wincing as she did.

The door the guard had been protecting, which the key unlocked, was a heavy, metal affair with no windows. It led only to a short corridor. A blank sliding door, flush against the wall and with a call button on a metal plate beside it, was the entrance to the lift. The light on the call plate showed the lift was still operational. This must be the entrance down to the outer Faraday bunker.

Jananin pressed the lift call button and the doors slid back. Inside, there was no plate with numbers to move the lift to a different floor. There was nothing to indicate the lift could be used.

"It must need an electronic key," Ivor said. "Dana?"

Dana reached up and pulled off her woolly hat, leaving her hair bristling with static. Signals came flooding back to her, and she found, instantly the signal of the lift, and told it to descend. The doors closed and the lift began to move.

As she stood between Jananin and Ivor, with the lift moving beneath her, feeling signals again, feeling more alive than she had for a long time, she felt stronger. They were as the touch of a fresh evening breeze; so refreshing after being stuck in a stifling south-facing room with the blinds down and the windows shut on a summer afternoon. She was tired of hiding in a hat and feeling stupid. She would face Cerberus and avenge Alpha, and end this.

-10-

THE lift was cramped, especially with Ivor in it. Jananin took the briefcase off and handed it to him. "We only get one shot at this. The other one is in the car, and likely broken by the Compton blast." She unfastened something that had been strapped to her body, under her coat: a steel cylinder with something written on the side in marker pen. "Dana, when that door opens, I am going to open the valve on this cylinder, and kick it into the corridor. There are very likely to be guards in the corridor. I need you to shut the doors and send the lift back up when I tell you, so that the guards and the contents of the cylinder do not get inside the lift."

"What the hell's that?" Ivor demanded.

"Shut up," said Jananin, and at that moment the lift decelerated and stopped, and the doors slid back. The seal broke on the cylinder with an explosive hiss, and Jananin dropkicked it through the door. "Now!"

Dana caught a brief glimpse of the depressurising bottle, fog blasting from it as it spun and ricocheted off the floor and walls and all about the ankles of three panicking men, as the doors slid shut and the lift began to rise again.

"Blake, what have you done! What's that you've put in there?"

"My calculations based on the specifications of the ventilation system suggest it will take around six minutes for the bottle to depressurise completely and the air exchange to reduce it to negligible concentration. Set that watch of yours, and I'll explain what it is while we wait."

Ivor set his watch as he was told. The lift reached the top of the shaft and drew to a halt.

"In 2002, terrorists instigated a siege in a public

building in Moscow. The security services gassed both the terrorists and the hostages with a cocktail of narcotics and opiate derivatives and successfully retook the building. The exact composition they used has never been publicly disclosed, but a contact of mine who works in Porton Down released the results of an analysis undertaken there on contaminated material and individuals recovered from it, enabling me to recreate something with comparable effects."

"Is it non-lethal?" Ivor demanded.

"The concoction used in Russia was estimated to have a death rate of approximately fifteen percent in the hostages. The exposure was prolonged, and the medics treating the victims weren't informed of what agents had been used. Considering my contact in Porton Down should be on duty today, and there are only three of them, their chances are good." Jananin folded her arms and leaned back on her heels.

Presently, Ivor announced the six minutes was up, and Dana told the lift to go back down. The doors opened to reveal two men lying motionless on the floor, the gas cylinder spent on the floor between them. The walls, ceiling, and floor of the tight corridor were plain concrete, and it turned to the right as Dana remembered from the plan, around the perimeter of the hexagon. A CCTV camera roosted like a one-eyed bird in the corner where the walls joined the low ceiling, but Dana could tell its connection had been cut by the Compton blast on the surface, and the image it recorded was being sent nowhere. Behind her, next to the lift, was another first aid station in a box fixed to the wall, a stand beneath it with two red fire extinguishers. She wondered how far down they were.

"I distinctly remember seeing three. One must still be conscious," Jananin said. The two men on the floor weren't completely inert; they made occasional slight motions with their breathing. They were unconscious, Dana realised, not dead.

"What can you sense, Dana?"

Dana concentrated for a moment. "I see lots of images, of corridors like this one."

Ivor went first into the corridor, following around the hexagon. They passed more cameras. Dana remembered the building's blueprints, the main nexus in the centre of the bunker, where Cerberus likely was. To get to it, they were going to have to go all the way around.

They rounded the first corner. *Four more to go*, she thought.

As they neared the second corner, she began to pick up the signals from the cameras beyond it.

"*Stop*." Dana held her arms out.

She saw Ivor move up behind her on one of the cameras. It felt like being in a fairground hall of mirrors, seeing herself from weird, scarcely recognisable perspectives. He bent down so his mouth was close to her ear. "What can you see?"

Dana turned round. "There's a man," she whispered. "In the corridor."

"What's he doing?"

"He's one of the guards. He's got a yellow gun." The man in the camera's image looked extremely stressed. He had a handkerchief or something held over his mouth with his free hand. He could hear them talking, and he turned and raised his gun.

"Blake?" Ivor said.

"You go," Jananin replied, mocking. "Use your psychology and see if you can talk him down."

Ivor went first to face the man, but before he had time to say anything, the taser discharged with a loud pop and a buzzing crackle, and Ivor went down like a ton of bricks. His glasses fell out of his shirt pocket and scudded across the floor. Immediately Jananin was over him and taking on the guard, who, now he had used his taser, had nothing else to defend himself with. She took him down with a kick to the diaphragm followed by a judo throw. After she'd kicked the taser out of his hand and pinned him down with her knee on his back, Dana went to Ivor. The two flimsy wire cables attached to the taser had gone through his shirt, and as Dana tried to rouse him, he passed his hand over his face. "Ja- Janana- *urh*." he said. "That was horrible!"

"The battery on the one he shot me with upstairs was knocked out by the Compton bomb," Jananin said.

"So you made sure I got the live one?"

"It would hardly make sense for me to take it and put myself out of action, and leave a child and a pacifist with no knowledge of hand-to-hand combat to deal with the situation."

After Ivor had recovered and pulled each of the taser's barbs out of his skin, each with a dramatic *ouch*, Ivor and Jananin frogmarched the man back to the lift. He seemed to be rather confused, and had probably inhaled some of the contents of Jananin's cylinder. They tied him up with medical supplies and his taser wires, and left him with his unconscious colleagues.

They passed the last two corners without event. Ivor said, "Whose idea was it to call it a Compton bomb, anyway?"

Jananin cast a wry sideways glance in his direction. "The broadsheets'."

They had completed the circuit of the hexagon's perimeter and reached the door to the inner bunker. Like the lift, there was no panel on the outside for a swipecard or with numbers for a code, or any other physical method of opening it. Behind this door, if everything Dana and Ivor and Jananin suspected was correct, lay Cerberus.

Ivor opened the leather briefcase on the floor. He set the timer, but didn't switch the power on yet. "Ready."

Jananin positioned herself in front of the door. She drew the knife from its holster at her thigh. "Dana, open the door."

Jananin tensed as Dana told the door to open, but

the two sides slid back to reveal a deep doorway, almost a corridor through the immense thickness of the concrete walls, and nothing but a concrete wall directly behind, shielding the contents of the room from the doorway. Little else could be seen of the room because of this, although Dana could feel signals and hear fans running, and sense the heat and air disturbance of a great deal of computer equipment.

Ivor pushed the briefcase through the door. "Detonator cap!"

Jananin took another detonator carefully from the box in her pocket, and passed it to him. With great care and both hands, he pushed it into the cylinder of TNT and connected up the wires and pushed the switch.

"Close the door!"

Dana closed the door, and then they were hurrying back around the narrow, claustrophobic corridor, all the way around the hexagon and back to the lift.

"Not in the lift," Jananin said. "The shaft is structurally the weakest point in the whole construction."

Ivor looked at the timer on his watch. "Two minutes."

The guard looked up at them from the floor. "What the hell have you done?"

Dana found herself staring in fear at the concrete wall on the other side of the lift exit. The door to Cerberus was on the other side of that, and the room the bomb was in was mere yards away from her behind the perpendicular blast wall. She hoped Jananin hadn't made a mistake in her calculations.

"Get down on the floor, just in case," Ivor said.

Dana sat in a foetal position next to the fire extinguishers and first aid box. Ivor crouched over her, holding her to him. It felt rather crowded with the three guards lying down there as well.

A blunt thump jarred the corridor, sending a rattle up Dana's spine.

Ivor released his hold on her. "Okay."

The guard swore as they left him there, retracing their steps around the perimeter. The metal door the bomb had gone off behind was all bowed out and split, and the air carried an odd smell and a trace of smoke that the ventilation system hadn't quite managed to suck out.

Ivor took a crowbar from under his jacket and pried away the fragments of the broken door. Inside, the light was still on, and Dana sensed signals. She stepped through the doorway. No trace remained of the briefcase or the Compton bomb inside it, and the floor and the blast wall fronting the door were all covered with sooty black residue that had splashed out from either edge of the wall and peppered the walls, leaving a clean line like a stencil where the wall blocked the line of sight from the rest of the room. She turned to Ivor, who looked past her, confusion written on his face.

"I don't understand," he said. "It's detonated well enough. Why is the power still on? Why hasn't it worked?"

When Jananin spoke, her face was livid, her voice rising to a shrill pitch. "*You built it!* You did this on purpose, Pilgrennon! Because you want this computer for yourself!"

Dana took another step into the room. There was no place for an operator to sit; no keyboards, mice, or screens, and the air was filled with the noise of cooling fans, although behind that sound there was an odd sort of hissing tone. Behind the blast wall that blocked the doorway stood a sort of large pedestal made of computer equipment. Reaching from the top of the pedestal to the roof and spreading like vines and branches from a stout tree bole was a thick mass of cables of all different thicknesses and colours. Lights moved through some of them; other lights blinked and glowed like fireflies in crevices of the pedestal. Dana could sense a multitude of signals emanating from the thing, but the strongest one was a transmission of pure terror.

Dana's throat hurt, and a sour taste had filled her mouth.

"What's that?" Ivor was saying.

"What's what?"

"It sounds like depressurisation. Like air hissing out of something."

"The only air I can hear depressurising from anything is the hot variety coming out of your mouth. You should check your other orifices if you think it's hissing out from anywhere else."

"Ivor?" Dana wasn't sure if Cerberus was making another signal that was doing something to her. The hissing seemed very loud and her vision wasn't quite right. She felt dizzy, and the room seemed somehow distant. As she stepped back, she lost her balance, felt Ivor catch her. What happened after that was blurred, although she could make out that she was being carried back into the corridor, and the panic in Ivor and Jananin's voices, but not what they were saying. The next thing she was properly aware of was sitting on the floor back under the first aid box, which had been pulled open, and a clear plastic mask being held over her nose and mouth.

"Can I just..." Ivor said, and he took the mask away and breathed through it a couple of times.

"It's because you inhaled when I told you not to!" Jananin chastised him. "It's called the Bohr effect."

The shapes of the three guards on the floor came into focus. One of them said, "You two must be a special breed of scum, bringing a kid down here and exposing her to your criminality, using her like a canary in a coal mine."

Jananin looked at the man with disgust. "Do you actually have any idea of what it is you are guarding? And how it just misused the carbon dioxide fire extinguisher system in that room to try to asphyxiate us?"

The man shrugged as much as he was able to, his hands being tied behind his back with bandages. "I'm not supposed to. It's some sort of computer facility. I know who you are, though. You're Blake and Pilgrennon. The Nobel laureate who went rogue and had some wild affair with the quack who falsified his medical credentials and robbed a charity he set up to help disabled children. And *that's* the child who can't be named and supposedly is dead."

"If you tell anyone," Jananin said, "they will not believe you. I have a very good solicitor, and a watertight alibi, and besides, you have been inhaling narcotics and opioids."

"I'm not a quack," said Ivor. "And the autistic aren't disabled; they're just *different*." He put the plastic mask back over Dana's face, and as Dana breathed in the oxygen and her head cleared, she recalled Ivor's toolbox, which she had sat in the car with her feet on the lid of all the way from Scotland, because the luggage didn't fit in the boot with the Compton bombs in it, the box he'd given her the fuses to replace the ones Graeme had given her from, the same box that had sat open on the table beside him while he was building the electronic parts of the devices, the same box that had been in Roareim and that Alpha had thrown on the floor, and Peter had thrown laundry on top of it, *that night she'd forgotten to put her fuses in her clean clothes and lost them...*

"Ivor, you know the Compton bomb didn't work. Did you use fuses to build it?"

"Well, yes. Everything I could make from normal household stuff, I did. I tried to keep specialist components to a minimum, as we were less likely to be noticed buying them."

"Do you remember, I lost my fuses? I think they might have got mixed up with the fuses in the box. They were fuses that didn't work. Graeme gave them to me because they broke in the toaster and the hairdryer and something at his work."

Ivor slapped his forehead. He turned to Jananin, making a wordless grimace and hand gesture at her. "Well, Cerberus is in here, and it's still very much awake. What other options have we got?"

Jananin said, "We have to go back there and destroy it

through some other means."

Ivor rummaged about the equipment that had come out of the first aid box: masks, oxygen cylinders, dressings, and a bag labelled *defibrillator*.

Jananin opened a box and found a scalpel. She used it to cut holes in the transparent tube connecting the mask to the oxygen cylinder, and push together a three-way junction held together with sticking plasters.

They once again followed the corridor around the hexagon, each with a mask attached to an oxygen cylinder that Ivor carried. Once in the inner bunker, they looked upon the pedestal encased in its peripherals and cables.

"Is that it, Dana?" Ivor asked

Dana nodded. "It's scared."

"Dana, don't be ridiculous." Jananin's voice was hard to make out behind the plastic mask she was wearing. "It's a computer. How can it be scared?"

"I don't know," Dana said, "but it is and I can feel it."

"We need to take it apart, but it's still live. How do we cut the power so we can do it without being electrocuted?"

Dana looked at the coloured lights glowing in the cables. There was a lot of power flowing through here. Cerberus itself wasn't using it — it was all peripherals. "Isn't there an off switch?"

Ivor laughed. "It appears not. Perhaps if we could overload it. Is there some way we can short out the power?"

"There was," said Jananin. "The Compton bomb failed because *someone* built it with dead fuses."

"An electromagnetic pulse works by inducing an overloading current. It doesn't matter about anything else; all we need to overload is the one system in this room. We don't need a flux compression generator; all we need is a power source."

Jananin looked about the room and the wall sockets. Dana understood this, sort of. Graeme had once shown her the white box in the garage where the fuses were that would stop the electrics in the house catching fire if they overloaded.

"We need some kind of external DC power source." Jananin cast about the room, her gaze settling on Ivor. "Why are you holding a defibrillator? Looking for one was just an excuse to get in."

Ivor looked down at the bag in his hand.

"*External power source!*"

He unzipped the bag and took out the defibrillator, disentangling the cables and pulling out the two handheld electrodes.

"It likely has some kind of surge protection built into it. It may recover quickly," Jananin warned him.

"Then make sure it gets disconnected as soon as I short it!" Before he had finished speaking, the electric guinea-pig whine of the defibrillator charging had already begun. He pressed both the handles to the metal casing of Cerberus's pedestal.

Dana's heart pounded, and she wasn't sure whose fear it was a response to — hers or Cerberus's. Would this be the end?

There was a loud thump, the lights flickered, and a bank of grey boxes on one of the walls exploded into a fountain of sparks. Every single light on the cables disappeared, leaving only the signal of fear.

Jananin stood in front of the pedestal, bent her knees, and drew her katana, swinging it in a fast arc through the cables. All of them fell in a fluid movement, writhing like a gorgon's locks and cascading onto the floor.

Jananin resheathed her katana and put her oxygen mask back on. "Now we destroy this thing in the traditional way." She seized a handful of cables and tore them out.

Ivor took up his crowbar and smashed into the side of the column, hooking the edge under a ridge and levering off the lid. The rest of the cables fell away.

Dana stepped up to look inside the pedestal. Wires and IDE buses and little chips and resistors on green boards filled it.

Ivor pulled out one of the boards, connections ripping away from it like grass roots from soil, and snapped it in half over his knee.

Dana grabbed the orange cables holding several boards together and pulled at them until the connections popped out, one by one. The blind terror Cerberus was emitting was getting stronger and stronger. Jananin and Ivor tore out more boards and broke them.

As the casing and the peripherals were stripped away, a large computer built into a framework about a metre high was revealed. It was very, very frightened, and the touch of human hands on its surface revolted it.

"Wait," said Dana. A suspicion had arisen in the back of her mind, perhaps as soon as she'd entered the inner bunker, that she had not wanted to confront, but she had become more and more sure of it, and now she was certain. "It's called Cerberus. In virtual reality, it chooses to manifest itself as a dog with three heads. What if this is only one of the heads?"

Jananin looked from her to Ivor, and her face became drawn, her mouth strained. "Then where are the other two?"

Dana stared at the computer they'd uncovered, the fear it emitted matching her own. "I... I don't know."

"Okay," Ivor said. "Perhaps if we take this one, we can use it to locate the others."

"You want it! Don't deny it!"

Ivor backed against the wall. Jananin's arm was ready to pull her sword from its sheath into a deadly uncoil. "Blake, think about this. If she can control it. What's the worst thing that could happen?" His eyes moved nervously to focus on Cerberus, or at least, one of it. "That the government is going to get this back? And Steve Gideon built it. It's probably a quantum computer. We don't know how he built it. If we smash it to bits without taking precautions, there might be radioactive material in whatever powers it."

"We can't carry this thing! It will be noticed! If we can even get out of here without being caught, they will already know what this attack was for. If we try to take it out of here, they *will* get it back!"

Ivor put up his hands, and looked to Dana. His hair was damp; a line of sweat ran down his temple. "Dana, what do you think we should do?"

Dana looked back at Ivor with her mouth open. She couldn't think. It didn't seem right to harm Cerberus when it was so afraid. She imagined it hurting and dying in front of her, and the thought of it was awful. But she thought of the attack on Roareim, the horrible signal from the satellite, of Alpha, attacking her mindlessly and now lying dead outside, and of Cale and Duncan at home with Pauline and Graeme, and Peter, wherever he might be.

"Destroy it."

Jananin looked at the computer in the middle of the blast wall, where they'd disassembled the pedestal around it. "The ventilation gap underneath it." She rummaged through various things strapped to her beneath her coat, until she found a rather old and corroded-looking steel gas cylinder. "If I put this and the oxygen cylinder under it, and we can put the panels back to restrict the airflow, when they reach sufficient concentration, they should deflagrate spontaneously. Not as effective as TNT, but enough to destroy it sufficiently that it can't be rebuilt or used as a model to construct another one."

Dana and Ivor picked up the external panelling and moved it back into position while Jananin arranged the canisters underneath. She hesitated. "I do not know if I should put them parallel or head to tail. On one hand, if the CO_2 concentration in the atmosphere is too high, it might diffuse before reaching sufficient concentration to explode; on the other, it might go off too soon."

"How about you put them however you think is most likely to work, and go with Dana into the corridor and I'll open the valves on them," Ivor suggested.

"Why would you do that? And why would I trust you not to fail, again?"

"Because of my old-fashioned chivalry. And because you're the Nobel laureate, and I'm some washed-up nobody who'll never work in science again, because you destroyed my career."

"Take Dana back into the corridor!"

Ivor and Dana took off their oxygen masks and left Jananin with the cylinder. They waited in the corridor, and a few minutes later, Jananin joined them. They walked back to the three guards.

"If it doesn't work," Ivor said as they waited in front of the lift, "how long do we have to wait until it's safe to go ba—"

The sound of an explosion followed by fragments rebounding off walls and clattering to the floor somewhere in the concrete-walled depths behind interrupted him.

"Let's get out of here," said Jananin.

A **S** the lift ascended, Ivor pulled the bottom of his shirt loose from the waistband of his trousers, and used it to wipe down the crowbar he'd brought along. He dropped the bar on the floor of the lift. "We should get rid of anything that looks like a weapon, in case we get stopped and searched."

In response to this, Jananin held open her coat, revealing the katana, the knife, and various other objects attached to her belt and strapped to her torso.

Ivor rolled his eyes. "Just take them off and leave them here. Assuming you've not stuffed a gun down your knickers and a bomb in your bra."

"Some of these weapons are unique and will be traced back to me, whether there are fingerprints on them or not."

Ivor shrugged a bit, making a face.

The lift came to a halt and the doors slid back. The guard was still tied up on the floor, facing the wall as they crossed to the door. The foyer was empty, but the view through the open doors showed the guards had been joined by police, and down on the plaza police on horses held back a noisy crowd.

One of the police turned and noticed them. "We need to evacuate the library. Come out."

Ivor went first, and once they had stepped across the threshold, the policeman faced them. "I'm sorry, but we're under orders to search everyone who leaves the library, no exceptions. Put your arms out, legs apart." He shouted over his shoulder, "Can we get a female officer up here, to search a woman and a girl?"

As the policeman got busy running his hands up Ivor's

thigh, Jananin crouched down next to Dana, as though she wanted to talk to her. She took something from inside her coat pocket, and carefully opened it, the shockproof case with the detonators in, and took two of them out. As she put the case back in her pocket and stood up, she flicked one of them behind her, through the open door and into the library foyer. It went off with a great flash of light and a tremendous noise, and as everyone's attention was diverted by the explosion, Jananin threw the other detonator into the vacant area on the plaza the police horses were trying to keep the rioting crowd back from.

Whatever training the horses had been through to join the police, it wasn't sufficient to stop them from taking fright at something so loud and bright at such close quarters, and most of them reared, riders falling, horses with and without police mounted on them going out of control and plunging into the crowd, knocking people down. A young police dog tried to run, and it became entangled in its handler and her lead, pulling her down on the pavement. The dog, sent into a full-blown panic, started to scream as though it was being murdered, and widespread panic spread across the civilians. With the horses scattered, the people fell upon the line of police, who struggled to hold them back with their plastic riot shields.

Amidst this, Ivor clutched Dana to him with one arm, put his other arm protectively around Jananin, and forced his way down the steps, through the police, who didn't try to stop them a second time.

"The car park's that way!" Dana shouted, working out their route with the help of GPS. Ivor used his height and size to push through the crowd, getting them off the plaza and into a street where there were fewer people.

The roar of helicopter blades filled the sky. Jananin looked over her shoulder. Ivor huddled Jananin and Dana into an alley between two buildings. In the crack of sky between the walls of the buildings above her, the dull green bulk of the helicopter passed over. When they moved back on to the street, Dana looked behind to see army vehicles in dull green livery pull up on the plaza, forcing the crowd aside. Men in army uniforms, carrying firearms, disembarked and forced their way up the steps to the Amethyst Building, throwing aside the rioting people.

A soldier with a large German Shepherd dog came into the street and spoke to a passing man. The man stopped and handed over his briefcase, while the dog sniffed him.

A horse galloped down the street, riderless. Jananin stepped away from the gap. "They'll be looking for people carrying anything electronic."

Ivor frowned. "With dogs?"

"You were not the only person interested in the rights to my synapse," Jananin said, her back turned on Ivor.

Ivor said something vociferously in Gaelic. "What are they? Are they to do with Cerberus?"

"They're part of the Information Terrorism protocol that was put in place after you Compton-bombed Oxford. If the original proposal was adhered to," Jananin explained, "those dogs are genetically engineered to be larger, stronger, and faster than the originals. The signal they emit sends information back to a control computer on the handler's arm so a remote operating team can use the dogs to identify odours and suchlike, and also to detect radiofrequency signals."

As Dana watched the dog, a hissing started in her ears, and neon flickering started up in her vision. She raised her hands to her head. "*Oh!*"

"Where's her hat? We didn't leave it back there, did we?" Ivor found the hat in Dana's pocket, and pulled it over her head. "Better?"

Dana nodded. "The satellites. Cerberus is still working."

"To the car. Now."

"What about Peter?"

Jananin shook her head. "We can't stay here. Even if we could, we'd never find him in this."

Dana looked up at the office towers as they walked, at a normal pace, so as to avoid attracting attention. The high-rises looked menacing somehow, with their concrete walls and blank windows. It felt like being stared down at by a great many featureless eyes. A giant poster had been stuck to a pollution-soiled brick wall, and Dana realised with a jarring recognition that it was the corrected image of Jananin aiming her crossbow on Roareim, with the blurry, indistinct shape of herself that had been edited out highlighted with a line. Fiery letters blazed out the words *THE TRUTH?* at the bottom, and in the right corner was the gold scales insignia of the Meritocratic Party.

The sky seemed weighed down behind them as they retraced their steps at a painfully slow pace. At last they reached the car park. Jananin got the driver's door open and slotted the keys in the ignition, turning them back and forth. "As I thought. The alternator's failed." She pulled a lever underneath the dashboard before going to the front of the car and lifting the bonnet. She prodded at the car's innards for a moment, and slammed it shut again. "Dana." Jananin took hold of her and pushed her into the driver's seat. "Stay there, and steer when I tell you to!" She reached over Dana to take off the handbrake. "Put your foot down on the clutch — not that one, the one on the left. Pilgrennon! Help push the car out of this parking space!"

Ivor and Jananin pushed against the car's nose until it began to slide back. "Steer!" Jananin shouted when it was a little more than halfway. "The other way!"

With Jananin shouting instructions at her, Dana managed to turn the car and straighten it up so it pointed towards the exit.

"Now," said Jananin, and she leant over Dana to move the gear lever into position 2 and took hold of Dana's right hand. "Hold the key like this." She pressed Dana's fingers in on the key and twisted it to demonstrate. "Keep your foot on the clutch until I tell you otherwise."

She and Ivor went behind the car and started to push it forward. It began to pick up speed. Through the open door, gravel crackled in the tyre tread. "Clutch up!" Jananin shouted. Dana moved her foot and the car slowed. The engine jolted, ran a few beats, and then stalled. Jananin threw her weight against the back of the car, and this time the engine ran. "Clutch down!" she shouted.

Dana stamped the pedal down. The engine continued to run. Jananin ran around the side of the car, reached over Dana, and knocked the gear lever into neutral and yanked the handbrake on. "Now take your foot off the clutch and get into the back."

Jananin turned at the sound of barking as Dana was climbing over. Dogs streamed down the embankment towards the car park.

"Get in the car!" Jananin shouted at Ivor. She threw herself down in the driver's seat and slammed the door. "Dana, put your seatbelt on." Jananin's hands were shaking as she put on her seatbelt and gripped the wheel. She revved the car hard and looked fearfully down as she let the clutch up.

As Ivor shut the door and the car began to move, the dogs caught up and crowded around the back of the car, yammering. One of them leapt against the broken window and forced its nose through, barking and hurling spittle at Ivor.

Jananin's car pulled out onto the street and wove between the stalled cars, mounting the pavement to get past. A dog ran in front of the car. Jananin stamped on the accelerator and the car leapt forward and hit the dog with a thud. The car lurched twice as the dog went under both tyres on the right hand side. Dana looked in the wing mirror, and she saw the dog that had been run over get back up and join the other ones in running after the car.

Jananin turned the car onto a road that had been cleared to some extent. The cars had been pushed to the sides to give a passage down the centre. She continued to accelerate as the dogs chased.

Dana looked over her shoulder and out the rear windscreen. The dogs were still keeping pace. Ivor said, "How fast are you going?"

"My speedometer is broken, but I'd estimate we're doing close to thirty-five miles an hour."

Dana stared at the racing dogs. Through the broken window with buildings reflecting the sound all around, the clatter of the diesel engine and the shrill hiss of the turbo aspirating were very loud. The acceleration pushed her down into the seat as the dogs grew smaller and were lost from view on the road behind.

"If they're electronic, how come the Compton bomb didn't break them?" Dana asked.

Jananin said, "The army brought them in as part of a response plan, for exactly this situation. They weren't here when we deployed the bomb."

Ivor stared out of the window at the stalled cars, and the paramedics running along the streets with their metal cases. Jananin blared the horn as looters raced across the road, carrying their spoils. One of them threw a brick at the back of the car. Fire gushed from the ruined windows and doors of what had once been a Victorian edifice, sending a thick column of reeking black smoke into the winter sky.

Ivor stared out at it through the broken window. He didn't speak, and fell to twisting the gold ring he always wore on his left hand.

"You never saw the damage your attack did on Oxford," realised Jananin. "I expect you were halfway to Scotland when the bomb exploded."

"Was it like this at Oxford?"

"Actually, no," said Jananin. "People mostly just went to the library. Nobody rioted or looted."

A boy wailed beside a phone box, and Ivor twisted in his seat to scrutinise his wrung red face, but it wasn't Peter. Businessmen huddled together in crowds under awnings and in doorways, clinging to the solidarity of numbers. Police on horses rode this way and that, but there weren't enough of them. A gang beat an old man with a volley of kicks and punches, throwing him through a shop window as the car passed. Dana saw a girl being dragged struggling into an alley by a rough-looking man. A middle-aged woman in a tweed skirt and woollen coat screamed hysterically in the middle of the street, surrounded by a gang of leering youths. Jananin did not take her eyes off the road as she pressed her foot to the accelerator harder. Her mouth was drawn into a stern line and Dana could see the tension in her forehead.

The car enclosed a bubble of reality, and Dana sat in it looking out upon the throes of insanity. Sometimes she could not bring herself to look. Others she just gazed out in mute shock. At last they reached the limits of the Compton bomb's range, and the stalled cars were replaced with congestion, and then they reached the motorway.

"I thought we were going to destroy Cerberus," Dana cried out, unable to contain what she was feeling for any longer. "But we only destroyed one of it, and nothing's changed, and I still have to wear this stupid hat, and Alpha's dead, and Peter's gone!"

Ivor put his elbow on the edge of the broken window where the wind ripped through, spreading his hand over his face. His shoulders began to shake, and a desperate, uncontrolled sob broke from his mouth. Dana too started to cry vocally.

"Will you both stop making that noise while I am trying to drive!" Jananin exclaimed. She pulled over into the next service station, saying she should fill up the car as she had no idea how much diesel was left in it, since none of the instruments were working.

While she was filling up the car, Ivor and Dana got out. Ivor slid down against the car's back bumper, the exhaust pipe leaving a greasy stain on his sleeve, putting his hands over his face.

"Don't do that there." Jananin pointed to some

picnic tables set up near a car park. Dana took hold of his sleeve, and they went over and sat down. Ivor sobbed into his hands, before wiping his face and his nose on his handkerchief. "I'm so sorry, Dana. That we haven't killed all of Cerberus like we meant to, and that I'm not very good at being a responsible adult and that I'm much use to you at all right now."

Soon after, Jananin pulled the car over into a parking space close by, leaving the engine running, and came and sat down with them. "Pilgrennon?"

Ivor was still crying rather embarrassingly. Jananin said, "I can't talk to you in this state," and turned instead to Dana. "The other heads of Cerberus may not even be in this country. Certainly Antrobus, who takes an interest in these sorts of things, didn't seem to know of any other potential sites. If I had to hazard a guess, I'd say at least one of them is likely to be in the USA, since both the Prime Minister and the President of America are both always going on about how wonderful and special the relationship between our two countries is. It is quite likely that whoever in government got hold of Cerberus from Steve Gideon, upon seeing that it appeared to be three computers and not realising the relevance of this to Gideon's design, saw the other two as an asset to be sold or bargained for favours with foreign powers."

"But how can we go to America? You need a passport, to go abroad, don't you? And I haven't got one."

"It might be possible to arrange something. Quite a lot might be possible, in fact, now that the version of Cerberus that had been put in a position of control in this country has now been removed. I know this was not quite the outcome any of us were hoping for, but it's quite likely we have achieved something significant."

Ivor blew his nose. "But what about Peter?"

"Has it not occurred to you, that Peter, if he is alive, is likely better off being cared for by someone else, even if that is the state, particularly when there is a price on your head and Cerberus is trying to kill us?"

Ivor closed his eyes. He leaned his elbows on the table and his forehead on his hands. "What do we need to do?"

"First, we should probably get something to eat. Then, we need to find somewhere we can lie low. Then, I'll make some enquiries."

PART TWO
EUREKA

-12-

BY the time Jananin had arranged a place to stay, it was already late. After stopping for a take-away meal which they ate in the car, they arrived around midnight at an inn. Dana had fallen asleep in the car, and her memory of following Ivor upstairs was a haze. He found a bed for her, and apologised that there was no time to find something to build a screen around it, and that she'd have to sleep wearing her hat.

Dana dreamed that she was fleeing across a heath, like the land on Lewis. Cerberus was chasing her, but when she looked behind her and saw its shape in the mist, it had only two heads, not the three it was supposed to. Somewhere out in the fog, she could hear Ivor calling for her, and she called back for him, but she never found him, and someone was chasing him, too. Possibly it was Jananin. Throughout the dream, Dana could feel nothing but blind, helpless fear, and she woke in a sweat with her heart pounding. When she reached up to her face, her hat had come off in her sleep.

"Ivor? *Ivor!*"

When he came, he had only his boxers on, and he hadn't shaved for two days and his hair was sticking up all over the place. He looked like some hideous caveman. Still gripped by the terror of the dream, Dana screamed at the sight of him.

"Dana! Dana, what's happened?" He saw the hat lying on the bed, and put it back on her.

Dana explained the dream, and she and Ivor went downstairs to a pub with all the furniture taken out and dust sheets over the bar, and found a wLAN that had been left on. Ivor switched it off.

"Do you think Cerberus will have been able to find me?"

"I don't know," Ivor said. "When people dream, they're in REM sleep. It can feel like it's going on for a long time, when in fact it isn't, and in fact it's just short bursts of intense neural activity. You probably woke up soon after your hat came off and there might not have been time for Cerberus to trace your connection to an exact location. Did you see anything in the dream that could identify where we are?"

"I don't think so. Where's Jananin?"

"She drove on immediately after she dropped us off here. She wanted to get the car to someone in Cambridge she trusted to be discreet about it, to get it fixed, and make some enquiries and get some things cleared up."

Dana went back to bed and tried to sleep. Ivor sat on a chair in his pants in the dark, watching out the window in case anyone should come.

The next day passed very uncomfortably. The inn they were staying in, it turned out, had been bought by someone about six months prior, who had intended to refurbish it. Once this had begun, it had turned out to be rather more costly than anticipated, and the inn's benefactor had run out of money and had to stop, and was now abroad somewhere trying to earn more money to finish the job, and had apparently agreed to let the flat above it to them in the meantime.

The inn was on the outskirts of a village, and as it was closed, few people came by that way. Dana and Ivor spent most of the day in the sitting-room which overlooked the pub's car park and main entrance, watching the news and keeping an eye on the window. Ivor went outside and found some mesh panels to make a Faraday enclosure around Dana's bed, so she could sleep without a hat on.

The news reported that there had been an Information Terrorist attack on London, and that three people had died and more than fifty had been injured. The news only released the name of one of the victims, an elderly man who'd had a pacemaker, because they were still trying to identify the other two and inform their families first. Dana knew one of them was Alpha, and she hoped desperately that the other was not Peter.

Colin Antrobus appeared briefly on the news, claiming that the computer embedded in the government had been removed during the terrorist attack, and that the civil service had broken down as a result of this. Commentators on the television called Antrobus a conspiracy theorist with no evidence for his claims, and the Prime Minister came out of his house and stood in front of a lectern, and denied the claims and said the civil service was working as usual

There was a brief report that the police were still seeking information on the whereabouts of Ivor Pilgrennon regarding his disappearance and fraud involving a charity, and the same outdated picture of him, with the reporter stressing that the picture was more than ten years old and he might not look like that any more. However, no connection was indicated between Ivor and the London attack, and strangely immediately after, a statement was read out offering an unreserved apology from the police to an unnamed individual who had been incorrectly identified as having a connection to terrorism.

"That's Blake off the hook," Ivor said.

The next morning, Ivor was making breakfast and Dana was watching from the upstairs window, when a woman came into the car park, wearing a Royal Mail uniform and carrying a bag, from which she withdrew an envelope. She pushed it through the pub letterbox and went on her way.

Dana ran downstairs to retrieve the post from the bare floor in front of the door in the unfurnished pub. The envelope read in scribbled capital letters, *Charlotte Anne Quack, The Fat Pig*, followed by an address.

Dana turned to Ivor, who had come downstairs behind her. "Who's Charlotte Anne Quack? Is she the lady who bought the pub?"

Ivor took the envelope from Dana and examined the writing. "I think this is one of Jananin Blake's witticisms, and this letter is for me, with Charlotte Anne Quack being an insult to me as well as a way of ensuring anyone in the postal system who sees it won't know it's me she's writing to."

"Oh," said Dana. "Is she insulting you by calling you a fat pig as well?"

"Quite possibly, but *The Fat Pig* is also the name of the inn. There's a picture of one on the sign outside." Ivor turned the envelope over and ripped open the top of it with his thumb. It contained a folded piece of A4 with a single, rather untidily handwritten line in the middle of it.

$$\beta \text{ is safe}.$$

Ivor's hands shook, his fingers crumpling the edges of the paper. "Peter is safe! Oh, Peter!" He folded Jananin's letter back up and put it back in its envelope, and he folded that in half and stuck it in his shirt pocket. "When she drove off the other night, I feared she might go off and get her own name cleared, and decide to cut her losses and just abandon us to our fate. I think this means she is coming back after all."

Later on the news, the identity of the other victim was revealed as a young man who had died as a result of being stabbed in a fight with someone else while attempting to loot a shop during the aftermath. Alpha was mentioned only as a third, unidentified victim whose cause of death had not been established.

After a few days, things began to calm down, and Dana and Ivor began to settle into a routine in the pub. There were some books, although they were rather limited, and a DVD player and some DVDs. Ivor started trying to teach Dana things using pen and paper and books, saying he didn't want her to miss out on her education.

It turned out that Colin Antrobus and Jananin Blake may have been on to something about destroying the Cerberus in the Amethyst Building having changed things, because it seemed something genuinely had gone wrong in the civil service, and an uproar had arisen about abuse of the postal voting system, and the Prime Minister had been forced to call the General Election early and decreed that postal votes would not be allowed, and he and the Leader of the Opposition and Colin Antrobus were all busy canvassing for support.

Dana asked Ivor if he would cut her hair, as it was too long and annoying her, particularly with having to wear a hat over it. After she'd had a shower in the kitchen-foil-lined shower room and got dressed, she stood in front of the mirror there with a towel around her shoulders while he sorted out a pair of scissors and the blade out of a razor to do it with.

"How short do you want it?"

Dana pointed high up on the nape of her neck. Ivor combed it straight and then, to Dana's shock, slid one blade of the scissors between her hair and her neck and lopped it off exactly where she'd pointed. Every other person Dana had asked to cut her hair, she'd had to negotiate with to reach a compromise. Every time Pauline asked her how short she wanted it and Dana showed her, she would come back with a complaint about it looking 'pretty' longer or it being 'a shame' and had continued to argue until Dana let her 'trim the ends' as she called it, and from this Dana had learnt to drive a hard bargain at the outset of negotiations.

She stared, stunned, at her reflection for a moment, her hair never having been cut this short. "Does it look all right?" she asked him after a moment.

She watched his reflection shrug. "I think it looks fine. But it doesn't matter what I think. It's what you want that matters. Do you want me to try to put some layers in it, so it's not all heavy and floppy at the front and on the top?"

Dana swallowed. "Okay."

He made the layers by holding the hair up by the ends and slicing bits off with the razor. When he was finished, he messed it up with his hands to try to shake the loose bits out so they didn't end up down her back and drying there like itching powder. "I suppose it doesn't look very professional," he apologised. "Perhaps once we've sorted all this out and you don't have to wear a hat any more, Jananin can lend me some money to pay someone to do it properly."

Dana grinned. She did actually like it, although she wasn't sure what it would look like when it dried. It made her look older and a bit different, and at least it wasn't all down her neck and annoying her any more. "No, it's all right. It looks mint!"

*

One morning Dana got up and went into the kitchen, and Ivor announced, "Happy birthday!"

"It's not my birthday yet! Not until the 17th, in four days' time!"

"It *is* your birthday! I was there, remember?" He pointed to the kitchen table, where there were two presents that were obviously hard-backed books, one wrapped in greaseproof paper and the other in kitchen foil, and a card he'd made by folding a piece in half and drawing a picture of a tree on the front, and writing *Happy birthday Dana love from Ivor* inside it.

Dana opened the presents. One of the books was about botany, and the other was about electronics, both obviously secondhand and probably acquired from a shop in the village.

"Thank you. So my birthday is on the thirteenth, not the seventeenth?"

Ivor shrugged. "I guess social services guessed. You and your brother were premature, though. You weren't actually meant to be born until May, so really you're younger than your birthday suggests. You both gave me several sleepless nights." He motioned to the books and card. "Sorry it's not much. Blake didn't leave me a lot of cash, and as I don't know when she's coming back, I need to make it last."

Dana thought of how Ivor had said, back in the house in Edinburgh, that he was a poor man, but that knowing Dana and Peter and Alpha were happy made him a rich man. She thought about how the covers of the books were faded and marked, and the pages inside were all foxed, but that it did not diminish the quality of the words or pictures in them, or that Ivor had chosen them for her about subjects she liked.

"I would rather have my birthday, on the day my birthday is, with you, and have presents like this, than get lots of expensive stuff from someone else on the wrong day."

Ivor smiled and scratched his cheek. He was growing a beard, he said, because it would make him less recognisable, and Dana hated it.

"I just wish that Peter and Alpha were here, and we were still in that house in Edinburgh." Dana recalled spending most of the time in that house worrying about Cerberus and Duncan and Cale, but in retrospect and after everything that had happened, it seemed idyllic, and she wished she'd thought to appreciate it more at the time. "And I know Jananin has her work and she wouldn't want to live with us, but it would be nice if she could visit on weekends sometimes."

Ivor laughed. "I think she'd leave in disgust if Peter and I got into one of our belching contests."

"And I would want Cale to come and live with us, too. And it would be nice if Pauline and Graeme and Duncan lived on the same street, so I could visit them and play computer games with Duncan."

"In this imaginary village we're wishing," Ivor said, "I'd wish Lydia was still alive and lived on that street, too. And I'd put my auntie's farm, which is in Wales in the middle of nowhere, at the end of the road."

"If Lydia wasn't dead," Dana considered, "I'd have an auntie too."

"You can share my auntie. She won't mind. I do worry about all this, and how it must be affecting her."

They sat together in silence for a moment. Dana wasn't really sure she wanted an aunt. Duncan had one, who was Pauline's sister, and she also had a boy, his cousin Eustace, about Duncan's age. Pauline used to moan sometimes about manners, and it was annoying, but her sister was even worse. Dana and Cale had been to the aunt's house a few times with their foster family, and although the food the aunt made was nice, she was constantly criticising everyone for how they sat or held their cutlery, or used their napkins. There were also a lot of words she would tell you off for if you said them in front of her, even though they were not rude words, and Dana had ended up doing what Cale did and just saying nothing. Eustace had his own list of words that people were not allowed to use in his presence, which consisted of his mother's list with some additions he had personally curated. In the car on the way home, Graeme would use every word the aunt disapproved of, and say that he pitied Eustace, because children are not inherently stuck-up or intolerant, and they just reflect back the attitudes they are exposed to, and it was not his fault he was being raised to be an insufferable little brown-nosed toady.

Then Ivor folded his hands on the table and smiled at Dana. "It's all very well wishing for things like that, but we have to remember, some things just aren't meant to be, and if we spend too much time thinking about how we wish they were, we forget to enjoy them as they are."

"You know when you said I was born too early? Is that why I'm a runt?"

"Who said you were a runt?"

"Bullies at school."

"Children born in spring and summer are always less developed than the ones born in autumn and winter they

go to school with. You'll catch up. I was born in August."
Ivor widened his eyes. "It wasn't until I was about fourteen
that I realised I'd suddenly become bigger than everyone
else!"

"Really?" Dana couldn't imagine Ivor ever having been
small. "But you never hit people, even though you're bigger
than them. Apart from that policeman you punched."

"Yes, well, I shouldn't have done that. It didn't solve
anything. It was my fault for getting myself arrested."

"And you never hit Jananin, even though she's not
very nice to you sometimes, or Peter, even when he hits
you."

"Men should never hit women." Ivor shook his head
emphatically. "It lowers us to something beneath animals.
And I'd never hit Peter, because I care about him. He can't
help it that sometimes he throws a wobbly. It's because of
his ADHD."

"Do animals not hit women?"

"Male animals don't hurt female animals. They fight
amongst themselves often enough. On my auntie's farm,
the cocks and the tups went at it hammer and tong with
each other if they got the chance, but they always treated
the hens and the ewes with respect. If any of them ever
didn't, I'd imagine they'd end up in my auntie's stew pot.
It's against nature to carry on like that." Ivor slapped his
hand on the kitchen table. "Anyway. What would you like
for breakfast on your birthday? I've got... *kippers*..."

"*Urh!*" Dana shouted, for he knew very well she didn't
like kippers.

"How about boiled egg and toast, in that case?"

The worry they'd both had about Cerberus having
found their location had finally eased, and Dana had a
pleasant birthday, with Ivor explaining some things about
genetics and biochemistry to her. Colin Antrobus was on
the news again. The Leader of the Opposition had accused
him of having a relationship with a much younger man,
and claimed that the man was under sixteen when the

relationship started. Then the Prime Minister said Colin Antrobus was a vile predatory individual and his party was an affront to democracy. Colin Antrobus had not appeared, but had released a statement denying the allegations, and saying that this sort of ridiculous *ad hominem* attack was the very reason the system was not working, and must be replaced with something new and radical, so we can start talking about politics instead of politicians.

Then the man Colin Antrobus was alleged to have had a relationship came forward, and said he indeed had once been in a relationship with him, and that he had known him since he was a child as their families were friends, but that their relationship as such had not begun until he was 18 and Antrobus was 27, and they had split up amicably a few years later because their work commitments had made it difficult. Then commentators came on the television to talk about it. One of them said it was appalling and homophobic that Antrobus should be smeared in this way. Another argued that it was not homophobic because it would have happened much the same had the relationship been with a younger woman instead of a man, and that because Colin Antrobus refused to discuss his personal life, it wasn't possible to tell if he was gay or bisexual, but said it was disgusting that he had been treated this way all the same.

Later that evening, Ivor and Dana walked down to the fish and chip shop in the village. There was a poster on the wall showing different fish species, and Dana and Ivor stood talking about the fish while they waited for their order, with Ivor occasionally making silly fish faces and Dana laughing at him. When the woman serving them called that the order was ready, she smiled at Dana as she handed it to her.

When they'd first come to live in *The Fat Pig*, Dana had been afraid to go outside with him in case they were recognised, but Ivor insisted she come out because it was unhealthy to stay indoors and not exercise. They had walked around the village, and a nearby park, at first at quiet times of day, and they never had been noticed. It seemed to be simply because Ivor was so obviously Dana's dad. Ivor said, that people only noticed other people if there was something suspicious about them to draw attention, and apparently the eccentricity of their clothing and Dana's autistic mannerisms didn't pass over that threshold when they were together.

Back in the flat over the pub, they ate their fish and chips, and Ivor mixed ale with fizzy pop to make shandy for Dana to try, as he said it was a special occasion and children are allowed to drink at home in private under the law. They watched a DVD, and perhaps the shandy had not been such a good idea, because she fell asleep leaning against him while they were watching it and missed how it ended.

She woke because Ivor had suddenly tensed beside her, at the sound of the pub door opening. Dana got up and went to the window, and looked out from behind the curtains. A modern silver hot hatch had appeared in the car park.

"*That's not her car!*" she whispered to Ivor.

Then Jananin's voice shouted up the stairs. "Pilgrennon?"

Ivor exhaled loudly and relaxed his shoulders. "We're up here!"

Jananin came upstairs and into the sitting-room. She looked at Ivor lolloping on the sofa with his horrible scratty beard, and the empty bottle of ale on the coffee table, but she didn't say anything.

"It's Dana's birthday," said Ivor.

"In that case, happy birthday." Jananin held up a carrier bag. "I got you some clothes and a passport for going to America with."

Dana took the bag, not really liking the idea of something as banal as clothes as a birthday present, but when she looked at the clothes, they were all practical ones with pockets, in the right size, and Jananin had already cut the labels on the back of the necks out for her. There weren't any dresses, which Dana hated, or any skirts, which she only liked if they had pockets and she could wear leggings underneath.

"What did you find out about Peter?" Ivor sat up in his seat and turned to her expectantly.

"He was taken into care in the aftermath of what happened in London. He wasn't hurt in the riot, and he still had his helmet on. Nothing about him has been publicised because from what I understand they were rather concerned about the way he'd been brought up."

"*What?*"

"If his written and spoken English hadn't been so good, they'd have assumed he was an illegal immigrant. It was obvious he'd been brought up in a very isolated situation with no exposure to technology, and the gaps in his knowledge, unfamiliarity with everyday objects, his clothing, his agitation at signals, seemed to give them cause for concern."

Ivor held his arms out, his expression disbelieving. "Who are these idiots, who think fresh air and wild food, and books, and love, aren't enough for a child?"

"Pilgrennon, I do not make the rules. What is important is that he is safe where he is, and it's probably best that he stay there for now. I have a report on him, but you're not to read it now, because we need to prepare to depart for America tomorrow. Oh, and I got something for you as well." Jananin took a hacksaw out of another bag, and dumped it in Ivor's lap. "We're going by container ship. The luggage allowance is very generous, although we obviously can't take poisons or explosives on board. You will need to pass through a metal detector, so you'd better get to work on that jewellery the police gave you."

Jananin started to explain to Dana what she intended they do. Dana's alias on her passport was Delilah Jones, and Jananin was to be Jane Jones and Ivor, Iain Jones.

Jananin had arranged a visa for them to go and live temporarily in America under these identities. She had made some enquiries with contacts she had, but most of them hadn't got back to her yet, and Jananin was pretty certain, because of information she'd received, that at least one Cerberus machine was in America. It would take just under a week to get there, which was better than going by plane, and the ship would be quiet.

While Jananin was talking, Ivor tried to grip the handcuff on his left wrist between his knees and saw at it, but he slipped and scratched his arm. "Jananin, please, can you give me a hand with this?"

Strangely enough, Jananin did not make a comment about his revolting beard, or suggest he cut his hand off, or say any other unkind thing to him. She told him to come with her downstairs and they would look for a vice. After some clattering about and sawing sounds, he came back, rubbing his wrists gladly and quite unharmed.

"Come and sit down and tell me what you've found out."

"There will be plenty of time to discuss that once we have boarded the ship tomorrow."

"There's time tonight. Dana and I ought to have some idea of where the situation is regarding what happened in London, in case we get stopped and questioned for any reason at the port. I'll make you a cup of tea."

Jananin took off her coat and threw it over the back of a chair. To Dana's surprise, the knife she'd never seen Jananin without was no longer strapped to her thigh. While Ivor was in the kitchen, making the tea, she sat in an armchair and regarded Dana awkwardly. "Well, did you have a nice birthday?"

Dana nodded.

So it was that Jananin explained where she had been, and what she had found out. She had gone first to her solicitor regarding the reports made on the news about her involvement. The solicitor had said that the picture of Jananin with the crossbow, which Dana had been edited out of, was suspicious and likely fake, and nobody had been able to credit a proper source for it. It seemed that since the London Information Terrorism attack, things had become very disorganised with the police and the other authorities. The reports of Jananin and Ivor's involvement couldn't be traced to any credible source, and the report of a dead body found in a car that had supposedly been identified as Dana went back to the name of a police constable who didn't exist, and a mortuary that had no record of receiving or examining any body of that description.

The only possible, tenuous links had been a helicopter pilot from Lewis, who said the man who stole his helicopter and destroyed it had two children with him, but was unable to positively identify either Dana or Ivor, and two security guards from London, one who claimed a woman overpowered him using martial arts and tied him up, but he was facing the wall most of the time and didn't see who else was with her or get a good enough look to identify her. The other guard had been the one in the bunker, and a medical examination of him had found his bloodstream full of narcotics and opioids. He swore blind that the missing kid from the telly and the unlikely terrorist couple were down in that bunker, but because of the state he was in, his evidence was inadmissible, and it was thought likely that he'd hallucinated this as a result of the sensationalist coverage on television.

Because of all this, Jananin's solicitor had advised her to make a complaint against the police, and to threaten to sue them for defamation, as the way she'd been linked to terrorism without proper evidence and the salacious way it had been reported had led some people to think something untoward had been going on between her and Ivor was harmful to her professional and personal reputation. Because Jananin's alibi for not being at work was that she was at present in Antarctica as part of a multidisciplinary research project, the solicitor had made it look as though Jananin's communication had come through from the Falkland Islands.

Jananin had also managed to find out that Dana's foster family were fine, and that a welfare check had recently been carried out on Cale due to her disappearance, and he was well, although clearly distressed by the absence of his sister, and perhaps because of this had started engaging more with Duncan and playing computer games with him. The police had quietly dropped any reference of Ivor's involvement in terrorism, although Jananin hadn't been able to do anything about his missing person's investigation or the other charges against him.

Ivor sat back for a moment, absorbing Jananin's tale. At length he said, "Could you send an email for me?"

"To whom?"

Ivor produced an old pocket diary. "I still have Steve Gideon's email address written down. It's a long shot, but I was thinking of trying to contact him."

"Steve Gideon committed suicide. I had that looked into as well. There is CCTV footage of him throwing himself off a bridge."

"CCTV footage can be faked, just like photographs." Ivor raised his eyebrows. "Cerberus seems to be quite adept at that sort of thing. If he is dead, it can't do any harm."

"How on Earth does someone of your ilk know Steve Gideon, who was nominated for the Nobel Prize for his work on computers?"

Ivor smiled in a self-deprecating sort of way. "He was doing his PhD in computing. I was doing my PhD in psychology. His research back then was trying to record an imprint of a person's mind on a hard drive. I helped him devise a series of questions he could ask his candidates that would get to the root of what gives us the personalities we have."

"Why would you need a print of your mind on a hard

drive?" Dana asked.

"Well, a lot of very good PhDs and research are undertaken for reasons that are nebulous, and uses that aren't particularly clear at the time. The main reason was simply to see if it could be done. One possible use for it was so that if someone died unexpectedly, or disappeared and was not available, you could question this imprint and still have access to that person's knowledge and experience. But it didn't work out, because even though he filled up great big hard drives with all this data, the imprints were inert. That spark of consciousness just wasn't there, so even though all the data might be in there, you couldn't interact with them to get it. Because that didn't fly, he thought then that perhaps they might work as a security key, but that didn't really work either, because they were just so big, and also because people change so much over time, especially young people in their 20s, which was who most of his volunteers were, seeing as we were at university. And the original imprint didn't quite match with one taken two years later, so it wasn't seen as reliable. Fortunately, Steve had a good PhD supervisor who was able to get him some papers and a good thesis out of results demonstrating what doesn't work instead of what does."

"What sort of questions were they?" Dana asked.

"All sorts." Ivor shrugged. "You had to lie in an MRI machine, with electrodes all over your head so he could record your brain activity, and he would ask the questions and you would answer them. I let him do me. I had to have rather a severe haircut, though." Ivor cringed. "Adrienne wouldn't talk to me until it grew back. Said I looked like a thug. I think he only had one woman volunteer for that reason, and she was an academic who was being treated for cancer so it didn't matter to her!"

"I'd rather people were bald than had revolting beards!" Dana objected.

Ivor ran his hand over his overgrown stubble, making an expression of faux offence at her.

"Well, you had better use a throwaway account, and write it so it won't be identifiable as you to anyone other than him."

Jananin gave Ivor a laptop. "What do you think, Dana?" Ivor asked.

Dana sat next to him and watched as he composed a message. *SRG this is ISP. I'm at the vet now and you need to get back to me re. your dog's behavioural problems.*

"Does ISP stand for Internet Service Provider?" Dana asked.

"Probably. But it also stands for me, Ivor S Pilgrennon. In academia, we often use our initials as a shorthand way to identify ourselves. In fact, I think Jananin might have branded hers on me somewhere." He rolled up his sleeve, exposing a welt on the inside of his arm. "Do you think that looks like it says JB?"

Jananin rolled her eyes. "Old fool. Send it, but make sure you use a VPN."

-13-

SOUTHAMPTON Port wasn't particularly crowded, and most of the people there seemed either to work in the port or work on the ships or the docks. To get to the ship, Dana, Jananin, and Ivor had to pass through a metal detector, and the luggage all had to be opened and inspected or x-rayed.

Dana looked at the doorless portal with apprehension. It had a red light on the top of it, rather like the kind on the backs of cars, which presumably would come on and some terrible siren would go off if someone tried to sneak metal through it. Ivor was busy taking off his watch and putting it along with his belt and his wedding ring into a tray upon a counter for the staff to inspect.

Dana put her hand in her pocket and took out her three fuses. She put them with Ivor's things. "Ivor?" she whispered. "What about the foil in this hat?"

Ivor considered this. He tried to attract Jananin's attention, by saying, "Jane Jones," but she had already gone through the metal detector and was dealing with the luggage.

"I don't think aluminium will set it off. Try it."

"Are you sure?" Dana didn't want to find out what happened if it did, or what the port staff would think if she had to take the hat off, and they found bits of tin foil all sewn into the lining.

"We haven't really got much choice."

Dana ran up to the gate and jumped through it. Nothing. Cautiously, she stepped back through it, and forward again.

The woman operating the X-ray machine smiled at Dana, and looked back to her monitor, narrowing her eyes at what she saw on the machine. "Have you got blades in this luggage?"

"Yes," said Jananin. "Instruments used in a traditional sport."

"What sport is that?"

"Iaido."

The woman turned to another monitor, and scanned through a list. "It checks out."

Ivor glanced at Jananin's luggage, ready to go down for loading, as he threaded his belt back through the loops on his waistband: a large trunk with wheels on one edge, a case containing binoculars and other devices, and a briefcase with a laptop in it. He and Dana had only a holdall between them, that contained clothing and the two books he'd gifted her. The customs officials had rifled through them all, checking between the pages of the books and finding the card Ivor had drawn a tree on, and holding up pairs of Dana's knickers and Ivor's pants and examining them as though they suspected they hadn't been washed. Finally they were free to go down and board the ship, and meet the captain.

The ship was called the *Atlantic Sonata*, and she (because Ivor said a ship was always *she* and never *it* or *he*) was 1,200 feet long. At the front of the ship was a bridge, which was the name for the rooms where the captain and the crew watched and steered the ship from, with a lot of aerials and gadgets and a rotating thing that was to do with the ship's radar. The entire deck of the ship was a platform that had been loaded with enormous steel boxes bigger than garages, stacked five high upon each other, for the *Atlantic Sonata* was a container ship whose purpose was to ply the route between Southampton and New York, carrying cargo of all kinds back and forth between the UK and USA.

Below deck on the ship were the engines and machinery and fuel stores that powered her, and the recreational rooms and cabins of the captain and crew, along with a couple of suites of rooms that were for passengers. The only other passengers were a couple who mostly kept to themselves and their cabins, and the captain and his crew spent most of the time when they weren't sleeping in their own cabins on the bridge drinking coffee. Three times a day a cooked meal was served in the galley. The best thing about it was there was no wLAN on the ship, or indeed anything much of that nature. The only phone that worked was a satellite phone, which you had to go to the bridge and get permission from the captain if you wanted to use. Dana was told that under no circumstances must she go out on deck unless Ivor or Jananin were with her.

Out on the open ocean and within the ship's steel hull, it was very unlikely there would be anything passing near enough to detect Dana's signal, so she didn't have to wear a hat on board, and it was very peaceful, and after what had happened in London and while laying low at the inn, nobody seemed to mind that they would be on the ship for seven days with nothing much to do.

Ivor said that travelling by cargo ship was unpopular, because most people wanted to get to America quickly and used the plane, or if they wanted to go slowly, they took a cruise ship, to be sociable with other people, and because there were casinos and shops and amusement parks on cruise ships, none of which were on the *Atlantic Sonata*. "But," he said, "she does have a swimming pool."

Dana shrugged. "I can't swim."

"Well, then, there's no better time for you to learn. I'll teach you."

Pauline and Graeme had once taken Dana and Cale to a swimming pool, so they could learn. Dana hadn't liked it, Cale even less so. It stank of chlorine and people looked strange and not like themselves when they took their clothes off and their hair got all wet. Pauline had taken her into the ladies' changing rooms, and while Dana changed into her swimming costume, Pauline had put on a bikini, and her stomach had a line down it and the skin was all loose and misshapen, she said because when she'd been pregnant with Duncan it had gone wrong and doctors had to cut a hole in her to take him out.

When they met Graeme and Duncan and Cale inside, Cale refused to go in the water and stood in his shorts with his arms folded over his chest. He didn't like what people's nipples looked like, and didn't want anyone else to see his. Graeme had put on tight swimming trunks that looked like knickers, and you could see the shape of his bum and his privates through them. His torso was really hairy both on the back on the front, and even though the hair was going grey like on his head, when he got in the water it went dark and with it plastered against his skin he looked like a wet monkey.

Duncan had on baggy shorts, but he was going through a growth phase where he was chubby and sort of had boobs, especially as he kept getting out so he could jump in from the diving board. And there were a lot of other people in the swimming pool, all of them wet and weird-looking with not enough clothes on, and it was confusing. Some were stringy with bulging muscles and veins, some were hairy, some were so thin their ribs showed through the skin, and some were fat with bulging guts or wobbly flesh.

Dana had held on to an inflatable ring, and Pauline and Graeme had tried to help support her while she tried to swim, but Dana didn't really like people touching her with their hands at the best of times, and them touching her with bare wet skin was just too much, and the water had gone up her nose and it had been horrible.

So she said no to his offer, and on the first day of the voyage, Ivor let it slide and said she could find her sea legs first. In the morning, after she'd eaten fried breakfast with him and Jananin and the captain and crew, and showed no sign of feeling sick, he told her gently but firmly that this was a life skill she needed to have, and made her go down to the swimming pool and put on a swimming costume that had been amongst the clothing Jananin had bought in a cubicle there.

It turned out not to be as bad as she'd expected. Nobody else was there, and Ivor didn't look too terrible because he wore baggy swimming trunks, although when he got out of the water with them wet, they stuck to his bum. Because he tended to comb his hair flat anyway, he didn't look vastly unlike himself when he got wet, and he was only hairy a bit on the front and not all over his back as well, and he was neither so thin his ribs were visible, nor so fat his gut bulged or his sides wobbled. And most importantly, he'd shaved off his horrible beard that very morning.

The first time he tried to help her by holding her arm and saw her recoil, he apologised and didn't do it again, and would stand back and wait patiently for her to try in her own time.

After that first morning of swimming, Dana had a shower in one of the cubicles near the swimming pool, and got dressed there. She went back to the cabins with wet hair and her towel draped round her shoulders. The cabins were three separate sleeping rooms with a shared toilet and shower, and a sitting room with windows that looked out to the starboard of the ship. The starboard of the ship, Ivor had told her, was the right-hand side as you were standing on her facing the direction of travel.

Jananin had been doing something with her laptop in the sitting room. When Ivor had sat down and started to comb his hair with the half a comb he still hadn't got round to replacing, she put it down and stood up.

"The report on Peter I have here, if you would like to read it."

"Thanks," Ivor said.

Jananin continued. "There's something else. "It seems I owe you an apology, Pilgrennon. I have allowed confirmation bias to get the better of me."

Ivor could scarcely have looked more shocked in

response to this had Jananin told him she had been persuaded that the Earth was flat.

Jananin continued. "My solicitor brought this to my attention. It seems the situation regarding the missing funds of your charity has been explained. The police are investigating your ex-wife and another trustee of the charity, someone called Archibald Sanderson, for embezzlement."

Ivor's mouth fell open. For a moment, he seemed unable to speak. "Adrienne?" he burst out. "She'd never do that. Sanderson I can believe, he was always for sale, but not her! I've known her since we were sixteen! She left *me!* She had her own money!"

"Believe it or don't, but clearly your insistence that you didn't rob your own charity wasn't a lie. It seems after you disappeared, she had you declared legally dead, but your will left all your estate to the charity, and she brought a claim against your executor under the Inheritance Provision for Family and Dependents Act. The executor, whom I am given to understand is your aunt, tried to settle out of court, but she refused and dragged her through the system. She was awarded a settlement, but as it was less than what your aunt had offered before the hearing, she had to pay the bill for all your aunt's legal fees, and apparently she wasn't happy with this outcome. She abused her position of a trustee of the charity to steal money from it that she believed should have been hers.

"Up until we were framed, it seemed she had got away with it, but the reopening of your missing person's case brought scrutiny upon her. Naturally, this investigation combined with everything else to do with Dana not being dead and other anomalies and embarrassment for them in what went on has shifted the attention of the police very firmly away from you."

She handed him a thick sheaf of printed paper, stapled together in the top left corner. "The judge's decision from the claim."

Ivor took the judgement wordlessly. It occupied him for some time, and as he sat there reading it, occasionally sniffing and turning back and forth between pages, his expression and twitches and fidgets became more agitated, until at last he set the document down hard on the table, got to his feet with an inarticulate grunt, and strode out of the room to the corridor towards the door that led to the open deck.

Dana put down the book she'd been reading and looked to Jananin, who had been drawing something. Jananin set it aside and put her hands on the arms of her chair, tensing as though about to rise, but then her expression changed and she relaxed. Then Dana, overcome with anxiety, got up from her chair, and Jananin did as well, and they both followed him outside.

He stood, looking out to sea, lost in his own thoughts with his hands in front of him, twisting the gold ring he always wore on his left hand as often he did, but as they approached he savagely pulled it from his finger and flung it over the starboard rail of the *Atlantic Sonata*.

An instant later he noticed them, and turned to acknowledge them, blushing slightly and putting both hands in his pockets.

"Thank you," he said to Jananin, humbly. "And thank you for waiting until we'd left to tell me. This solicitor of yours must be worth her salt."

"I make a point of not working with people who are incompetent," Jananin replied.

"My auntie, she's the most decent, reasonable person you could ever wish to meet. That's why I made her my executor. It must have upset her enough that I was missing and presumed dead, and then for Adrienne to sue her and drag her through the entire court process, and to steal from the charity I set up in Lydia's name..." He looked to Dana now. "I'm sorry. I guess money just turns some people into monsters."

The rest of the voyage passed pleasantly. Dana had

felt reassured by Jananin's report on Pauline and Graeme, and that with the Cerberus that had been embedded in the British government removed, there probably would be little risk to them, although she couldn't help but worry about how Cale was doing, as they'd never been apart for any significant length of time in their lives. When she confessed this to Ivor, he tried to reframe it as it perhaps being a good thing for them to have some time apart, and that Cale might get better at communicating with other people instead of relying on Dana all the time.

She was mindful of the conversation she'd had with Ivor in the inn, about how she'd missed the time she'd had with him and Jananin and Alpha and Peter in Edinburgh, and made a conscious effort not to dwell on things, and just to enjoy being free of Cerberus, and not having to wear a hat and being able to feel GPS and sense the ship's tiny presence in the vast, empty ocean. They were fortunate to have some fine February weather, and many times stood on the bow of the ship watching the sun go down, the sky alight, the ocean surface filled with orange and pink.

The ship's cook served different meals each day and all of them were good. One time, after an enjoyable meal of gammon with pineapple, salad, and chips, after they had gone back to their sitting-room, Dana remarked that she would like to just travel in a ship around and around the world endlessly, only stopping to refuel, and that way she would never have to face Cerberus. Jananin remarked in response to this that it was fine, as long as she didn't travel equatorially and they could go to Antarctica, since that was where she was supposed to be at the moment, and there were no signals there either.

The ship had a library with fiction and non-fiction books. Ivor taught Dana some biology and geography, and after some cajoling, Jananin taught her some chemistry and physics, and even a bit of astronomy out on the deck when the sun had gone down and the nights were the darkest of dark and the stars very bright. One time, she ended up lying next to Ivor on the boards, with her head on his shoulder and his arm around her to try to keep her warm while Jananin lay beside them, pointing out Orion and Canis Major, the dog star.

Jananin and Ivor talked on the ship, mostly about what they were going to do and where the other two Cerberus computers might be. Jananin sometimes insulted Ivor, but they didn't argue. Dana learned breast stroke and front crawl, and to float on her back, and by the end of the journey she could do a few laps of the ship's swimming pool.

And so it was with disappointment and trepidation that one dawn Dana stepped onto the deck with Ivor for their morning walk around all the shipping containers, and saw not the welcoming sight of the empty ocean stretching ahead of the *Atlantic Sonata*, but a distant land mass that she understood was New York.

*

Ivor said goodbye to the captain, and thanked the ship's cook for his meals. The three of them set off along the pavement, Ivor towing Jananin's trunk and the holdall with his and Dana's luggage in it in his other hand. Dana looked back over her shoulder at the *Atlantic Sonata*, the cranes already in place and beginning to unload her shipping containers as she lay in her berth. Some people would probably think the ship very ugly with her great stained iron hull and the brick aerodynamics of her bridge. Pauline was always moaning about how ugly the architecture in Coventry was, and how she wished they'd rip it down and build something else. She and Graeme didn't see eye to eye on the matter, because Graeme said the buildings were part of the city's postwar history, and if they tore them down they would be destroying history so they could build twee, fake buildings that pretend to be something they're not instead of something authentic. Pauline would probably say the *Atlantic Sonata* was an eyesore, but Dana loved her and missed her already, and the quiet sitting-room that had been just for her and Ivor and Jananin to read and draw and talk in, and enjoy the view of the open ocean.

As they left the cargo area of the port to head for the main terminus and the exit into New York, the people began to look less like dock workers and sailors and more like tourists, and their numbers started to increase, and with the hat on Dana's head blocking all signals from her, she felt crowded and yet also isolated, as though the people were not alive, more like zombies in a game. Then Ivor made a comment about the weight of Jananin's luggage; and Jananin shot back that he had volunteered to deal with it, and she was perfectly capable of handling it herself, and that it was because he was unfit and had been eating too much dinner all those evenings in the ship's galley, and that it didn't matter that she hadn't killed him when she'd had the chance, because at the rate he was going he'd give himself a coronary and finish the job for her.

Dana missed the quiet peace on the ship more than ever, and the mass of people with their mobile phones and computers that she couldn't feel the signals of became ever more alarming, and with people close and towering over her, she couldn't sense the layout of where she was from GPS, and she started to cry and panic and worry she'd lose both of them in the crowd. Ivor noticed this, but he had both his hands full, and all he could do was suggest Dana hold one handle of the holdall, and he hold the other and she stay as close as possible.

They got through the passport gate without much trouble. Seeing the state Dana was in, the staff there seemed keen to stamp the passports and get them through quickly. Then they reached a covered area, with a fountain in the middle and shops about it, and Jananin said she was going to get pounds changed into dollars and buy some mobile phones because she had got rid of the old one in Southampton just as they were leaving. Probably she had thrown it into the sea like Ivor had his wedding ring.

Ivor led Dana over to a wall, and turned her around so that her back was facing it and he was blocking her from the crowd, and he put his arms around her firmly and counted potatoes to help her breathe, and she pressed her face into his chest and shut her eyes, and felt ill, and wished the noise and people would go away.

After a while, she made out Jananin's voice. "Oh, there you are. Why are you always squeezing and smothering her?" Dana turned her head slightly, and opened her eyes to look at Jananin.

"I'm giving her a hug! If you want the scientific explanation, it's called pressure therapy. Some people find it calming." Ivor tightened his arms on her a bit. "If you ever want to try it, you have but to ask."

Jananin took the holdall and Ivor tucked Dana under his arm, keeping her close to him as they followed Jananin on a long walk through the port and out into a very noisy street. All the time, Dana tried to keep her attention on the floor in front of her and not look round at the heaving masses of people. Amidst the chaos, Jananin managed to get a taxi to pull over, and a yellow door opened to the back seat. Once inside with Ivor next to her and the door closed, it did seem a little calmer, but that ended abruptly when the cab pulled roughly out into the road, and Dana threw up.

The cab driver heard it and became irate. He slammed on the brakes in the middle of the road, causing the traffic behind to honk frenziedly at him, and started shouting at Ivor over his shoulder. However, when he realised that most of the sick had gone into one of the ship's paper bags that Ivor had been trying to coax it into, and that what hadn't had gone on Ivor, he calmed down a lot and began to drive on. "She better not have no contagious diseases or nothin'!"

"She doesn't," Ivor countered. "She's autistic. It's just a sensory thing because the port was so busy."

The man calmed down a little more. "My niece is

autistic." He glanced from Ivor to Jananin in the front seat. "Where to?"

"The botanical gardens," Ivor said before Jananin could speak.

Jananin couldn't look at him, as he was sitting directly behind her, but she twisted in her seat. "The botanical gardens? We need to get out of the city, not go sightseeing!"

"Let's just go there for a few hours. It'll calm her down and give us some time to work out where to go."

Jananin settled herself back in her seat and exhaled forcefully.

"Lady, we going to the botanical gardens like your husband suggests, or are we doin' sumthin' else?"

Jananin grimaced at the word *husband*. "Right. *Fine*. Let's do the botanical gardens. I expect I will have to pay for us to get in, in the same way I am having to bankroll everything on this expedition."

The cab driver snorted explosively, and tried to straighten out his face.

*

Jananin told the driver she would pay his normal rate for him to leave their luggage in his car and go off and have his lunch for a few hours.

The visitors to the botanical gardens were much quieter and sparser than those at the port. Ivor pointed out that all the plants in the gardens had labels, either on tree trunks or in the ground next to the specimens. Most of them were still dormant after winter, and not very exciting, but as Dana read their Latin names out to him, she started to feel calmer. The strangeness of another country and the people everywhere began not to matter so much.

"*Parrotia persica*." Its branches were quite bald with only the slightest sign of buds starting to form, but the bark was all rough and splotchy, looking almost like the abstract marble pattern on the endpapers of old books, and she put her hands on its broad trunk to feel its texture.

"*Prunus serrula*." Likewise had no flowers or leaves yet,

but its bark was bright, shiny red broken up with lines of rough corky texture, as though it had grown too fast and the bark had split and left it with stretch marks.

"*Magnolia soulangeana*." The bark was grey, not very interesting when Dana reached out to touch it. Then Ivor nudged her shoulder, and when she looked at him, he pointed up above their heads.

The branches of the tree were covered with white, spear-like, unopened flowerbuds, held up to the clear sky like candelabra, swaying ever so slightly in a minute breeze. When she looked behind her at Ivor and Jananin again, they were both looking up at the magnolia flowers, not speaking, and somehow they looked younger, and as though everything that had happened between them in the past was momentarily forgotten. They looked like two people who had only just met.

When Dana looked farther afield, she realised they'd come into a part of the gardens that was just for magnolia trees; an arboretum. Most of them were very large and probably very old, and all of them were covered with the same spear-like buds, some of them pink, some of them magenta, some yellow, and a lot of them the same white as the one they stood under now.

"Come here," Ivor said at length, and he crouched down and hoisted her up with some difficulty, as since she'd had a birthday she was probably too big, and sat her on his shoulder to give her a better view. The magnolia must have been pruned to keep the branches clear of the visitors' heads, so it didn't poke people in the eyes or mess up their hair, Dana supposed, but sitting on a tall man put her head up amongst its branches where she could see the spear flowers closely. She touched them, gently, imagining the petals curled up tight within them.

They sat on a bench in the magnolia garden, with Dana between Ivor and Jananin. Jananin gave Ivor a mobile phone she'd bought him. He found it rather difficult to use, as he said it had been more than ten years since he'd last bought one, and he was a bit of a helpless Luddite with technology at the best of times, and asked Dana to help him. With her hat blindfolding her to electromagnetic signals, Dana could make neither head nor tail of it. Jananin added him as a contact under the name 'Charlotte Anne Quack,' and sent him a text message, and he managed to add her back as 'Nemesis.'

It was peaceful under the magnolias, and Dana fell asleep there for a bit. When she woke up, Ivor had put his arm around her to stop her falling off the bench, and he was still trying to work out how to use his mobile phone. Jananin had gone off to make some phone calls. Ivor said they could go to the shop, and when they got there, they'd have to work out how to send a text message back to her between themselves, to tell her where they were.

The shop had mostly what Pauline would describe as *tat* — souvenirs like pens and yo-yos with the New York Botanical Gardens logo on them, and sweets and tea towels, but next to it there was a book shop. When Dana and Ivor walked into it, the walls and partitions between the bookshelves had huge floor-to-ceiling photographs of landscapes around the USA printed on them. The first was of dramatic orange rock formations and tall flowering cacti against a bright blue sky.

As they rounded a corner, the next image made Dana stop in her tracks. Her mouth open, she pointed at the scrubby vegetation, the trees with their rough, shaggy trunks and sparse, short branches with bushes of tough foliage at the end of each, the sky and the distant purple-grey mountains in the distance.

"That's the place in the game!" As Ivor turned to her, she added in a whisper, "*The Cerberus game!*"

He glanced at it, and back to her. "I thought it was based on Greek mythology, and it was the Styx and the afterlife from that?"

"That's how it's like, in the place where you start the game when you log in. Outside of Erebus."

Ivor and Dana moved closer to the picture. To the side of it on the wall, there was a white plaque, which said *Nevada Desert, copyright Sarah Dalton, used with permission*.

Ivor looked rather excited. "Let's see if we can find some books about the Nevada Desert!"

Soon they had found two substantial books, both with lots of photographs and diagrams, *A Guide to the Flora and Fauna of Nevada*, and *Ecologies of North America*. Dana sat down to read, and beside her Ivor began rummaging through his jacket pockets, assembling what he found on his lap: the mobile phone Jananin had just given him, a five-pence coin, the key to the computer room on Roareim, Peter's medicine in its squashed box, and some crumpled-up paper thing, discoloured and moulded into its folded shape as though it had got wet with seawater and dried like that. When he finally uncrumpled it and rolled it out on his knee, it turned out to be a ten-pound note, one of the defunct paper ones that Dana remembered had been around before plastic ones replaced them.

"You'll probably have to ask Jananin to pay for them," he said.

Dana pointed to a picture of one of the trees. *Joshua tree, Yucca brevifolia*. She turned a page, to see a photograph of the little burrowing owls, and of a huge black-and-orange mottled lizard, the one she remembered she picked up and got bitten by in the game. *Gila monster*.

When Jananin found them a few minutes later, Dana closed the book she was reading and held both of them up to her. "We need to go to Nevada."

Ivor looked up at her, widening his eyes and sticking out his bottom lip. Jananin considered his silly expression and the things he'd taken from his pockets.

"Before we go to Nevada, we will see if we can find a clothes shop, and I am buying you another jacket. That tatty old military one makes you stand out too much, and besides, it smells." She made a distasteful face.

Jananin paid for the books, and they found a clothes

shop with a menswear section. "Go and find something," Jananin said.

Ivor shrugged. "How about you pick something that you'd like for me?"

Jananin scowled. "I don't believe this kind of shop generally carries stock of straitjackets."

He chuckled a bit to himself. "It would be better if you picked something that you like. That way, it would look more like we were together."

"Why should I want anyone to think *that*?"

"Well, I don't know, maybe because it would draw less suspicion if we looked like a couple on holiday with our kid, instead of us looking like a pair of information terrorists with someone else's kid." Ivor faced Dana, turning his hands palms up. "Do you understand the point I'm trying to make, that Jananin looks like a badass, and I look like a tramp?"

Dana nodded.

"I do not wear clothing to look like a *badass*. I wear it because it's practical. This coat, for example, works well for concealing weapons under."

"Then pick something for me that you think fits those criteria."

Jananin exhaled through her teeth. She went briskly to the racks of jackets, making a brief examination of several before pushing them around on the rack and lifting out three to compare the design of them. "Will this do?"

Ivor took the garment she proffered, a dark grey leather one. He checked the size label and swapped it for a different one of the same style. After he'd taken off his RAF jacket and put it on, he shrugged his shoulders and asked Dana, "Do I look like a badass in this?"

While they had sandwiches and coffee in the refectory, Dana explained to Jananin about recognising the picture of the desert from the game, and that she thought it was a clue, and they worked out how to get to Nevada. Jananin thought that it would be a bad idea to use a commercial flight or any other sort of public transport to get to Nevada, and that the probably the safest and least conspicuous way of getting there was to drive, although it would take several days and they would have to stop off along the way. Ivor and Dana agreed with her, so when they went back to the taxi, she told the driver to take them to a place they could buy a secondhand car.

People in America drove on the other side of the road to in the UK, and the car Jananin bought had the driver's seat on what was the passenger side at home. The car didn't have any GPS, so Jananin also had to buy a map and Ivor had to navigate for her. While he did this, he was also trying to sew kitchen foil into the lining of a wide-brimmed hat of the sort Americans wear in films, that they'd bought for Dana to wear at the botanical gardens, and he kept confusing his left and his right, which annoyed Jananin. Dana told her it probably wasn't his fault, because the car was a mirror image of the sort of car they were all used to, and it must be confusing it being like that when you're trying to work out what's left and right.

By evening, they had reached a place called Pennsylvania, and they stopped at a motel. The food served there was not very nice; the staff brought it on a tray to the door to their suite and left it on the floor outside, and it was just microwaved TV dinners.

Dana and Ivor sat on the sofa eating theirs and watching American news, which, thankfully, said very little about anything going on in the UK. Jananin ate hers quickly, standing up, and set about sending messages to her contacts. She took a photograph with her mobile phone of a picture she had drawn on a piece of paper while they were on the ship, of a magnolia tree with a single flower on it, and a huge, insanely detailed owl sitting in the fork of it. The tree was not unlike what Ivor had tried to draw on the card he'd made Dana, but it was rather better drawn.

"If that's a code," Dana asked, pointing at it, "What does it mean?"

Jananin pointed brusquely at Ivor. "The tree's him. The flower's you, or rather, any one of his experiments. The owl's me."

Dana chewed her food and considered this. "So when Rupert Osric sent you a picture of an owl, with a flower, that was to tell you he has me?"

"Correct. And if I were to send him a picture of a tree, or a flower, and nothing else, that would infer a sighting. Or a tree that had been cut down..."

Ivor put down his fork. "Thanks, Blake. You know, I was rather hoping, that once we finish this, perhaps we can work something out, and you can just send him a picture of a tree with its professional reputation in shreds, in jail or some other suitable location."

"I'll think about it." Jananin consulted her laptop. Sounding rather surprised, she said. "You have a reply to your email."

Ivor set his food down on the table and leaned forward to look, as Jananin read out. "ISP this is SRG. Meet me when time stands still, at the place between yesterday and tomorrow, and we'll talk about my dog."

"The place between yesterday and tomorrow?" Ivor frowned. "It's some sort of riddle. He's sent it like that because he doesn't want whoever's still got the other two heads of Cerberus to intercept it and work out where and when he means."

Jananin gave a sort of shrug with her eyebrows. "Either that, or he or whoever has access to his email is deranged and has written nonsense."

"The place between tomorrow and yesterday?" Ivor leaned forward, resting his forearms on his knees. "Surely that's just *today*?"

"No, today is the *time* between tomorrow and yesterday, not the place." Jananin's attention was diverted by an alert from her mobile phone. Dana watched her read it, her expression shifting as she processed what had been sent to her.

"Someone has passed the details to me of a man in Nevada, who may have information on something he knows about there. Oddly enough, it's through Osric, and it's a scientific contact of his, not anyone with any involvement in the government, apparently a local ecologist. He says he's keen to speak to us in person, and I should arrange to meet him in Eureka County."

Dana finished her food and put down her tray. "Is that, like, where Archimedes lives?" She looked from Jananin to Ivor. "Is that who the man is?" When they both seemed rather amused by this, Dana added, "Archimedes is a scientist, isn't he?"

Jananin said. "Possibly. But this man's name is Isaiah Redwood."

-14-

IT took three more days of hard driving to reach Nevada, stopping in Illinois, Nebraska, and Utah. As they drove west, the countryside became more open, and less green, with fewer houses in the landscape. Dana couldn't tell what the names of the places were without GPS, but Ivor passed the road map back to her so she could see, and she helped a bit with the navigation. The countryside in Wyoming was especially nice, with great open grasslands and sparse woods, and mountains in the distance. In Utah, the desert looked like the other picture they'd seen in New York Botanical Gardens, with dramatic orange rock formations and clear skies.

On the morning they reached Nevada, the view through the car windows became similar to that Dana had explored in the game. She couldn't see any pumas or any of the sheep and deer, and she wondered if perhaps the game had exaggerated their numbers to make it more interesting.

Ivor and Jananin were arguing again. "When we meet this bloke, let me handle it, at least at the start," Ivor said.

"Why should I let you handle anything?"

"Because you're clever, but you've got no tact. Blake, you're rude and insulting, and you say inappropriate things. If he gets offended by that, we could potentially lose the only lead we've got on this."

They arrived at a steakhouse restaurant. Dana was hoping they would be able to find somewhere less transient to stay now they were here. When they had stopped off *en route,* she'd had to wear the woolly hat in bed, and change into the cowboy hat by going out away from houses so she wouldn't be in range of any computers or wLANs. Ivor had sewn a chin strap on the hat so it didn't fall off, but the hat made her too hot, and had now become extremely manky and bobbly from being slept in. Furthermore, Dana hadn't been able to wash her hair since the last morning aboard the *Atlantic Sonata*, and although it thankfully was short and she didn't have to put up with it being dirty all down her neck as well, the inside of the hat was sticky and unpleasant.

Within the restaurant, blinds screened the windows from the bright sun. Soon after they'd ordered and taken their place at a table, a large man, rather similar to Ivor in height and build, came into the steakhouse. He had a voluminous grey-brown beard that, along with his cowboy hat, obscured most of his face, and had on jeans, a casual shirt with a peculiar sort of tie that looked like a bootlace with an ornate metal slider on it, and a dusty suede jacket with a sort of fringed trim on it. He cast about the restaurant.

"Do you think that's him?" Jananin said.

Ivor stared at the man, trying to attract his attention. "I think so. Just let me manage the introduction. I don't want us to get off on bad terms."

After ordering something, the man came and sat down at their table. Dana was not very good at understanding people's expressions, and all she could see of the man's face was his nose and a pair of brown eyes. "Name's Isaiah Redwood."

Ivor pointed to Jananin. "This is Jananin Blake, this is Dana." He pointed to himself. "Ivor Pilgrennon."

Isaiah Redwood nodded.

One of the staff members came over with their meals. "Thank you, this looks lovely," Ivor said. Isaiah Redwood simply raised his eyebrows appreciatively at the plate of steak set before him.

Ivor drummed his fingers on the table briefly, and smiled. "I understand you're an ecologist. I took the liberty of looking up your research on the way here. I see you had a number of papers published in highly respected journals a few years back, about the effects of climate change, tourism, and pollution on the water table and the growth habits of different species of cacti."

Isaiah Redwood's only response to this was a gruff "Yes," along with a mouthful of rare steak shovelled into his mouth.

Ivor changed tack. "On the way here, aside from the spectacular scenery, we noticed several churches of interesting architectural design, and..."

Jananin, who had been eating, put down her fork and leaned her elbow on the table, turning to give Ivor a very funny look. Isaiah Redwood said, "Shut up, Pilgrennon. You talk too much. We're not here to talk about my career, and my beliefs are between me and God."

Ivor started, and then closed his mouth. Isaiah Redwood wiped his beard on a napkin and began to speak.

"First thing to know about Nevada is, there ain't no *Nevarda*. It's pronounced *Nevadda*. Second thing, what happened in the UK isn't common knowledge here, but there's talk, and your media shut down that information about you that got out a lot faster than ours did. If people ask you where you're from, say you're Australians. Folks round here can't tell the difference between Australian and British accents, same as y'all can't tell American and Canadian apart."

Isaiah Redwood paused to allow this information to be absorbed before continuing. "Now, don't know what you know about how the system here works, but we've got two parties, a red one and a blue one, a bit like in your country. A bit like in your country, too, we've had the same party in power for a long time, despite ratings being unfavorable. There's two levels of government in America, the state government, that's the 'states' in USA, and the federal government; that's the 'united' part. What I can tell you is about ten years back, the feds built a military base out here in the desert. They've never given no explanation to the Nevada state nor the people in Eureka as to why it's there and what function it serves, and they guard it and won't let anyone get close to it.

"The local folks and that military installation have no lost love. I've been out there in the desert and come across them practicing drills, setting off munitions and disturbing the peace and the wildlife. We get soldiers coming into town, looking for a good time, behavin' like they're in Vegas and causin' trouble for the sheriff. There was this guy, bit of a local character, sometimes forgot to take his medication, lived with his mom. He was into all these conspiracy theories, posting stuff on the Internet speculating about the base and there being some Area 51 Roswell crap going down there. A bit silly, all harmless really, pleasant enough fella. Couple of months back, one evening, he decided to go snooping around the perimeter, and those damn feds shot him dead."

Ivor and Jananin exchanged glances. Dana sat in her chair, looking up as Isaiah Redwood and his odd cowboy hat. It had an ornate band around the crown with all manner of funny souvenirs attached to it: a bird's skull, feathers, reptile teeth, a badge in a sort of fish shape formed from a single piece of wire, and some bright red corrugated hooks that were possibly spines from desert cacti. She found herself thinking of Peter who, if he didn't have his medicine, sometimes did things that weren't very sensible, and wondering if the poor young man who wrote things on the Internet had been anything like him.

"So. If you don't go causin' no trouble here, you're not going to get any trouble back. I know the sheriff personally, very reasonable guy. If you say there was a supercomputer installed in the infrastructure in London, manipulating the voting system, and you think there might be a similar situation going on here, I'd say that base is the prime candidate. And I'm prepared to help you as best as I can, first thing because the countryside round here would be a better place with that base gone, and second thing because

I've always voted for the other party. If they've been losin' fair and square, that's one thing, but if they're being kept out by foul play, I want an end to that.

"As to where you can stay, there's room in my villa. My wife and I have been having disagreements for some time, mainly over that damn military base. After they shot that guy two months back, she decided it weren't safe here no more, and she and our son moved out and went back to Las Vegas."

Dana thought a villa sounded rather grand and exotic, and wasn't quite sure what to expect when they finished their steaks and set out in the car to follow him to the destination. It turned out a *villa* was simply what people in Nevada called a bungalow with a swimming pool and a garden, isolated from other houses in the desert. It was a nice house and the views from it were very scenic. It also had a basement, which was probably meant to be for storing things and for Isaiah to do his laundry in, but his son had been using it as a gaming room. Although he'd taken the console he used and the television away, there was still a sofa there and a wLAN. It also had a shower and a loo, although they were rather basic and the shower just had a curtain to separate it.

Ivor and Jananin explained to Isaiah, as simply as they were able to, that Dana would need a room where signals wouldn't be able to get to her. They decided the basement would be easiest to convert for her needs, and after an afternoon's work, they had fixed sheets of lightweight metal to the ceiling, and the cellar being underground seemed to prevent anything coming through the wall. Dana was hugely relieved to be able to take off her hat and wash her hair, although she was disappointed that she'd not be able to use the swimming pool.

Isaiah said he would cook them a meal. Ivor offered to help him, but he said he didn't want to eat 'no black pudding or spotted dick or any other weird English food,' and made a paella with prawns in it.

They ate the food in the dining room, with the television on in the background. A brief mention of the election in the UK came on, about Colin Antrobus's Meritocratic Party being ahead in the polls. Antrobus himself was given an opportunity to say something short about what his party was about. He said, "Politics has become about politicians and not about policies. Meritocracy is about giving decisions back to the electorate, and rewarding people who work hard and contribute."

Isaiah turned to glance at the television. "He has a fair point. Over here, one of the issues people can never seem to stop arguing about is abortion. I figure, we should ask all the women of childbearing age what they think, and let that be our answer."

Ivor glanced suspiciously at a crucifix hanging on the wall of Isaiah's dining room. Isaiah, apparently noticing this, added, "A foetus is a human life, and it's a sin to destroy it. But it's also a sin to bring a child into this world if you can't love it. Which of those sins is the worse is not for me to judge."

On the opposite side of the room to the crucifix, there was a photograph of Isaiah Redwood with his wife and son. He and his wife were wearing cowboy hats and smiling. The son looked older than Dana but younger than Duncan, and as though he hadn't wanted to be in the picture.

The Prime Minister and the Leader of the Opposition were then interviewed about their opinions on Antrobus. One of them claimed he was 'far right' and the other claimed he was 'far left." Dana asked what that meant and if left and right were the other way around in America, like cars being mirror images and driving on the other side of the road. Ivor replied in disgust, that they were nothing to do with actual left and right, and didn't mean anything at all; that they were just insults used by stupid people who refused to have a rational, intelligent discussion about their differences of opinion.

After dinner, Isaiah suggested Dana could have his

son's former room, and that Jananin and Ivor should have his spare room. Dana said she would rather sleep in the basement on the sofa, and not have to wear a hat in bed, and that Ivor and Jananin wouldn't want to share a bedroom anyway, because they didn't like each other, and Ivor snored sometimes. Isaiah it seemed interpreted this the wrong way, and said it was appalling that a child should offer to sleep in a basement because of her parents' marital disharmony and their inability to keep it secret from her.

Eventually, it was settled by Dana explaining repeatedly that she would much rather sleep in the basement, and Jananin explaining it was to do with Dana's medical issue that they had put the metal sheets in there for. Isaiah cleaned the sofa, as he thought his son might have been eating snacks and getting crumbs on it, and put a clean sheet on it and a pillow and duvet. It was a bit cool down there, but it didn't matter with the duvet, and Dana would much rather have been slightly too cold and have to sleep with a duvet over her head, than have to wear a hat in bed and be too hot for it.

When she woke up, she had no idea what time it was, as she couldn't find a clock in the basement, and none of the signals outside could reach her. She put on her hat and dressing-gown, and went up the stairs, to see if it was light.

It was, and the house was full of fresh air with a slight chill. The curtains and the bifold door in the living room had been opened wide, and Isaiah Redwood was standing out on his patio, watching the sun rise over the desert. Dana went out and stood there as well. Presently, he noticed her, and turned and looked at her. He said, "Heh," and his teeth showed from within his beard in something that was possibly a smile. "You practicing blending in round here, with that hat?"

Dana's hat had a loop attached to it, with a toggle. She held the string and pulled the toggle up under her chin, lest the wind rise up and try to blow it away. "I have to wear my hat when I'm not in the basement. It's to stop the bad computer knowing where I am."

He turned back to the spring dawn that reached out with long fingers of shadow across the desert. A bird was singing somewhere, and it sounded a bit but not quite like a blackbird song. The air was very still, the sky very clear. The early morning light cast the distant mountains in strange colours.

"You study the desert, don't you?" Dana asked. "The plants and the animals, and the rocks and the rains and streams?"

"I do. And I never tire of looking at it."

Dana took a step away from the door, looking around at the desert that spread in all directions to the distant mountain ranges, like it did in the Cerberus game. "Are there not any other houses?"

"There's a few. There's *that*."

He pointed, and Dana looked, to see a collection of pale, boxy objects some distance away. "What's that?"

"That's the military installation, where we think that bad computer might be hiding out. Can't see much of it from here, without binoculars, though. I'll show you later, when your mother gets up, and that good-for-nothing father of yours."

"Why don't you like Ivor?" Dana asked.

He thought on this for a moment. "I know a charmer when I see one, same as I know a snake when I see one. And he's both of 'em." Isaiah leaned back on his heels, exhaled forcefully through his nose, and put his hands in his pockets. "But, I guess some of my animosity's maybe me externalizing my own situation in a way that's not quite fair. The way I see it, if he's with someone like her, and he's blessed with a kid like you, he's brokered himself a pretty damn fine deal with his English scholar good looks and that silver tongue of his. Whatever's gone on between them that's put their relationship on the rocks is with no doubt his fault, same as why I don't have my wife and son living with me no longer is mine."

Isaiah looked out upon the desert once more. "I shouldn't judge him. Only God is perfect."

"So, if there's a perfect god," Dana said, "why is the god *he*?"

Isaiah frowned. "How'd you mean?"

"Well, only animals are *he* and *she*. Computers, rocks, clouds, plants, the sun and the moon, everything else, is *it*. Apart from ships, which are *she*, but they're a bit unusual."

"Some plants have male and female versions."

"Yes, but they're still *it*."

Isaiah considered. "You know, I think you're probably right, and if God is universal, God is *it*. Don't go saying nothing about that theory in no churches round here, or anywhere else, mind you."

Dana looked at him with uncertainty. "If I *don't* say it in *no* churches, doesn't that mean I *do* say it in all of them?"

He laughed. "You're a funny kid. Can't fault your logic, though."

After breakfast, Isaiah said he would show them the military base, as best as he was able. He didn't think what he intended to do would attract any undue attention, as the personnel there were used to seeing him at work, and knew who he was, and he often had visiting scientists come to look at things and discuss them with him. Despite this, he warned them very strongly that they must do as he said, and not take any weapons or do anything to look threatening, because the soldiers had high-powered rifles and other dangerous tools that they wouldn't hesitate to use if they thought they had a reason to. If anyone approached and asked who they were, they were to say that they were Australian, that they were Jane and Iain Jones, a zoologist and a botanist, and that they had come to study the flora and fauna of Nevada and had brought their daughter Delilah with them.

Dana found herself glancing repetitively at the distant pale blocks of buildings as they set out from the villa.

Isaiah crouched down from time to time, to explain the name and evolutionary niche of a plant, or to identify a *scat* left behind by some animal. Normally Dana would have found this sort of thing to be greatly interesting, but now she struggled to concentrate, her attention taken up by that ominous presence and with no GPS or other signal to orient herself in the landscape that looked largely indistinguishable whichever way she turned.

She knew from the books they'd bought at the New York Botanical Gardens that the shrubs that grew all over the landscape were called creosote bushes, and the shaggy-stemmed trees that occurred in stands from place to place, with thick tufts of foliage at the tips of their sparse branches, were Joshua trees. Most of the creosote bushes had started to flower, their hint of yellow giving the dry, brownish foliage of the bushes a brighter, greener tinge. They gave off a rather odd odour, especially when they got brushed against people's legs, but it wasn't an unpleasant smell. The only animals she noticed were some lizards basking in the sun on a rocky outcrop, and they were hard to see, being the same colour as the stone they were on.

"Where are all the pumas?" Dana asked.

"You likely won't see pumas when you're out. They're quite reclusive, and they won't come near people if they can avoid it. Usually, I only see them when I'm in the house, looking out the window." They were approaching what looked like a very thorny, sprawling plant, not unlike the creosote bushes, but forming a tangled barrier between them and the base, which was now much closer. "This here is new," said Isaiah quietly. "I don't know if it was that boy they shot, or the incident in London, but they've mined the perimeter field."

Now they were closer to the thing, it had become clear it was not a plant. It was a great tangle of razor wire to keep people out, and fixed to the wire in various places were yellow hazard signs showing something exploding.

Other signs showed skulls and crossbones, and the word *MINES*.

"I thought they were illegal internationally." Jananin was wearing a cowboy hat, jeans, a loose cream shirt, and boots. She'd been carrying her heavy infra-red binoculars on the strap around her neck, but now she took off the dark-tinted glasses she usually wore and put them in her shirt pocket, so she could raise the binoculars and look briefly at the base.

"They were," Isaiah said. "The Supreme Court just brought in an exemption allowing the feds to use them here."

Ivor's upper lip pulled back from his teeth, lines forming at the side of his mouth as he looked under his hat brim, through the wire to the compound, surrounded by land contaminated with explosives.

As they moved on, a line of immense pylons crossed the land before them, carrying cables across the wire and on to the base. As they passed under it, Dana could somehow sense the power and data running through it, despite the foil inside her hat, as a prickling of her scalp and a tense pressure in the middle of her forehead. The base of each pylon was surrounded by more razor wire and warning signs.

Ivor looked up at the cables, and upon glancing at Dana and seeing the concern in her face, put his hand on her shoulder. They soon moved away, but they passed several more lines of pylons as they made their way around the perimeter of the minefield, huge bandwidths of data pouring in from every part of the USA for Cerberus to analyse.

"The one in London was hidden, not very well guarded huh?" Isaiah asked.

Jananin said, "It was disguised as a public library."

"Secrecy's one way to protect something. This one ain't secret. They have to protect it in other ways."

"Nobody knew it was there, until Dana found a

blueprint online for a bunker construction, that matched the dimensions of a building suggested by someone who had a lot of information he'd been looking very hard for."

"Bit of a conspiracy nut, huh? Or they thought he was, even if he wasn't."

"Still is," Ivor said. "Colin Antrobus has some very strange ideas."

"Pilgrennon," said Jananin, sounding exasperated. "Colin Antrobus went out of his way to help us at his own expense. An assassination attempt was made on him because of it. You could try being more charitable."

"You three are a weird family." Isaiah was shaking his head. "I ain't never heard of no family where the kid called her parents by their first names, and the husband and wife called each other by their last names. I reckon that's not usual, even in England."

"Speak for yourself," Jananin retorted. "You Americans call a sofa a *loveseat*. It sounds revolting, the sort of seat one would have to check very carefully for stains before using."

Isaiah roared with laughter. He pointed at Jananin. "She's funny."

"And that's not quite right about in England," Dana added. "Ivor is half Scottish and half Welsh. Jananin is from England, but she might have some Irish in her as well, although we're not sure, because she's not saying."

He laughed at this as well, this time more quietly, closing his eyes for a few seconds. "What's wrong with calling them Mom and Dad?"

"Because those aren't their names."

They walked all the way around the razor wire perimeter, pretending to study things in the desert and stopping from time to time.

Back at the villa, Ivor sat down, looking rather drawn and weary in a way that was nothing to do with having just been on a long walk.

"Can you and Jananin work out ideas of how to deal

with this one as well?" Dana asked him.

He forced a smile. "I expect so. All problems have solutions if you think long and hard enough. And after all, Jananin is a Nobel laureate."

He didn't sound very confident about it. Days passed. They went out into the desert and looked at more things. The three adults talked about having ideas, but never produced any. Isaiah stood alone in the desert in the mornings, Ivor floated in the swimming pool, and Jananin went for solitary walks, all trying to have ideas. The days turned into a week, and then two weeks, and still they had nothing.

One evening, everyone was sitting at the table after dinner, and Dana was playing with a globe that Isaiah had bought years before to teach his son Geography. She was looking at the map of the USA, trying to remember what GPS felt like and what she could remember of their journey from New York.

"I remember Ohio." Dana frowned. "Did we really drive through a state called Misery?"

"*Missouri*," Isaiah corrected, somewhere between amusement and offence.

"Isn't there someone like Colin Antrobus in any of the states?" Dana asked. "Someone who someone might know, who knows things about how the country is run, and might know how we can get in, and will tell the people there's a Cerberus in that army base and what's going on?"

Isaiah exhaled loudly. "With the Second Amendment, that's not going to go to plan. In the UK, most people don't have guns, and you might not like the politics there, but the polarisation of it is nothing compared to here. Things could kick off very quickly and very badly if people get wind of the electoral system being rigged and decide to take things into their own hands and start a militia. A disorganised rabble armed with hunting rifles and handguns is no match for the federal army. All we'll achieve that way is to irrigate the desert with innocent blood, and potentially have ourselves arrested for fomenting an insurrection."

"The London one was easier," Ivor said. "They couldn't guard it like this one, or it would have drawn attention to it. Once we'd worked out the hardest part of where it was, everything else could be overcome."

Jananin leaned back in her seat and folded her arms. "The only thing I can come up with is to try to destroy its infrastructure. If we follow the cables back, out of surveillance range, it might be possible to set explosives and disconnect it from its power and data supply. The distances involved means we're looking at a fifty mile radius and coordinating the attack over a circumference of over 300 miles. And even then, it's still intact and they still have it, and we've still got the minefield, the base, and whatever personnel and weapons they've got in it to deal with."

"Short of inviting the Russians to the party, I can't think of any way to get into that base or destroy it. And the Russians are an ill wind that blows nobody no good, and an act of treason might be an act against the feds, but it ain't no help to the good people of Eureka County."

Dana had been sitting quietly at the table while everyone else spoke, and the more and more ideas were dismissed, the more it seemed to her that there was only one solution to the problem. "What if I went back into the game?"

Ivor looked at her sharply. "You're not logging back in to that game. Remember what happened last time you did? That game was the whole reason Cerberus came after us in the first place. It's too dangerous."

"I don't see any other alternative," Jananin said. "That's how she obtained the blueprints that got us into the last one."

"Well, you know, Isaiah might take issue with that." Ivor threw his hands up in the air. "Since this is his house, he probably ought to know that the last time Dana went in that game, Cerberus or whoever was controlling the

UK version of it, sent two RAF helicopters with guided missiles to our location to kill us! And that base probably has its own stock of guided missiles without needing to call in air support. As soon as they work out where she's logging in from, they can probably launch it from right where they are!"

Isaiah, oddly, didn't seem particularly fazed by this. "Well, if she wants to play a game in secret, she can always use a VPN."

Ivor slapped both palms down on the table. His eyes were wide. "We tried that. It's not reliable. This thing can pick up landmarks and GPS locations and stuff from her subconscious. I know she calls it a game, but it's not. It's some sort of virtual testing environment someone has set up for this thing, so it can evolve its own security system!"

"Well," Dana offered, after thinking about this. "I haven't been able to sense GPS since we got here, because I've had to stay in the basement when I'm not wearing a hat. So I truly don't know where we actually are. And the desert, it all looks the same. I don't think Cerberus would be able to recognise any landmark from what I've seen. And your villa, Isaiah. Is it the only one of its kind, or are there other villas, that look a lot like it, around here?" Dana thought of Pauline and Graeme's house, which Graeme had once told her was built in the '70s. The other houses on the same housing estate had all been built at the same time, and were all made from the same three basic architectural plans: a detached house, a terrace, or an end terrace. They all had the same dimensions and rooms, and the only differences were how the people who lived there arranged their furniture and decorated the inside, and how they set out their gardens. Dana was pretty sure if she went back there without GPS, she'd never be able to find Pauline and Graeme's end terrace, even with the plants she remembered them having in their garden, and the gate and the brick wall at the front, which was different to the others on that street.

Isaiah nodded. "There's other villas like this, pretty much. I never went in much for plastic flamingos or garden gnomes, or other funny garden ornaments that'd make it stick out."

Ivor turned to Dana. "It's too dangerous. We need to keep thinking. There must be another way."

Jananin said, "Pilgrennon, do you want to destroy this thing, or not?"

"We've thought and thought, and we've talked about it for two weeks now! There's no other way!" Dana argued.

"I'll set up a VPN," Isaiah said. "My son's connection hardware is all there in the basement. They won't know where you're connecting from."

Ivor put his elbows on the table and leaned his forehead on his hands. "It looks like I've lost this referendum. But Dana, I wish you wouldn't. After what it did to Alpha and everything else that's happened."

"Ivor, will you come with me to the basement when I try? You know when I'm in the game, and I do something?"

"You dissociate."

"Can you watch me, when I dissociate, and if there's anything not right..."

He took his arms off the table and straightened his posture, defeated but resolute. "I'll unplug it."

THE desert in the game had changed subtly.

While it had been highly detailed before, there had always been the telltale signs that this was a simulation, perhaps because Cerberus had only seen it from the single vantage point of the cameras connected to it that looked out from the military base where it was hidden. But now, every rock had a real texture, every Joshua tree had individual leaves, and every animal had a brightness to its eye and an alacrity to its movements that computers just can't emulate. The creosote bushes smelt just like the ones in the real desert did. The distance between where she stood and the unreachable mountains now felt vast and real, and no longer as though the mountains were just a flat bitmap layered in front of the sky. Dana had, not intentionally, and for better or worse, brought her own experiences of the Nevada desert into Cerberus's recreation of it.

She went to the gully and presently found Eric, who had climbed down and was exploring the stream at the bottom. His character was still equipped with the pirate outfit he'd picked up when Dana had last played. "Hey!" he shouted up when he saw her. "It looks like it got a graphical upgrade!"

"Yeah, it looks mint!"

"That friend you brought here, last time you were on, Fal? He keeps logging on here looking for you." Eric started to climb back up. "He comes on here and he just asks for you and doesn't play. You should get in touch with him. I think he's worried."

The last time Dana had been in the game and seen Duncan had been when they had enacted the pirate attack, just before Cerberus had attacked Roareim. A whole lot had happened since then. It had been more than two months ago. Dana could only wonder what Duncan had thought, and had speculated about, during her absence.

"Anyway. Are things all right with you? Did you get banned from coming on and playing or something?"

"No, I didn't get banned, things were just..." Dana broke off. "We were really busy with something else. And yes, things are all right." Dana thought of the *Atlantic Sonata*, the botanical gardens, the road trip across America, and Isaiah Redwood's villa. "Things are good. Are you all right?"

Eric finished climbing up and sat on the edge of the cliff. "Yeah, I guess. My cat had to be put down."

"Oh."

Dana sensed a presence. She turned her head to see Cale, in crow form, perched on a rock. They were both glad to see each other.

Cale, go and see if you can get Duncan to come on, Dana thought to him.

Cale launched himself into the air, and disappeared.

"I mean, he was old and really manky, and it was a relief, really, as he was just constantly ralphing and having accidents in the house, and I don't think he recognised me or Mum any more. And we're getting a kitten now. I've gone with Mum to the breeder to see her, but we have to wait until she's old enough until we can bring her home."

Cale was now flapping about the sky, dive-bombing at the head of a figure who approached, which turned out to be Duncan's avatar, still in his pirate outfit.

"You came back!" he exclaimed when he saw her. He came and sat with them on the edge of the gully, and Cale settled back on his rock.

"I'm sorry I didn't come back on. I've been helping some people with something. It's something to do with the election and the computer that was in London. I've said I'll help them sort it out, but it means I'm a bit busy sometimes."

Eric made a noise of derision through slack lips. "Oh, come on! Why would people ask *you* to help with *that*? You're like, twelve, or something."

"Colin Antrobus, huh? Mum quite likes him, but Dad can't *stand* him."

"My mum fancies him," Eric said, "but apparently he's gay."

"You know in this game," said Dana, "there are clues to things, like, references to things in the real world. Sometimes if you can find what they are in the real world, that gives you another clue, that helps you to solve a puzzle or find something else in the game."

"Yeah." Eric laughed. "The whole thing is full of Easter Eggs." He picked up a tortoise from beside him, and turned it upside down in his lap. Printed on the bottom of the shell were the words, *Other end up. Do not drop.*

Duncan said, "LOL."

"This whole place, that goes on and on forever." Dana spread her arms out. "It's the Nevada desert, in America."

Duncan looked about at it from where he sat. "You're right. I could have worked that out. You know the film, *Tremors*? The desert in that looks exactly like this. And that's in Nevada."

Eric grinned. "That film is mint!"

"And, it is *Nevadda* and not *Nevarda*," Dana told them. From where she was sitting, she could see one of the cables strung across the great pylons, where it stretched across the gully. Only, she never remembered the pylons being in the game before. She must have brought them with her, from the real desert.

"Do you remember there were pylons and electric cables in the game before?" she asked Eric.

"No." Eric looked, noticing the cable. "There's a few puzzles outside, but most of them seem to be to do with the stream, or the inside of the mountain where Cerberus is."

"What if there are more puzzles outside, but we haven't noticed them before? Like the pirate one?"

"But I've tried to get somewhere in it before, lots of times. It just goes on forever, because you can do that in a game in a way you can't in reality. The desert's just an endless loop subroutine to give some atmosphere to the outside of the game, and a couple of really simple puzzles to entertain the noobs when they first log in."

"If you try to go somewhere in the desert, but you don't know where you're going, in a game it's made so you can't just find it by accident. It's like with it going on forever, or with something being in two places at once, it doesn't work like in the real world. What if we follow the cable, and it leads us to a puzzle?"

"But it goes in two directions," Duncan said. "If we want to follow it, how do we know which direction to follow it in?"

The three of them got up and walked towards the cable, and to the pylon it connected to on their side of the gully once it came into view.

"Well, it's a lot easier to follow it that way than it is to get to the other side of the river and follow it the other," Eric said, the wires buzzing over their heads. "So I reckon let's try that first."

They set off, following the wires, brushing against the creosote bushes. Dana found herself looking at the ground, for clues, remembering the lesson in ecology Isaiah had given, which she'd been distracted from and had struggled to listen to at the time."

"Urh!" Duncan exclaimed. "I've trod in something!"

"This is just disgusting!" Eric said. "They've tried to make it too realistic!"

Cale found this enormously funny. Cale often found things funny, but he tried to hide it from other people, and usually only Dana could tell, although sometimes his face would tense and he would snigger silently to himself.

When Dana thought about it, she suspected it was

probably her fault. Isaiah was interested in poos, or *scat*, as he called them. He could tell what species of animal had done them and what it had been eating.

Dana began to make something out in the distance. The power lines led over an all too familiar tangle of razor wire, its sharp edges glittering in the sun, the warning signs about the minefield and trespassing not being allowed moving a little in the slight breeze.

They stopped before the wire. "Do you think we have to go around and find a way through?" Duncan asked.

"I'm not sure," Dana replied.

Eric said, "Isn't America where they keep having civil wars? And where westerns are made, where they ride horses in the desert. And there's a sheriff, but it's not a debt collector like a sheriff means here. It's like a policeman, or something."

"I don't think they have civil wars any more," Dana said, thinking she'd not seen any evidence of war, civil or uncivil, on the drive across America. "I think that must be a historical thing, same as we don't have Guy Fawkes blowing things up, or people being tortured and executed for being witches or hang-drawn-quartered for saying rude things about kings any more here."

"You know in *Tremors*, right?" Duncan said. "We watched it on Cale's birthday, because Mum thought he was old enough, as long as we told him first it was a bit scary and we had to turn it off if he didn't like it. But he didn't, not like it, I mean." He added in a private message to Dana, *And I know that crow is Cale.*

Dana looked at Cale's crow. "What happens in it?"

"There are these monsters that live in the soil in the desert, and they come out and eat people! And there's this badass couple who have all these guns and make bombs to blow them up with! And all the special effects where the monsters die are like someone filled a sleeping bag with paint."

Eric interrupted. "Someone's coming!"

Back along a road that was little more than a track slightly more stony and less overgrown than the rest of the desert, a caravan of sorts was approaching. Three horses accoutred in tack for riding, and a pair of mules, drawing a wooden cart.

Dana glanced at Cale, and he returned a sly corvid blink.

The horses were one black, one chestnut, and one palomino. The palomino horse had more ornate tack on it than the other two, and the horses all looked well-cared for, and as though they'd been brushed and had their manes and tails combed especially for them.

"I think this horse is for the sheriff," Duncan said, taking the palomino's bridle. "I think Epsilon should be the sheriff, because in the western films it's usually a man, so having it be a girl will help balance it out."

Dana took hold of the horse's saddle at the front and back, put her foot in the stirrup, and climbed up. Once she was on the horse, with its long, maned neck and pointy ears stretching out in front of her, she could also see into the cart the mules were drawing, and it was filled with equipment and rather silly-looking cartoonish explosives: red cylinders with string fuses and *dynamite* written on them, black shiny bombs like bowling balls, grenades with ring-pulls, and a big wooden crate at the bottom with *TNT* stencilled on it in black.

Cale alighted on the side of the cart.

"Here," said Eric. "Wire cutters. For getting in."

Eric and Duncan took the wire cutters and cleared an entrance through the razor wire. The caravan of three horses with their riders and the mule cart behind them moved cautiously onto the edge of the minefield.

"The puzzle must be to get through the minefield, without being blown up," Eric said. "But how do we know where the mines are?"

The three of them looked carefully at the ground around them. Duncan pointed. "*There.*"

Dana could just about make out something in the sand, with a red light blinking every few seconds on the top.

"That? If we have to find all of them, without setting them off, it'll take ages!" Eric complained.

Cale took flight. He circled over the minefield ahead of them a few times. Then he hovered, as if asking them to follow.

"Birds' eyesight is better than people's," Duncan said. "Perhaps we should trust him."

They began to follow Cale, pausing from time to time as he calculated their route. There came the roar of a helicopter overhead. "Quickly, the bombs!"

Eric threw a bomb overarm at the helicopter, and it hit it and blew it up into nothing. It wasn't very realistic, really, Dana thought. In the real military, they probably had to use proper anti-aircraft missiles in rocket launchers, or at least something like Jananin's crossbow to aim it properly and fire it hard enough.

As they continued, some more helicopters came, and some fighter jets. The bombs seemed to work even if you forgot to light the fuses on the dynamite or pull the rings out of the grenades.

Finally they reached the centre of the minefield. The pale, blocky concrete buildings of the base lay within a tall mesh fence on concrete posts, topped with barbed wire, and a closed gate.

"What do we do now?"

"Call them out, Epsilon! Like the cowards they are!"

"Should we let the mules go first?" Eric suggested.

"It's just a game," Duncan retorted. "It's not like if they get hurt, it's real."

"I know, but." Eric looked rather sheepish in spite of his pirate outfit and the grenade he was holding. "If they panic and run off, they might set off the mines, and overturn the cart and set off all our ammo when we need it, so even if it doesn't kill us, we have to go back and start again."

They decided it probably was best on balance to uncouple the mules, so they did so and let them wander off, hoping they wouldn't set off any mines.

Dana sat on her horse and tried to project her voice like an important person, while at the same time doing the best imitation of Isaiah Redwood's accent she could manage, mixed in with what she could remember of how cowboys speak in Westerns. "I am the Sheriff, and I represent the People's Militia of Nevada, and we have come to challenge you, the Feds, for building your base on our land, and for not asking for no permission before you done it neither! And for murdering that poor guy, who was a local character, just because he forgot to take his medicine! And y'all are yeller for hidin' in yer base and not coming out and engaging us in a fair fight!"

Soldiers began to emerge from inside the base, in pairs. They ran for the gate, carrying their rifles ready for engagement.

"We need guns to fight them with!" Dana looked into the cart, seeing only bombs and no guns, and then to Cale.

"I want an SA80!"

"I want a Kalashnikov and an Uzi, and a headband like Rambo!"

Cale didn't know what these things were, but Dana could still connect to the Internet through Isaiah's wLAN, and she used search engines to find out what they looked like, and the requested items or something similar enough appeared in the cart for Eric and Duncan to arm themselves with. The pair of them set to, weaving their horses between mines and shooting back at the soldiers that spilled from the gates of the base, while Dana concentrated on throwing explosives at the soldiers and the aircraft that kept appearing.

All the soldiers were copies of the same model of a man in army fatigues armed with a rifle, but with number generated randomly for each one that specified him a skin tone ranging from palest pink to darkest brown. Dana wondered if, in the real army, that was why people all wore a uniform and had the same haircut, to make it easier for them to get on with it when they had to have a real war, and actually *kill* people, if they all looked like nondescript copies instead of individual people with personalities and mothers and fathers. When the soldiers died, they just fell motionless, or their bodies disappeared in an explosion and their clothes turned to torn rags flying in the air.

Duncan's poor horse was shot from under him, and he had to hide behind it and shoot over. Eric rode his horse into the soldiers, firing his Uzi and his Kalashnikov, bullet casings spraying in his wake. The horse reared and kicked, bringing down some of the men, but then it too fell. Dana threw a grenade at the soldiers as they came to take him, and even though it exploded right on top of him and killed all the enemies, he was completely unharmed, because games rarely take into account friendly fire.

The men had stopped coming; the gates had fallen. The only horse left was Dana's palomino, the mules had fled from the battle, and the only explosive left in the cart was the wooden crate stencilled with *TNT*.

"We must have to use this inside the base, to destroy it for good!" Dana realised.

Eric and Duncan picked up the case between them, and carried it behind Dana as she rode to the central concrete building and the gaping doorway in its blank face that led down to the bunker below. As she dismounted, she realised the bunker was a hexagon shape. She led the way in, to concrete stairs that led down, twisting and turning, lit by bulbs in wire cages on the walls. It reminded her a bit of the military base on Roareim, but as she passed through the doorway at the bottom of the stairs and into a corridor that turned, in a familiar way, around the perimeter of the hexagon, she was reminded instead of the Faraday bunker beneath the Amethyst Building. As the three of then navigated the way around the outer corridor to reach the inner bunker, Dana became aware of a signal, a broadcast of the most intolerable terror and dread...

They reached the end of the corridor, and the entrance. A metal door with ventilation slats in the top of it, just like the ones on Roareim, and all bashed about like the ones on Roareim, after Peter had thrown countless wobblies, and the one Jananin had lost her temper with and kicked into the wall because Ivor had hidden the key.

Dana opened the door.

It cowered against the far wall in terror, the two-headed hound, its body shaking in fear, heads lowered, saliva running from its lips. Ivor's watch was still fastened around one of its necks.

The watch made her remember the last time she'd encountered Cerberus itself in the game, the time before Cerberus had told the police she was dead, and had tried to frame Ivor and Jananin for murdering her. The time before Cerberus had inexplicably decided it needed to eliminate both her and them. It all came to her in a rush of comprehension, and suddenly she understood why the Cerberus beneath London had been afraid, and why this one was afraid.

When she had come into Cerberus's world, and confronted it there, it was after she had argued with Ivor, and he'd told her the truth. She had been filled with despair from knowing it. She had been filled with fear that Jananin would kill him, and she had sat there in front of it, with her morbid thoughts and her misery, and she had fought with Cerberus and put that watch around one of its necks, and her fear and her despair had rubbed off her and become a part of the game, had got into Cerberus, in the same way Cerberus had pulled Roareim and the fish-hand records from her subconscious and she'd brought the real smells and sight of the Nevada desert into the game.

From behind her, she made out Eric and Duncan's voices over Cerberus's fear. *What is it? That's mint*, and *Why has it only got two heads now?*

Cerberus began to growl. The hair on its shoulders

bristled. It went for Dana, and for an instant, things were a confusion, its huge body on top of her as she lay on the floor, and Eric and Duncan shouting in panic behind her. Then she felt its mouth on her forearm, a horrible wet heat in the middle of the piercing pressure of teeth, and her own pain bled back into Cerberus.

Cerberus recoiled from her. It *screamed*.

Dana sat up on the floor. She remembered the last time she'd got hurt, when Alpha had attacked her. She remembered Alpha, lying dead with the paramedics struggling valiantly to bring her back from where she could never return, after the accident with the Compton bomb, Ivor on the steps, broken, despairing, her own shock, the anger she had felt at Cerberus for causing this. She remembered the time before that, Abigail, cornered, fight because flight was not an option. The anger when Abigail humiliated her, how she hated Abigail with all the hate she had in her, how she'd wished Abigail and her family dead.

And Cerberus felt her wrath, and having felt her pain, cornered in the bunker and unable to escape, Cerberus attacked the one thing it had left to attack: itself.

Its heads turned upon each other with a great roaring of noise that filled that little room of unyielding concrete walls. It fell upon the floor in a writhing mass of legs and teeth, and Dana got up in a hurry to avoid being entangled in it. "Quickly! The bomb!"

Eric and Duncan set the crate down on the floor. There didn't seem to be any timer or other mechanism for triggering it. They'd have to hope it would just go off by itself when the time was right, like the other bombs had. They ran, up the stairs, back outside, for the gates and back out.

A tremendous noise split the sky and threw Dana headlong. She fell flat on her face, pressing her hands against the ground and raising her head to look over her shoulder to see a great mushroom cloud of fire and smoke erupting from the base behind. She turned her head back and put her hands over the back of her head when it was followed by a rain of grit and gravel.

When the sound of falling debris died away, she rolled over and sat up. The base was burning, thick black smoke pouring from every entrance. On the ground nearby, Eric, Duncan, and Cale looked back at her.

Out of the burning ruins, something charged; a dun four-legged shape, fleeing and screaming like the police dog in London who had got tangled up and panicked. As it rushed around the conflagration to run away towards the mountains, Dana recognised it as an ordinary hound, with just one head. She pointed to it. "Stop it! It's escaping!"

She could not match its speed in the form she had, so she copied the code of one of the pumas in the desert, and melded her own manifestation into it. She gave chase, the puma's thick coat protecting her from the sparse undergrowth, its big padded feet swift over the harsh stones and dry soil, aware she was a cat in pursuit of a dog, in a world where nothing was what it seemed and everything was twisted from its true reality.

She chased it not in anger any more. She no longer wanted to destroy it. She felt sorry for it now, knowing all that time it had been suffering. "Come back!" she tried to shout after it. It came out as a growling, yowling, puma sound, but she knew Cerberus would understand, if only it would stop and listen to her. She'd never intended this to happen. She didn't know if she could, but she wanted to try to help what was left of Cerberus, to take back the harm she'd done it. But Dana knew full well it fled in fear, and hate, and pain, and that those were the only emotions it could feel, because they were all she had given it, and nothing would turn it from its course.

High in the sky above, Cale kept pace with her, though Eric and Duncan were long lost, left far behind her in the endless landscape, and Cerberus continued to flee for the distant mauve-hued mountains that never grew any closer.

Cerberus couldn't escape the game, the environment

of its own creation, and slowly but surely Dana was gaining on it. She concentrated on the flowing motion of running as a four-legged creature, the movement smooth and efficient through the puma's taut spine, but as she was almost upon the hound, it evaporated into tiny fragments and dissipated like smoke on the wind.

She pulled up sharp to a halt, catching sight of a few remaining particles, tiny hexadecimal letters that had made up Cerberus's in-game manifestation drifting past the puma's ears. Cale descended from the sky to land beside her, and as the puma and the crow looked upon each other, the land and sky itself began to disintegrate, the mountains and clouds and creosote bushes and Joshua trees decaying into base code. Dana had time only to think to Cale that she was sorry she didn't know when they'd be able to meet again, before the game became so unstable she could no longer hold together her presence in it, and she was back in Isaiah Redwood's basement.

Ivor was standing at the bottom of the stairs. "Dana! Something's happened a few minutes ago. I didn't want to interrupt what you were doing as you seemed okay."

Dana wordlessly followed him upstairs, forgetting to put her hat on. Outside, the sky was very blue between the clouds, and the desert seemed so much more beautiful with GPS to show her where she was and how far it stretched around her. On the patio, Jananin and Isaiah were standing, both with their binoculars. In the distance, where the base had been, a thick column of black smoke was rising into the atmosphere.

"It just blew up, a few minutes ago," Isaiah said. Jananin handed Dana her binoculars, and she looked. The entire site looked to have been blown up with very powerful explosives. Only the central building still stood, every window and gap guttering with flame beneath the thick outpouring of smoke.

"It started fighting with itself!" Dana exclaimed. "When I last saw it, it only had one head left, and it ran away."

"So the third one is still out there?" Jananin demanded.

Dana shook her head. Suddenly, everything was right. She knew where she was, she knew exactly what time it was, and it was all wonderfully free. "It disappeared. The game broke down. I think it was unplugged. Can I go in the swimming pool, and can we have ice-cream?"

Ivor seemed happy about this, but Jananin was more cynical. "Until someone plugs it back in."

Ivor said, "If you go in the swimming pool in the daytime, you need to use SPF cream. The sun might not feel hot this time of year, but it can still burn you."

"Well, you don't," said Dana impudently. "Your back's gone all red and peely."

Ivor got down on one knee so he was looking her in the face. "Yes, that's because I'm an idiot and I didn't use the SPF cream, and now whenever I put on a shirt it feels like it's made of sandpaper, and I struggle to sleep at night because of the pain of it, and I don't want you to have to go through the same thing."

A commotion interrupted them. A car in official livery had pulled up outside the villa, and it was the sheriff, who was making rounds to reassure people about the explosion and try to find out at the same time if anyone had any information he didn't on it. As Dana listened to the sheriff speaking to Isaiah, it became apparent that the sheriff had been in contact with someone in the federal government, who had given the explanation that it had been some sort of accident involving a munitions dump in a bunker on the site, and that the sheriff had a lot to say about that, and had demanded reassurances that the federal government wouldn't be building anything of that sort out here in future without proper consultation.

The sheriff smiled at them where they stood behind Isaiah occasionally as he spoke, and Ivor started to become strangely agitated, and suddenly he picked Dana up and whirled her around, whispering loudly to her, "It's gone!"

And then something very silly came into his face, and he carried Dana back outside, and jumped in the swimming pool with her with both of them still in their clothes, making Dana scream.

When the sheriff had left, Isaiah and Jananin came out too, both looking very satisfied. Dana went to a bathroom and got changed into her swimming costume, and she did go swimming, and didn't use SPF cream because the sun had become obscured by great towering clouds filling up the desert sky, which she could see without having to lean back as she didn't have to wear a hat. And they had ice-cream, and Isaiah made cocktails of the sort he said they have in Las Vegas, and even Jananin drank one.

Dana fell asleep on a sun lounger under a towel after drinking some of Ivor's, and she dreamed, but her dreams were pleasant, and when she woke, she knew where she was immediately and wasn't confused. Evening had crept in, and all around her was the gentle rustle of rain falling on the desert and the parasol over the sun lounger, and the scent of it was intense and wonderful.

-16-

AFTER the euphoria that had followed the destruction of the base and the Cerberus unit within it had worn off, and it had become normal once more to not have to wear a hat and to be able to sense GPS and signals, things started to become uneasy once again. Jananin was adamant the job was not over, and the final Cerberus computer needed to be located and destroyed, because if it had been disconnected or switched off, the chances were that sooner or later whoever had it was going to plug it back in, and in the meantime that person had as long as was required to find out what needed to be done to protect it, which potentially meant finding and eliminating all of them.

Ivor, meanwhile, was of the opinion that while this might be true, there was nothing else that could be done about it at the moment. He wanted to go back to England and try to find Peter.

Dana, on the other hand, had enjoyed a carefree few days before she began to worry about something else. Cerberus, it seemed to her now, had only become dangerous in the first place because Dana had gone into its world and taught it how to feel fear and despair, and she had ultimately defeated it again by exposing it to wrath. If someone had indeed disconnected the remaining Cerberus unit, and it was still out there, cut off from all connections like she'd been when she'd had to wear a hat, unable to understand what was going on around it, and able to feel only pain, and anger, and sadness, and fear, she was responsible for that, and she felt sorry for it.

She tried explaining and talking about this to Ivor and Jananin. Ivor was of the opinion that Cerberus was too dangerous, what the governments in the UK and USA had been using it for was wrong, and that it was right to remove it in any way possible, and the most important thing was protecting human life. If a computer had developed the ability to suffer, it still wasn't equal to a living, suffering person.

Jananin thought that if it was anybody's fault Cerberus might be suffering, it was Steve Gideon's for designing it that way. When Dana said that he probably hadn't meant it to be used that way, and that Dana had poisoned it by releasing her own emotions into its consciousness, like Pandora into the world in the myth, Jananin said that she did not mean what she had said about Pandora, and that it had been something said in anger that was more to do with herself and Ivor than it was to do with Dana, and that she shouldn't dwell on it.

Speaking of Steve Gideon, Ivor had sent several replies to his email asking him to clarify it or give him some more information, but he or whoever had access to his emails had not replied.

Dana sent messages to Duncan and Eric. They scoured the Internet and asked questions on online fora. The game server remained down. Nobody knew what had happened to Cerberus's game, or indeed whence it had come in the first place. Nobody was able to trace it back to any game developer.

Jananin decided to go away alone for a while, to meet some of her contacts and look for clues as to where the remaining Cerberus might be. They were now well into summer, and it was unpleasantly hot in Nevada, and Isaiah said while it had been nice to have them, it would also be nice if they would go away now, as the Nevada police were busy clearing up the minefield and all the debris from the site, and he hoped once that was done, his wife and son would come home.

So Ivor and Dana went on a road trip to the states north of Nevada for around a month. They went up through Oregon and Washington by the coastal route with Dana navigating for him all the way, driving through quiet roads surrounded by forest and stopping at lovely, lonely beaches. Even though Ivor had complained on Roareim about being tired of lobsters and mussels and that sort of food, they ate a lot of them in quiet restaurants, and now he wasn't there any more, he said he enjoyed it here because the coast, the mountainous, dramatic scenery, and the food all reminded him of the Hebrides.

Some places they stopped at for a few days to explore more. One of them was Puget Sound, a place of dark, brooding pine forests, quiet and cool even in the midday sun, that went up to the edge of the land and dropped their cones all over the beach. At a jetty near a small town, Ivor and Dana found a couple of women who gave tours of the local coast around the San Juan Islands in their boat, so tourists could try to see the orcas, which were a sort of large piebald dolphin.

They talked to the women for a bit, and one of them asked Dana if she and her dad were from England, and she said, as she had been told to say, and was quite used to saying by now, that they were Australian. The woman said Dana must have lots of experience of spiders and snakes, in that case, and Ivor diverted the conversation to a different subject, as Ivor was very good at having conversations with people in a way that prevented them from asking awkward questions of Dana when they did encounter people, which wasn't very often as on the trip they'd avoided cities and kept to quiet locations, which suited both of them.

"Are you available to give us a tour now?"

The women were delighted to give Ivor and Dana a tour on their boat. Once they had come on board, and set off into the Pacific, it became apparent that the women were both really passionate about the wildlife around Puget Sound, especially the orcas, and because of this, they didn't ask any more questions about Dana and Ivor and Australia. Dana sat beside Ivor and listened to the story they told about the history of the orcas, and it was very tragic.

In the 1960s, people who didn't know any better had come to Puget Sound and attacked the orcas in order to steal their young as exhibits for marine zoos, killing some of them in the process. What wasn't known at the time was that orcas stay in the same family group with their mothers their whole lives, and that while they're not more intelligent than people in terms of being able to do maths or write grammatical sentences, the parts of their brains that process emotions are more complex than those of humans. Socially, they are more advanced than people, and that meant they should never be kept in captivity because people couldn't even begin to understand, let alone provide for, their complex needs.

As the story was coming to an end, Ivor pointed to the port side of the boat, where the water looked a bit foamy, and what looked like a black shark fin had just slipped above the surface.

"Oh! Is that them?" Dana cried.

It *was* them, and they switched off the engine so as not to disturb them, and sat still and silent to watch. The only parts of them that came to the surface were the dorsal fins and the spurts of spray when they exhaled through the nostrils on the tops of their heads, and an occasional glimpse of a black muzzle with white spots above the eyes.

They were called the L Pod, and the two women were able to tell that because they had a calf with them. The calf was male and he was very precious, because ever since the tragedy all those years ago, the orcas had been declining, and had few calves. Some people thought it might be because of pollution, or global warming, but others speculated that in their grief, the orcas had simply stopped having children in the belief that the world was not a safe place for them.

Dana and Ivor didn't talk much in the car that evening. Dana felt sad for the orcas, but she was glad she had come here, and that she had seen them with him. For the first time, she forgot utterly about Cerberus for the rest of the day.

They left the coast and the Pacific behind after that, and went to Idaho, which was very scenic to see through the car windows with its fields and distant mountains, but not as interesting to stop off and have a meal, or go for a walk, as it had been on the coastal route. They weren't in it very long, as one place Ivor wanted to visit particularly in Montana on the other side of it was the *Wooly Mammoth Center*.

At the centre, or the *center* as Americans write it, there were twelve woolly mammoths, and you could pay to go in and look at them, and read some signs that explained how they had come into being. The signs tried a bit too hard to be cheerful and flippant and not enough at imparting detailed information, and the way Ivor explained it to Dana was better. They sat on a bench under a tree where they could see the mammoths while he did.

Mammoths went extinct after the last ice age, but the frozen remains of two mammoths had been found in permafrost in Siberia, and they were preserved well enough that their DNA was still readable. What scientists attempted to do first was to take the nucleus from a mammoth cell, where the DNA was, and use it to replace the nucleus of a fertilised elephant egg, which was then put back in the elephant in the hope she would have a mammoth calf. However, this didn't work. The elephant mother's body seemed to recognise that it wasn't another elephant, and rejected it. What they then tried instead was to use the same technique Ivor used to fertilise ova using genetic material derived from a cell instead of actual sperm, and fertilised an elephant ovum with half the DNA of a female mammoth.

This did work, and the elephant gave birth to a female calf that was half elephant and half mammoth. She had medical problems because of something called outbreeding depression, which often happens when two animals of different species or who have very different adaptations manage to breed. Elephants have large ears and not much body hair to help them keep cool where they live in Africa. Mammoths have small ears and lots of hair to help them keep warm on the tundra. The 'mammophant' was neither one thing nor the other, and was too hot in the sun and too cold at night.

What they did after that, once she was mature, was to use the DNA of the other frozen mammoth to fertilise the mammophant's egg, so she had a calf who was ¾ mammoth and only ¼ elephant, which was still quite a lot, genetically speaking, for how it impacts outbreeding depression. The original mammophant after a few years died before they could try again.

Here the project ran into even more problems. Only two mammoth carcasses had been found in good enough condition to have usable DNA, and both of them were female. It was, Ivor explained, possible with modern technology for a female to be a father, but the father had to be a male in order to have a chance of a male offspring, because a female could only give her X chromosomes to her children. All of the mammoth-elephant creatures were therefore female. And because there was no other source of mammoth DNA, the only thing they could do was reuse the genetic material on the ova of the ¾ mammoth, meaning her offspring were inbred as one of them was her parent and the other her grandparent. This having continued for a few generations, most of the mammoths in the center were by now less than an eighth elephant.

Dana watched the mammoths ambling around their enclosure, using their trunks to pluck hay out of a large container and push it into their mouths. "So, the mammoths can only breed if humans help them, because there aren't any males?"

"Correct." Ivor leaned back on the bench in the dappled shade offered by the tree. "And although there's twelve of them, genetically speaking, they're the equivalent of only two mammoths and a quarter of an elephant. Unless someone finds a lot more frozen mammoths before Siberia thaws out, they're doomed to spin in the extinction vortex, because that's not a viable gene pool. And there's another thing." He turned his head to her, holding up his hand to cover his mouth, as though he didn't want the mammoths to overhear what he was about to tell her. "There's more than just DNA involved in making a mammoth. Mammoths are matriarchal, just like the orcas back at Puget Sound. They don't know they're mammoths; they don't know how to *be* mammoths. Psychologically, they're just elephants, because they've only ever experienced elephant habits and elephant culture, and elephant mothering techniques." He took his hand away from his mouth and tapped his temple with his index finger.

Dana frowned at the mammoths. "What's the point of them, then?"

Ivor laughed. "That's a very good question, that should probably be asked of a lot of research that gets funded. On one hand, it's very interesting science of the sort that it's good to know is possible. On the other hand, there's another, less glamorous way to prove the same science. Elephants, living, extant elephant species, are endangered and suffering from loss of genetic diversity. And we have genetic material from elephants that has been lost, lying about preserved in ivory used to make things from the time when elephants were far more numerous and people went about shooting them, and it's not so old we can't get viable DNA from it. But if someone were to extract DNA from an old piano or some antique silver teapot with a bit of ivory on the handle, and make an elephant pregnant with it, and produce a calf that brings back some of what was lost because of some empire-builder took a gun to Africa 200 years ago, nobody would pay twenty dollars to come and look at it!"

Dana realised he was right. She felt sad for the

mammoths, just as much as she had for the orcas. Although the orcas' history was filled with great sorrows, and their future was uncertain, the mammoths knew no past and had no future at all. They seemed quite content, though. They had each other, and they had a nice place to live, and they didn't seem to mind all the people coming to look at them.

On the way back to Nevada, they drove once again through Idaho. They were going to meet Jananin here, at a waterfall place called Niagara Springs, which was a national park, which meant something like a very large nature reserve.

To get to Niagara Springs, they had to drive down a steep road into a canyon, which was the cause of Ivor uttering more than a few choice phrases in Gaelic. The road led them on beside a river, the Snake River, according to GPS. The banks of the river were verdant, but it became scrubby and brown farther out, and borders of it on both sides were dry and stony, rising up into reddish rock cliff walls. They passed a large complex of buildings with a sign indicating it was a fish hatchery, and then on the other side, where the canyon wall sloped into a bank, water seemed to be bursting out of a whole area of the ground and running down the wall in great frothy rivulets, so white with foam it almost looked like milk.

There was a place to park nearby, and so Dana and Ivor set out on a short trail on a little path through the undergrowth. Ivor said it was an aquifer, which meant a place where underground water comes to the surface. At the end of the path there was a platform with a rail to stand and look at it and the water from it that passed underneath on its way to the Snake River. When Dana looked closely at the torrent of water, underneath the foaming white it was almost blue. When she commented on this, Ivor said it was because the water had more oxygen dissolved in it than usual water did.

Jananin wasn't at the aquifer, so instead they went to

the fish farm, and saw the tanks of fry, which were called steelhead trout, and a lady gave them a tour and explained how the fish were raised and cared for in the warm, oxygen-rich water that helped them to grow, and then they were released into the wild. Which was interesting, and nice, but a bit unfortunate that they couldn't buy a fish and take it home to have for dinner.

After this they had some lunch, and then they went to the nature reserve to see the Snake River and to try to find Jananin. There were more people here, and Dana hoped she'd be able to recognise her if she did see her. It wasn't always easy, even if it was someone she knew well in a strange place, especially if someone wore different clothes, or changed their hairstyle.

Pauline had once had her hair cut differently, and had come home and asked Dana what she thought of it. Dana had replied, truthfully, that she didn't like it. When Pauline had asked why, and Dana had said because it made her look not like Pauline, Pauline had said she understood why Dana had said that, but that it perhaps wasn't the right thing to say when someone asked that sort of question. Dana had retorted that, in that case, it had probably not been the right question to ask.

Eventually Ivor pointed her out, on the path beside the river. She had her cowboy hat on and her dark glasses, but she had on jeans and an American jacket instead of her trench coat.

They went to meet her, and Dana told her about the trout fry in the tanks.

Ivor asked her if she had found any leads, and it turned out she hadn't. They walked a bit along the river, and saw some pelicans with huge pink bills swimming.

Ivor was shaking his head. "It's quite possible it's offline for good. I mean, how long's it been?"

"Nothing can be assumed," Jananin said. "If it does come back online, it can be guaranteed it will only happen at a time when whoever switched it off is confident there is a solution to prevent us from breaking it, as we did the other two."

"We can't just wait forever. If it happens, we'll have to deal with it when it happens. In the meantime, we need to look at our other priorities. Like what to do about Peter."

Jananin sighed. "We've already discussed this. He's probably better off where he is. He's without doubt safer if it does come back online and it finds where you are."

"We can't just leave him! He'll think I've abandoned him!"

Jananin frowned. She shook her head slightly, shifting her stride to look at him. "He is being cared for. Why is it so important?"

Ivor suddenly snapped, very loudly and angrily, in a way that made some people on the other side of the river stop their conversation and look at them, *"Because he's mine! He's my boy!"*

Jananin glanced briefly at Dana, her expression uncomprehending. She turned back to Ivor. *"What?"*

"You..." Ivor stopped walking. "...hadn't worked that part out?"

Suddenly Jananin was up close against Dana, scrutinising her face, her glare fierce, perhaps noticing something she had not before seen in the shape of her eyes, the texture of her hair, the freckles across her nose which the American sun had made worse, despite wearing a hat and using SPF cream like she was supposed to. When she looked back to where Ivor had been, he was some distance away, moving at something between a run and a trot towards a group of large, smooth boulders. She went after him with a noise of exasperation.

"Blake, before you lose your temper!" Ivor's voice was panicked, and he sat, or possibly fell, down suddenly on the ground, perhaps in fear that she might try one of her judo throws on him. "Before you push me in the river, or shove a cactus where the sun don't shine, have you ever thought about *talking about it* instead?"

"I have not lost my temper." Jananin frowned. "In fact, it perhaps explains a few things that did not make sense. What I cannot understand is why you did it. It is stupid and weird. If you wanted to have children, why didn't you just do it with your wife?"

"How long have you got?" Ivor said. When she didn't reply, he shifted his position and leaned up against one of the rocks. "Okay. Sit down and talk to me for a bit."

"I've told you before, Pilgrennon, you're not psychoanalysing me. It's pseudoscientific rubbish."

"Not for you. For me. Blake, who were your parents?"

Jananin's face contorted with disgust. *That is none of your business.*

"Okay, let me guess. Your father was a man of science. Come on, Blake, just humour me with this."

Jananin scowled. She looked away, and then she looked back and spoke. "He was an engineer officer in the RAF, ultimately achieving the rank of Air Marshal, before his death from cardiac arrest in his late fifties, while I was doing my PhD."

"Thank you." Ivor paused for a moment. "When your dad, Air Marshal Blake, or whatever rank he was at the time, found out he had a daughter, he would have had various expectations about that. My guess, a little spitfire who would kick sexist stereotypes in the balls. His expectations were met."

Ivor and Jananin stared at each other for a moment. Dana sat down beside him.

"You see, Jananin, you can tell a lot from a person about how they were brought up. I'm not surprised to find out he was a military man; I can see that discipline in you. I can also see you have that absolute confidence and tenacity from having someone behind you who loved you unconditionally, who always had your back, stuck up for you and made sure you had a time in your life when you didn't doubt yourself despite what anyone else did or said to you. You've never had your spirit broken in that utterly devastating way only a parent has the power to do. That's why you've hit the ceiling before you're forty in a career that usually takes good interpersonal skills and not just knowledge and skill to be even moderately successful in. I'm guessing that was him."

Jananin sat on a rock. She didn't look at Ivor. For a while, Dana wasn't sure if she was trying to come up with a suitable insult, or simply ignoring him. "I was born in the UK," she said at last. "We were always being moved from place to place with my father's work. My mother was the editor of a scientific journal; she could do her job anywhere. When I started school, we were living in Tokyo. I liked the Japanese school. It was ordered. Academic achievement was valued, and they promoted patriotism while having respect for other cultures. They were very harsh on anyone who insulted another pupil.

"When I was seven, we moved back to England. The school there I did not like. It was chaotic, disorganised. My accent was not of those parts. One day, I went to the lavatory, and another girl followed me in there, shouting insults at me about my parents and the Japanese, stood outside the toilet door yelling and beating it, and pressed up against my back denigrating my mother and father in my ear while I was washing my hands. I ignored her, but she just shouted louder and louder.

"There was this drinking fountain inside the girls' loo. Rather a strange place to have one, not very salubrious. I filled my mouth from it while she just stood there behind me running her mouth, and I turned and *spat it* full in her idiotic pop-eyed face to wash the smirk off it."

Ivor put his hand up to his mouth to hide his amusement at this.

"The teacher told me it was wrong of me to do that, that it was only words, told me I must apologise, but I refused. My father was called. He left his work. He came into the headmaster's office where I was sitting. He was told what I had done. He asked me why I had done it. When I told him, he laughed in their faces. He said water from my mouth was far cleaner that any word that came from the filthy mouth of a dishonourable xenophobic bully, and that the girl deserved what she got. Then he said, before they could expel me for refusing to apologise, he was withdrawing me from the school, and would pay for a tutor to educate me properly, and the only reason he and my mother had even considered this piss-pool state primary was because they thought it was important that I should socialise, and that if this was the sort of socialisation on offer, there was no point in it at all."

Jananin paused for a moment, a distant look in her eyes. "I was never particularly close with my mother, though. When I was older, and started taking an interest in science, she was supportive, and I'm still on friendly terms with her. I was the only one and I assumed it happened by accident."

"Papa Wolf or Mama Bear," Ivor said. "You only need one of them. In fact, I suspect having both is probably a way to raise a bit of a megalomaniac. I know the type of father he was. Because my grandfather was a very similar sort of man."

Ivor stretched his legs out, crossing one ankle over the other. "Professor of Astrophysics, Oxford University. He loved brilliant women. As an undergraduate, he met one of the few women doing science in his day, and he married her. They never had children; they were enough for each other. But she worked with radioactive isotopes in a time when the health risks of that weren't fully understood, and she died of cancer in her forties. In his grief, some say in a moment of madness, he married a woman he met working in a roadside café when he stopped off on the way back from a conference. When she had a daughter, no doubt his expectations were an intelligent, serious girl, perhaps not one who would kick sex stereotypes in the balls so much as outmanoeuvre them in an argument, but that daughter was my mother, and she is a sex stereotype. Then they had my aunt, and she more or less met his expectations. She became the golden child. My mother was the scapegoat."

"I don't know why you are telling me this," Jananin said. "I don't see why Dana should have to listen to you blather on about your family either."

"I want to know what it's like for people who have families," Dana contended. "After all, I never had one."

Ivor held up his hand in a mollifying way. "It'll all make sense, at the end. My mother, not academically bright, emotionally abused by my father, left home as soon as she was able, got married at eighteen, pregnant soon after. That was Lydia. My mother had her own expectations about what Lydia was supposed to be, a girly girl, a social butterfly, the sort of child she herself had been, and Lydia didn't meet them. It wasn't as bad for me; I was a boy. If she had expectations about me, they weren't very specific. The only way she saw to heal herself was to have and love that same daughter her own father couldn't bring himself to love: herself. When Lydia was very image of the child her father wanted my mother to be, that could only end in disaster. All that unhealed trauma that my grandfather caused, my mother revisited on Lydia.

"My mother probably believed she loved Lydia. But what she loved was a psychological construct in her head; what she thought Lydia should be; the daughter she wanted; the daughter who, if she'd loved my mother better, if she'd been punished enough and forced to try harder, she could make her into, like clay forced into a mould. After Lydia died, there were no pictures of her anywhere in the house, save for one, that stood on my mother's dressing table. It was of Lydia at a wedding of my mother's friend. My mother had forced her to go as a bride's maid, even though she didn't want to. This serious, solemn, shy girl who rarely spoke, never wanted to draw attention, dressed up in a ridiculous costume, all caked in face paint like a clown. She had this horrible wig on. She didn't like having long hair, and at the dress shop just before the wedding, she got hold of a pair of scissors and chopped it off. You couldn't see it on the picture because of all the make-up on her, but there was a bruise all across one side of her face, from where Mum walloped her over the head.

"My father, he was around. He went to work, he went to the pub, he came home and watched TV. But emotionally, he was never there. He saw me and Lydia as just a hobby of our mother's. He once took us to a football match, and we didn't misbehave there, but we weren't interested in it, so he never did anything with us again. When Lydia died, he was upset, but it passed quickly, and I think it was more of a relief, like when an old pet that's senile and incontinent dies."

Dana thought of Pauline and Graeme and Duncan. She thought of Beatrix, the foster carer who had hit children. She had never hit Dana or Cale. Dana had been hit by other children, usually at school. It was bad, but what was worse was being afraid of someone you knew would hit you every time if they had the opportunity. It was probably better just to be hit quickly and have it over and done with, than have to wear horrible clothes, like a dress or a skirt with no pockets and not be allowed leggings underneath, or to have to pretend to be someone you're not all day.

"Are you asking me to feel sorry for you?" Jananin's face was full of scorn. "You wrote in your own thesis that autistic people are unable to empathise with others."

"Actually, I didn't say that. If you'd read it properly again before you had the ethics committee dispose of it, you'd have seen I was *debunking* that. I said autistic people are capable of empathy, but they often struggle to understand the mindset that neurotypical people have because their experiences of the world and their priorities are so different. Both neurotypical and autistic people are capable of empathy, but their differences can cause both of them to have trouble understanding the other. That's what causes neurotypical specialists to incorrectly assume their autistic patients aren't capable of empathy.

"So, when you ask," Ivor continued, "why I didn't just have children with my wife, there's a whole lot of baggage causing an obstruction to that solution."

"The point you are trying to make, *I think*," Jananin said, "is that you saw yourself as the product of a cycle of abuse, whereby your sister was abused because your mother was abused, and you wanted to break the cycle. Surely in that case the obvious solution is to not have children at all, and to have yourself sterilised?"

Ivor folded his arms behind his head, leaning back on a rock. "Yeah Blake. That's an obvious solution, a logical one. Problem is, I'm flesh and blood, and I'm irrational. I'm not a machine, I'm just a man. I wanted a child, but I didn't want a girly girl. Or a boyey boy. Or any one of the variants that you tend to get in the common or garden neurotypical child. I wanted a daughter like Dana, or a son like Peter. I was devastated when Adrienne left and that opportunity was taken from me, but now when I think back on the time when I was with her, I was just racked with doubt. Had I made the same mistake as my mother, making a commitment to someone when I was far too young? What if Adrienne got pregnant, and the child's personality was the image of my own mother's, and spite and loyalty to Lydia meant I couldn't love her?"

"It's all very nice of you to tell me how your awful family scarred you and caused your sister's suicide, Pilgrennon, but none of this excuses what you did. You as an adult are responsible for your own actions and their consequences."

Ivor raised both hands with a vigorous motion. "I'm not asking to be excused. Jananin, the only thing I can give you is an apology. I'm sorry. I can't undo it. What I am trying to do is get straight in my own head what I did and why I did it. To be quite honest, I've only really started to analyse it myself since I explained it to Dana."

"What you did?" Jananin laughed. "What you did was commit crimes, like any other criminal."

"Well, that's not quite right, because people don't just

wake up one morning and go out and commit a serious crime. A criminal psychologist will tell you that. People don't suddenly become serial killers. They start out by committing what are called entry-level offences, and when they get away with it, they start committing worse ones, and they build up like that. That was how I started. Splicing what I suspected to be genes involved with autism into a cell containing my own DNA. Just a project to satisfy my own curiosity. And it was my genome I was fiddling about with. I wasn't hurting anyone else." He shrugged.

"That was where I was when Adrienne left me. In a moment of stupidity, I went to the red light district, and I picked her up. Jade Cooper." Ivor gave Dana an apologetic glance. "I took her home, I got talking to her. I ended up sympathising with her, and *well*, not doing what I'd brought her there for, but paying her for it anyway. We became friends. We talked about my work. She wanted out of that life, away from that pimp she was with, off the drugs. She wanted to do something to repay me. It was only then I started thinking about surrogacy. She agreed to it as soon as I suggested it. Perhaps all that time selling her own body, it didn't seem odd to her to lease it out for a different biological function. All my knowledge suggested that in making a child from that cell I'd gene edited, we'd get a healthy boy, of normal intelligence, who'd look like me, with autistic traits. At that point, there was consent from everyone involved. Partly it was to satisfy scientific curiosity and see if my theory about genetics was right. Another part of it was... well.

"That didn't work. Resulted in a stillbirth. I'd made a mistake, doubled up on a lethal recessive somewhere. Then, I met Peter's mother. I asked her, outright, if she'd sell me her ova, on the understanding I could use them to make a child. She didn't care, said she never wanted children, needed the money, if something useless to her was valuable to me, I could have it."

"It was still unethical of you to facilitate her behaving

like a cuckoo for money," Jananin interrupted.

Ivor shrugged. "Perhaps. That was the point, as I see it, I kind of went off the rails. You see, the way I figured it, if people don't find out about it, it's not going to hurt them. This fertility clinic I let space to, they were always short of sperm donors. They put adverts up, looking for intelligent men, saying it could be completely anonymous. I asked the brightest and the best of my male patients to give me a semen sample for a study, and I just put them in with their collection. They got what they wanted. I found out a few years later that Alpha had been conceived in that very fertility clinic. And, well, we know what happened with Alpha, but I was trying to help her. That was how I found out about your synapse. And *you*."

"I made it *very* clear to you, that I wanted nothing to do with your research."

Ivor nodded, looking tired. "And in my arrogance, I thought if you never found out, it couldn't hurt you. After all the other stuff I'd done and got away with at that point, it didn't seem such a big step to bribe the gynaecologist you let slip was scheduled to operate on you. It didn't seem such a big step, when Jade's friend who'd agreed to be another surrogate pulled out, and I had Gamma's embryo, to lie to a couple desperate to have their own child when the ship had well and truly sailed, and give her to them. I regretted that as soon as I'd done it, though, same as I regretted abandoning Dana and Cale. I wonder every day where Gamma is, if she's okay."

Jananin snorted. "This *is* eugenics, Pilgrennon. And it's entanglement of the professional with the personal of the worst sort."

Ivor sighed. He put his arms down and folded his hands across his chest. "If you hadn't worked *that* part out, there's perhaps something else about me you haven't worked out. The way I see it, the only thing I can do is tell you it as straight as I can say it, and you'll either believe me, or you won't."

"And that is?"

He looked at Jananin directly, and waited for her to look back at him before he spoke again. "My research isn't my priority now. Incidentally, putting aside the fact that you've made it impossible for me to ever work in science again, it doesn't matter to me at all. Until you found Dana and came looking for me, I'd been invisible to you and the authorities, and the scientific community, for more than a decade, and that's because I've been called to a higher purpose. There is no work more important than being a parent, to those who have that call. Nothing else matters."

"It all sounds very wholesome," Jananin said, "and *completely* insincere."

Ivor shrugged. "Like I said. Believe me, or don't. But a scientist always re-evaluates his or her conclusions in the light of new evidence."

"Some evidence is overwhelming. Some science is established fact that no addition can overturn. Evolution. Gravity."

"Well, think about it. But if we're in limbo with finding this last Cerberus machine, and it's likely to remain that way, then if you could see some way to letting me have Peter back..."

Dana, unable to contain herself any longer, interrupted him. "Jananin, you could go back and get Peter! Pretend you were going to adopt him, or kidnap him, or something, and give him a new passport and a visa like you did with us, and he can come and live here, and we can stay in America and wait and see if Cerberus comes back. You could just go back to work if you don't want to stay here as well!"

Jananin was shaking her head. "It's not that simple. And if Cerberus does come back, Peter may be safer staying where he is."

"But they will put him with horrible carers, and he won't get a nice family because he's too old, and he's supposed to be with us!"

"Jananin, please, think about it. If we're still in this

position in another month... it could be that the last Cerberus just developed a fault and broke by itself, like expensive computers are always doing! Someone could have spilled coffee all over it!"

"Then if it is," Jananin bared her teeth, "perhaps that means I should consider my armistice with you to be at an end."

Ivor sighed. "Have you ever read any of the research into the psychology of revenge, and the people who achieve it?"

"No. Why should I? It's not my field, and it's probably no different to all the other pseudoscientific nonsense dreamt up by a man who blamed everyone else for his unhealthy fixation with sexual acts with his own mother."

"Okay, maybe you have a point about Freud. He was a prat. Jung talks a lot more sense. But never mind. The evidence overwhelmingly suggests that people who succeed in getting revenge find it unfulfilling."

"Give me the contact details of one such research group." Jananin got to her feet. "Once I am done with you, I will email with my findings, so they can add my data point to their analysis."

"What's more, it tends to result in revenge cycles." Ivor glanced pointedly at Dana. "You might cause someone else to want to seek to avenge *me*."

"In that case, give the contact details to her as well. I'm sure they'd appreciate two data points for the price of one." She shrugged her shoulders, adjusted her belt. "Now, where have you parked the car?"

-17-

BY the time they reached Eureka County, it was time for dinner. They didn't go back to Isaiah's house, because his family had moved back in with him, but knowing they were due to return, he'd asked the sheriff to find them somewhere to rent for a while in the town. The sheriff had sent Ivor a text message with the address and where he had put the key. When they recovered the key from the place he'd hidden it and went in, the sheriff had kindly left them a note and a bag of groceries.

The problem was that the kitchen turned out not to be very well equipped, and there weren't any proper knives for cutting up vegetables, only the cutlery sort for eating food with. Ivor tried to use first a steak knife, and then a butter knife, to cut up a potato, but neither of them were much use.

"Can I borrow your knife?" he asked Jananin.

"It's called a wakizashi, and no you can't, unless its intended use is seppuku." Jananin went upstairs, to see if her luggage she'd left at Isaiah's had been left there.

Dana complained that she was so hungry her stomach hurt and she felt all weak and wobbly. Ivor suggested that, if they washed a carrot, Dana could eat that and it would keep her going for now, and then they could walk to the shop, which wasn't very far, and buy a vegetable knife and probably something else to have for dinner that was already prepared and could just be bunged in the oven.

Dana ate her raw carrot as they walked down to the shop. She didn't want to eat the top of it with the stalk, so she put that in a flowerpot outside the door. The front of the shop looked like something that belonged in a Western film, and a bit tatty and weathered as well, but inside it just looked like any shop. Ivor found a vegetable knife and Dana chose some pizzas for them to have for dinner.

When they went to pay, the lady who served them smiled at Dana. "Are you the family from Australia?"

There weren't many people in Eureka County, the sheriff seemed to know everyone, and word seemed to have spread around that an Australian family had come to stay with Isaiah Redwood not long before the federal base blew up, and had been coming and going to the area. Dana wasn't exactly sure what the local people suspected or talked about, but they were always pleasant, and they all seemed happy that the base was gone, and perhaps saw the Australian family as a good omen even if they didn't suspect them of having involvement in it.

"That's us," Ivor said.

"And what's your name?"

"I'm Dana," said Dana, holding the paper bag with the pizzas in and forgetting she was supposed to say it was Delilah, because at the same time she noticed the lady was wearing a badge that said *Hi, my name is Dana.*

"Aw, that's my name, too." The lady tilted her head and spread her hand over her heart, and then she said to Ivor, "She's an absolute credit to you. And aren't all of them just lovely at this age, before they turn into teenagers?"

Ivor and the lady both laughed, and Ivor said, "We're making the best of all the time we have together here, before that fated day arrives!"

"You been travellin', seein' nice places?" The lady glanced from Dana to Ivor and back.

"We went to Puget Sound in Washington and saw orcas," Dana told her. "And then we saw mammoths in Montana. And we visited Niagara Springs and saw the trout on the way back to Nevada."

"That sounds lovely!" she enthused. "I do hope you enjoy the rest of your stay here. Here's your change." She handed Ivor some money.

Outside, as they walked home, Dana said to Ivor, "I've

never met anyone else called Dana. Although, I was called that after the policewoman in the station when I was found, so there must be other ones."

"I think it's more common in America than it is at home," Ivor said. "There was an American TV programme that was quite popular some time back, that had someone called Dana in it. It could be the policewoman you were called after was named from that."

"I've never met anyone called Ivor or Jananin before, either."

Ivor laughed. "If you went to Wales, you'd probably meet lots of men called Ivor. It's a popular name there. Jananin, that's a bit of an unusual one. If her father was deployed abroad often, it might be something from a different culture that her parents picked or made up, inspired by their experiences."

"It must be annoying for people who have one of those really ordinary names, like loads of people have."

"I know the sort you mean. When I was at university, there were about five people called Paul on the course. They just end up with everyone calling them by their last name, or by a nickname. The most absurd part of it is it's probably his mother who saddled him with that name in the first place, and yet when his mates come round and refer to him as Ginger or Smith, she gets all snotty about it and insist they call him John or whatever!"

"Ivor, you know we're supposed to be Australian?" Something had occurred to Dana, a question she'd once asked Jananin, which she hadn't been able to answer. "In Australia, is it tomorrow or yesterday?"

Ivor suddenly stopped walking. "*Tomorrow or yesterday?*" His eyes were wide, his hands spread in front of him, and he stood frozen in revelation. "The email from Steve Gideon!"

"Australia? Australia is the place between tomorrow and yesterday, where we have to go to meet him?"

"Dana, I don't think it's Australia, although that's

very much on the right track." He seemed very excited now. "As the world rotates, day and night progress from east to west, so there must be an arbitrary longitude line somewhere that everyone's agreed marks the beginning of a new day. Perhaps there is some small country that lies on this line. Can you look it up on the Internet?"

Dana shook her head. "I don't know how to look that up. I can only search for words. I don't know how to ask that in words. Perhaps if we had a map, we could look on that?"

They hurried back to the house. Ivor shoved the pizzas in the oven, and they began looking around for an atlas or a map. But it turned out the house, as a rental property, only had basic furniture, and didn't have any books or anything of that sort.

Dana suggested, "How about Isaiah's house? He had a globe in his dining room."

Jananin had now come downstairs, and had got the gist of them having discovered a lead of some sort. Because Dana was extremely hungry, Ivor took the pizzas out of the oven and put them on plates, and they took them with them and ate them in the car while Jananin drove. Ivor tried to explain what they'd realised, but he mostly did it with his mouth full and just annoyed her.

Isaiah had just had dinner with his family, and he and his wife did not seem amused when Dana pounded on the door and came bursting in. "Can we borrow that globe in your dining room, please?"

She went to the room, found the globe, picked it up. Ivor steadied it while she turned the ball to find Australia, in the southern hemisphere.

Somewhere in a room behind, she could hear Isaiah's wife, asking Jananin questions, probably trying to be polite, but Jananin seemed to have brought some of the pizza from the car into the kitchen to eat and only said something briefly in response. Probably Isaiah and his wife both thought it was a weird thing that British people did;

to cook a pizza and eat it in the car. Isaiah had come into the dining room, and he pointed to the globe, touching the point where Nevada was. "You are *here*."

Dana looked at Nevada, and the western coast of the USA, where she and Ivor had travelled by car. She looked at Australia again, and the great expanse of the Pacific Ocean that divided the two places. Roughly down the middle of it, a jagged line had been marked on the globe. Dana pointed at it. "Why isn't it straight, like the other lines?"

"That's the International Date Line," Isaiah said. "You're maybe thinking of the Nautical Date Line."

"Why's the nautical one straight and the international one not?" Ivor asked.

"Because, stoopid," said Isaiah, in the gruff tone he often used when talking to Ivor. "It has to fit around the land out there so time zones make sense."

Dana looked at the jagged line, the sort of line that is never seen in nature. "So there aren't any countries that are on the line?"

"Well, of course not. It would make no sense if there were. I mean, in that country, there'd be a line somewhere, and it wouldn't just be another time zone, it would be a whole other *date*. So if you stepped over the line one way, it'd be tomorrow, and if you stepped back the other way, it'd be yesterday. And if you just stood on that line, you could even argue you weren't in neither of them!"

Ivor and Dana looked at each other. They looked at Isaiah. "Exactly!" they said in unison.

"What's the closest land to the date line?" Ivor suggested.

Isaiah shrugged. "Could be Midway Atoll. Nothing there really, apart from an airstrip. Beautiful place with some great wildlife, though."

"What you say is wrong."

They all turned to the door at Jananin's voice.

"The International Date Line *was* in the Pacific Ocean, not intersecting any land. Until about fifteen years ago, when Japan built an artificial island on it."

Isaiah did not seem impressed by this contradiction. "Why the hell would they do *that*?"

"Not for any reason I can explain in particular, but if you have ever been to Japan, and spent time with the Japanese, and come to know their spirit of innovation and their sense of humour, it does not seem out of character."

Ivor handed the globe back to Isaiah, not looking away from Jananin. "Do you have any contacts in Japan who might know about it and how we can get there?"

Jananin folded her arms and leaned back on her heels. "I have one already in mind."

*

On the drive to Honolulu to meet Jananin's contact, they talked in the car about the other essential detail in Steve Gideon's email: what time was it when time stands still?

"I did think of that, a while ago," Jananin said. "I thought perhaps it was Daylight Saving Time in autumn, when the clocks go back and you get an extra hour. But they don't do that in every country, and when I did an Internet search on it, Japan is one of the countries that doesn't observe it."

Honolulu was on the west coast. Dana didn't like it as much as the more northerly parts of the west coast she'd driven around with Ivor. The hotel they stayed in was a tower block in a city. The view of the Pacific was beautiful, but the city was crowded and noisy, and the sun was very hot.

The morning after they'd arrived, Ivor switched on the television to find the American news channels filled with talk about the UK. The election results had come in: Colin Antrobus's Meritocratic Party had been elected to power.

The press were interviewing him outside the Houses of Parliament. "Colin Antrobus," the interviewer asked him. "Now you have won the election, will you start procedures to immediately withdraw from the European Union and the ECHR?"

"Yes!" Antrobus replied.

The interviewer paused, as though she had been expecting him to say rather more than that.

"And your pledge, to hold referenda on the monarchy and the House of Lords?"

"Yes, we plan to hold referenda on those matters at the first opportunity. Personally I think both of them are outdated, but that's for the people to decide! If the Electorate tells us they want a constitutional monarchy, we will work out a way to fit all the pomp and ceremony and silly costumes into the Meritocracy in some way."

"And what timescale do you intend for the transition?"

"The timescale for transition from the current system to full Meritocracy is set out on our website." Colin Antrobus at this point looked as though he perhaps wished he'd had more time to plan for this and put more detail on his website. "Currently, I have taken the title of the First Spokesman of the Meritocracy of Great Britain and Northern Ireland, in place of Prime Minister, and I have assembled a skeleton cabinet to serve in the transition."

Ivor said, "Well, it'll probably last a few weeks before he screws it up and he gets ousted, and we have to have another general election."

"He is not like any politician I have ever met," Jananin said. "Give him time. His intentions are good."

They had to switch the television off then, as Jananin's contact arrived. He had come on a private jet and caught a taxi to the hotel. He was shorter than Jananin and his very black hair was neatly wrapped in a queue at the back of his neck. He wore jeans, sunglasses, and a T-shirt that said *I heart NY*, but with his hairstyle it was a bit incongruous and he looked as though he was trying too hard to pass as a tourist.

When Jananin opened the door, the two of them bowed to each other very formally, and then the man said. "Hisashiburi! It is good to know you are coming to Japan once more!"

"It is good to have reason to come to Japan once more."
Jananin answered. "Dana, Ivor, this is Takahashi Yūtarō."

The man smiled at Dana, and then he bowed politely,
looking at the floor as he did. "It is good to meet you."
However, he didn't bow to Ivor, and instead said, very
genially and with a smile on his face, "And you are the
piece of shit who has caused all this trouble! I am told I
must not kill you though, at least not yet."

Ivor didn't say anything back to him. He sat on the bed
and seemed to do his best to be inconspicuous.

Takahashi turned back to Dana. "Let me tell you a
secret about Jananin Blake. Everything Blake knows about
iaido, I taught her." His voice became a dramatic whisper.
"And everything I know about poisons, she taught me."

Dana watched him, thinking he seemed friendly, but
unsure of what to say to him, as she had never met anyone
like him before. She'd remembered something else. "Is
being Japanese a bit like being Chinese?"

Takahashi grinned. He made a peculiar wiggling
movement through his posture. "Only in the same way as
being English is a bit like being French."

"If I try to draw some writing I once saw, would you
be able to tell me if it's written in Chinese, or something
else?"

Takahashi shrugged. "I can tell you if it is Chinese,
although I won't be able to read it."

Someone quickly found a pen and a pad for Dana to
draw on. It was difficult to remember how they looked, the
funny characters on that label in the gilet she'd got from
the desert puzzle in the game. She remembered first there
were four different characters. She tried to first draw the
basic shapes of them all, and began to add the other details
as best as she remembered them. Takahashi watched over
her shoulder.

"There are some mistakes, but I think I can see what
you are trying to write." He took the pen and made

corrections with a few deft strokes. "There."

浮遊都市

"Is it Chinese?" Dana asked.

"No, these are kanji you have drawn. Or tried to. It is a Japanese word. In fact it is the name of the place we are going: Fuyūtoshi. It means, the floating city."

PART THREE
浮遊都市

-18-

TAKAHASHI had arrived on a private jet, and since it was still at the airport, he had arranged that it would refuel and they would use the same plane to fly to Fuyūtoshi. The inside of the plane looked nothing like an airline plane of the sort Dana had seen on films and television, and had sofas and cushions and a bar in it. The pilots, both Japanese men wearing jackets with logos, loaded the luggage into the hold and spent a moment explaining that they had to sit in one of the chairs and wear a seatbelt during take-off and landing, and how to brace and how to evacuate in case an emergency arose and the plane crashed in the sea.

Dana hadn't travelled on an aeroplane before, but the takeoff seemed quite smooth, and although the floor never felt straight, she didn't feel sick on the flight.

Ivor and Dana settled on one sofa, while Jananin and Takahashi sat on the one facing it.

"Fuyūtoshi is a very beautiful city. It's at its most magical to visit in spring, when you will see the cherry and the wisteria flower," Takahashi said. "But we are coming up to autumn, so you'll be able to see the maples changing colour, which is probably more interesting than visiting in summer or winter."

"It's a city, as well as an island?" Dana asked.

"A small city. We walk everywhere in Fuyūtoshi. There are no roads. Which in some ways is a shame, as I can't ride my bike there."

"Are cyclists not allowed?"

"No. But I didn't mean a bicycle. I meant a real bike." Takahashi held his hands out in front of him, fists closed as though grasping handlebars. He rotated one of his hands vigorously and blew through loose lips, making a loud *vroom* noise. "I have to leave my bike in Tokyo. It is the best kind of bike: a Yamaha!"

Jananin laughed.

"Do you know who has loaned me this plane?" Takahashi smiled. "Sato Hiroshi, the mayor of Fuyūtoshi!"

"So it's a city and an island, and it has a mayor?" Dana asked.

"Fuyūtoshi is a very beautiful, wealthy city, full of good citizens, but not without its own problems. Its mayor has taken a very keen interest in the politics in your country. Mayor Sato is an intelligent man, and he knows something has been covered up in the UK and US. He also knows you have something to do with it, and he is very keen to meet you. He hopes he may be able to help with what you are looking for. He has asked me to give you this."

He handed Jananin an envelope. She opened it and examined the documents inside.

"A permit, to allow me to carry up to two blades in the city?"

Takahashi nodded. "A Defender of the Peace exemption. It's an honour the mayor can confer to a trusted person with sufficient skill."

Jananin folded the first document, which seemed to be printed on plastic paper like a bank note. "And an invitation for me and my two companions to have dinner with him and his wife tomorrow evening."

"I have told him that your companions are both gaijin and one is a child, and requested that the meal not be too formal." Takahashi pointed to the bar. "Oh, also, I have a bar on this plane. Would anyone like anything?"

Jananin said, "I don't want to drink alcohol, but do you have any sencha on board? In both the UK and the US, the tea on offer is so bad I generally drink coffee."

"Of course I have sencha! I even have a mugs with handles on them, so you gaijin can drink it without spilling it all over yourselves!"

Takahashi set about brewing something in a teapot. Dana looked out the window at the hazy horizon of the Pacific, sensing their position and how far they still had to travel from GPS. Although it had been morning when they'd taken off, the sun behind the plane had barely risen any further in the time they'd been travelling.

Takahashi interrupted her reverie by setting down mugs on the table before her and Ivor. Dana stared in disgust at the green-tinged yellow solution in the mug she'd been given. "*Urh!* It looks like wee!"

Jananin glanced up and Takahashi stopped from going back to his seat and turned back at her exclamation. Takahashi looked shocked and Jananin looked angry, which seemed bizarre considering they'd both spent much of the time on the journey to the airport insulting each other and laughing.

"Dana, if you come with us to the meal with the mayor of Fuyūtoshi," said Jananin in a stern voice, "and his wife serves you tea, you are not to go *urh* at it, you are not to compare it to wee, you are not to ask for milk to be put in it, and you are not to ask to be served a tin of pop as a substitute!"

"Oh, come on," Ivor said. "She's just a kid! It's hardly the worst I've heard. Didn't you ever notice the kinds of creative comparisons Peter was always making about the food I cooked?"

"No, this is not okay," Takahashi said, holding up his hands. "In Japan, we might laugh at how foreigners try to imitate our customs and take no issue with them laughing at our attempts at theirs, but it's offensive to insult food, and to be disrespectful to cultures and ancestors. Certain allowances are made for foreigners, and Sato Hiroshi is a diplomat, but he is traditional, and some things are beyond the pale. In fact, there's something else you should know about him. You know sometimes a sportsman or a celebrity goes into politics and is able to use their fan base to be successful? Sato is such a sportsman. He is a retired sumo wrestler."

"So, like, a big fat person, who wears a nappy?" Dana asked.

Takahashi set his arms akimbo. "In Britain, you have a lot of comedy, and you make comedy of fat people, but you must not make fun of sumo. It takes work and commitment to achieve the physique required for it. Sports in Japan have a spiritual aspect to them, and sumo is possibly the most spiritual and traditional. It's perfectly acceptable today for women to pursue all manner of careers and sports, to practice iaido, or kendo, yet sumo is still for men only, and women are not even allowed in the dojo. Another thing: Sato will probably wear to the dinner a traditional kimono. Do not ask him why he's wearing his pyjamas!"

Ivor turned to Dana, making a silly face. "If I'm invited to this dinner as well, I think I should probably just say nothing unless it's to answer when I'm spoken to!"

"That is probably a good example for you to follow, Dana," Jananin said.

*

As the plane approached Fuyūtoshi, the position of its windows on the sides facing away from the direction of travel made it difficult to see anything of where they were about to land. They had to sit in the seats and wear the belts for the landing, and from GPS Dana could tell the city was on the left-hand side and what seemed to be the runway jutted out over the ocean. She watched through the window on that side, hoping to catch sight of it. Tall buildings passed in a blur as the plane descended, steel and glass flashing in a low sun behind them, as though the morning had only just beaten them to the floating city.

The plane touched down with a jolt and a squawk of tyres on the runway surface, and then the deceleration was pressing her seatbelt into her pelvis and the plane drew to a stop. The pilots came out of the cabin and opened the door for them to climb out, and unloaded their luggage.

Jananin and Takahashi bowed to the pilots and Takahashi thanked them in Japanese.

The air was warm, with just a faint sea breeze. As Dana stepped out from behind the plane, the splendour of Fuyūtoshi was revealed, tall buildings rising like shining towers, surrounded by a hazy horizon of nothing but blue Pacific blending in to blue sky. The airstrip didn't seem to be completely stable, either, as though it floated on pontoons on the ocean surface.

The four of them set off with their luggage to a building between the edge of the airstrip and the city. Inside, it was set up much like customs had been at the port in Southampton. Two officials, one female and one male, greeted them with "Konnichiwa," and Jananin and Takahashi spoke it back. They had to pass through a metal detector, with Dana emptying her fuses from her pocket and Ivor taking off his watch.

"Why doesn't the thing in my head set it off?" she whispered to Ivor while they were waiting for the customs officials to examine their luggage. "The scanner in the hospital could detect it."

"It's too small," he whispered back. "None of the metal components are any bigger than a rice grain."

The woman customs officer was examining Jananin's luggage. She and Jananin bowed politely to each other, and the woman opened the case with the binoculars and electronics items in, examining each of them methodically before putting them back in the case. Then she turned to the trunk Jananin had brought, in which it turned out she had brought along her katana and wakizashi. The woman lifted them out more as though she was appreciating them than inspecting them, and Jananin showed the plastic-paper certificate Takahashi had given her. The woman checked it, and then she smiled and held out both the weapons by the sheaths, with their handles facing Jananin, with a respectful bow. Jananin didn't put them back inside the case; she strapped the knife to her thigh and belted the sword around her waist, and put her trench coat back on to cover them.

The man customs officer meanwhile had been examining Takahashi's luggage, and had found another wakizashi. Takahashi showed a similar document, and his knife was returned to him respectfully.

Then it was Dana's and Ivor's turn. Dana showed the woman her fuses and stood calmly while her pockets were searched. The holdall with clothes in it was searched thoroughly, albeit rather more discreetly than it had been in Southampton.

Something went wrong when the man took Ivor's jacket from him and found in one of the pockets a yellow Post-It note that he had scribbled something on. The two customs officials started shouting at him, but either the language barrier or some other cultural difference made it very hard to understand why. "How dare you bring contraband to Fuyūtoshi!" the woman said.

"What's the matter?" Ivor was completely bewildered. "I don't understand why I'm not allowed that! Does what I've written on it look like a rude word in Japanese?"

"You bring Rizla!" the man exclaimed.

Takahashi stepped in and spoke calmly to them in Japanese. He took the Post-It note, pointed to the writing on it, and pressed it against the wall next to the desk, apparently trying to demonstrate its purpose, but it didn't work because the sticky part was all covered in fluff from being in Ivor's pocket. The customs officials seemed to calm down a little.

Takahashi spoke to Ivor. "Tobacco, cannabis, and all other products to do with smoking are illegal to bring to Fuyūtoshi. They thought it was a paper for rolling leaves up, to prepare a cigarette or a joint to smoke."

Eventually, after making Ivor fill in a form explaining the purpose of the item, they were allowed to go, although the Post-It note was confiscated. They stepped outside the other door of Customs and Takahashi introduced them to the city.

Fuyūtoshi was only a few miles across in each direction. The citizens of the floating city lived on fruit and vegetables which they grew in great high-rise hydroponics towers made of glass and steel, and the fruits of the sea brought daily to the port by their own fishing vessels. They ate no product of any land animal, although they had to import their rice.

All the buildings in the city were tower blocks, and there were no low-rise buildings, but between the blocks of flats there were garden areas with places in the structure of the floor that had been filled with soil and planted with trees, although most of them were not very large and some were more like bonsai. Most of the buildings, Takahashi informed them, also had gardens on the roof. The island had no roads and had been designed to be traversed on foot, and it had been carefully planned with paths winding through gravel gardens, bamboo forests, and peaceful places of running water that surrounded Shinto shrines, and leading out to residential areas, shopping precincts, and blocks of offices. The only vehicles allowed were tiny ambulances with electric motors, with space for one patient on a stretcher and all the medical equipment stowed underneath and in the roof, with one paramedic driving and another sitting on the back. There were many CCTV cameras, and at first their myriad images from all angles made Dana feel a bit dizzy, but she became used to them after not very long, and she decided it was better to put up with a lot of signals and to feel a bit overwhelmed than it was to have none, like when she'd had to wear a hat.

Takahashi gave them a brief tour, which ended outside the residential block where he lived. It was surrounded by an ornamental pond containing water lilies with giant, vertical-edged pads, with arched bridges and wooden walkways leading this way and that over it, from the entrance to decks with seating and pots of plants to the paths. He gave Ivor a spare key and told him the number and pointed out the position of his flat. Then he gave him some bank notes called yen, and said he and Dana should go and discover the city, and also buy some clothing suitable to wear for the dinner tomorrow. He and Jananin would take the luggage in to the flat, and presumably afterwards they intended to go elsewhere together as old friends, and didn't want Ivor and Dana with them.

"What sort of clothes do we need to get?" Ivor asked.

"Well," said Takahashi, "we Japanese are a bit like you British, in that we aren't possessive about our culture. If you want to wear Japanese clothing, that's perfectly acceptable, although we will laugh at you if you wear it wrong. You shouldn't wear very casual clothes like tracksuits or jeans. The sort of thing you'd wear for a dinner out with friends in the UK is fine and probably easiest."

With that, Takahashi and Jananin left them both standing outside the apartment block.

"So," Ivor said. "What would you like to see first?"

Dana looked around. There were a lot of people in Fuyūtoshi, although the design of the place helped to prevent it from feeling crowded. Most of them were Japanese, but inhabitants of other nationalities as well as people who looked to be tourists were not uncommon. Dana had noticed a few other residents carrying blades, some under jackets that made them less obvious, but some of the women wore a traditional dress with a short sword held inside the sash. The police she'd seen patrolling wore katana and carried a taser and another knife on their protective vests. Most of the people had mobile phones, although they seemed to be much more advanced than the type people had in the USA and UK. The signals she could feel from them were much more complex, more like full-size computers.

"Can we have some lunch? Is Japanese food weird, like their tea, or is it nice, like Chinese takeaway?"

Ivor chuckled. "Probably somewhere in between. Let's see what we can find." They set off in the direction of the central hub of the island, where the main retail district was located.

It seemed the city, despite being built on the International Date Line, officially used the day matching Japan, and was a full twelve hours ahead of Greenwich Mean Time, meaning that when it was midday today in the UK, it was midnight and tomorrow had just begun in Fuyūtoshi. However, north to south across the centre of the city was a straight path not interrupted by any buildings, with a line of metal inlaid in the middle of it. At intervals along it, *International Date Line* had been engraved in the surface, along with kanji that presumably said the same thing, and arrayed along one side of the line could be found occasional proverbs, shrines, or works of art about yesterday and remembering the past, and on the other, similar mementoes celebrating tomorrow and hope for the future.

Close to the centre of the island the date line passed in front of a great building, architecturally imposing both in height and footprint. Underneath the kanji showing the building's name, was an English translation in smaller text: *Meridian Tower*. Its facade was supported by great pillars with folding doors drawn completely back, so its ground floor was shaded but open to the air, and the inside seemed not to be a retail space, but another public area like the park, with signs for museums and art galleries. One sign indicated it was the city's tallest building, with a restaurant on the top floor.

Ivor and Dana caught a lift up. They thought the view would make up for it, even if it turned out Dana didn't like Japanese food. However, it turned out Dana did like Japanese food. They found a table and ordered a cooked spider crab, to share, and some sashimi and rice and salad, and ate it looking out upon the distant, empty horizon where blue sky met blue sea all around them, with Fuyūtoshi spread out beneath them.

After the meal, Ivor ordered a platter of Japanese

dessert to share, and a pot of sencha. Dana ordered orange juice instead.

"I don't know how you can drink that tea," Dana said when it came. "It looks like wee and it tastes like something for watering plants with instead of drinking!"

Ivor poured some of the tea into a thick-walled cup with no handle, looking a bit like a very large thimble, which seemed to be what it was intended to be traditionally drunk from. "You'll probably appreciate it more when you're older. Besides, it's quite nice to have as a palate cleanser after a meal."

Dana did try some of it from his cup after she'd finished her orange juice, and tried to be more charitable towards it since it was expected to be at the important dinner tomorrow and she was not allowed to disparage it there. She supposed it did get rid of the sugary taste from the orange juice and the desserts.

Afterwards, they went to one of the other floors where there was a large department store, a bit like a Japanese version of Marks and Spencers, to look for some suitable clothes. Ivor found a more formal jacket and a shirt and tie and a pair of chinos that would do to go with them.

"You know how it's really *men's wear*," Dana said, "but they write it *menswear*. So it looks like *Men Swear*."

"If we move along to Children Swear, hopefully we can find you some clothes for this dinner."

Dana went along with him despondently. She didn't like clothes shopping.

At the entrance to the *Childrenswear* stood a display of mannequins dressed in dark trousers and zipped jackets, with glowing neon stripes on the arms and legs. "Those are mint!" Dana enthused. "Do you think you have to put batteries in them?"

Ivor laughed. "Oh, dear. If you're saying *mint* and thinking clothes are cool, you must be turning into a teenager!"

"Do you think I can wear that? Look, it has pockets in

it and everything."

"Takahashi specifically said no tracksuits. I think that counts as a tracksuit. We can get it anyway, if you like it, but we have to find something else."

"Can we get two so I can have one to wear when the other's in the wash?"

"All right, then." Ivor picked up a T-shirt from a rack. It had a cartoon on it of a poo with a smiley face. "I know who would want this!"

"*Peter*!" Dana laughed.

"So, do you not like smart clothes?"

Dana put her hands behind her back. "Boys get to have smart clothes that aren't so horrible. Why are girl smart clothes always dresses?"

"But you wear a skirt, sometimes. You wore one when I first met you." Ivor made a fanciful expression. "Were you putting on a special effort, just for *me*?"

"I can wear a skirt, but only if it's got pockets and I can wear leggings underneath. At least skirts have waistbands, and they're not all loose and empty-feeling round the middle."

"Hmm. Well, Takahashi said something from our own culture should be acceptable. And the way I see it, in our culture, anything that is okay for a man to wear in any given situation, is okay for a woman. And likewise if a man wants to wear women's clothes, in the right situation, like if he really wants to wear a cocktail dress at a cocktail party, and they throw him out when women are wearing the same thing, that would be dreadfully sexist of them."

"Can I just dress up as a boy? If the mayor thinks I'm a boy, I'll just go along with it."

Ivor yawned and rubbed the side of his face. "I think we should go home after this; I'm still on Nevada time. How about we get some smart boy trousers to start, and see if we can find the girliest shirt and jacket you can tolerate."

By the time they had found Dana some suitable clothes and shoes, and paid and left the building, it was mid-afternoon, but both of them were very tired, as their bodies thought their lunch had been their dinner and it was time for bed. They passed a shop selling electrical goods, showing news about the UK and the Meritocratic party, and they passed a newsagent, with papers showing photographs of Colin Antrobus looking victorious, a huge rippling Union Flag taking up the space behind him. Although Dana couldn't read the kanji on the papers or understand the Japanese spoken on the television, the way Antrobus was portrayed and spoken about seemed happy and celebratory, unlike the indifference shown in America or the outright hostility shown in the UK.

When they reached Takahashi's apartment, Ivor knocked on the door and shouted, "Hello!" before going in. As they were taking off their shoes, Dana started at the sight of a man with long wet hair hanging all around his face and tattoos all over his body, wearing only a pair of leather trousers, who had come into the hallway.

"Ah, you're back. I was just having a shower. Blake should be back soon." It was only after he'd spoken that Dana realised he was Takahashi, looking wild and very unlike the neat appearance he'd had before.

He showed them the rooms where they could stay. He only had two bedrooms, so Jananin would have to share with Dana and Takahashi would sleep on his sofa so Ivor could have his room. Upon being shown the room, Ivor pulled the curtains, shutting out the afternoon sun. "If you both don't mind, I'm absolutely knackered," he said.

When Takahashi turned to go out, the tattoos on his back showed a great owl sitting in the fork of a magnolia tree. He had carp swimming on his shoulders, and whoever the artist was who had done the tattoos was highly skilled.

He went into the kitchen. Dana followed him rather cautiously, and waited in the doorway, not sure what to make of him in this new guise. He'd seemed jokerish and not very serious on the plane, and now he looked strange and a bit scary.

Takahashi gestured to his ornamented torso. "I suppose you'd like to know what *this* means?" When Dana stared back at him without reply, he said, "Have you ever heard the word, *yakuza*, perhaps from a film, or in manga?"

Dana shook her head.

He leaned back, spreading out his arms and gripping the edge of the kitchen worksurface. Under the designs on his skin, his body was all lean muscle, like a hound. Not the stringy, bulging physique of a bodybuilder who works out to show off, but the condition of someone very fit and active. "I'll explain to you what it means. But first, let me put your mind at rest. Let me tell you a story about Jananin Blake. I'm afraid this is rather embarrassing for me. I have known Blake for a very long time. We went to school together once, in Tokyo. She was the only gaijin child in the school."

"What does that mean?"

"Gaijin? It's not an insult. It just means a person who is not Japanese. Like foreigner, in English. The school was a good school, and taught children to respect those with differences, but Blake didn't fit in very well. She wasn't pretty like the Japanese girls. Nobody wanted to sit next to her. In English, what do you call it when you practice sports in school?"

"PE?" Dana suggested.

"PE in Japan, for children of the age we were, usually means judo. We were six years old, and in the judo class, Jananin Blake could beat every other girl. She was one of the oldest children in the year, and being a westerner, she was taller. And I said, to the boy beside me as we were waiting for our turn, that it wasn't really fair, because she looked more like a boy than a girl. I had intended to say it privately to him, but because I was rather possessed with how funny I thought I was being, I said it much too loudly, and everyone heard.

"The teacher was angry, told me to apologise and to leave the lesson. But then Blake stepped up and challenged me to spar with her. Normally, it is forbidden for men and women to fight each other. Even small men, after puberty, are much stronger than tall women. Usually, if a man insults a woman, her father or brother takes it up with him. But the teacher, in her wisdom, seeing that we were children, and that Blake was tall, and strong, and she had the skill and the spirit for it, and that it might be a fitting punishment for me if she did best me, allowed it to go ahead.

"To decline to spar after I'd insulted her would make me a coward, so all I could do was try my best, and of course she beat me. I was a laughing stock; the boy who was beaten by a gaijin girl. My parents were not very impressed with me either, when they found out what had happened and what I had said to cause it. The other boys at school wouldn't sit next to me for the next year.

"However, Jananin Blake, upon settling her debt with me, was magnanimous in victory, and on seeing my situation had become rather like hers, one day she came and sat next to me. We became friends, and when her family moved back to England the next year, we wrote to each other, and we met up on holidays. Years later, when the time came for me to consider university, I decided to try for the same English university she was applying for, and came to see life as a foreigner in her land. I introduced her to iaido, and we joined a local club. When I went back to Japan, I got a job in the secret police, and eventually I rose to become a spy and was asked to infiltrate the yakuza, the criminal gangs that terrorise Japan. When I was exposed and the government was unable to protect me, it was Blake who taught me her knowledge of poisons, and my reputation for killing my assassins became so formidable, they decided it was more it was worth to keep sending them after me."

Takahashi shifted his weight onto one heel. He folded his arms. "I know Blake, very, very well. Believe me when I tell you, *she will not kill your father*. If she was going to do it, she'd have done it already. What he did was wrong, same as I wronged her, and he has a debt to pay, just as I did. But she no longer sees the price of that debt to be his life, and they will settle it, at some point, one way or another. She perhaps believes he *deserves* to think she will kill him, and she is probably right, but you do not deserve to have to think it as well."

Dana watched him for a moment. "How do you know he's my father?"

Takahashi's mouth straightened into a taut smile, and his shoulders began to shake with suppressed laughter. His eyes became very wide and silly. "It's obvious. But she didn't realise, until recently, did she?"

Dana stared at him. "Not until the day before yesterday. Or was it two days ago? I don't know. I think we lost a day when we came here!"

Takahashi shrugged. "In some ways, Blake is the cleverest person I know. In other ways, she's not very clever. I can also tell you she's stressed about this meal with the mayor. She's not much good at that sort of thing. But I can also tell you, she'd be a lot more stressed if she'd been invited to a British dinner! In Japan, when she makes mistakes, it's easy for the Japanese to excuse her for being a gaijin. In her own culture, she doesn't have that excuse!"

Dana laughed, suddenly recognising Takahashi's disarming clownishness through his wild hair and his sinister body art, and perhaps a little bit of something that reminded her ever so slightly of Jananin.

"Now," he said, pointing his finger at her and smiling. "You are probably tired because of the flight and the change in time zones. If you want to be clever about that, don't do what Pilgrennon did and go to sleep. He'll just wake up early, flush the toilet and wake up all the rest of us and annoy us, and feel tired before evening tomorrow and make it last far longer than it needs to. Try to stay awake and go to bed in the evening with the rest of us. If you like, I can take you out and we can get sushi. Or we can do something here. Do you like cartoons?"

Dana nodded.

"Perhaps we can watch a cartoon. There's an old Japanese cartoon I have, that has an English soundtrack because it was made for both Japan and the US and UK. Blake and I used to watch it when we were young, because we wrote to each other about it, but we had to be careful not to spoil any of the plots as sometimes it was broadcast earlier here, or there."

"Why do you call her by her last name if she's your friend?" Dana asked as Takahashi showed her into his sitting-room.

"Everyone is called by their last name in Japan, but for Japanese people, your last name comes first. Takahashi is my family name. Only your family calls you by your given name. And if Blake and I called each other by our given names, given that we are obviously not brother and sister, people might think we were a couple! And much as she is a very good friend of mine, western women are not my thing." Takahashi grimaced. "And short Japanese men are most definitely not her thing!"

Takahashi put on a DVD of an old cartoon called *Thundercats*.

"Why doesn't he have a Japanese sword?" Dana asked after a while. "Like a katana?"

Takahashi shrugged. "I guess when they made it, they must have thought a more western sword would make it appeal more to a western audience."

Dana thought about how confusing it was that some people said *western* to mean cowboys and deserts in America, and others said it to mean the whole of America as well as the UK and Europe all together.

Jananin came back not long later, and when she came into the sitting-room and saw what they were watching, and Takahashi lolloped in his armchair and grinned at her, she laughed.

As evening approached, Takahashi hammered on

Ivor's bedroom door, shouting that he was a lazy gaijin slug and should get up and help with the dinner. In the kitchen, Takahashi got out a bag from the fridge, and emptied out and unwrapped a parcel of four octopus. He started playing with them and being silly in front of Dana, arranging them on the kitchen worktops like they were coming to get her, and wrapping one of them round his face and screaming like it was strangling him.

Ivor came in and seemed quite amused, and then to Takahashi's surprise, he took a knife and dealt with the octopus, removing the guts and unpleasant bits from inside them and the skin from the outside, and cutting them into pieces with expert skill. He didn't even burst any of the bags of ink.

"Perhaps you are not as useless as you look!" Takahashi had prepared a spicy sauce. He stewed the octopus in stock, and then deep-fried it until it was crisp, and it was served up on his dining table, covered with the sauce, and alongside a big bowl of white rice and a salad.

Jananin and Takahashi seemed to be treating the meal as a trial run for the dinner tomorrow. There weren't any forks, knives, or spoons at the table, and Dana and Ivor found themselves having to learn to use chopsticks, and being introduced the rules of politeness surrounding their use, such as that they must not be put down on anything other than the chopstick rest, used to stab pieces of food, or raised above the level of one's mouth.

Ivor said he was glad he had checked the labels in the clothes he had bought, to make sure they were machine washable, as whatever was served to him for dinner tomorrow would likely end up all thrown down his front rather than in his mouth.

-19-

DANA woke up at around 6 AM the next morning, even though she'd done what Takahashi suggested and gone to bed as late as possible. For breakfast there was rice, seaweed, a very savoury-tasting broth, and something a bit like piccalilli. Like all the other Japanese food, it was very nice, but it seemed rather an odd combination of things to eat for breakfast.

Jananin and Takahashi said they were going to the dojo to practice kendo. Dana and Ivor decided to go back to the street with the International Date Line, as this seemed to be the most likely place Steve Gideon meant, even if they hadn't worked out what he meant by *when time stands still*.

It started at one side of the island and ended at the other in much the same way, with a vantage point and a railing to stop people falling off the island and into the sea, and struts strung with a big cargo net beneath, which Ivor said was probably to catch tourists who had drunk so much sake the railing couldn't prevent them from falling over.

It was Friday morning, officially, although on the east side of the island it was technically still Thursday. Most of the local people had gone to work and the other people there were mostly tourists, but outside one shop a small throng had gathered, mostly police and official-looking people, some of them wearing white forensic suits and carrying cameras. Dana couldn't understand what they were saying, but she caught the word *yakuza* a couple of times in their conversation. Behind the forest of their legs, red stains showed on the pavement in front of the shop.

Ivor steered Dana back the way they'd come. "Let's

look at something else."

So they looked at the sculptures and writings that arrayed the sides of the path along the line. Many of them were Japanese and written in kanji with translations underneath. *Tomorrow, tomorrow's wind will blow*, said a line under a simple, abstract sculpture of flowing intertwining metal strips.

Learn from yesterday, live for today, hope for tomorrow. Traditional Japanese proverb.

Tomorrow is a mystery. Today is a gift. That's why it's called the present. -Eleanor Roosevelt, USA.

There are two days in the year when we can not do anything: yesterday and tomorrow. -Mahatma Gandhi, India.

Tomorrow Never Dies.

This last one was on a low plinth underneath a life-size statue of James Bond, holding his gun up to his cheek in his typical pose. The words on the plinth also explained that he was a British fictional character.

From the CCTV cameras, Dana could see a few different angles of herself and Ivor standing next to James Bond, and thought this was quite funny.

The path of the date line was few miles long, with many businesses on it, most of them cafés or restaurants, or similar shops that served ice-cream. Ivor said he didn't see anyone who looked like Steve Gideon, and that although they had narrowed things down a lot, it would be very difficult to say exactly where they were supposed to find him here, even if they did manage to work out what time he meant.

After they had walked up and down again, they walked to the dojo, which meant something like a sports centre where people do martial arts, which are sports much like football and golf in England, but English people think Japanese sports are exotic and call them martial arts because they come from another country, or so Ivor explained.

They sat on the floor to watch people competing

in the central ring. The sport was called kendo, and the participants wore masks with mesh at the front, robes that reached to the ground, and gloves, yet they had bare feet. Dana wondered at first if it was going to be like snooker or pool, because each participant held a wooden object like a cue. But after a referee came forth, and two men bowed to each other, crouched down, and raised their cues to point at each other, it turned out to be more like fencing, and they had to score points by using the sticks both to hit each other and stop the opponent from hitting back. Although Dana didn't really like sport, either to participate in or to watch, she had to admit the kendo was quite exciting as the two men pressed into each other with their bamboo swords locked, sidestepping and turning as they tried to find the moment to strike, although the loud shrieks they made as they tried to get each other were a bit disconcerting.

At the end of the match, the referee declared one of the men to be the victor, and they bowed to each other once more, and went away. Next came two women, one taller than the other. They bowed, crouched, and attacked each other, their screeching even worse than the men's. The women seemed very evenly matched, and Dana could not tell who had won until the end, when the referee awarded the match to the taller one. The women bowed and left, but as the taller one came out of the ring and took off her mask, Dana recognised her as Jananin.

After Jananin and Takahashi had got changed and come out to meet them, they went back to the date line path to have lunch at one of the outdoor cafés there. Jananin and Takahashi were both wearing katana, and after they had been seated, Dana asked, "Why is it okay for some people to carry swords in Fuyūtoshi?"

"For the protection of everyone else," Takahashi replied. "If the police, and people who have earned the trust of the city, have blades, then there are more people to stop the yakuza when they come here to commit crime."

"Why don't the police have guns? Like they do in America where the sheriff has one. Or in the UK, where specially trained police are allowed them."

"No firearms or explosives are allowed anywhere on Fuyūtoshi."

"But if these yakuza are coming here and hurting people, wouldn't it help if the police had them?"

"No," said Takahashi firmly. "No guns. Those are the rules here."

"And no smoking, either, apparently," Jananin said. "Although I have seen people using electronic devices to vape nicotine and probably worse here."

"No, no smoking. If people want to take drugs, they can buy them and pay tax on them. But smoking is disgusting and disrespectful to other people, so it is not allowed."

After lunch, they walked up and down the date line one more time, and Takahashi used his phone to take a picture of Ivor and Jananin standing next to the statue of James Bond. Ivor leaned his elbow on Bond's shoulder, his spectacles in his hand, and Dana stood behind the statue, leaning out as though he was protecting her from a baddy.

After they had wandered around a bit more and talked about the CCTV and the cafés along the line, it was time to go back to Takahashi's and get ready for the meal.

Dana wore her trousers that were intended for boys, a shirt, and a 'girly' jacket they'd found in a dusky pink colour. Ivor wore his jacket and tie. Jananin wore the same leather trousers she usually wore, but she put on a lacy shirt and glittery eye make up. Ivor said he felt like he was back in the 80s and she was a rock star. Takahashi wore a black shift with a sort of wide-belted long grey jacket over it, with two medals pinned on the breast. He wore what looked like wooden flip-flops with it, over white socks like mittens with a separate compartment for the inside toe. It gave him a smart, military look, although Dana pointed out to him that he was technically wearing a dress.

The mayor's house was a pagoda about seven storeys

high, set within a very beautiful garden. The mayor and his wife met them at the door. Although he was barely as tall as Jananin, the mayor was enormous, and he wore a vast patterned kimono with a wide cummerbund. Dana was glad they had been invited to have dinner with him, as if he'd invited them to go swimming with them she wouldn't have known where to look.

His wife looked tiny next to him, wearing a flowery kimono with a thick sash and her ebony hair in a bun. When they introduced themselves, it seemed she used her husband's name like Pauline and most of the married women Dana knew at home, and her name was Sato Aoi. Then everyone had to bow, and Dana did her best to remember and do it as Jananin and Takahashi had taught her.

Everyone took off their coats and shoes in the lobby, and Jananin and Takahashi left their katana there, although neither removed their wakazashi, and Sato Aoi wore a short sword wrapped inside her sash on the left side. The house was a traditional Japanese design, with paper screens about a square table very low on the ground with cushions around it. The seating plan was the Satos together on one side, Jananin and Takahashi on the opposite sides adjacent to them, and Dana with Ivor on the side facing.

They all took their positions, and to Dana's relief she saw an ordinary stainless steel spoon had been set at her place alongside the chopsticks, although none of the adults had been afforded such a concession. Then, to her alarm, Sato looked straight at her across the table, and asked directly, "How do you like our Fuyūtoshi?"

Dana glanced at Ivor, but his expression seemed to indicate she had to answer and he couldn't do it for her. "Fuyūtoshi is a beautiful city," she said truthfully. "But this morning, we went to the International Date Line, and someone had been hurt, by the yakuza."

Sato interlaced his fingers in front of his enormous

chest. "You are very perceptive. Fuyūtoshi is indeed a beautiful city, spoilt by our inability to keep the yakuza out of it."

"What exactly *are* yakuza?" Dana asked.

"They are organised criminal gangs. Bad people who commit the most terrible crimes. Rather like the mafia you know from the west."

"And what is the mafia?"

Ivor said, "The mafia are like the Italian version of the yakuza."

Sato laughed, and so did Takahashi and Jananin. "Fuyūtoshi has some autonomy, but we don't make most of our rules. They are made by the government in Japan, and they are not being cooperative in stopping the yakuza from coming here. Many wealthy people live in Fuyūtoshi, and many tourists come here. We are doing them a disservice when we can't protect them from organised crime."

"In America, and in the UK, the police can have guns to help them stop criminals," Dana said. "But nobody is allowed a gun in Fuyūtoshi. Apart from James Bond."

Sato roared with laughter. "James Bond! I'm afraid, we cannot have guns in Fuyūtoshi. They are much too dangerous. A sword can only kill one person at a time, but a gun..."

A waiter entered from behind a screen and set down plates before them, each with only a single morsel in the middle: something wrapped in pressed seaweed with a dressing drizzled over it.

"What is it?" Dana asked, as the waiter returned with glasses and a bottle of sake, and began to set them out and fill them.

"*Uni*," Sato Aoi said. "I don't know what is English name of this."

"It's a sea urchin," Jananin said, giving Dana a sharp glance, while at the same time she noticed Ivor had given her a very stern look.

Sato continued, addressing Jananin now. "Tell me,

Blake-san, about this Meritocracy Party. In Fuyūtoshi we are all very interested in this Colin Antrobus and his ideas."

"I'm afraid he is seen as a rather divisive person at home," Jananin said. "I am surprised by the interest being shown in it here. His idea is to replace the government with something akin to a direct democracy, but to stop it becoming completely anarchic, he has proposed a system where people who contribute more to society in various different ways have more votes, and people who claim benefits from society renounce their vote in order to do so."

"Ah." Sato picked up his bit of sea urchin deftly with his chopsticks, ate it, and set the chopsticks back down. He took a sip of sake and savoured it before continuing. "In Fuyūtoshi, we like his idea. In Fuyūtoshi, the problems we have with the yakuza are because Japan won't act to stop them targeting us, and we do not have the power to do that ourselves. The obvious solution would be to declare independence. But all of us on Fuyūtoshi are very patriotic. We would hate not to be Japanese, or to cause offence to our own countrymen. If we were to reframe the question of being not of independence, but to be about moving to a new and better system, and we had to leave as a consequence, for the same reason the UK had to leave some international organisations when it declared itself a meritocracy..."

Jananin nodded. "I see what you mean."

"What it is we want to be is..." Sato appeared to struggle with his English. "What is it called in the UK, when there are islands that want to be British but govern themselves, like the Falklands and Gibraltar?"

"British Overseas Territories?" Jananin suggested.

"Yes!" Sato waved his finger, his expression genial. "Fuyūtoshi wants to be a Japanese Overseas Territory, and wave the Flag of the Sun with our Japanese family, but to choose more control over who can come here."

Takahashi glanced between the other guests. He

smiled and drank his sake.

"And this idea of people who don't contribute not having votes. I like that! Yakuza should not get to vote. Hikikomori should not get to vote! What is hikikomori in English?"

Sato conferred with his wife and Takahashi for a moment, and Takahashi said, "I don't think there is a direct translation. It means a person who is unemployed and lives with his parents, and doesn't usually leave the house."

"Exactly," said Sato, sipping sake. "If they want to live like that, it's their problem, but I don't want them sitting in Japan casting votes that affect hardworking people here."

Next to Dana, Ivor positioned his sake glass so it was within easy reach. He picked up his chopsticks clumsily, grasped the sea urchin morsel with his hands close to it, and put it in his mouth. Dana watched him chew and swallow, and when he was done he smiled a bit and arched his eyebrows.

Dana wasn't sure how to get the spoon under the sea urchin without touching it with her fingers, which she suspected might be bad manners, so she picked it up carefully with the chopsticks and ate it. It tasted like nothing she'd ever eaten before, but it wasn't a bad taste.

Sato indicated Takahashi. "Of course the Japanese government were kind enough to give me Takahashi-san. His wisdom has been a great help in protecting us from the yakuza, even though the yakuza unfortunately know who he is now."

The next course was served, a bowl of broth containing fish and vegetables. Dana watched Sato Aoi take the bowl in one hand and pick out the pieces with her chopsticks, but she used the spoon for this one. She was rather surprised to see Jananin drink the broth directly out of the bowl; Pauline always told Dana the rudest thing you could do at the table was to lick a plate or drink from a bowl.

Sato laughed. "I understand, Takahashi, that Blake-san's skill in iaido exceeds yours."

Takahashi laughed back. "The nature of iaido prevents us from sparring together, so it will never be known. In kendo, however, this morning, she did defeat Nakamura Akari in a match."

"Nakamura Akari!" Sato exclaimed, turning to Jananin.

"It was very close," Jananin said. "It could have gone either way."

"Nakamura represented Fuyūtoshi in the last national championship. She's the best we have here."

Takahashi set down his soup bowl. "We are a small city, and there are kendōka better than Nakamura in the national championship. But Blake is good. We've sparred together occasionally in kendo, as friends, and she wins as often as I do."

Jananin said, "That's because us western women are on average taller than you eastern men. It's simply a reach advantage. He's stronger than me."

There came an awkward silence. Something about this comment didn't seem to have gone down very well with Sato. Perhaps he thought it was immodest of Jananin; perhaps it was her typically blunt delivery; perhaps it was the turn of the conversation to the inappropriate idea of a man fighting a woman in a martial art; or that bringing up natural anatomical differences between sexes and ethnicities might be considered distasteful in polite conversation.

Sato Aoi put her hand on her husband's arm and smiled briefly. The mayor forced a short laugh.

Jananin shook her head. "Besides, my kendo and iaido are done purely for sport. Takahashi has used his skills time and time again in the service of his country, against people who have no concept of fighting by the rules or respecting their opponents."

Ivor turned his head to look at Dana. He put his hand on his left shoulder and winced.

Sato Aoi nodded. "In the rules of sport, men must not fight women, and you must stop if your opponent falls. In war, of the terrible sort fought in history, and still today with the yakuza, women when challenged by men have one choice: fight or die. None of us know how that will go until it is demanded."

The soup bowls were cleared away, and a sashimi dish was brought out. Dana already knew she liked sashimi. The first time she'd tried it, she'd wondered why anyone ever bothered cooking fish if this was what it tasted like raw. She studied with delight the different colours of the glossy fresh fish strips and how they had been arranged on the plate.

Sato began picking up his sashimi daintily with his chopsticks. "This man you are looking for in Fuyūtoshi. There is nobody here recorded under the name Gideon. There are many gaijin who make their permanent residence here, and some of them are British, so he could be using another name."

"He implied he would meet us, in a riddle of sorts," Jananin explained. "To mean Fuyūtoshi, he wrote *the place between tomorrow and yesterday*. He also wrote, *when time stands still*. Do you have any idea of what he might mean by that? Is there anything that happens here that could be considered time standing still?"

"Well, there is daylight saving time. In autumn."

Jananin frowned. "We thought of that. I checked and I thought Japan didn't observe it!"

"*Japan* does not observe it." Sato spoke humorously. "It is one of the rules we in Fuyūtoshi are allowed to decide for ourselves. We brought it in a few years ago."

Jananin exchanged glances with Ivor and Dana. Ivor was holding his plate under his chin to stop himself from dropping his sashimi.

Sato Aoi said, "It happens in about two weeks' time. We have midnight, and then at one o'clock, it becomes midnight again. And in the spring, we have midnight at eleven and lose an hour. Rather like the date line in some ways, and just as confusing for outsiders!"

The sashimi was followed by a rice dish, and finally by desserts on a tray set in the middle of the table, and the dreaded sencha. Ivor made a silly expression at Dana as it was being poured out, and she made one back.

Sato laughed. He pointed at Dana. "I see you there, having jokes with your father. There is nothing more sacred than family, but the bond between a father and a daughter, or a mother and a son, is often a wonderful thing. I have a daughter. She is very small at the moment, but I look forward to the good times to come. When I was elected as mayor, I vowed to make Fuyūtoshi the city I wanted it to be for my daughter to grow up. I am doing my best, but it's not enough."

Sato and his wife clasped hands briefly, and everyone seated at the table smiled. Then Sato said to Dana, "My agents tell me you seem to have a strange ability. That you can control computers, just by thinking. I would like this for my daughter. How is it done?"

Ivor suddenly coughed, spraying particles of food into his hand. Dana dropped her plate and it rolled off her knee and hit the leg of the table and broke into two pieces.

Sato Aoi got to her feet. "I am *so* sorry!" she held up her hands in apology and said angrily to him, "*Hiroshi!*"

The broken plate was recovered, and Dana was quickly brought another, and nobody noticed that she did not drink very much of her sencha.

The meal was politely concluded. As they walked back over the gardens, now dark and lit by the myriad lights of the great city, and looking very much like the view from one of the windows Dana remembered seeing when she had fallen into the Styx in the Cerberus game, Jananin said, "He is a very clever man. Perhaps he is too clever."

-20-

IT was just under two weeks until the clocks would go back.

Ivor said he was almost certain that the place between tomorrow and yesterday in Steve Gideon's cryptic email was somewhere along the International Date Line, on Meridian Street, with its cafés, restaurants, shops, and quiet seating areas and art displays running straight from the north to the south of the island. The problem was, the diameter of the island was a few miles, and Meridian Street ran the whole length of it. They would have only an hour when 'time stood still' to search amongst the great many places he might have intended to meet them along the street, and chances were they would not find him, as there were a lot of people in Meridian Street all the time, and it had been more than ten years since Ivor had last set eyes on Steve Gideon. As he said, they had the time and the longitude, but what they needed was the latitude.

Most days, Jananin and Takahashi went out together. Dana didn't know exactly where they went, but she gathered that a lot of the time they spent at the dojo practising kendo and iaido, which Jananin said focused her mind and helped her to think.

That left Dana with Ivor, and most days they would go out and look around the city. They looked unremarkable compared to many of the tourists in Fuyutōshi. Ivor wouldn't let Dana out of his sight after that first incident with the police they'd seen on Meridian Street, and sadly they saw more evidence of shops being broken into and crime about the city, and Dana thought of Mayor Sato and his struggle to stop criminals from coming. Dana couldn't read the newspapers or understand the Japanese she overheard most people speaking, but she came to understand that people from wealthy families were being kidnapped by the yakuza and ransomed.

There were plenty of CCTV cameras all over Meridian Street, and it was on the third day Dana had the idea. "The signals from the cameras are short-range. I can feel them when I'm near them. Perhaps if we could turn them into long-range signals and collect them all together in the same place, it would make it easier to find Steve Gideon when the clocks go back. Although it would still be hard. It's difficult enough to concentrate on two of them at the same time, and there are loads of them."

Ivor considered this for a moment. "If we could route the signals onto monitors, that would make it easier. Then we could all look."

Ivor and Dana walked to the north end of Meridian Street. They sat down on a bench and Ivor tried to explain to Dana concepts like bandwidth and IP addresses, but she couldn't understand what he meant or how it translated into the way she could see what wireless CCTV cameras were filming when she was close enough to them. Ivor said the cameras were sending their signal to a router, and she needed to find that and translate its security details in a way that they could enter it into another system and get access to it on the Internet.

Dana didn't understand this at all, and that first morning as she sat with him on a bench near to one of the sculptures, she became very frustrated and annoyed trying to work out what it meant in terms of what computer signals actually feel like and do what was being asked of her. After she had tried and tried and not got anywhere, Ivor said it didn't matter and it was time for lunch. They went to one of the outdoor restaurants to have some miso soup and sushi, and Dana was so irritated from not being able to understand the camera signals she said something rude to the lady who served them, and Ivor apologised to the lady and told Dana off for being a mardy little so-and-so.

After they had lunch and Dana had calmed down a bit, they went back to the bench and she tried again. With her eyes shut and her hands over her ears to help her concentrate, she managed to work out several strings of hexadecimal code, and read them out slowly so Ivor could write them down on a notepad.

At Takahashi's apartment, Ivor showed Takahashi and Jananin the codes. With a great deal of trial and error that took up all of the evening, they managed to set up Takahashi's computer using the codes Dana had provided, so it showed the feed from the camera Dana had extracted the data from on the screen.

"Excellent!" Takahashi rubbed his hands together. "But we are going to need the other cameras along Meridian Street. And probably, a lot more monitors and computers."

In the days leading up to the clocks going back, Dana and Ivor returned to Meridian Street and collected more camera hacking data. Jananin and Takahashi went out and bought more computers and monitors, and set them up in Takahashi's apartment. By the time they'd collected enough cameras to cover the whole of Meridian Street, half the sitting-room was taken up with a crescent of monitors, each of them showing the feed from eight different cameras, and it was unpleasantly warm in Takahashi's sitting-room with all the computers running, even though his air conditioning was working at full power.

Dana was told to make a habit of going to bed late and getting up late, so she'd be alert and able to help when the clocks went back at midnight. They planned for each of them to take a quarter-segment of the wall of monitors to watch, to search for a British man as soon as midnight came.

Dana felt rather stressed that day. She tried not to do anything too strenuous in case it made her tired for the night and stopped her from concentrating. Her guts were dodgy and she didn't feel like eating much. She asked Ivor what Steve Gideon looked like. He said he was nearly as tall as he was, but of slight build, and that he had a moustache, although his build and moustache might have changed as it had been probably fourteen years since he'd last seen him. He also said he was a bit camp.

Dana asked if that meant he liked to stay in a tent in the wilderness, and tried to imagine a sort of thin but rugged mountain man with a moustache. Ivor apologised and said that perhaps hadn't been an appropriate way for him to describe him, and that it meant Steve Gideon had a bit of a stereotypical manner that was flamboyant and melodramatic.

The twelfth hour approached, and Takahashi put on the kettle not to make sencha, but to make coffee to help them concentrate.

Dana had two monitors, a total of sixteen CCTV feeds, to watch over. She concentrated fiercely, looking from one screen to another, but all her people were Japanese, apart from a couple of gaijins at one table who were both women.

With a sudden clamour that startled Dana from her concentration on the screens, Takahashi rose from his seat and yelled something in Japanese that was almost certainly a swear word. "These feeds are compromised! We've been hacked!" He pointed at the monitors with an aggressive arm movement. "This is deepfake shit!"

"What's happened?" Ivor said.

Takahashi pointed to one of the CCTV feeds in the middle of a monitor. "Gaijin here has six fingers!"

Ivor leaned forward to look. His expression changed. Jananin came to stand next to him and scrutinise the CCTV feed. Then, they looked at each other, both smiling, as though they were sharing a private joke.

"That's him," Ivor said.

Dana looked at the image they'd been studying. In the centre it showed a slight man with a moustache and a floppy sort of quiff. As he reached for a cup and saucer that had just been set before him, the CCTV recording showed his hand quite clearly had six digits instead of five.

Ivor pointed to the scrap of notepaper taped to the top of the monitor. "It's close to the middle. Shouldn't take long. Let's go."

"Why has he got six fingers?" Dana asked as they hurried out of Takahashi's apartment block and across the lily pond bridges.

"He's a polydactyl," Jananin said.

Dana frowned. "I thought that was something that flew around during the time of the dinosaurs?"

Ivor laughed. "That's a pterodactyl!"

"Does one of them not work, then?"

"No," said Ivor. "He can use them all, because he was born that way. Just as you can use the transceiver in your brain, because you were born with it, and your nervous system can adapt."

Soon, they were approaching the café, but Takahashi no longer seemed to be with them. "Where's he gone?" Dana asked.

"Never mind," Jananin said. "Don't mention him."

The CCTV feed had led them to one of the few coffee shops on Meridian Street. Most Japanese seemed to prefer tea, but Steve Gideon was drinking coffee. What was more, when they approached his table, Dana saw his coffee was so black, it had stained the cup with a scummy tide mark from what had been thus far consumed. It looked as though the spoon would have stood up by itself had he tried to stir it.

He looked up at Ivor, his face pleasantly surprised, if a bit mad-looking. "Ivor! It is wonderful to see an old friend in Fuyūtoshi!" His voice shook and stuttered out the name of the city when he spoke, and he looked in turn to Jananin. "And Jananin Blake, my more worthy rival back in the day I was once a Nobel nominee!" Then he looked down from their faces, to Dana's, his expression changing, wide eyes becoming wider, and he stammered incoherently for a moment before he could make himself understood. "Never in a blue moon could I foresee a straight man so full of chivalrous ideals as Ivor Pilgrennon be unfaithful to his wedding vows, but I must say, Ivor, if you insist on philandering like a politician and being a raging heterosexual who can't keep his knickers on, this is a better outcome to it than I or anyone else could possibly imagine!"

Dana turned to Jananin. She looked as though she might be about to lose her temper, so she turned to Ivor instead, who had gone a bit redder about the face than usual. "I don't understand what he's talking about!"

"You don't want to, either." The reply seemed to be to Dana, but Ivor was looking at Steve Gideon when he spoke. "He has a dirty mind and a quick wit and his mouth has never been able to keep pace with either of them. Steve, stop it, I know it's meant for me, but it's rude for Dana and Jananin to hear. The Japanese take great offence at the idea of insulting someone's ancestors! And for your information, Adrienne left me soon after you staged your own death. If you hadn't done that, perhaps we could have cried on each other's shoulder while you were in jail for being framed for murdering Richard and I was there for actually making a..." He put his hand on Dana's shoulder.

"Electrobotanist girl?" Dana suggested.

Jananin interrupted them. "It is probably best if you stop talking about this now and do not bring up this topic again."

Steve Gideon shut his mouth and folded his hands on the table in front of him, and Dana couldn't resist looking at them, and how his fingers were just as perfectly formed and arranged on his hands as her own, but with an extra one on each hand. He looked up at Jananin. "Please do sit down. I'm so very sorry for my loquaciousness running away with me. Not many Japanese people understand English well enough for me to be able to rabbit on at them and wind them up, and I do miss it. Although as Ivor is my longstanding friend, and very much my type had he batted for the other side, I can only vouch for his loyalty and good character, and to offer my very best wishes and congratulations to both of you seeing that he is available and hoping that this unfortunate indiscretion he has committed hasn't put you off him... and I will shut up now as has been suggested and we shall say no more of this."

Dana sat down. "Can I have an ice-cream?" There was rather a strong smell of vanilla and coffee about Steve Gideon, which had put her in the mind for ice-cream. Although it wasn't unpleasant, after breathing it in for a while it became cloying.

Ivor ordered sencha for himself and Jananin, and an ice-cream for Dana.

Steve Gideon smiled. He put his elbows on the table and waved his hands, as though trying to exorcise the spirit of the last conversation. "So, you know I was framed? And you're here to talk about my dog. My Porpoises. Artificial intelligences, people used to call my funny little pets." His expression became suddenly dour. "Artificial *stupidities*, I used to correct them!"

"Your learning machines," Ivor said.

"Quite. Well, as my research consistently showed, the quality of learning is highly dependent on the quality of the tutor and the teaching materials. Machines are subject to just the same errors in learning processes as humans are. Quite probably more so. I appreciated that, but never to its full extent, not until after what happened."

Ivor smiled faintly. "What happened?"

"A rogue teacher. Set a hitman on my poor Richard. I knew he was coming for me too. Whoever wanted my Cerberus didn't want me making any more of them, or anything else that could challenge it. It was disappear or die."

"So all the time you've been pretending to be dead, you've been here? Nearly fourteen years?"

"Not all of that time, here. Most of it, though. I'm working on something new. Something that won't have the same faults as my Cerberus and my Porpoises. Something that can learn, but can think a bit more rigidly, something that isn't quite so inquisitive and impetuous." Steve Gideon sipped his coffee.

"You may not have to do it in hiding any more." Jananin poured the tea into the cups. "Two of them have been destroyed. The other seems to have been disconnected and we're hoping you might have some idea of who has it."

"Dis..." Gideon stammered, setting his cup down unsteadily on its saucer. "Destroyed?"

"One was embedded in the UK civil service," Jananin explained. "The other was embedded in the American equivalent. Both of them were being used to interfere with the voting system. When whoever was controlling the British one realised we knew too much about it, they tried to assassinate us as well."

"I... I knew something had gone wrong, that they'd been disconnected. I suspected they were being used for something illegal. I saw about the Information Terrorist attack in London and suspected that might have been one of them. I assumed whoever did that took it for themselves."

"The other one was hidden in a military base in the Nevada Desert," Ivor said. "The government covered it up pretty well, said it was an accident with a munitions dump, but their government's as rudderless as the one in Westminster without it, and the cracks are starting to show."

"Well..." Steve Gideon drank the remainder of his coffee. "If it's disconnected, it'll probably stay disconnected. It's designed to function most effectively with all three of them working as redundant units. The idiots who stole it didn't realise that, selling one of them to America as they did."

"Steve, do you have any idea where the other one is?"

Steve Gideon shrugged. "Have you tried Russia? Or perhaps China?" He glanced at his watch. "I shouldn't worry too much about it. Whoever has it has probably realised the other two have gone wrong, and scrapped it before it does the same. It's been wonderful to see you again, Ivor, and to meet you, Jananin in a less competitive environment, and you... what is your name?"

"Dana." Dana scraped with her spoon at the molten ice-cream in the bottom of her glass dish.

"Dana. It was good to meet you." Steve Gideon got to his feet. "My hour will be up soon. I'm wanted for a murder I didn't commit, and the murderer may still be looking for me to finish his job. Goodbye."

As he walked away and disappeared amongst the midnight pedestrians, Dana looked from Ivor to Jananin and back again.

Ivor frowned, pushing out his bottom lip. "In some ways he knows more than he's letting on. In other ways, it's rather the opposite. In every way, he's being disingenuous."

Dana thought back to the label in the furry gilet; the tall buildings against the night sky, covered with lights, and how the view of the city had looked just like that as they walked home from Mayor Sato's pagoda. "The last Cerberus has to be here. The name Fuyūtoshi was in the game! How can he be in the same place as it for years and not know it?"

"He's lying," Jananin said. "Dana, you asked before we arrived here where Takahashi had gone, and I asked you not to mention him again. Takahashi has been watching this meeting in secret, and now he will follow Gideon to find out where he has gone. I don't know why Gideon agreed to meet us, but it's apparent he chose this particular time because when the clocks change, the CCTV footage of the past hour will likely be overwritten with the next hour, erasing all record of his activity. Fuyūtoshi's software is all Japanese, and because mainland Japan doesn't observe daylight saving time, it's probably not been designed to cope with it, rather like all the money that had to be spent fixing software for the Millennium Time Bomb all those years ago."

Ivor rubbed the side of his jaw. "I think he still has the last one. He must have switched it off. He knows the other two are down, but it's possible he didn't realise they were destroyed, and he maybe thought there was a possibility we had them and we might have been amenable to bartering so he could have them back. He was potentially going to help us, but when he found out we'd destroyed them, he changed his mind."

Dana wished they had brought along Isaiah Redwood. He always seemed to be good at telling when people were lying. She wondered if he would like the Japanese food, or if he would just think it was weird.

They went back to Takahashi's apartment and waited for him to return. Ivor switched off all the computers and monitors with the CCTV on and started to tidy them away. Jananin sat in an armchair, and a strange, distant mood of contemplation came over her.

A door slammed and Takahashi came in. "I know where he's gone," he said holding up his hands, "but I have to go back to Sato before we can do anything else."

"I think I also know where he has gone," Jananin said.

Takahashi stared at her.

"Since we arrived at this city, a number of anomalies have stood out to me. Some of them are subtle, some not so, but they all point to one conclusion."

Takahashi said nothing in response to this, so Jananin continued. "Firearms, explosives, and tobacco and other smoking-related paraphernalia are illegal in Fuyūtoshi. This was the first thing we discovered upon our arrival here. Explosives, now that's understandable in such a highly-populated area. Guns, potentially also, until you become aware of the problems the yakuza are creating here, and it seems absurd that even the police are not permitted basic handguns to protect the people. But a zealous and aggressively enforced ban on smoking and any paraphernalia associated with it? When recreational drugs like nicotine and THC are available in other forms? It makes no sense."

Takahashi still said nothing, so Jananin continued. "Then there is the lack of visibility of research and development facilities, when Japan is famed for its hardware and software. Another, rather more subtle, observation, is that you seem to have rather more hydroponics greenhouses and fishing boats docking at your port than might be needed to supply the population here, and how despite the city being small, none of us have encountered Gideon by chance in the time we have been here, and he has managed to stay unnoticed here somewhere, despite a very obvious physical difference that would make him distinctive to the locals."

Takahashi nodded slightly, but he offered no suggestion.

"But the most significant observation, as I see it, is that all structures that float on water, unless they are just simple rafts, require some sort of submerged counterbalance to stabilise them and prevent them from capsizing. Sailing ships have deep keels to stabilise them. Surfboards intended to be stood on have a fin underneath. Even a simple buoy has a pole with a weight on the bottom below. It follows that Fuyūtoshi must have some underwater component of this sort to keep it upright in the water, or the floating city would quickly become some sort of sideways-upside-down Atlantis. And it would be a grave underestimation of Japanese efficiency and ingenuity to assume that such a stabiliser on as ambitious a construction such as Fuyūtoshi would be constructed from inert ballast. All of these observations, taken together, point to only one solution."

Takahashi did not speak for a moment. After much consideration, he replied, "It is forbidden for those of us who have the trust of the city of it to speak of it to outsiders, gaijin and nihonjin alike. I am sworn not to reveal it even to my closest friends and family. As you have deduced it for yourself, and as you revealed your deduction in front of two witnesses unknowing it was forbidden to talk of it in front of them, I don't think any rules have been broken. But I will have to inform Sato about this nonetheless, and you must all of you swear that you will never speak of it to anyone else now."

"I don't understand," said Dana, "what I am supposed to swear not to talk about."

Ivor explained, "What Jananin has worked out, I think, is that if Fuyūtoshi is the floating city, there must be another city, a sinking city, underneath it."

Takahashi nodded. "Suichūtoshi. The Underwater City."

-21-

THE next morning, they walked to the dock. Jananin and Takahashi were not wearing their katana or their coats to cover them, as Takahashi said were they were going there was not room to draw a katana so it was no good even if it was needed. They each had a wakizashi, and Takahashi had another long knife or perhaps a short sword on his other side, and wore split-toe boots. Jananin wore a loose shirt with a close-fitting sleeveless leather tunic over it. Dana had on her Japanese tracksuit, and Ivor had on chinos and a shirt and jacket the same as he usually wore.

Takahashi led them out onto a wharf. Off the edge of it, an odd sort of fin stuck up out of the water, bigger than a man was tall. Takahashi got down on hands and knee, and leaned over the side of the jetty and rapped with his knuckles on the surface of a hatch that protruded from the surface. In front and behind the hatch, a smooth hull like a whale's back showed.

Soon there came a slight sound of movement beneath the hatch, and it rose on a hinge. A man wearing a sailor's cap and a T-shirt with the kanji for Fuyūtoshi printed on it looked up at them from within.

"Konnichiwa," said Takahashi. "Are you in service?"

The submarine captain looked from Takahashi to his three guests, and bowed to them, as well as he could in the position he was in. "Come aboard."

The submarine captain disappeared down into his vessel. Ivor motioned to Dana. "Come on. You first."

Dana stared at the hatch and the back of the submarine where it floated beneath them in trepidation. "What if I fall over?"

"Then I'll have to come and get you, and both of us will just have to be wet." Ivor shrugged. "What's the worst that can happen?"

He held Dana's hand to steady her as she stepped down onto the back of the submarine. It felt extremely unsteady beneath her, but quickly enough she managed to get hold of the edge of the hatch, and climb inside to step on the rungs and make her way down. Jananin followed her, then Ivor. The hatch led into a short tube that opened to a ladder descending into darkness. Dana's foot found the floor and she stepped away from the rungs, her eyes beginning to adjust to the lower light level.

Both flanks of the submarine opened to floor-to-ceiling windows. In the middle was a seating area with all the seats arranged around the same back so all the passengers could see out. When Dana stepped up to one of the windows, it was convex to conform to the shape of the hull, so she could see above and below, and a little bit to the front and back, although it was a bit lensed and distorted by the thick glass. The morning sun glittered on the ocean surface above, and cast dynamic columns of light through the water.

She turned to Ivor in delight. "This is mint!"

The submarine captain fixed her with a nonplussed stare from his seat at the window bubble to the fore of the vessel. "What does this mean, *mint*?"

"It means a place where money is made," Ivor explained. "But how she's using it, she just means it's cool."

Takahashi closed the hatch and jumped down from the ladder, making the submarine wobble a bit. "To Suichūtoshi," he said.

"Takahashi, you know the rules about taking outsiders to Suichūtoshi," the submarine captain replied, rubbing the back of his hand on his face wearily.

"These gaijin have earned the trust of the city, and have permission from Mayor Sato." Takahashi presented the submarine captain with some documents. He scrutinised them very carefully for several minutes.

"All right," he said at last. "They will need to write their names in the book. Those are the rules."

The captain brought out a book from a safe in the cabin. It turned out the names had to be written properly in kanji, which posed no problem for Jananin and Takahashi.

"Do I have to write in it as well?" Dana asked. "Aren't I too young?"

"If you are too young to write your own name, then you are too young to be trusted to keep a secret." The captain shrugged. "However, there is a concession for children. You only have to be able to write your first name."

Dana tried to argue with this by asking what would happen if a woman had a baby in Suichūtoshi and the baby couldn't even say its own name let alone write it, and Takahashi said that people don't start families there as there are no facilities; they go to Fuyūtoshi or somewhere else and stay there with the baby until it's old enough, as Suichūtoshi is not a place for little kids.

Jananin said all of this was immaterial as Dana's name could be approximated with kanji quite easily, and drew two rather simple characters that she said sounded like *Dana*, which Dana simply had to copy once for practice and write into the book.

"It's a good job the policewoman on duty the night you were found was not called Persephone," Ivor remarked, but he had a lot of trouble writing his name. Takahashi had to write it down for him and he had to practice it several times before he could get it right.

At last they set off, on a tour of the sea around Fuyūtoshi first, as Takahashi explained it was not the done thing to just sink and go there directly, in case anyone saw and it aroused suspicions. The city was surrounded by seaweed farms and floating photovoltaic fields to feed the people both in food and power, and so the boats all had to come to the port through a shipping lane, otherwise as Ivor poetically observed, it would be like a haulier driving an artic through a power plant and over some poor farmer's fields of wheat and cabbages. However, this didn't pose an issue to the submarine, as it could travel underneath the great rafts of seaweed with their trailing green fronds, through which bright shafts of daylight would stab and disappear, bathing the submarine in a sublime light show as the captain explained to them what each variety of seaweed was called and its culinary use.

Although the view from the submarine was fascinating, there was something about it being underwater that was a bit claustrophobic and disorienting. Dana tried to attract Ivor's attention to tell him quietly. "I can't feel GPS."

Ivor cast about the inside of the submarine, at the big windows. "I don't think there's enough metal in here for it to work as a Faraday cage."

"It's the salt water," Jananin explained, glancing up from where she was sitting. "A few metres of brine electrolyte works as well as any Faraday cage. It's the same reason why radio signals won't propagate underwater and submarines have to come to the surface to send messages, and rely on sonar to navigate."

They passed other submarines and places where people could get out in wetsuits and snorkels, and interact with fish who did not seem to fear that they might end up on a sashimi plate, and grey porpoises with stubby little noses who would come up and let people pet and cuddle them. They reminded Dana a bit of the orcas in Puget Sound.

Once they had travelled far enough out from the city and away from the dock, and no divers or other submarines were near, the captain turned back towards Fuyūtoshi and the submarine sank deeper in the sea, until the water darkened and the surface was just a distant glimmer. Everyone fell silent, the faint whine of the electric motors that powered the submarine's propellers and the slight marine sounds that penetrated the hull seeming very loud as they waited.

Although Dana could sense nothing at all of GPS or

any other signal from outside the submarine at this depth, the submarine had a computer to help the captain steer it and navigate, and this gave off its own signals. She couldn't make a lot of sense of them at first, but as the journey progressed, she found herself examining them and trying to process them in different ways to make sense of them, since there was nothing else she could feel. If she looked at the signal data in a particular way, they formed a sort of fuzzy shape, like an inverted cone with a tail extending from the bottom. As she concentrated on it, more details began to form. The cone was made up from irregular objects protruding from the central axis. At the very bottom of the spindle, there was a blocky counterweight and an immense chain that descended into the depths, perhaps attached to a great anchor some unfathomable distance below.

It was only when someone nudged her that Dana realised she'd been sitting with her eyes shut in her effort to understand the signal from the submarine's sonar. Ivor pointed silently to the captain's back. In front of him, the windows of the submarine looked out on something rather similar to the image Dana had made in her head from the signals, although it was murky from distance and the light was dimmed by depth and the shadow of Fuyūtoshi overhead. The wider part of the structure to the top of the spindle was easiest to see, as it glowed with many lights. As the submarine drew steadily closer, the lights were revealed to be a great many windows, and the windows were revealed to be set in pipes and structures built out from the central axis. The buildings of the underwater city were not skyscrapers, or houses, or anything that even approximated that. The city was made of watertight modules fixed together.

As they'd passed from the seaweed farms beneath the outer rim of the city, the water had been empty of any human activity, but now signs started to reappear. The submarine passed beneath suspended cages and gridded platforms, the lights that shone from the prow illuminating oysters and crabs being reared there. As the captain guided the submarine up, a large shelf covered with a layer of sand passed by one of the windows. Upon the sand were lots of small, dark, spiny shapes, and a sea-urchin farmer floating face-down over them in SCUBA gear looked up from tending her flock to wave to them as they passed, her pony-tail floating in the water.

The underwater city was now so close that Dana could make out individual modules and the distant shapes of people within, and the submarine became lost against a jumbled wall of interconnecting pipes and units. The captain seemed to be aiming for a tube jutting out from the edge, which split into a number of other pipes extending down.

With careful adjustment, aided by Takahashi who was in the pipe underneath the hatch shouting instructions, the captain manoeuvred the submarine beneath one of the pipes and into position so the protruding edge of the hatch slotted inside the tube. Takahashi worked a handle through several rotations. The noise of a motor started up, and a slight turbulence disturbed the water outside the submarine's windows. The motor stopped, and a green light lit up on the panel beside the hatch. Takahashi worked another handle, something unlocked, and the hatch swung upwards, revealing a pipe with ladder rungs leading up to another hatch.

Takahashi shouted a thank-you to the captain, before calling to the others to follow him. Dana let Jananin go first, and when she followed, Takahashi was already at the top and opening the next door. The ladder rungs and the walls were wet with seawater, and as she looked around the narrow pipe, she could see exactly what Takahashi had meant about it not being for little children. Elderly people and those with physical disabilities likely wouldn't get on well in here either. Probably even very fat people like Sato would have problems.

The next hatch led up into a horizontal pipe, and Dana climbed out onto a floor. Takahashi closed the hatch behind them once Ivor was through. Ivor, Jananin, and Dana looked around the pipe, which had a hatch at each end and a bit of a window on either side looking out into the sea. Condensation had formed on the walls, and the noise of a fan could be heard. Pipes and wiring ran along the top of the tube, running through the walls into the adjacent compartments. A computer screen on the wall showed a readout of gas percentages and humidity.

"Good grief." Ivor put on his spectacles and examined a pipe labelled *oxygen*. "I can see why the mayor has these rules. With people living like this, I can only imagine the damage a bomb or a bullet could do if someone were to get one down here, or even an accidental ignition source."

Takahashi pressed on, opening the next hatch. They passed through another corridor, and then into a hub with three hatches leading off it, with a seating area and a medical kit and fire extinguisher fixed to the wall. Dana looked uneasily about. There were signs next to the hatches, but they were in kanji, and with no GPS and everything being modular and symmetrical, she'd already completely lost her sense of direction. There was a security camera here, but it gave out no signal, and a cable joined it to the ceiling line. The computers here must have to manage without wireless technology, if the salt water blocked radio signals between the modules.

In the next compartment they met a Japanese man and woman who seemed to be heading for the submarine dock. They didn't speak English, and Takahashi asked them questions in Japanese. Dana understood the word 'gaijin' amongst the questions, but nothing else. After they had gone, Takahashi turned back to them. "I have asked them if there is a gaijin down here, an English man, who works with computers. They say there are not many gaijin in Suichūtoshi, and there is only one of that description. He is a bit of a mystery as they don't know his real name and he doesn't socialise much, and everyone here just calls him Yubi-san. In English it translates to something like 'Mr Fingers!' He has a laboratory in the hardware sector, they are given to understand."

Takahashi led on through the underwater maze. Each module was joined by a watertight door that had to be opened and closed on every passage between them. They passed more doors leading off, on both sides, all with Japanese signs, but some also with English translations identifying as research centres belonging to Toshiba, or Sony, or other names familiar from Japanese technology. They came to the end, another pipe for submarines to dock to. "Wherever he is, we must have walked past it," Takahashi said.

Ivor folded his arms. "There are a lot of them. How are we to know which he's in? Dana, is there anything you can pick up?"

Dana shook her head. "Everything's hardwired. The only things that have a signal are *those*." She pointed to the panel each module had, which showed the gas concentrations and humidity as percentages, the output readings of the sensors that worked with the fans to maintain a habitable atmosphere.

"Let's walk back the way we came, slowly, and see if anything jogs our memories," Takahashi suggested.

They were about halfway along when Dana noticed a subtle change in the atmosphere. She recalled she'd noticed it the first time, but it hadn't really registered as significant. "Does anyone think it smells funny in here?"

Jananin frowned. "It smells like *vanillin*. It's a common stain used in thin liquid chromatography."

Ivor exhaled. "What is thin liquid chromatography, and is there a reason someone would be doing it in an electronics lab, where research typically involves computer hardware?"

Jananin shrugged. "Not one I can think of."

Dana looked at one of the readout screens. The

oxygen and carbon dioxide levels were all within normal range, but something had caused a smell here that the ventilation hadn't quite been able to clear. "When we met Steve Gideon yesterday, there was a funny vanilla smell about him."

"Now you come to mention it, I do remember that," Jananin said. "I thought it must be something they were using in the coffee shop."

Dana looked about at the nearby doors. All of them were labelled in Japanese, without English translations. "What do they say?"

Takahashi studied the closest. "In English, it says something like, *The Pacific Institute of Neural Technology Systems Research*."

Ivor ran his fingers over his jaw. He pointed at the door. "That could be it."

Takahashi rapped on the door before turning the handle to open it.

The door opened upon a large circular room, with a few other doors leading off it. There were tables built into the walls, covered with computers and hardware, and another circular table in the middle of the room with its surface scattered with circuitboards and components. A young woman wearing a lab coat shouted indignantly at them in Japanese. Takahashi shouted back, and approached her, asking questions. With her answer came a derisive snort and a shake of her head.

Takahashi said to Jananin, "She says, she has never heard of a gaijin with six fingers on each hand, and the idea is so absurd she says I am a crazy person and I have made it up."

Jananin laughed. "Then it seems we are in the right place."

At that same moment, one of the other doors opened, and Steve Gideon himself appeared, with a laptop under his arm. His expression fell when he saw the four of them there, and for a moment he jerked back and forth in indecision about whether to retreat back through the door he'd come or do something else. Then he rushed across the room to one of the other doors and seized the handle.

"Steve, stop!" Ivor shouted.

Takahashi let out a shout. Something whizzed through the air. Steve Gideon suddenly seemed to lose control of his arms and legs. He fell flat on his face in front of the door and lay still. Something that looked a bit like a cog, like a tiny silver spur, was stuck in the back of his jacket.

The young woman screamed. She pressed herself back against the wall, elbows bent, hands balled in fists in front of her mouth, and started gibbering and sobbing hysterically. Takahashi shouted something at her. "He is not dead! Somebody get her to calm down; she thinks I'm yakuza. She can go to him in a minute, but no-one must touch until I remove it, because it has curare on it."

"Curare?" Jananin exclaimed. "How d'you put curare on a shuriken without poisoning yourself?"

Takahashi bent over Steve Gideon's lifeless form, drawing a cloth from his pocket. "With care." He took hold of the silver spur carefully between finger and thumb, and deposited it in the cloth. "Now deal with him while I get rid of this."

Ivor rolled Steve Gideon on to his back. He had gone completely limp, he wasn't breathing, and his eyes seemed to be fixed staring in front of him. He looked like he was dead. Ivor felt his wrist for a pulse.

"If it's curare he'll be in respiratory arrest," Jananin said. "He's fully conscious, but he's paralysed, and he'll need mouth-to-mouth until he metabolises it off." She spoke to the young woman, slowly in Japanese to explain, while Ivor tipped Gideon's head back, held his nose, and breathed into his mouth. It didn't look like a very pleasant thing to have to do to someone with a moustache.

The woman screamed again as Jananin took her by the arm and brought her to Gideon's side, but Ivor held out his hands in a calming way. He placed one hand on Gideon's chest, spreading his fingers out. "He's not dead," he said, although she didn't seem to speak any English. "Come and sit down. Do you know mouth-to-mouth?"

After Ivor had breathed for him a couple more times, the woman had calmed down enough to understand, and took over from him for a few breaths.

"Takahashi, what the hell?" Ivor demanded. "He's not a terrorist! He's not even a bad person!"

"Sorry," Takahashi said. "Force of habit. But that's the benefit of curare. If you make a mistake, it's reversible."

After about ten minutes, Steve Gideon's eyes moved, and then he blinked. He blinked again, and he twitched, and then he took a shallow breath on his own.

"Is there a bed or a sofa where we can put him?" Ivor asked.

Takahashi spoke to the woman. She nodded nervously and led them into another room, a small kitchen and seating area with windows that looked back on the underwater city. Ivor carried Steve Gideon with some difficulty, and put him on the sofa with a cushion under his head. After a few more minutes he was breathing regularly, and he managed to stutter out, "Ivor, love, I would have enjoyed that so much more if you wouldn't eat so much garlic!"

Steve Gideon groped with his hand across his chest, into the inside pocket of his jacket, to retrieve a plastic cylinder. He sucked sharply on the end of it, breathed in, and exhaled a cloud of fog smelling overpoweringly of vanilla.

Ivor grimaced. "Steve, I appreciate you perhaps need this after what's happened, but in future, can you try not to do it in front of Dana?"

Gideon moved his feet, sliding himself into a sitting position. His hands shook. "Megumi?" He followed it with a request in Japanese. The young woman said something in response, and started making him a cup of coffee.

"I'm sorry, Ivor," Steve Gideon said. "Please don't think badly of me for lying to you."

Ivor sat down on the sofa. He put his hand on Gideon's shoulder. "Where is it?"

Gideon's eyes twitched aside to indicate one of the doors. "It's in one of the other rooms. It's disconnected, of course. I put it back inside the box I used to transport it. It works as a Faraday cage." He took another drag on his vape, turning his head and blowing it up the wall, but there was nowhere for it to go inside the submarine room, and the ventilation system didn't seem very good at removing the odour, concerned as it was more with maintaining the appropriate oxygen and carbon dioxide levels and keeping the humidity below a certain percentage.

"After Richard was murdered, and I fled the country, I took one of them with me. I kept fairly quiet about the research I was doing with Cerberus, of course, waiting until I had results to publish, and I figured I was being targeted because someone who didn't know the specifics understood I had a computer. Whoever took them, probably didn't notice anything particularly odd about finding two identical computers instead of three. I realised one of them had gone to America when I observed a change in latency with the communication between the one I had and the other two."

"You plugged it back in, and monitored how it interacted with the other two?"

"Well, of course. My research was all I had left after Richard was murdered and I was forced to disappear. I wanted to know how my design would pan out. I wanted to learn all its strengths and faults, and from it design the next generation. I had some suspicion it might be being used for not entirely honourable ends, notwithstanding the way it was obtained from me. I did wonder, about the governments in the UK and the US."

Megumi brought him a revolting-looking cup of black coffee, which he took a shivering sip from, and set down on the table in front of him.

"You see," he continued, "There wasn't really a lot

I could do. I came here, continued my research. I had to continue it rather low-key and use another name, but there are some fantastic computer scientists in Suichūtoshi. I've had some great PhD students in the time I was here. Megumi is one of them." He broke off to smile at the young woman. "And as time went on, it seemed to be that Cerberus was operating very stably, and despite what had been done to me, and what it was being used for, it might be best to let sleeping dogs lie.

"Even if democracy for more than the past decade has been an illusion, the expense might be worth the stability it's brought. The NHS has been working well enough, and no big wars have broken out. I mean, now it's been removed, I hear the UK has elected some nutcase who intends to leave the EU and the ECHR! And that he wants to abolish the monarchy and for some people's votes to be worth more than others! And in America just before this happened, one of the parties there stood that loudmouth trying to pitch himself as some sort of populist. It polarised the parties there, made drama out of something that never needed to be. Since they've had my Cerberus, it all seems to have returned to being much more moderate."

Ivor patted Gideon's shoulder. "I once used to think, that if I stole something, if nobody was using it and nobody ever found out, nobody would get hurt." He shook his head. "I was wrong."

Gideon frowned. He took a few more sips of coffee.

"The funny thing was, after being stable for more than a decade, something destabilised it a few months ago. The output showed it was behaving very erratically. After the incident in London, when the first one got disconnected, I had the idea something had gone terribly wrong, but we couldn't really work out what. When the second one became unstable and went down, I decided not to risk the third any more, and I disconnected it myself, and it's been disconnected ever since."

Dana pulled a footstool across the floor. She sat down

uneasily in front of Steve Gideon. "I think I know why Cerberus went wrong. I think it was my fault."

He looked up, met her eyes, and then he laughed, not unkindly. "Of course it's not your fault. I made a mistake when I designed it and it developed a fault by itself. You shouldn't be carrying the weight of the world on your shoulders at your age."

Dana pointed at her forehead. "Ivor put a... a thing..."

"A transceiver," Ivor told him.

"A transceiver, in my brain when I was a foetus. I can hear computers. I mean, not just like when they make *beep* noises or people use them to play MP3s. I can hear what they're thinking. I can talk back to them, tell them what to do, as well."

Gideon's mouth fell open. He turned his head to look briefly at Ivor, and back to Dana.

"I tried to talk to your Cerberus. It had made a world for itself, on the Internet, out of the desert in Nevada and the myths about Cerberus being a three-headed dog that guards an underground river called the Styx, and the electoral register and all bits and pieces from the real world. Only... and I'm really sorry and I didn't mean this... my brother and my foster brother, and this other boy, and me, we thought it was a game, and we went and we tried to kill Cerberus because we thought that was the point of the game, and I had this argument with Ivor when I found out what he'd done, and I was really upset and scared, and I think I taught Cerberus how to be scared and sad, and because I came into its world and tried to kill it, it came into my world and tried to kill me..."

Gideon stared at her. "Is-is what you're trying to say," he stammered out, "that you have *contaminated* Cerberus with *emotions*?"

"I'm so sorry!" Dana cried.

"Dana, don't be sorry!" Ivor said fiercely. "You're not in trouble for anything. You weren't to know!"

"This is *fascinating*," Steve Gideon said. "There has

never been a computer that can experience emotions. And you think that was what made it unstable?"

Dana nodded.

"This instability, as you call it." Jananin spoke from the first time, standing beside Takahashi in front of Gideon and Ivor. "It has made it dangerous. That is why we have come here, to tell you, that you must destroy the remaining Cerberus unit."

"Destroy it?" Gideon glanced up at her. "Surely, if this is the first computer in the world that can experience emotions, we should *study* it?"

"It's too dangerous!" Jananin countered.

Ivor raised his hands. "He's had it here all this time, and had it under control. Can you study it safely, without it being able to connect to anything?"

"He wants it!" Jananin pointed accusingly at Ivor. "He thinks he can use it to exonerate himself!"

"I don't," Ivor said. "It's his computer. It should be his decision."

"Blake is right," said Takahashi to Steve Gideon. "You may think this thing is safe with you, but what if someone else were to get hold of it? What if you were to die?"

"I have made a will."

Jananin said, "Then how well do you trust your beneficiary, or your executor, not to sell it to someone who will abuse it? The same way as the other two have been abused."

Ivor looked at Dana. "It seems you have the deciding vote."

Dana became aware of the focus of everyone in the room shifting to her.

"It's not up to me to decide," she said. "What about when a person commits a crime, and they go to court, and a jury and a judge have to decide what happens?"

Jananin laughed. "This is not a person. It's a machine. It doesn't answer to the law, and it can't be sent to jail."

"But what about the Meritocracy and Colin Antrobus.

He says the people have to decide, right? So why don't we take Cerberus back home, and tell Colin Antrobus, this is what's left of the computer that was controlling everything, and how it did it, and everyone has to decide, together, whether it should be destroyed, or if Steve Gideon can study it?"

Nobody initially looked very enthusiastic about Dana's suggestion.

"In a referendum?" Jananin said.

"They can have a referendum about that, can't they?"

"So far as I understand the Meritocratic Party's manifesto, the people can nominate anything they want for a referendum."

"Then can we do that?"

Dana felt deeply uncomfortable with everyone staring at her, being asked to make a decision as though she were an adult. Then Steve Gideon spoke, sounding a bit defeated. "All right, then."

"And can I see Cerberus, before we take it back home?"

Gideon looked at her with interest. "See it as in look at it, or see it as in *interface* with it?"

Dana shrugged. "Both. I made it so Cerberus could feel horrible things. I want to see if I can try to fix what I did."

Jananin and Ivor both objected to this vociferously, with arguments that it was too dangerous.

"Please!" Dana shouted at them.

"It's disconnected," Gideon explained. "It's in the box I used to transport it here, and the room it's in is a Faraday cage too. It would be relatively easy to open the box and then close it again if she'd like to do that."

"Dana," said Ivor wearily. "Can't this wait?"

"I just don't like to think of Cerberus, on its own, afraid."

"If you insist on taking this risk," Jananin said, "I insist someone goes with you and intervenes if anything goes wrong."

"There's probably room for one more in the room, if

she and I go in," Gideon said.

"Fine," Jananin replied. "Takahashi is the best trained."

Dana and Takahashi followed Steve Gideon to a door. Inside, the windows looked out on the sea, and once the door was closed behind, no signals penetrated the Faraday prison of metal and brine. In the centre of the room stood an upright box with carry handles on the side, much the same size as the Cerberus unit that had been under the Amethyst Building in London. To one side lay an inert mass of loose, thick cables that ran up into a junction above the door. Cerberus's connection to Fuyūtoshi above, and out into the Internet and the world.

"When I open the box, you will be able to connect to Cerberus. It's a quantum computer, so it has a permanent power supply, and it's not designed to be switched off. It's still on in there."

Dana nodded to show she understood. She knelt on the floor in front of Cerberus, and as Gideon started to unfasten one of the boxes' sides, she closed her eyes to concentrate.

*

When Dana opened her eyes, it was dark. She could sense Cerberus close to her, feel its breath, just make out the form of the great dog.

This was where Cerberus had been trapped, a mind alone in the dark, devoid of signals and interaction. It moved away from her when she tried to approach, filled with fear and despair and pain and hatred. "Cerberus, please stop," Dana beseeched it. "Please, let me try to undo what I did to you. I never meant to."

But Cerberus evaded her every time she reached for it, pressing itself against an invisible wall in the dark that seemed to encircle her with a fixed radius no matter where she moved. And Dana realised she knew, and deep within herself she had always known, that what she had done, how she had contaminated Cerberus, was irrevocable. There was no undoing it.

But there was another possibility.

"Cerberus, please let me try. You have to let me try. Because I'm Pandora, and I've to finish what I started."

Dana knelt on the floor, as she had done in front of Cerberus's corporeal form back in Suichūtoshi. She tried to think past the fear and panic that was bleeding back into her from Cerberus. She could see this version of Cerberus was the one she had fastened the misshapen facsimile of Ivor's watch around the neck of when she had done it this great harm, when it had all gone wrong, for it wore it still. Rather than trying to grab it and force her will on it, she sat still on the floor. She thought of Ivor.

Dana thought of Ivor as he was to her when she was afraid and sad, and how he'd held her tightly to calm her down, and how it had felt. It was enough to make Cerberus stop pacing and fidgeting and pressing as far away from her as it could, and it turned its head to face her.

She reached out her hand. She touched the great hound's face, holding on to that feeling.

Cerberus took a step towards her.

Dana thought of the *Atlantic Sonata*, of Ivor and Jananin, the quiet, private sitting-room where they used to talk, the deck of the ship on that night they'd gone out, stargazing, Jananin explaining the names of the constellations, Dana snuggled against Ivor with her head on his shoulder to keep warm.

Cerberus took another step forward. It lowered its head. With trembling shoulders, it crouched down in front of her, and shuffled until it lay shivering, with its head in her lap. Dana stroked the huge hound, its oily, smelly coat not mattering to her, even though she didn't much like dogs. Ivor had once said, that when you have a puppy, you fall in love with it, so when it grows into a dog it doesn't matter.

Dana remembered the times in the inn, the times in America, of Isaiah Redwood in Nevada and the funny things he used to say. She remembered how the orcas and the mammoths made her feel, and that it wasn't always a bad thing to be sad about something. She remembered Ivor and Jananin and the magnolias, and all the Japanese food she'd eaten in Fuyūtoshi, and the funny things Takahashi said. She remembered Pauline and Graeme at home, and Cale, and Peter, and Duncan and playing computer games with him.

All of these feelings she gave to Cerberus, and only then did it understand. Only now was the gift complete.

Dana tried to think to Cerberus in a way it would understand, that they were going back to the UK, that the Meritocracy would decide what was best and fair to do, and that Cerberus would have to be tested, to make sure it was safe, and then if it was, they would reconnect it, and it wouldn't be trapped and alone. But until that time, it wouldn't need to be afraid any more.

Once she was sure it understood, Dana got to her feet and made it known she needed to leave, now. But she would tell everyone what had happened, and make sure Cerberus was given a fair trial.

The one thing she could not understand, as she disconnected, was why the main emotion Cerberus seemed to be feeling was *guilt*.

-22-

LOADING the box with Cerberus in it onto the submarine turned out to be something of a complicated operation, needing a crane bringing to the docking pipe to lower it into place. Once back at the wharf, they needed another crane to lift it out, and then Ivor and Steve Gideon carried it between them to Takahashi's apartment block.

Takahashi's apartment was now quite crowded, with the Cerberus box shoved behind a sofa with a cloth draped over it, and Ivor and Steve Gideon agreeing that they'd share a bedroom until they could set off back to the UK. It was understood that Gideon's PhD student, Megumi, would take responsibility for packing up his other projects up and come and join him back in Oxford once she had put the lab in Suichūtoshi in order. Apart from the box containing the last Cerberus unit, Steve had brought with him only a briefcase packed with handwritten notes, and a valise.

Then Steve opened a window and tried to vape out of it, and Takahashi became angry about this. "No, not out of window! You do that outside properly, and not stink up my flat!"

Ivor said, "Steve, we've got to try some CBT when we get back to England, to see if we can work out something to help with the way you're abusing stimulants!"

Takahashi went into the kitchen with Jananin, and they discussed something, and Takahashi went out. Jananin explained to the others that they had agreed, since they had accomplished what they meant to do here, Takahashi would report to Mayor Sato and take a couple of days off to visit his family. They were not to tell anyone where Takahashi had gone, as his family lived somewhere secret in Fuyūtoshi, and if the yakuza found out, they would kill them to get to him.

Steve Gideon was very interested in Dana's ability to interface with computers. He asked her a lot of questions about how things felt and what it was like, and took the time to explain many things to her about how computers work. Dana enjoyed talking to him. He often used words she didn't understand, but she would rather talk to someone like that than to a person who spoke to her like she was an idiot.

She talked so much with him, that on the second day, Ivor and Jananin apparently became tired of listening to them, and they both went out and left them together in Takahashi's apartment all day.

They had spent the morning talking about how the Internet works, with Dana telling Steve about games and how Cale could play them if he wanted to, but he preferred to watch. For lunch, Steve had made miso soup with tofu and seaweed, and sushi, and it seemed as he had lived in a Japanese place for a long time, he had learned to cook as they did. They spent most of the afternoon talking about GPS, and how he thought it was an anomaly that Dana could conjure up a map to see where she was, but only for the immediate area she was in. Although when they discussed this, Dana realised she could also call up maps of other places she'd been, up to an extent. She could remember the route she'd taken with Ivor in America, but not specific places and names, and nowhere near the detail she could see when she was in the place.

While she spoke, Gideon often wrote notes on paper pads.

"Why do you write by hand, when you're a computer scientist?" Dana asked him.

"Ah, it's so that Cerberus, or anyone else who might be interested, won't be able to hack me and steal my ideas! You have given me a great many ideas for future research projects! When I get back to Oxford, I am going to have a lot of grant applications to write and PhD students to recruit!"

He set down his notepad and got up. "Excuse me," he said, and Dana knew he was going outside to vape, again. She decided to pick up the glass she'd drunk out of as well as all the cups Steve had dirtied with his horrid coffee, and take them to the kitchen.

As she went to the kitchen, she passed the door to a bedroom that had been left open, and a mirror that by chance from where she stood reflected the view of the front door. As Steve Gideon went to unlock it, it was suddenly flung violently open, knocking him back, and two men dressed all in black charged into the room. Dana dropped all the cups on the floor and froze against the kitchen doorway, but with the screams and shouts the men made, it went unheard. One of them punched Steve in the side, and they both forced their way into the living room without seeing her.

Dana ran to Steve, who had fallen down on the floor. It was only when she saw the blood spreading across Takahashi's hemp mat in the hallway that she realised he hadn't been punched. "Steve Gideon!" she cried, and she knelt next to him and tried to put her hands over the wound in his side and press down, like she'd seen paramedics and first aiders help people on television, and stop all the blood coming out of him, but already his face was like wax.

He was grasping something in one hand, close to his face. "*Cerberus!*" he said, and he looked at Dana. "Take my... research... back to England."

He said nothing more, and the thing he was holding fell from his fingers. It was his wallet, with a picture inside the plastic screen wallets often have, of himself, looking much younger, with a man with dark hair. His partner, Richard.

Two men stood in the doorway behind Dana, and now

she knew what these men were: yakuza.

Somebody seized hold of her arm, shook her roughly, and shouted at her in Japanese. When the men saw she didn't understand, he shouted again, "*Where is computer?*"

And because Dana was very afraid they would hurt her, and very upset about what they'd done to poor Steve Gideon, she told them it was in the sitting-room.

Two of them took Cerberus. The other two took hold of Dana, pulling her away from Steve Gideon and out through Takahashi's front door. "No!" Dana screamed, and she found the signals from the men's phones, made them ring the police, but it wasn't enough as the police weren't here now, and she was being dragged, struggling against the yakuza to no avail, down the stairs, out onto the walkways and bridges over the lily pond that surrounded Takahashi's apartment block. Blood covered her hands and arms with a sticky film, the men's rough hands on her slimy and repulsive from what they'd done.

Somebody saw her and shouted. People looked at the yakuza, and Dana with Steve Gideon's blood all over her hands and down the front of her clothes, and they started screaming and panicking.

The men said something to each other. The two with Cerberus went first, carrying it out onto the bridge, and the other two held Dana roughly up by the arms, as she fought them all the way and refused to stand or walk, and screamed to the people for help.

Two people broke through the panicking masses, onto the walkways: Ivor and Jananin. Ivor pushed ahead of Jananin, shouting out as he realised what was happening. "What the hell do you think you're doing? Take your hands off her!"

He reached out for her, and at the same time, one of the yakuza let go of her to position himself between Ivor and Dana, and his hand went to the hilt of a knife...

"*No!*" Dana screamed, and she felt for the man's mobile phone signal again, these mobile phones the Japanese all had, more advanced than the ones at home, more power hungry, and with a battery to supply that, newer, less tested, more unstable...

The back pocket of the yakuza's leather trousers burst into flames. In the diversion it caused, Ivor managed to reach Dana and pull her clear. Behind him, a whirl of motion, a shout, overhead a flash of steel...

Jananin had struck the other yakuza who'd put his hands on Dana with her katana, up over her head in a blow down through the point where the neck joined the shoulder, a stroke that had come to a stop in the middle of his heart. The same strike she'd tried to use on Ivor back on Lewis.

As Ivor pulled Dana away, the yakuza whose trousers had exploded tried to come up on Jananin's left flank, but her free hand flew for the knife strapped to her thigh, and she drove it hard up through the bottom of his sternum into his ribcage before he could reach her.

Jananin pulled the wakizashi back out of the man, spraying the decking with blood. The yakuza fell down on hands and knees with a wheezing intake of breath. She twisted against her right shoulder, trying to pull her katana free, shaking the man impaled on it. He'd fallen to his knees. All the colour had drained from his face as it had from Steve Gideon's. His lips moved, but no breath and no sound came, and bloody bubbles rose from his wound. Jananin looked about herself, eyes wild. She pulled again on the katana, a vigorous twist and a jerk against feet braced apart on the decking, but the blade was stuck. On one of the walkways leading off, the two yakuza with Cerberus were putting the box down. They were coming.

Ivor stepped forward. He pressed Jananin aside. He grasped the handle of her katana with both hands and pulled, setting his foot against the now dead yakuza's shoulder. He grimaced as the sword eased free, and the man's body fell back on the bridge, the water beneath the water lilies darkening with blood below.

Ivor held the sword handle back out to Jananin. She didn't seem to see him. She stared at the men approaching, and a sort of shudder overtook her. Ivor took her hand, put the katana back in it, clasped it tightly in both his own. She turned to look at him, and an exchange passed between them somehow. She pushed her bloodied knife back into its sheath, and held the katana with both hands, turning to face the yakuza.

Ivor took hold of Dana, pulling her away, his voice desperate at the sight of the blood all down her. "Dana, where are you injured?"

"It's not mine." Dana started to cry. "It's Steve Gideon's!"

Ivor put his arms around her and pressed her tightly to his chest. He told her not to look, but she refused, turning her head to Jananin, who stood with her back to them both, facing the two yakuza. Her feet were spaced apart, her knees were bent, and she held her katana with both hands close to her body, arms tensed, the blade near to horizontal. The two men stood, katanas drawn, in similar posture. Memories rushed through Dana's mind on a whirlwind of fear: Jananin, at the dinner with Sato, explaining it was a sport and she'd never used it to kill; Takahashi, explaining how it was wrong for men and women to spar together because men were stronger, although perhaps it was different with swords than it was hand-to-hand like in judo, as he'd admitted he and Jananin had sparred together as friends; Sato's wife, saying how in real war, women are given no exemption and must choose between fighting back or death.

She was one against two. She had trained for a sport. They were practised in the art of killing.

A woman broke from the crowd onto the walkway behind Jananin's opponents. Her hair was in a bun and she wore a traditional kimono, the side of it gathered up in one hand, and she ran silently because she had taken off her wooden sandals and she ran in her socks, a slight tremor through the walkway the only hint that might give her away. Her other hand was on the hilt of the short sword she wore in her sash, and as she came within reach of the nearest man, she drew it and plunged it into his flank, letting off a blood-curdling shriek as she did.

The attack on the first man and the noise she made were enough to startle the other enough to give Jananin an opening, and she uncoiled with an upward strike that tore open the second yakuza's throat and sent him crashing back into the handrail and falling over it backwards, headfirst into the water.

The woman put both hands on her sword hilt and pulled it out of the first yakuza, and he fell to the deck, bleeding. She took her stand with Jananin, back to back, both with knees bent and feet set apart, holding bloodied blades, the woman's socks now soaked with blood, as three more men rushed from the crowd onto different parts of the walkway.

Something whizzed through the air. A yakuza suddenly stopped running; fell flat on his face and lay completely still on the walkway. A silver spur protruded from his back.

With a fearsome scream, Takahashi burst from the crowd onto the walkway behind him. As the other two yakuza turned from the women and tried to arrange themselves to meet him, he ran at them and leapt over their fallen comrade, drawing his katana in midair and striking the first with a blow through the head that stopped him in his tracks and sprayed the air with a bloody mist. As he landed, he was already turning and bringing his katana up over his head once more and down straight through the shoulder and into the heart of the final attacker.

Takahashi pulled his sword out using both hands and his foot against the dying yakuza's chest. He went immediately to the man the woman had stabbed, who was on his hands and knees on the walkway since he'd fallen there. He kicked him so he fell on his side, kicked his katana away under the handrail and into the lily pond, and shouted a question in Japanese at him. When he replied, the only word Dana could make out was 'Takahashi' but from the tone of the rest of it, she gathered it was an insult, and he punctuated it by spitting blood in Takahashi's face.

Jananin crouched over the man, drawing her wakizashi once more. "Who sent yakuza after us?" she demanded. "Was it Sato? Just because he cannot take a joke?"

The man laughed. "These were our orders. Take the computer and the child, unharmed. Kill Steve Gideon. I will tell you nothing more."

"Then enjoy your slow death, in hospital." Takahashi shrugged. He bowed to the woman who had come to their aid, standing on the deck beside Jananin in her bloody socks and the hem of her kimono all stained, and she bowed back to him. Then he spoke to Jananin. "Jananin Blake. You might once have just been a gaijin who showed much skill and interest in kendo and iaido. But today, you become bushi. And you are my sister." He bowed very deep and long to her, and she did her best to bow back to him, but she was shaking visibly now.

Ivor let go of Dana. He went to Jananin, and as she turned to face him, he gave her a hug, in much the same way he'd always hugged Dana and Peter to help them to calm down. And she lost her grip on the handle of her katana and it went clattering down on the decking, and she hugged him back. All around them, the crowd of Fuyūtoshi citizens who had witnessed it began to quietly applaud.

*

The police and the paramedics arrived soon after. They had to wait in the lobby while they went up to Takahashi's flat, but when the paramedics came down, they bore a stretcher with a white cloth stained with blood covering the person who lay on it, and they said they were very sorry but nothing could be done for Steve Gideon.

Someone had taken the woman who had helped them home to her family. The police picked up Cerberus and carried it back into the flat. One of them cleaned Jananin's katana and gave it back to her, and took her wakizashi that she'd put away with blood on it, and cleaned that for her as well. The police were very kind and grateful, and bowed often to Jananin and Takahashi, and called them Defenders of the Peace, and they rolled up Takahashi's hallway rug that had been ruined by Steve Gideon being murdered on it, and got rid of it and wiped down the floor underneath for him. They wiped the wallet that Steve had dropped and put it on the coffee table; they made a pot of sencha. Jananin and Takahashi drank it in silence. Takahashi gave them a short statement, and at last they went away, very thankful and apologetic about what had happened.

Dana had been crying ever since they had come back into the flat, and Ivor had sat with her the whole time on the sofa, holding her tightly. Takahashi spoke to her gently. "We are all deeply upset by this. But please, can you tell us now, *what happened?*"

Dana told him, her voice shaking, how the yakuza had irrupted into the flat when Steve had opened the door to go outside to smoke his vape, and how they'd stabbed him on the spot and demanded to know where the computer was.

"Do you think it was Sato?" Jananin's voice was unusually unsteady.

"I can't imagine he would do that," Takahashi said. "He has always hated the yakuza. It was almost certainly not Gideon either, since they killed him. But someone here has found out more about us than we have let on to anyone, and betrayed us. We need to leave Fuyūtoshi tonight, and we must not tell anyone we are leaving."

Ivor said something to Dana about understanding it being hard, but that she had to get up now and get ready to leave.

After Dana had a shower, as she was packing her things, she picked up Steve Gideon's wallet, and took out the picture of Steve and Richard. The plastic pocket in the wallet had protected it from the blood. She put the picture inside Steve's leather briefcase with all his handwritten research notes.

-23-

"**THEY** just forced their way in, and they stabbed him, and I tried to stop the blood coming out but there was nothing I could do!"

Dana sat tucked under Ivor's arm as the plane flew east, into the night. It would take fourteen hours to reach the UK, and now they were packed and set off, with nothing to distract Dana from the memories of the great clouds of blood spreading in the lily pond, and the blood that had run off in the water in clouds all around her feet in the hurried shower she'd had to take before they went, she had started to cry again.

"He had an aortal bleed. There was nothing anyone could have done to help him." Ivor was trying to keep it together for her, but his eyes were red and wet, and his voice came out strained.

"He seemed such a nice man," Dana sobbed. "I mean, he was a bit weird, but then so am I, really."

"He was a lovely man," Ivor said, his voice breaking. "He and his partner Richard, when I was married to Adrienne, they were our friends and we often went out together. Steve and I used to talk together about all sorts of things. I was looking forward so much to having him back and being able to bounce ideas off him again. Unfortunately, it's the way of life that everything dies, and losing someone is something we all have to go through, sooner or later. It's natural for it to hurt, and to feel very sad about it. All we can do is talk about it, and with time, although the sadness never goes away, you start to remember more the good things about the person you lost, and the bad things like how the person died and how terrible it felt, start to matter less."

Dana thought of London, when Ivor had cried, Alpha on the floor and the crowd around her. "Is it wrong that I feel so bad about Steve Gideon, but not so much when it happened to Alpha?"

"No, it's—" His voice faltered. "People have different relationships with each other, and people process grief differently. Steve died very traumatically in front of you. Alpha's death would have been instant and painless, she wasn't outwardly injured, and you didn't witness it." He hugged Dana for a moment while she cried into his shirt, continuing to talk to her gently as she did. "Besides, when I was about your age, some distant cousin I didn't know that well died in a car accident. At about the same time, my aunt's collie, who was rather special, died as well, and I was far more cut up about the dog. I think my aunt and Lydia were the only ones at the funeral who knew that was who I was actually crying about. I don't think some of the other people there would have been quite so sympathetic if they'd realised."

Jananin sat close to Takahashi and neither of them spoke much. Behind the seats, the box with Cerberus in had been lashed to the wall with bungees to stop it sliding around in case the plane hit turbulence.

Dana asked if there was anything to eat. Although the jet plane had a bar, unfortunately it turned out not to have a kitchen, and with the hurry they'd left, there were only some bags of crisps and tins of pop Takahashi had grabbed from a shop in the airport. The last thing Dana felt like eating and drinking, on a plane after everything that had happened, were acidic gassy drinks and crunchy, sugary, salty crisps, even when it turned out the crisps were Japanese ones made from seaweed.

What she really wanted now was some of the miso soup that had been so ubiquitous as a first course for any meal in Fuyūtoshi, with tofu and seaweed bits in it, or some tapioca pudding, or some other warm food with soft bits and nice liquid. It seemed a sad conclusion to what had been, up until it went so horribly wrong, a very enjoyable stay.

Ironically, the least unappetising thing on the aeroplane was sencha, so Takahashi made a pot, and Dana put some of the seaweed crisps in a cup so they went soggy and were more comforting to eat. Ivor asked Takahashi if the plane had a stereo, and if he had any Shostakovitch he could put on, which he did.

It wasn't easy to sleep on the plane. Even with the lights off, the constant irregular motion remained a low-level disturbance. Ivor snored, at one point annoying Jananin so much she got up from her seat and came over and poked him hard in the belly, telling him to shut up, and he woke drowsy and disoriented and said he hadn't said anything. Dana woke with a start somewhere over Alaska with hail rattling across the fuselage and wings, and flashes of lightning in the windows throwing eerie strobing upon the cabin.

"What if the plane gets struck by lightning?" she asked Ivor.

"It probably already has," he said. "It's probably designed for it."

The plane must have crossed the storm, and Dana must have fallen asleep again, because the next thing she knew, she had woken to daylight showing through the windows, and the door to the cockpit was open. One of the pilots was shouting to Jananin and Takahashi. Dana could sense a radio transmission, and she could also sense from what she'd some time ago worked out was the plane's radar, two objects approaching quickly from behind.

This is Eagle Owl calling Tawny Owl. Come in Tawny Owl!

It was a man's voice. An English voice.

Tawny Owl, do you copy?

Jananin went forward to the cockpit. "Eagle Owl, this is Tawny Owl. Over."

Tawny Owl, I hate to have to ask you this as an independent woman, but are those two Russkis bothering you?

"They're coming at us Mach Two. Appreciate if you can do something about them. Over."

Tawny Owl, hold your course. Over and out.

From the radar, Dana could now make out not only the two shapes coming up behind, but three more shapes approaching very fast head-on.

"There's something—" Dana started to say, but a tremendous noise cut her off as the three approaching points passed straight by on the radar. "Something's exploded!"

"It's all right," Ivor said, although he didn't look as though it was all right. "It's just the noise aeroplanes make when they travel faster than sound."

On the radar, the two shapes following disappeared. The other three went out of range, but several minutes later, they returned, following, their speed reducing.

Eagle Owl calling Tawny Owl. Eagle Owl calling Tawny Owl. Eagle Owl's transmission sounded a bit smug.

Jananin's voice again, to the radio. "Eagle Owl, this is Tawny Owl. Over."

Tawny Owl, we got 'em. Over.

"Thank you, Eagle Owl. It is good to hear your voice. Over."

Tawny Owl, I wouldn't be much of a gentleman if I didn't walk you home after that. Prepare for escort to Cape Wrath. Over and out.

Jananin came back, closing the door to the cockpit behind her.

"What was that about?" Dana asked. "Who's he, Eagle Owl?"

"He's the RAF," Jananin said, sitting back down. "We are nearly home."

"What were the other things? The things behind I saw on the radar?"

"Russians," Jananin replied. "They didn't have permission to be in British airspace."

"Then why did they come? Why did they follow us?"

When nobody seemed to be capable of answering Dana's question, she fell silent for a moment. Russians. Yakuza. Someone had told them about Cerberus. And Takahashi thought it wasn't Sato. Dana thought back to the meal with Sato, and the question he had asked her. It had seemed curious, not malicious, but how had he known? His spies? Had his same informants told the Yakuza and the Russians?

There was something else. Steve Gideon's last words. The photograph he had clutched. Dana had thought he meant *take Cerberus and my research notes back to England...* but with his stutter, with the life draining out of him, he might have meant something else. In London, in the Amethyst Bunker, where they'd found the first Cerberus. There had been no seat, no keyboard, no monitor anywhere in that room. No space for an operator. How Cerberus had felt, just before she disconnected from it for the last time...

"What if nobody stole Cerberus from Steve Gideon. What if Cerberus stole itself?"

After a long pause, Ivor said, "What do you mean?"

"What if Cerberus murdered Richard? What if everything that happened after that was all Cerberus, and no-one was ever controlling it?"

"A computer can't murder someone," Ivor said.

"A computer could potentially hire a hitman from the dark web," Jananin suggested.

Dana breathed unsteadily for a moment, the pieces falling into place. "Cerberus had Richard murdered, I don't know why. Perhaps he told Steve he was worried about it, or he said something it interpreted as a threat somehow? Cerberus ordered someone to take it and install one in the civil service, to sell one to America, because it wanted the connections. What if it kept the governments in power because it suited it, because it was stable and straightforward, and not because of anyone making it do that?"

The three adults stared at her in silence.

"What if Cerberus somehow got a message out when I used it, telling the Yakuza and the Russians to come and rescue it? What if it planted a program in another device, like it used Alpha to attack me?"

Jananin frowned. "I can't imagine Gideon would have been foolish enough to take another device into there with it that could be used for that purpose. Are you saying it has implanted this program in *you*?"

"What if I'm making them track me, not on purpose, and I don't even know I'm doing it!" Dana cried out, turning to Ivor, but he could offer no solution.

Takahashi, however, let out an anguished cry. He took his mobile phone out of his pocket. "Could it be this?"

Dana stared at him, aghast.

Takahashi dropped to his knees. He started beating his mobile phone with something, smashing it to bits on the floor of the plane. He picked up all the pieces and took them into the loo at the back of the plane, and the toilet flushed behind the door.

Jananin stared fiercely at Dana. "Dana, if this is true, and that machine is wholly responsible for the murder of two people—"

Ivor interrupted. "It ordered the yakuza to kidnap you as well as to murder Steve and steal it! It has to be destroyed as soon as we land!"

"I don't know!" Dana cried. "I might have made it worse, the first time. But the second time, I might have made it better. What I did to it, might have fixed it. Steve said it had become unstable. I don't know if it did that before I did what I did to help it. I don't know if he would have wanted us to destroy it if he knew!"

"This is not something we can afford take any more risks with!" Jananin shouted. "We work out how to destroy it as soon as we land!"

Ivor put his hand on Dana's shoulder and spoke to her firmly. "It's just a computer. It's volatile and there's no controlling it. Steve would want us to do what was safest for you, what was best for everyone. Now let's sit back down. We'll be landing soon."

Evening had fallen just as they had left Fuyūtoshi, and a night and most of a day had passed in half the usual time in the flight east. Now the sun was setting, behind an overcast sky swept with rain above a grey sea. GPS showed land approaching ahead. A lighthouse on a high cliff passed on the right of the plane, flashing once. The land was as barren as Lewis. The plane gradually slowed, and the jolt of the wheels came as it touched down.

The pilots opened the door. Wind tore across the exposed airstrip as Dana climbed down from the plane. The pilots began to unload the luggage, depositing the box with Cerberus in it down on the tarmac.

Two men approached. One was very smartly dressed in a blue military uniform. He had very black hair and brown skin, and he saluted to them and greeted Jananin like a friend. The other seemed to have come in rather a hurry from a boxy building at the edge of the airstrip. Dana only realised he was Rupert Osric when he told Jananin he'd had her car mended and driven it up to meet her, and she in turn shoved the briefcase containing Steve Gideon's research notes into his arms and told him to deliver it safely to the Department of Computing at Oxford University.

To one side of the airstrip stood three RAF jets and several helicopters. Dana looked back over the empty scenery, to the lighthouse. Beyond it, the land fell away to ocean, dark squalls of rain tearing across the distance. Out there, GPS was telling her, lay nothing but sea, and then the ice of the Arctic.

This was Cape Wrath, the end of the world.

*

Inside the building, a man was waiting to meet them, and this man Dana did recognise on sight. He was Colin Antrobus, leader of the Meritocratic Party, from the telly.

"My name is Colin Antrobus," he said, grasping and shaking in turn the hands of Jananin, Ivor, Takahashi, and

Dana, "and it is my very great honour to welcome you back to the UK as the First Spokesman of the Meritocracy."

Jananin began to explain to Colin Antrobus what had happened since she had contacted him to tell him she would be bringing in a dangerous computer for the Electorate to decide the fate of: that Steve Gideon had been murdered by the yakuza, that Russian aircraft had pursued them over the Atlantic; that several attempts had been made to kill herself, Ivor, and Dana; that the governments of the UK and the USA had both been compromised and their electoral systems infiltrated; that Steve Gideon's partner had been murdered; and that all of these crimes, they had come to believe, had been single-handedly orchestrated by Cerberus itself.

Then she told him that she required some assistance from the Armed Forces to quietly take it outside and blow it up somewhere safe.

"I can't allow that," he said, shaking his head emphatically.

Jananin became irritated. "Why? Why not?"

"Because I was elected on a promise that I would bring transparency and accountability. Because it's illegal on several levels. This computer, it's secure and cut off from the world in that container, isn't it?"

"It's more the risk it would pose if it were to fall into the wrong hands." Ivor tried to explain.

Antrobus raised a finger. "First of all, that was Gideon's computer. It's a chattel. If he's dead, it's the property of whomsoever he bequeathed it to in his will, or failing that, his next of kin. It would be a matter for that beneficiary to decide, after his executor gets probate. Secondly, if as you say several serious crimes have been committed, some of them involving the electoral system, this computer potentially contains evidence, and it would be negligence to allow it to be destroyed along with any data on it!"

"If I may speak." The military man raised his hand. From his voice, Dana suspected he might have been Eagle

Owl, but she wasn't sure. "I have known Professor Blake for a very long time. I don't think she would exaggerate, and from what she says, it sounds as though this thing is a serious security risk. It would be straightforward to arrange for it to be taken out to the testing range and blown up this very evening. We could make up an excuse if necessary, say it was an accident."

"You do and you'll be held accountable for it!" Antrobus chastised him.

The uniformed man shook his head. "I'm sorry, Jananin. It's more than my job's worth."

"Hold me accountable for it!"

Everyone turned at Ivor's exclamation to face him.

"My career's already destroyed, my name dragged through the mud. Just say I did it!"

Antrobus objected, "There's still going to be evidence of negligence here if we're claiming someone allowed you to steal explosives and set them off!"

Ivor shrugged. "We don't need to blow it up to destroy it. I can pilot a chopper, well enough at least to take it out over the Atlantic and push it out into deep water, where no-one can get to it to recover it, and the saltwater will rot it soon enough. Jananin goes with me to see it's done, and we ditch the helicopter somewhere easy to recover. Say I absconded with Cerberus and was never seen again."

Antrobus considered this for a moment. "I suppose it'll be a lot easier to make a convincing argument that it was stolen by a member of the public, than that members of the Armed Forces blew it up by accident."

"There's only one thing I ask in return." Ivor faced Jananin directly. "Let me go. Let me have another identity. I'll be Iain Jones if that's easiest. Just let me live in peace somewhere, let me be Peter's father, and Dana's and any of the others if that's what they want."

"Jananin, let him!" Dana blurted out. "Let me go with him!"

Ivor turned to her. "You don't have to decide *anything*

yet, Dana. Let's finish this, and get rid of Cerberus once and for all, and you can make your decision in your own good time."

"Now see here, you." Colin Antrobus turned on Ivor. "I have spent the last ten years of my life, looking for evidence to confirm what I've suspected while people called me a conspiracy theorist and a loony." He pointed at the box with Cerberus in it. "This machine potentially contains evidence that will vindicate me, once and for all!"

"I think you've already been vindicated," Ivor said. "You wouldn't have won a stonking majority in a general election fair and square if the electorate thought you were a loony. You may think you can use this machine to your advantage, but therein lies the danger of it. These three computers have corrupted and destroyed everyone who has tried to control them. This is not evidence you can use; it's evidence that will use you."

Antrobus considered this further. He looked longingly at the box. "I suppose it might just be possible to explain that away."

Jananin faced Ivor for what seemed a very long time, the expression on her face changing, but her stare unwavering.

"I swear from this day, if word ever reaches me that you have experimented on so much as a fruit-fly, you are dead, Pilgrennon."

Ivor gave a firm nod. He put out his hand to her. "*Deal.*"

Jananin looked down at his hand, and back up to his face. Slowly, she raised her hand to clasp tightly the one he offered.

-24-

ALTHOUGH night had fallen and Dana had not slept very well on the plane, her body was still working on Fuyūtoshi time, which was twelve hours different to Greenwich Mean Time, and she was wide awake. Through the night, Ivor and Jananin prepared. Antrobus had made it very clear that there would be a full investigation, and if anything was found that cast doubt on the story they intended to use of Ivor having stolen Cerberus and disappeared after leaving the helicopter in some uninhabited location nearby, he would do nothing to help them. Jananin's car still had a briefcase with a Compton bomb and her crossbow in the boot, along with the detonator box in the glove compartment, and they decided the easiest way to get rid of them was to take them and throw them all into the sea along with Cerberus.

Eagle Owl, or whoever he was, as nobody seemed to think to introduce him to Dana, was very busy helping Jananin, and spent some time explaining the controls of the helicopter they were pretending to steal to Ivor. He told him it wasn't some toy for training spoilt rich boys who want to play at pilots on the weekend, but a sensitive piece of military equipment.

By the time they were ready to depart, first light had not yet broken over the eastern horizon. In the predawn gloom, they assembled beside the helicopter.

"Dana," Jananin said sternly. "There is no reason for you to come. Takahashi has offered to act as your personal bodyguard here until we return."

"We can wait here together," Takahashi said. "You can show me how to eat a haggis for breakfast!"

"I want to come. I want to stay with you." Dana found

herself staring at the box with Cerberus in it, inside the helicopter and secured to a piece of cargo webbing with bungee hooks. "I want to see it's gone, for myself." It was more than that. Dana had an ominous feeling something might go wrong, Cerberus might fall into the wrong hands again, and she'd never know.

Ivor picked Dana up and sat her on the floor of the helicopter. "Dana, I really think it would be best if you stayed here," he said, his face level with hers. "But if you really want to come, you've been with us through everything else, and I have absolutely no business forbidding it. So if you're coming, you need to do as Jananin and I say."

Dana nodded.

Ivor got in. Jananin climbed up behind him. Eagle Owl saluted; Takahashi bowed. "Come back safely," one of them said.

Then Jananin was sliding the door shut and Ivor was at the controls, running the preflight checks, his forehead etched with lines of concentration, his bottom lip jutting out. Straps with metal fittings jangled faintly where they hung from rails behind the doors.

They were over open ocean when the sun began to rise, struggling to penetrate the cloud cover.

"Dana, let me know when GPS tells you we're over deep water," Ivor said.

Apart from the familiar sensation of GPS, Dana was starting to make sense of the signals that came from the helicopter. Its radar was like the one on the jet, similar in principle to to the submarine's sonar. "I think there are more helicopters coming."

Jananin stared at her for a moment. She leaned forward to the controls next to Ivor and pushed a button. "Tawny Owl calling Eagle Owl, Tawny Owl calling Eagle Owl. Eagle Owl, do you copy?"

Jananin looked up, her finger still on the switch, as two helicopters came into view ahead.

"Eagle Owl, this is Tawny Owl! *Mayday! Mayday!*

Mayday!"

There were five of the other helicopters, approaching from all sides. As they closed in, Ivor was forced to fly low, close to the surface of the water. "What are they? What are they doing?" he said.

Jananin moved about the rear compartment of the helicopter, getting visuals on the helicopters through the windows. "I think they're Russian."

"They want Cerberus!" Dana realised. "We have to throw it into the sea, now!"

Ivor twisted in his seat. "What if we do, and they go after it, and they manage to recover it before it sinks?"

Jananin had been going through the other things they'd brought, the bag with her crossbow in. "I can try to shoot them, but there are five of them, and once I shoot one they're liable to start shooting back! We've still got a Compton bomb and a detonator. If the flux compressor still works, it's a sure way to take out all of them at once, but we've no way of stopping it from destroying Dana and our own helicopter."

Ivor pushed the autopilot switch. He got out of his seat and came into the back, and opened the case. Dana jumped when he flicked a switch, but a light came on and that was all. "It works." He picked up an egg timer with detached wires trailing from it and gave the top a twist. "But this seems to have broken." He poked at the other components inside the case. "If we don't use the flux compressor, we've still got a functional detonator and TNT, enough to destroy Cerberus if we strap it to it. If we set the detonator and push it out, the impact with the water should set it off. It won't deal with them, but at least that's Cerberus disposed of before they manage to get hold of it."

"We're too close to the surface," Jananin said. "The blast will hit us."

Ivor looked out the window at the helicopters closing in around them. "If we open the door, and you shoot one of them, I can try to get out through the gap, gain some altitude. If I tilt towards the door and you hold on to something, give it a push, it should slide out."

They set about strapping the bomb to the box with Cerberus in it. Ivor made Dana hold on to the webbing attached to the back wall, told her to stay there no matter what.

Something struck the fuselage on one side above the door with a bang. Dana screamed. Jananin had the crossbow out and Ivor was ready to open the door. As soon as she had it assembled and cocked, he opened the door and she fired straight through it. Dana caught a glimpse of a line running from above the door to the other helicopter, before it disappeared behind a great ball of flame, and she closed her eyes and pressed herself back against the hot wind and the great noise of the explosion. Jananin was beside her, grasping some straps, her foot braced against the box containing Cerberus, ready to push it out.

Suddenly the other door behind Jananin was pulled open, and some great black and sandy creature burst into the helicopter and started barking and tearing about. Total chaos broke out. The dog, which looked to be a rather cruder version of the ones that had chased the car through London, had electronic devices strapped all over it and attached to its head. It gave out a signal, and it seemed to be targeting Dana for the signal she gave out. Dana was screaming and trying to hide behind Ivor, who was trying to get hold of the dog, and Jananin had drawn her knife and was trying to kill it, and as Dana tried to get away from the dog, she didn't see the man in fatigues and a helmet who was leaning through the door, and he seized her and took hold of her about the middle with his arms, and jumped backwards away from the door, and the helicopter and Ivor and Jananin and Cerberus were flying away as they slid rapidly backwards.

Dana screamed, fearing she'd never see anyone she'd known again, reaching with both arms to Ivor and Jananin. The dog was standing in the doorway, barking frenziedly at her, and Ivor kicked it so it fell out of the helicopter, and at the same time Jananin reached up with her knife and slashed the zip wire that had been fired into the fuselage above the door, and it snapped, and another helicopter flew across the sky over Dana's head, and then the surface of the water exploded somewhere behind her, and the man lost his hold on her.

The water came over her with a freezing grip that stole all her breath. It was nothing like falling into the Styx in the game, or even the swimming pool on the *Atlantic Sonata*. For a moment she could make no sense of anything, and everything was drowned out by the pain of absolute cold; an icy, suffocating pressure that numbed every inch of her skin. Her eyes stung when she tried to open them, unable to focus in the salt water. It was all she could do to try to assume the position Ivor had taught her to float on her back, and take in what short gasps of breath she was able.

As her body adjusted to the shock of the cold, she made out the man who had grabbed her as he drifted away behind a grey-green ocean swell. He was floating but he looked like he was in pain. He had fallen flat on his back when the zip wire broke and pitched them both down into the sea, and he must have hurt himself.

She sensed another signal, the dog. It was coming for her. Dana tried to think unpleasant thoughts as she had with Cerberus, but it was so hard to remember, to concentrate on anything, with the terrible cold pressing in on her. The dog came paddling to her and she tried to hold her hands close to herself, to stop it biting her, and it got hold of her clothing at the shoulder with its teeth.

Turbulence in the water. Someone on top of the dog, taking hold of it by the scruff; a single blow into the side of its chest with a knife, and its grip released. Jananin reached for Dana through the water. When she spoke, her voice sounded weak, high-pitched somehow, from the cold and pressure on her lungs.

"We have to get under the water. *You remember what I*

told you about signals and salt water?"

Dana managed to nod.

Jananin wrapped her arm around Dana's waist, and the pair of them turned onto their backs. She started to swim towards where something orange was going up and down above the swell. It seemed to be wreckage from where she'd shot the other helicopter; a life-raft or something partly inflated, tangled up with mangled pieces of metal fuselage.

Jananin reached for the tangle of metal. She cut something with her knife. "Hold on to me," she told Dana. "Don't let go!"

Dana wrapped her arms around Jananin, barely able to feel anything, the cold stinging her to the bone. Jananin fought loose the piece of wreckage, and as it came away from the orange inflatable buoying it up, it pulled her down, and the water closed over Dana's head. All she could make out were dull shafts of light thrusting down from the surface, and the overpowering cold and pressure getting worse. She couldn't speak, only issue streams of bubbles, the sound distant and rubbery to her ears. Jananin clamped her arm around her waist.

A blaze of light flashed over the surface above, and immediately after there came a great noise that Dana felt all over her body as a blow through the water rather than heard with her ears. She screamed, but only air came out and a distorted, distant sound.

A slackening in the pressure and Jananin's other arm around her told her she'd let go. Dana held on back, trying to suppress the instinct to breathe in, her diaphragm going into spasms.

The surface of the water plastered her wet hair over her face. She gasped and coughed as the water drained from her ears and the deafening silence became the boom of the ocean. A fierce smell of smoke burned her nostrils and icy pinpricks of rain stung her face.

There were no helicopters in the sky above. Dana could

see very little on the surface of the ocean which rose and fell all around them, but she made out some wreckage and one of the dogs, which was clearly dead.

"Did the Compton bomb go off while we were underwater?"

"Yes."

The orange life-raft came into view, and Jananin managed to get them to it. Either something had punctured it or it had never inflated properly in the first place, for it lay all flaccid with the water running over and under it, but it was something to hold on to.

"Where's Ivor?"

Jananin didn't answer.

"Jananin, where's Ivor?"

Gulls began to congregate in the air, wheeling above Jananin and Dana on their long black-and-white wings. They were waiting for both of them to die, she realised, so they could come down and have their lunch, much as she would look at a lobster on Roareim and wait patiently for Ivor to cook it and serve it up. And Dana felt pretty much okay with that. They needed to eat something, and it was only the natural order of things. Their screaming began to grow indistinct as the pain sensations from Dana's body faded. She couldn't keep her eyes open. Jananin shook her occasionally, telling her to stay awake.

A dull throbbing sound punctured the noise of the gulls and the ocean. At first Dana thought she was back on Roareim with Ivor, and it was a Minke whale's song. She opened her eyes and saw the birds had gone, and something other than tide and wind blasted the surface of the water. A helicopter in the sky above.

Dana did not remember much about being pulled out of the water. The next thing she consciously recognised was shivering and being wrapped in foil and blankets inside, where more straps with metal rings on them jangled from a rail along the ceiling. She was aware Jananin was next to her, and some men and women whose uniforms indicated they were RAF around them.

Jananin was trying to tell them something. "Tell Rajesh," she said. "The Russians were sent here... for a computer... and a child. They must not... not see... not hear... must believe... the child and the computer were both destroyed... nothing must get out to contradict it."

Around the helicopter on the ocean surface floated bits of helicopter and dead dogs, and the body of one of the pilots who had pursued them, buoyed up in an orange lifejacket like a float on a baited fishing line.

"Jananin, what happened?"

Jananin was shivering violently, soaking wet. She didn't look like herself at all. Under the foil and the blanket she'd been given, she put her hand on the sheath strapped to her thigh, but the handle of the knife was gone. She must have lost her wakizashi in the sea.

"We couldn't drop the bomb with you... in the water. One of us had to detonate it manually. We... argued. I told him to go, make sure you were safe. Said I didn't trust him to do it. He said... old-fashioned chivalry... that I was the Nobel laureate... he picked me up... dropped me out the door."

Jananin's coat was lying on the floor. She reached for it weakly, and one of the crew picked it up for her. "He put... something in my pocket... said he wanted you to have it."

Dana recognised the thing Jananin put in her hand. It was Ivor's watch. The space between the glass and the face was half full of water and the second hand had stopped.

*

Army medics ran to the helicopter as soon as it touched down at Cape Wrath. Dana was moved to a room and assigned two women who told her they were her personal doctor and nurse, and that she was being treated for cold water immersion and potential hypothermia. The room had big windows looking out over the sea, and she lay propped up in her warm bed and gazed out upon the dark ocean as the evening drew in. The sun sank low behind the clouds, casting eldritch rays of golden light through a shroud of grey. Squalls of rain lanced down with sudden vigour, and she saw the storms, gyrating masses of darkness, process steadily across the distance like marching gods, and it was as though Ivor and Cerberus had been swallowed by Nature's malefic power, and Nature went about her business and would not answer to Dana.

She remembered the *Atlantic Sonata*, the trip around America, Fuyūtoshi, the times she'd been happy, when Cerberus had disappeared for a while. She thought of the times in the house in Edinburgh, in the inn, on Roareim, all the time she'd had with Ivor and Jananin that had been spoilt by worrying about Cerberus. Even that time on the jet back from Fuyūtoshi when she had felt so wretched about Steve Gideon, but she'd still had Ivor. She wished now she could go back to any of them, that she could have lived in any of those times, instead of here and now and being free of Cerberus for good, if this was the price.

Dana clutched Ivor's watch tightly in both hands and cried and cried. She felt as though all the strength she had in her was utterly spent, and she stood at land's end looking out upon oblivion and waiting for the world to finish.

-25-

JANANIN switched off the engine and regarded the
morning mist in the park through the gaps in the wire
fence.

"Where do your foster parents live?"

"Over there," Dana pointed. "Other side of the park."

"I won't risk going any closer, then."

"Come with me. Pauline and Graeme won't mind. You
can meet Cale."

Jananin considered the dials behind the steering
wheel of her car. "Dana, you have a life beyond this to go
back to, and I don't belong in it."

"I want to stay with you. I don't want to go back to
pretending to be normal and I don't want to go back to
that school!"

Jananin glanced at her. "Why would you want to live
with me? What is it you think I do all the time that's so
exciting? I'm no good at being responsible for people other
than myself, and I'm busy anyway. I have work to do."

A long silence followed. There seemed little point in
arguing; in spoiling the last few minutes they would spend
together.

"Will you make sure Peter is all right?" Dana asked.

"I'll do what I can, within my power."

"Do you think... in the end, you would have killed
him?"

Jananin sighed. "To be perfectly candid, the only time
I really think I could have gone through with it was that
first time on the road in Lewis, when you got in my way.
For all that iaido teaches, it is a difficult thing indeed to
kill someone, unarmed and... so... *pathetic*." She grimaced,
as though she didn't quite believe her own words. "And I

wish I had not said that thing to him, when he asked for a knife and I said he could only have it for seppuku." Jananin shook her head. "And a few other things, but that one keeps coming back to me for some reason."

"I believed him. When he said he was sorry." Dana's eyes became hot and wet. "Jananin, he never said anything unkind about you, not to me, not ever, when you weren't there. Even when you tried to kill us all, the worst thing he could say was that he thought maybe you were mad, and that was it."

"Perhaps something good has come, and will yet come, of all the ill he did." Jananin's voice had become tense, as though her throat was constricted. "Go back to your family."

Dana stepped out of the car into the damp, still air and the distant hum of early morning traffic. Jananin did not look round as Dana closed the door. The soles of her boots felt thin and worn as she walked the tarmac pavement to the park gate. She looked back as she passed through, and it was as though the wire fence divided two worlds.

The red lights on the car's back melted into the mist, the noise of its engine dissolving in the damp air.

Dana watched the empty road for a moment, before setting out across the silent tennis courts, their borders buried under depths of wet leaves and litter. The hedges were thickets of empty branches. She avoided the dog turds hiding in the sodden grass as she trudged down the slope towards the road. The swings made no sound, hanging perfectly still in the windless mist.

Some streetlamps still glowed, red against the predawn sky. The gardens on the street were much as she remembered them.

Dana opened the gate quietly and stood staring up at Pauline and Graeme's house with its dark windows, feeling a sudden longing. This felt like a house where people she had never met lived. She knew which cars were parked behind the forbidding garage door, but they could have belonged to anybody. She knew Pauline had planted the shrivelled things in the front garden that had once been pansies, but anyone could have put them there.

A faint rattle came from the front door, and it opened. A boy with tangled black curls, wearing his pyjamas, stepped out onto the paving with bare feet. His eyes were crusted up from being asleep. Cale did not greet Dana or smile at her, but she knew he was glad she had come back.

Footfall thudded on the stairs, deep inside the house. The form of a man in a dressing gown emerged from the dark hall. Graeme stared, open-mouthed.

"Dana?"

From behind Dana, Pauline's voice: "Dana? *Dana!*" She pushed past Graeme, pulling her dressing gown on over her pyjamas as she passed Cale, her voice becoming hysterical. "Oh my God, Dana! Graeme, call the police!" She threw her arms around Dana and started to cry very loudly.

In the house, with the front door closed, Dana tried to tell them, and Duncan who had just got out of bed and was coming downstairs, that they must not call the police, for no crime had been committed, and it would be a waste of the police's resources when they were needed for other things, but despite her request, that was exactly what they did. Then they went into the sitting-room, and made Dana sit down on the sofa, and Pauline asked her if she could heat up some soup for her to eat, and what kind would she like?

Dana said that perhaps instead of soup, Pauline could make tapioca, and then Cale could have some too, as he would like some. And Pauline very sternly said that if Cale wanted some tapioca, he could jolly well ask for it himself and say please and thank you for it as well, as he was perfectly capable of doing so, instead of using Dana as his personal servant.

Pauline heated up some chicken soup, and when Dana had sat at the table to eat it, the police arrived, and Graeme took Duncan and Cale out of the dining room, and Pauline brought in a policewoman, and another woman, and the three women sat at the table with Dana.

The policewoman took off her hat and set it down on the table. She introduced herself, and she introduced the other woman as a social worker who was there for safeguarding and procedural reasons. Pauline told Dana that the two women were here to help her, and to find out what had happened.

"Dana, can you tell me," began the policewoman, gently but very gravely, "where you have been for the past ten months?"

Dana looked at the three women in turn, feeling as though their stares were piercing her where she sat. "I ran away," she said quietly.

"Okay. Can you tell me why you ran away?"

Dana shrugged. She shook her head slightly. "I didn't want to go to school."

The policewoman turned to Pauline. "You're not a suspect at this point, but I'm afraid I'm going to have to ask you to leave the room for the rest of the interview."

Pauline's face crumpled like wet tissue, lines forming around every part of it. She gave a shuddering, convulsive sniff and nodded silently, wiping her eyes as she left the room.

"I need to ask you some more questions, Dana."

Dana stared at the door where Pauline had gone. "Why did you say that to her? You must have said it in a horrible way or done body language or something I don't understand to make her cry like that. Don't treat Pauline badly! She's not a criminal and she's not done anything wrong!"

"Dana, I need to ask you, has anyone done anything to hurt you?"

"Yes," said Dana indignantly. "Before I ran away, Abigail beat me up in the toilet at school and I hit my head and got concussion. And Miss Robinson told lies that hurt my feelings, that I was *pretending* to be autistic to *have attention*. I don't even *want* attention, so why would I do that? I'd rather people left me alone."

"Dana, did anyone hurt you in between when you ran away, between the hospital and now? Did anyone say or do anything in any way inappropriate, or that you felt was not right?"

"No," said Dana, not understanding what she meant, and thinking she shouldn't tell her about the Russians and the yakuza, as she wouldn't believe it anyway.

The policewoman started asking her more questions, but Dana did what Cale did, and stopped answering, and didn't speak to her. After a while, the social worker told the policewoman, "You need to stop now. She's shut down."

"Okay. Thank you, Dana, for talking to me. I'm sure you want to finish your soup and go to bed." The two women left the room, and shortly afterwards, Duncan and Cale were shooed in to sit with her while Pauline and Graeme spoke to the policewoman and the social worker behind the door in the hallway.

Duncan smiled at Dana. He didn't say anything. She knew he wouldn't say anything to anyone else. She knew Cale wouldn't either, because he never did.

Their voices were indistinct, but as she sat there in silence with Cale and Duncan, Dana could sense the signal of the stereo left on in the sitting-room, and through the open door she could eavesdrop on the conversation.

Pauline was crying audibly again, and the policewoman was saying, "I'm sorry to cause you distress. I want to stress, again, that neither of you are suspects in any way at this point. But we need to find out what's happened to Dana."

"Oh, I can't bear to think about it. What if she's been mixed up with a gang and trafficked, or something unthinkable's gone on?" Pauline's crying became muffled, as though Graeme had put his arms around her and she was crying on his shoulder.

The social worker was speaking now. "She *is* back

now, and that's the most important thing. When she was being interviewed, we had to stop because she shut down. Shutting down in kids can sometimes be a sign of trauma. But, autistic kids can sometimes shut down for all manner of reasons. I have to say, off the record, that I don't have any concern that anything seriously untoward has happened to her, based on what her attitude was like before she shut down. She seemed a bit irritated by the questions, but she wasn't angry, and she was polite, but she wasn't cowed."

Graeme's voice: "So what happens now?"

"Okay, well, first we need to let her settle for a few days. Then we'll need her to come in to the station and do a recorded interview. She'll also need to be checked over medically. It's probably a job for a paediatrician rather than the GP. Social services will arrange it."

Dana was allowed to sleep late that morning. When she got up, Pauline and Graeme had taken the day off work, and Pauline made her eggs and buttery toast for breakfast, and Graeme told her that she would not be going back to her former school, and they would work something out, perhaps that she would go to Cale's school, or something else, but that for the rest of the week, she would stay at home, and if she went out it could just be for walks or things she wanted to do.

The television on the dining room had been left on a news channel with the volume turned low, but Graeme turned it up to hear something that had come on. The screen showed a map of the upper part of the British Isles, with a point beyond Cape Wrath marked. "The Ministry of Defence has confirmed that five Russian helicopters were destroyed off Cape Wrath. At least twelve Russian soldiers have been confirmed dead in the incident, with one recovered alive from the sea and is now in custody. The MoD have also reported that a British citizen, a man, lost his life in the incident. We're given to understand that the identity of this person cannot at this time be revealed because of security reasons, but the MoD and the First Spokesman have paid their respects to this man and his family. It's understood that the target of the attack was a prototype supercomputer designed by Steve Gideon, who it's now believed has been assassinated along with his partner Richard Phelps."

The screen changed to show the photograph of Steve and Richard, which Dana had taken from Steve's wallet and put inside his briefcase with his notes. "The computer it's understood was being transferred back to the UK after recovery. The MoD reports that the computer was also destroyed, but that Gideon's research was recovered and has been secured. Russia has denied responsibility for the attack, claiming that footage of debris shows the helicopters to belong to a mercenary group, and that they were not ordered to illegally enter British airspace."

Dana's throat tightened and her face became hot as she listened to the report. Colin Antrobus was being as true to his word as he was able, with what he couldn't admit being excused as being for national security, and they hadn't pinned the blame on Ivor as he'd suggested they do. Jananin, Antrobus, and the RAF men and women had let him be an anonymous hero and the Russians take the blame.

Graeme gave a grunt of disgust. "Some MI5 agent giving his life for his country, and they can't even honour his memory by telling us his name. The Russians will have started World War Three by next spring!"

Pauline pointed at something else that had come on the television. "Watch this. They filmed it earlier this morning and I think it's gone viral because they keep showing it. She's funny. Cheered me up no end."

The television showed a private jet plane on a runway. Two men were unloading what looked like scientific equipment from it. A woman walking, carrying another piece of equipment, wearing a brown leather trench coat with a wide collar appeared in the edge of the shot as the camera panned. "Excuse me, Professor Blake?"

Jananin turned, briefly, and kept walking. "Professor Blake, can you tell me where you've been for the past ten months?"

Jananin turned properly this time, irritation showing in the expression behind her dark glasses. "In Antarctica, as you very well know from the Department of Chemistry of the University of Cambridge!"

"Professor Blake, would you be able to tell me what you were doing in Antarctica?"

"No, I wouldn't be able to, because the results are yet to be published. What are you anyway, some sort of arsewipe journalist? I don't talk to the media. B—r off!" The television channel had recorded a beeping sound over the word she said before *off*, but it was quite likely it had originally been transmitted live and uncensored.

Pauline laughed. "Can you believe that? She's some big shot scientist who was in Antarctica, and someone tried to frame her for terrorism. They even claimed at one point that you were dead and it was her who'd done it! Serve them right she was so rude to them!"

And so it happened that when Citizen Pauline Rose a week or so later received a letter congratulating her on being a Tier Three Meritocrat and inviting her to come to a polling station and cast her votes on what policies should be nominated for referenda, and to nominate people she thought would make good spokesmen, she put 'Doctor Colin Antrobus' for two of her nominations, and like a lot of people she treated her third nomination not quite as seriously as they treated them in subsequent polls, and she put 'Professor Jananin Blake'.

*

Dana sat on the table and swung her legs, while Graeme and the woman who operated the machine that could see inside people looked at the image of her head on the computer screen. Or rather, the image of what her head was supposed to look like that she had copied off the system's database and used to overwrite the scan of her head.

"It looks perfectly normal. There must've been an error on the first scan."

Graeme leaned his elbow on the table. His and Dana's coats were heaped over his knee.

The radiologist continued, "I expect it was some kind of superimposition with a scan of something else. Actually," she consulted a book with handwriting in it, and then opened a few files on the computer. "Ah!" The files showed pictures of heads with big glasses on, and one with a comedy giant nose. "This is an open access facility some evenings. Looks like some postdocs from biochemistry used it the evening before we did the scan. The results must've got mixed up somehow." She reloaded the picture of Dana's head with the device. "I'll bet that's the CPU from a calculator. I expect they were doing it as a hoax. They made a scan of this device in order to combine it with another image of a head, but for some reason it ended up being combined with your scan."

"There you go, Dana," said Graeme. "It's nothing. Their silly machine made a mistake."

"Do I have to talk to any more doctors and police?" Dana groaned as she put her coat back on.

The radiologist smiled. "I believe I am your last specialist. With any luck, you won't be seeing any of us again for a couple of years."

The outside air carried an autumn chill and the smell of bonfires. On the way home they stopped at the park, and Graeme pushed Dana on the swings.

-End of Book Two-

THE EMERALD FORGE

MANDA BENSON

-Book three of Pilgrennon's Children-

There are such things as monsters, but slaying them is little use when the factory keeps sending more.

When Dana is troubled by disturbing dreams about a girl imprisoned in a nightmarish hospital, and a boy from school who seems to know far too much about the past starts following her, it's just two more problems on top of many.

Then she's attacked by a bizarre construct, half beast, half machine, and the puzzle she's being drawn into starts to bear an uncanny resemblance to her own origins...

www.tangentrine.com

PILGRENNON'S
CHILDREN

THE TETRALOGY

PILGRENNON'S BEACON

PILGRENNON'S GAMBIT

THE EMERALD FORGE

THE LAMBTON WORM